George Park Fisher, Making of America Project

Life of Benjamin Silliman, M.D., LL.D.

late professor of chemistry, mineralogy, and geology in Yale College - Chiefly from

his manuscript reminiscences, diaries, and correspondence - Vol. 1

George Park Fisher, Making of America Project

Life of Benjamin Silliman, M.D., LL.D.
late professor of chemistry, mineralogy, and geology in Yale College - Chiefly from his manuscript reminiscences, diaries, and correspondence - Vol. 1

ISBN/EAN: 9783337332587

Printed in Europe, USA, Canada, Australia, Japan

Cover: Foto ©Andreas Hilbeck / pixelio.de

More available books at **www.hansebooks.com**

LIFE

OF

BENJAMIN SILLIMAN, M.D., LL.D.

LATE PROFESSOR OF CHEMISTRY, MINERALOGY, AND GEOLOGY IN
YALE COLLEGE.

CHIEFLY FROM HIS MANUSCRIPT REMINISCENCES, DIARIES,
AND CORRESPONDENCE.

BY

GEORGE P. FISHER,

PROFESSOR IN YALE COLLEGE.

IN TWO VOLUMES.

VOLUME I.

NEW YORK:

CHARLES SCRIBNER AND COMPANY.

124 GRAND STREET.

1866.

RIVERSIDE, CAMBRIDGE:

STEREOTYPED AND PRINTED BY

H. O. HOUGHTON AND COMPANY.

PREFACE.

Professor Silliman, after he had retired from active duty in College, spent considerable time, at the request of members of his family, in writing down reminiscences of his life. His first design was to describe the establishment and growth of the departments of instruction in Yale College, which had been so long under his care; and for this reason he commences with his appointment as Professor of Chemistry. From the beginning, however, he introduces other facts relating to his personal history, and before he has proceeded far, he announces such a modification of his plan as gives to the work, during the period which it covers, the character of an Autobiography. The narrative terminates with the resignation of his Professorship. From this date, — and, indeed, for several years previous to it, — his Diary is a full repository of public and private events, until within a few years of his death, when other occupations left him less time for keeping up this daily record. In addition to these valuable documents, there are found among his papers an autobiographical fragment relating to the period of his childhood; an extended sketch of the character and military services of his father; a manuscript volume pertaining to the family of the second Governor Trumbull, whose daughter he married, and to society in Lebanon, where they resided; another similar volume containing his Recollections of Colonel Trumbull, and remarks upon his paintings; and various other writings having a biographic value, besides a voluminous mass of correspondence.

In undertaking, by the invitation of his family, to prepare a Memoir of my venerated friend, it appeared to me that the work should be, as far as practicable, in his own words; that extracts from the Reminiscences, and, when they terminate, from the Diary, should furnish the basis of it; that letters and other contemporary papers should be interlaced at the fitting points, — breaking, however, as little as possible, the continuity of his own narrative; that his friends and scientific contemporaries should be called upon to communicate their personal recollections, and their estimate of his character and influence; and that these various materials should be cemented and illustrated by such additional statements as might be found requisite for this end.

In carrying out this plan, it has been an important part of my duty to select from the copious autobiographical manuscripts named above, the matter which might properly be inserted in these volumes. While performing this delicate and responsible task,

I have been anxious not to transgress the limit of propriety in bringing out the details of private life; but I have equally guarded against the prudish reserve that would suppress harmless and characteristic incidents and expressions of personal feeling. That in every case I have judged with discretion, is more than I dare claim. At all events, the reader will see Professor Silliman as he was, in the different periods of his life, and, I venture to predict, will rise from the perusal of this work with no diminished appreciation of his excellence. Although the use here made of the documents referred to is one, it is believed, which he would have sanctioned, yet it should be distinctly stated that they were composed primarily for the entertainment of his own family. They are written, therefore, in the frank and artless style of colloquial narrative, and with no attempt to guard against the imputation of egotism. Hume begins his Autobiography by remarking that " it is difficult for a man to speak long of himself without vanity." In truth, it is inevitable that the semblance of egotism should belong to whatever a man writes about himself; but it will be found that Professor Silliman really set a modest estimate upon his talents, acquirements, and services.

Not all the parts of this Memoir will have an equal attraction for every reader. For example, details respecting the history and progress of Yale College will naturally be of more interest to the graduates

of this Institution than to others; and yet even the
European friends of Professor Silliman, into whose
hands this work may fall, will, perhaps, be interested
in marking the steps by which the higher Institutions
of learning in this country have risen to their present
degree of prosperity. On other topics, also, details,
which might appear to some gratuitous, I have frequently admitted for the reason that they served to
fill out a picture, or were characteristic of the Author.
Little circumstances that aid us in reproducing the
features of social life in the past, have a constantly
increasing value.

But a small part of the correspondence on the following pages has to do with strictly scientific inquiries. Professor Silliman did a great work for
science; but he was not given to speculation, nor
did he devote himself, as under other circumstances
he might have done, to original investigations. Hence
his strictly scientific correspondence is mainly that
of an Editor, and affords comparatively little matter
of permanent value. But his epistolary intercourse
with men of science was, nevertheless, large, and is
probably of more interest to the general reader than
if it were predominantly made up of scientific discussions. To the persons who have granted me the
use of correspondence, I render my thankful acknowledgments. In the case of a very few foreign letters,
it has been inconvenient to consult their authors;
but these letters contain nothing of a private nature,

and are inserted merely to illustrate the relations in which he stood with eminent men abroad.*

A number of unpublished letters of General Washington, addressed to Governor Trumbull, were in the possession of Professor Silliman. Two of them were written in the last year of Washington's life, and embrace highly interesting observations on political affairs. They contain a response to the suggestion that he should save the Federal party from division and defeat, by allowing himself to be brought forward once more as a candidate for the Presidency. † In connection with the letters to Governor Trumbull, other letters of historical value, addressed by John Adams, Lafayette, and other distinguished persons, to Colonel Trumbull, the Artist, are printed in the Appendix.

Not a few references by Professor Silliman to persons who are still living, have been retained. It would have been difficult to erase them, and since his notices are always kindly, it seemed unnecessary.

* Notes which I have added either to letters or to citations are distinguished by the initial, F.

† These letters supply a deficiency which is noticed by Mr. Sparks in his collection of "The Writings of Washington," Vol. XI. p. 444. Referring to the request in regard to the Presidency, addressed to Washington by Governor Trumbull, Mr. Sparks observes: — "Similar sentiments were expressed in letters from other persons. No answer, nor any remarks on the subject by Washington, are found among his papers. See Sparks's Life of Governeur Morris, Vol. III. p. 123." The letter of Governor Trumbull, to which the first of the two letters mentioned above is a reply, is given by Mr. Sparks on the same page with the foregoing note.

In the notes which relate to his labors in Boston, where, as he considered, his highest success was obtained, such personal allusions are frequent. These notes are important, not only as disclosing the associations into which he was brought, but also as revealing the intellectual processes and the feelings involved in the preparation and delivery of his public lectures. There is one circumstance which he at least would have regretted. It has been impossible to make mention of more than a fraction of the great number of persons in different parts of the land, whose names are coupled, in the manuscripts before me, with some expression of gratitude or esteem.

Without further explanation, I present these volumes to the numerous relatives of Professor Silliman, and to the more numerous and widely dispersed family of his pupils, in the hope that they will prove to be a not unsuitable memorial of his worth and services.

G. P. F.

New Haven, March 1, 1866.

CONTENTS OF VOL. I.

PART II.

FROM HIS APPOINTMENT AS PROFESSOR TO THE COMMENCE-
MENT OF HIS CAREER AS A PUBLIC LECTURER.

1802–1834.

CHAPTER IV.

APPOINTED PROFESSOR: A STUDENT OF CHEMISTRY IN PHILA-
DELPHIA.

CHAPTER V.

THE BEGINNING OF HIS WORK AS PROFESSOR.

CHAPTER VI.

VISIT TO EUROPE: RESIDENCE IN LONDON.

CHAPTER VII.

VISIT TO EUROPE: RESIDENCE IN EDINBURGH.

CHAPTER VIII.

VISIT TO EUROPE: RESIDENCE IN EDINBURGH.

CHAPTER IX.

GEOLOGY AND MINERALOGY IN YALE COLLEGE: THE WESTON METEOR.

CHAPTER XIII.

PART III.

FROM THE COMMENCEMENT OF HIS CAREER AS A PUBLIC LECTURER
TO THE RESIGNATION OF HIS COLLEGE OFFICE.

1834–1853.

CHAPTER XIV

CHAPTER XV.

CHAPTER XVI.

LIFE OF BENJAMIN SILLIMAN.

CHAPTER I.

HIS CHILDHOOD AND EARLY HOME.

His Birth. — Origin of the Family. — His Father. — His Mother. — His Father's Capture by the British. — An Early Journey to Stonington. — Anecdote of Dr. Franklin. — Manners and Society in New England. — Death of his Father. — His Early Religious Training. — The Assembly's Catechism. — His First School. — Slavery in New England. — His Preparation for College. — Society in Fairfield: Mr. Eliot; Mr. Burr; Dr. Dwight; Judge Sturges. — His Love of Natural Scenery.

BENJAMIN SILLIMAN, the most eminent of American teachers of Natural Science, was born in North Stratford (now Trumbull), Connecticut, on the 8th of August, 1779. His life opened in the midst of stirring scenes of the Revolutionary conflict. The home of the family, from which his father had lately been forcibly carried away as a prisoner by a party of British soldiers, and from which his mother, to escape the perils of war, was now a voluntary exile, was situated in the town of Fairfield, at the distance of a few miles from the place of his birth. To this home his mother was speedily restored; and here his childhood was spent, on or near the spot where his ancestors on the paternal side had lived for several generations. Daniel Silliman, the first of the name who settled in Fairfield, was understood in the traditions of the family to have been an emigrant from Holland. Later discoveries, in which Professor Silliman was much interested, indicate that the family was of Italian origin. At the epoch of the Reformation, persons bearing the name of *Sillimandi*, and professing the Reformed faith, removed from Lucca, in Tuscany, and took refuge in Geneva, then the common resort of persecuted Protestants. Their descendants, who had dropped the terminal syllable *di* from the name, are now found established in Switzerland. They have among them the tradition that a member of their family named Daniel Silliman, who had held a civil office in Berne, left that city for political reasons, and went to America about the time of the Puritan emigration from England. There are strong reasons for believing that the first Daniel Silliman of Fairfield was either this emigrant from Berne, or a near relative. In this case Holland may have been a place of temporary sojourn, and, at any rate, from Holland he would naturally embark for America, — which will perhaps account for the tradition connecting the progenitors of the Fairfield Sillimans with that country.

The Sillimans of Fairfield were settled from the beginning upon an eminence about two miles from the village of that name, and called, in consequence probably of the reputed origin of Daniel Silliman, Holland Hill. It is a piece of elevated land stretching for a considerable distance, and rising to a sufficient height to command very fine views of Long Island Sound, with the adjacent country extending down to its shores. In full view from the Hill, at the edge of the water, lie the towns of Fairfield and

Bridgeport, of which the latter, however, at the time when Professor Silliman was born, was only an insignificant hamlet. Answering in some degree to the local situation of the family, was the consideration which they appear to have enjoyed in the community in which they resided. In earlier times in New England the communal feeling was stronger, the distinction of ranks more marked, and social affairs more under the guidance of recognized leaders or leading families, than at present. Such appears to have been the rank of the Sillimans of Fairfield in the last century. Ebenezer Silliman, the grandfather of the subject of this memoir, was a graduate of Yale College in the class of 1727; he pursued the profession of law, became a Judge of the Superior Court of the Colony, and was a member of the Governor's Council. He was the proprietor of a large landed estate, and an influential man in public affairs. His son, Gold Selleck Silliman, the father of Professor Silliman, was likewise graduated at Yale College in 1752. After engaging for a short time in business, he studied law, and became a successful practitioner at the bar, as is indicated by his holding the office of Prosecuting Attorney for the County. He had interested himself in military affairs, and at the outbreak of the Revolutionary struggle was a colonel of cavalry in the local militia. But during the most of the war he held the rank of Brigadier-General, and was charged with superintending the defence of the southwestern frontier of Connecticut, which, on account of the long occupation of the city of New York, and West Chester County, as well as Long Island, by the British, was a post

requiring much vigilance and efficiency. He took
the field at the head of a regiment early in 1776, was
in the battle on Long Island; and both in that retreat and in the retreat of the American forces from
the city of New York, his command was placed as the
rear-guard. He bore a perilous and honorable part
in the battle of White Plains, and on this, as on several other occasions, narrowly escaped the balls of
the enemy. While serving in the camp of Washington, General Silliman enjoyed his confidence.
Disparaging remarks, made by Adjutant - General
Reed with reference to the New-England troops, had
stirred up much ill feeling among them; and Washington chose to evince his disapproval of the Adjutant's conduct by showing marked courtesy to General Silliman and one or two other well-known New-
England officers. General Silliman descried the
British fleet when approaching to land the troops
for the destruction of the military stores at Danbury
in 1777, and rapidly collecting the militia, he, in connection with Generals Arnold and Wooster, inter-
posed a resistance to their progress, sustaining the
attack of superior numbers in the conflict at Ridgefield, and harassing the enemy on their way back to
their vessels. The estimate that was put upon the
value of his services is attested by the enterprise
undertaken by the British in conjunction with the
Tories, which resulted in his being detained in cap-
tivity for nearly a year.

On his mother's side, Mr. Silliman was directly
descended from Pilgrims of the *Mayflower*. His
grandmother, whose maiden name was Rebecca
Peabody, was the daughter of Elizabeth Peabody

who lies buried in Little Compton, Rhode Island; and *her* mother was the daughter of John Alden and Priscilla Mullins, the legend of whose love, which brought disappointment to the hopes of Captain Miles Standish, has been commemorated in Mr. Longfellow's verse. Mr. Silliman well remembered his grandmother, who died in her eightieth year in his father's house; and she was fourteen years old when *her* grandmother died. On her who caressed him in his childhood had rested the hands of one who was nurtured by emigrants in the *Mayflower.* The grandfather of Mr. Silliman, in the maternal line, was Rev. Joseph Fish, a graduate of Harvard College, and for fifty years the pastor of a church in North Stonington, Connecticut, whose reputation as a man of exemplary piety is sustained by his letters, many of which have been preserved. His ministry was disturbed by the divisions excited in his parish by the Separatists, whose subversive movements followed the great religious revival of 1740, and against whom his principal publication, a collection of Sermons, was directed. His eldest daughter, Mary Fish, the mother of Mr. Silliman, was first married, in 1758, to the Rev. John Noyes, son of the pastor of the First Church in New Haven. Mr. Noyes died in 1767. Her marriage with General Silliman took place in 1775. He had been previously married, and a son, William Silliman, the fruit of this earlier marriage, was now a youth. Three of her children also survived, Joseph, John, and James Noyes, the last two of whom ultimately became faithful ministers of the Gospel, and died at an advanced age. In 1804 she was married the third time, to Dr. John

Dickinson, of Middletown, who died in 1811. Her own death occurred in 1818. She combined in her nature a woman's tenderness with a remarkable fund of energy and fortitude. The mild blue eye that looks down from her portrait, and the compressed lip, indicate the mingling of gentleness and resolution that marked her character. Her devoted love to her children was reciprocated by a most warm and reverential affection on their part, and seldom has filial love so fine a combination of virtues to fasten upon.

The story of the capture of his father, and the picture of his early home, which follow, are from Professor Silliman's own pen. The extracts are taken from the biographical Sketch of his Father, and from the fragment of an Autobiography, — both written in the very last years of his life.

My father's vigilance made him obnoxious to the Tories, and he was so much an obstacle in the way of British incursions that it became an important object to make him prisoner, especially as the British in New York were, as it now appears, about to devastate the coast of New England, plundering and burning their towns and destroying their resources; and as Connecticut, on account of its strenuous opposition to British aggression on the rights of the Colonies, was, in their view, peculiarly worthy of chastisement, it was determined to make this hated colony the first object of their resentment. A secret boat expedition was sent by Sir Henry Clinton from New York — manned chiefly by Tories: this craft was a whale-boat; the crew were nine in number, and only two of them were foreigners. They entered Black Rock Harbor at Fairfield, drew up their boat into the sedge, and leaving one of their number as a guard, the remaining eight proceeded across the hills, two miles,

to my father's house, which at the midnight hour was all
quiet and the family asleep. On May 1st, 1779, between
twelve and one o'clock A. M., the house was violently as-
saulted by large heavy stones banging against both doors,
with oaths, imprecations, and threats. My father, being
awaked from a sound sleep, seized two loaded guns standing at his bedside, rushed to the front windows, and by the
light of the moon seeing armed men in the stoop or portico, he thrust the muzzle of a musket through a pane of
glass and pulled the trigger, but there was only a flash in
the pan, and the gun did not go off. Percussion caps
were then unknown, and muskets were fired by flint and
steel. Instantly the windows were dashed in, and the ruffians were upon him. The doors were opened, and he
became their prisoner. William his son, although ill with
ague and fever, was aroused from his bed and became also
their captive. These rude men, bearing guns with fixed
bayonets, followed my father into the bedroom, — a terrific
sight to his wife, she being in bed, with her little son, Gold
Selleck, not yet eighteen months old, lying upon her arm.
The invaders were soothed by my father as if they were
gentlemen soldiers, and were desired to withdraw from the
presence of his wife. They sulkily complied; and my
father, by tossing my mother's dress over a basket containing the sacramental silver of the church * of which he was
deacon, thus concealed from them what would have been a
rich prize. He also secured some valuable papers before
he, with his son, was hurried off to the boat, leaving my
mother disconsolate and almost alone.

The capture of my father took place on the Sabbath
morning of May 1st, 1779, and my birthday was August
8th — three months and eight days after the midnight surprise and assault which made my father a prisoner during
a year with the British at New York and on Long Island.†

* It was sacramental day, and the sacramental vessels would have been
used on that Sabbath.

† The fact of Gen. Silliman's capture is reported to Gen. Washington by

The capture of the father was soon followed by the retreat of his wife to a place of greater safety.

My mother had secured an asylum in the house of Mr. Eliakim Beach at North Stratford, now Trumbull, and had made all necessary arrangements for her own removal and that of a part of her family. A British fleet and army, which had paid a hostile visit to New Haven between July 4th and ,7th, sailed from New Haven on the evening of the 7th, and on the morning of the 8th disembarked at Kinsey's Point on the beach at Fairfield. My mother and family from the top of our house witnessed the disembarkation of these troops, and that was the signal for their own retreat to North Stratford, a distance of seven or eight miles, where, with several members of her family, she was comfortably established and kindly treated.

In their progress on their pilgrim journey the cannon began to roar, and the little boy Gold Selleck, amused with the sound that brought sorrow to many hearts, at every report cried, *bang ! bang !!*

"To our ears," writes my mother, "these were doleful sounds;" and she adds : — "Oh, the horrors of that dreadful night! At the distance of seven miles we could see the light of the devouring flames by which the town was laid in ashes. It was a sleepless night of doubtful expectation." "I returned," says my mother, "to visit our house, and found it full of distressed people whose houses had been burned, and our friend, Captain Bartram, lay there a wounded man."

My mother's cheerful courage contributed to sustain her; and I ought to be (I trust I am) grateful to my noble mother and to my gracious God, that the midnight surprise, the horror of ruffians armed for aggression, and the loss of her husband, as perhaps she might fear, by the hands of assas-

Gen. Putnam, in a letter dated May 7, 1779. (Sparks' *Correspondence of the American Revolution*, II. 294. F.)

sins, had not prevented my life, or entailed upon it physical, mental, or moral infirmities. Hope and comfort returned to my mother with the assurance of my father's safety, and with the restoration of correspondence, although restricted to open letters and to the surveillance and jealousy of war.

At the expiration of a year, General Silliman was restored to his home.

The family were all presented in the porch or portico before he crossed the threshold. My brother, then two and a half years old, was brought to his paternal arms, and to this day remembers his first sight of the unknown gentleman in his military garb; while the little Benjamin — nearly nine months old — was retained in the house until the first interviews were over; and until William, the only son of a departed mother, and the three Noyes, sons of a departed father, had paid their *devoirs;* when the little stranger was brought in the arms of his cousin, Amelia Burr, who said, "Here, uncle, is your little boy." That "little boy," now the veteran of more than fourscore, can only thank God for the signal mercies of which he was then unconscious.

While looking through my mother's letters, and those of my father at this crisis and in other years, I made some brief memoranda — outline sketches — which may interest my children. Some of them I will annex, just as they were jotted down upon a loose sheet.

1779; *May* 11*th.* *To her Son, Joseph Noyes, at Stonington.* — "As we have strong fears on account of the Tories, we have every night a guard of armed men — as we believe, faithful and true; and as it would be a very desirable thing to the enemy — our foes — to recapture my husband, he does not always lodge at home. I fear very much, if you were here, the enemy would be for carrying you off too."

Of the Little Boys, to their Father on Long Island. Dec. 4, 1779. — " I never enjoyed a better state of health. I never made so good a nurse to any of my children as I do to the dear babe now in my lap. He is a fine little fat fellow, as good as possible at night, and so in the daytime too, if properly attended to. His little brother is very fond of him ; they both sleep with me, and both awake before sunrise, when I get up and leave them to play together, — a sweet sight to a fond parent. Selleck and Bennie are my only constant companions; and sweet little sociable beings they are. I long that you should see them." A year later, my mother remarks in a letter : — " Little Selleck, three years and three months old, is a little chatter-box, and Bennie, sixteen months old, begins to use his tongue."

My father's manners were those of a dignified gentleman of the old school, softened by a benignant amenity and affability which made his society attractive in an uncommon degree ; and being a man of great intelligence and large intercourse with his fellow-men, he was an object of great respect and confidence. He had high conversational powers, enjoyed society exceedingly, took great satisfaction in female society, and held woman in high regard. He taught us, his sons, to be very attentive and respectful to ladies, and always to give them the preference. I have, at the distance of seventy-two years, the most distinct recollection of his person and manners.

He was a decidedly religious man, but had no austerity or bigotry. The family prayers were punctually attended, as far as practicable, by all the circle, — negro domestics as well as hired white people. He was not willing that any member of the family should miss the opportunity for religious influence, or that any of his household should be absent from public worship on the Sabbath, although in a large family it was not easy to send all to church, especially as there were little negro children to be taken care of, and we lived two miles from the town. As, however, we had usually half a dozen horses and two chaises, we were tolerably provided for; and the horses under the saddle sometimes carried two,—a female riding on a pillion or a blanket, behind a man or a lad. My brother and I were sometimes instructed to take each of us one of the daughters of our clergyman, — the Rev. Mr. Eliot, — who had more girls than horses; and we were at an age when the jeers of our school-fellows made this a rather embarrassing duty. At our Sabbath evening prayers there was always a hymn sung, and as the members of the family were most of them good singers, this addition to the usual service was very interesting. . . . . .

The Sabbath was considered as beginning on Saturday evening at sunset, and ending on the next evening at the same hour. All farm-work and other labors, as far as possible, were adapted accordingly. Family visits and calls of particular friends were, however, interchanged on Sabbath evening, and the children were indulged in moderate play with the setting sun and the appearance of the first stars.

My Maternal Grandmother, Rebecca Fish. — This venerable lady, after her husband's death, in May, 1781, removed to Fairfield and became a member of the family of my father and mother; and although she died when I was only between three and four years old, I retain a distinct recollection of her person and manners. She took the charge of dressing and undressing us; she knit our warm stockings for winter; and I have no doubt taught us our early prayers and hymns, although this latter fact I do not remember. We were always accustomed to kiss grandma for good-night, when we were about retiring to bed; and on one occasion we were told that grandma was sick; and I well remember her appearance as she lay in the bed, the last night that we saw her alive and received her last kiss. The next day, when we came to bid grandma good-morning, she did not speak to us as usual, and they told me that

she was dead. I inquired what that meant, (for I believe I
had then no distinct idea of death.) They replied that an
angel had come in the night and taken grandma's soul up
to heaven through the window. This was my earliest
impression of death, and I believe it has not been without
an influence upon my feelings in subsequent years in relation to that solemn event, diminishing its terrors by the
association with an angel visit.

In connection with the memory of my maternal grand-
parents, I will mention my visit to Stonington in 1792.
My mother, then fifty-six years of age, my half-brother,
Rev. John Noyes, then thirty, and myself, thirteen years
old, formed the little party. We had a chaise, and a saddle-
horse on which I rode, mother and brother being in the
chaise. At Norwich we lodged in the hospitable house
of my mother's affectionate friend, Dr. Joshua Lathrop,
whose lady was daughter of the Rev. Mr. Eells, my grandfather Fish's particular friend and neighbor, as well as min-
isterial coadjutor, as he was settled over another parish in
Stonington. These families visited each other often. The
house of Mr. Eells was situated up a narrow lane some
distance from the road. My grandfather had sold a swift
Narragansett black mare, which he and the family had
often rode to the house of his friend; and this horse came
into the possession of Dr. Franklin, who, in one of his
journeys to Boston, came unconsciously opposite to the
lane leading to the house of Mr. Eells; (for gentlemen in
that day travelled chiefly on horseback.) The horse instantly wheeled towards the house, and the rider applied
whip and spur and voice in vain to force the animal along
the public road. At length he gave her the rein, and away
she flew for the house, and was soon at the door. The
family, seeing a strange gentleman ride up, soon lined the
windows; and the reverend gentleman coming out made a
courteous bow to the traveller, as if to bid him welcome.
He raised his hat in turn, and added, "Sir, my name is

Benjamin Franklin, of Philadelphia. I am travelling to Boston, and my horse appears to have some business with you, as he has insisted upon coming to your house." " Oh, sir," replied Mr. Eells, " that horse has often been here before. Pray alight and come in and lodge with us to-night." The invitation so cordially given was as frankly accepted, and it resulted in a permanent friendship ; and Dr. Franklin, whenever he travelled that road, found here a welcome and a happy home. He used to remark that he believed he was the only man who was ever introduced by his horse. This anecdote I had from my mother. The two ministers were six miles apart.

In our progress through Stonington we were everywhere greeted warmly by the people, who were rejoiced to see the only surviving child of their revered and beloved minister, with two of her sons. The population were principally substantial farmers. . . . . There were few public roads, but many private avenues to the farm-houses. Often I dismounted to let down the bars, or to open the great gate ; and sometimes the final access to the house was over a stile. . . . .

People in those days were not so much hurried as now ; there was more leisure in the family, and personal friendship was cherished often through long lives. Thus my mother through life cultivated the kind regard of some persons belonging to her father's pastoral charge. I remember her correspondence with Miss Hannah Fellows, of Stonington,— a single lady, whose friendship she highly valued and retained through life. Those who were born and educated under the primitive influence of New-England sentiments and manners, when population was yet sparse and personal friendships still partook of the simplicity and sincerity of colonial manners, — the good people of that early era, — appear to have felt and cherished the social sentiments as a part of their nature, and the hospitality which characterized that state of society offered a welcome

asylum to the travelling friend. My mother was born and
educated under such influences, and a refined standard
of deportment in the parental home added graceful attractions to her manners.

Among the first people in New England there was a
graceful dignity blended with winning kindness, — and, in
the case of acknowledged friends, crowned by a cheerful greeting when they met, which produced reciprocal
feelings and a cordial response. These traits were conspicuous not only among persons in elevated position, but
in a good degree also in those gradations in society in
which refinement was not dependent on wealth, and limited
resources demanded even a frugal hospitality. Such was
the case with the clergymen, who, being usually men of
education, and often — as well as their families — possessing very interesting manners, caused their homes, with the
aid of manly sons and lovely daughters, to present delightful family circles. My mother was very attentive to our
manners. We were taught to be very respectful, especially
to older persons and to ladies. If we received a book or
anything else from her hand, a look of acknowledgment
was expected, with a slight inclination of the head, which
she returned. In a word, she wished to form our manners
to a standard at once respectful and polite. We must not
interrupt any one who was speaking, and never speak in a
rude, unmannerly way. We were taught always to give place
at a door or gate to another person, especially if older. Of
course all profaneness and levity on religious subjects, and
all coarse and indelicate language, were prohibited. The
family manners in those early times were superior in some
respects to those which are often observed at the present
day. The blunt reply to a parent, without the addition of
sir or *ma'am* to *yes* and *no*, was then unknown, except
among rude and unpolished people.* The change is not
an improvement. The omission of terms of reverence and

* Of course I do not refer to the Quakers or Friends, with whom plain-
ness of speech is a religious habit.

respect tends toward the loss, or at least the weakness of the sentiment itself. Reverence towards parents and others superior in age, position, or character, enables us the more readily to manifest and feel reverence for our Creator and Redeemer. As to my mother, in the course of long experience I do not remember to have seen a finer example of dignity and self-respect, combining a kind and winning manner and a graceful courtesy with the charms of a cheerful temper and a cultivated mind, which made her society acceptable in the most refined and polished circles. Her delightful piety, adding the charm of sincerity and benevolence both to her action and conversation, attracted the wise and the good, and won the thoughtless to consideration. It is a great blessing to have had such a mother. I loved and honored her in life, and her memory is precious.

Of the circumstances connected with the death of his father he retained a full recollection.

About sunsetting, at the close of a bright and beautiful summer's day, when all was brilliant without, our father, sitting by the side of the bed in the old arm-chair, experienced a strong rally of mind, a last effort, such as often precedes death; when, being close to the northern window, he cast his eyes abroad upon the face of nature, as if to bid the world farewell, and then, in a clear and distinct voice, calling us around him, said to our mother, "My dear, I am going the way of all the earth; take good care of our *dear* children." He repeated the hymn —

> "Show pity, Lord, O Lord, forgive,
> Let a repenting rebel live:
> Are not thy mercies large and free;
> May not a sinner trust in Thee?"

I know not how many verses he repeated, but enough to show the state of his mind. He also added, "I have that peace of mind the world can neither give nor take away." He repeated also several times, " *The morning of the resur-*

rection!" These effusions of the dying Christian were followed, or perhaps preceded, by a fervent prayer for himself, for us his children, and for our dear mother. He prayed for forgiveness of his own unworthiness. How beautiful, how consoling was this closing scene! His sun broke out from the clouds, and shone with cheering splendor, and then the night of death closed in. . . . .

The morning after his death, our heavenly - minded mother sat down in the room where our father lay a corpse, and taking her two young sons, one on either hand, read to us passages of Scripture containing God's promises to the widow and fatherless. During her widowhood, in the absence of male friends of proper age and feelings, she prayed aloud with us and in the family, using her own language. . . . . . The earnest injunction of our dying father was most faithfully fulfilled by the best of mothers. During the twenty-eight years that she survived my father, she was at liberty during twenty-one of those years to live most of the time with her children in their families, and she was ever received as an angel of love. She was indeed the best of mothers; and she, chiefly from our limited paternal inheritance, courageously gave us brothers a public education, while the solvency of our father's estate was still hanging in doubt, although it proved in the end solvent, and but for the Revolution would have been ample. Her beautiful, benignant portrait continues to smile upon us from the wall of the drawing-room of our house; and had I a Cowper's poetical talent, as I have his filial love, I too would dedicate "a poem to my mother's picture."

My recollections of my childhood and early youth will be perhaps unmethodical, and will often present my only brother of the whole blood, as we were almost constant companions from our infancy until we had finished our college education, when I was nearly seventeen, and he almost nineteen years old.

For our early religious training we were indebted chiefly to our mother. She taught us prayers and hymns, and every morning heard us read in the Bible and other religious books adapted to our age. In mild weather we usually resorted to the parlor-chamber, the best chamber in the house, which was also reserved for our guests. Here, while our mother combed the hair and adjusted the dress of one, the other read or recited passages of Scripture or hymns and sacred poetry. Our mother also gave us the best advice and instructions from her own lips. These opportunities were precious, and were repeated in other places of retirement, as was convenient. I still possess the large folio Bible which was my father's, — London edition of 1759, — one hundred and three years old. It was printed on beautiful paper, with a clear good type, and was fully illustrated by engravings of Bible scenes, and by maps and plans. In the settlement of my father's estate, this Bible went out of the family and was carelessly used. A few years ago I bought it back and had it put in order : the text is all perfect; the prints and maps are all preserved ; and those works of art which were the admiration of us children, now in my old age bring back very interesting reminiscences, and always of our blessed mother. Our father, as I have said, was a decidedly religious man, without austerity, and was a strict observer of the Sabbath, and of all the laws of morals and religion. Although he was much engrossed by public and private duties, and therefore left our religious training chiefly to our mother, his daily life shed a holy influence over the family. Thus we breathed in a religious atmosphere, and our sentiments and manners were influenced and formed by a Christian standard of thought and action.

The Assembly's Catechism was in those days taught, not only in the schools, but was recited by question and answer in the families of religious people, especially of the Congregational and Presbyterian denominations. It is indeed a very able summary, and may be read with advantage by mature minds; but it is not easy for children to comprehend the doctrines or to master the language. Still it should not be discarded; it has been an important educator, although all its views are not adopted in this age. It is also an interesting historical document, illustrating the religious character of the century that succeeded next after that of the Reformation. On Sabbath afternoon, the public service being concluded, we, my brother and myself, with the younger servants who were negroes, — the children of the older servants, — stood up in a line, and recited as much as we could of the catechism; (the Assembly's was the one that we generally rehearsed.) With the plainer parts we did tolerably well, and could repeat the commandments; but we found it difficult to remember, and perhaps still more difficult to understand, the complex illustrations of the commandments. I well recollect the restlessness of the colored children, and all were glad when this exercise was finished. Still, an impression of solemnity was left on the mind, and I find that catechism still deeply lodged in my memory and engraven in my religious temperament.

The writings of that excellent Christian instructor and charming poet, Dr. Watts, were ever delightful to my brother and myself. His catechism, both the longer and the shorter, were quite intelligible to our young minds, and to recite them was a pleasant employment. There was also in them a kindness and gentleness that attracted us; they seemed like the voice of an affectionate Christian parent, or of the Saviour himself. The hymns for children were lovely; some of them remain among the permanent stores of my memory, and ever bring up to my mind refreshing visions of the days of childhood.

> "How doth the little busy bee
> Improve each shining hour,
> And gather honey all the day
> From every opening flower.

> How skilfully she builds her cell;
> How neat she spreads her wax;
> And labors hard to store it well   ·
> With the rich food she makes."

These verses, written from recollection, are among the charming reminiscences that flit through my memory like angel visits in a dream, and like other dreams they vanish on waking to the realities of life. . . . . . The anxious and wise care of our excellent mother extended to the period when we arrived at full manhood, and her life was continued, as an inappreciable blessing, until we had almost reached our meridian. I was almost forty, my brother almost forty-two, when our mother died, July 2, 1818.

It is my recollection that the elements of English reading were taught us by our mother at home along with our religious instruction.

I am not quite certain as to priority of time, but it is my impression that our first school for reading and spelling was in a small schoolhouse on the hill in the road to Fairfield town. It was not over a quarter of a mile from our house, and was situated upon a basis of granite rock, with loose masses and cliffs of the same rock on the descending hill; and upon and around these masses we children played in the recess from school, unconscious that these loose rocks, as well as the firm ledges of granite (a name then unknown to me), were historical records of the planet. . . . .

The discipline of our almost infant school was parental and not severe discipline. The rod was rarely or never used; but milder methods were employed. On one occasion our *ma'am* — for that was her familiar title — detected a little girl and a little boy in whispering and playing. The punishment was, that a double yoke of limber branches of willow was adjusted to the necks of the offenders, and they were required to walk home as yoke-fellows. The little girl, not at all abashed, addressed her shrinking companion by epithets of endearment: he was compelled to bear the sly

titter of his school-fellows, — a punishment not soon forgotten.

There was a fine fishing-ground at some distance from
the shore, and the long clams standing erect in the sand
afforded the requisite bait. Fishes also for the seine flowed
with the refluent waves into the narrow inlets in great numbers, especially at the head of Black Rock Harbor, among
which the striped bass were the most esteemed; and sea-
fowl flitted across the spit or bar which ran out almost
a mile from Fairfield Beach, and at low water appeared
a naked rocky reef, resembling an artificial breakwater.
We boys loved to wander, when the tide was out, on the
hard flats, which were so firm that the human foot made
hardly any impression, and they were hardly marked by
the iron shoes of a horse, resounding to his tread.

One afternoon, as Mr. Fowler — who was our first male
teacher — did not arrive with his usual punctuality, a rumor
was circulated among us that he was not coming, and that
we were then to have a holiday. " *Quod volumus facile
credimus*," and away we went under the leadership of some
master-spirit down the narrow lane * to Fairfield Beach.
Smooth shells and polished pebbles decorated the beach,
and there were numerous islets of hard sand peering above
the waves, but soon to be submerged again with the returning tide. To one and another of these islets we wandered,
wading through the shallow channels by which they were
surrounded. Like thoughtless children, as we were, we did
not heed the rising tide until the channel became filled and
the water too deep for most of us to pass with safety; and
few of us could swim. By the exertions of the taller
and stronger boys, however, the shorter and feebler were
helped over the strait, and glad were we to be once more
on *terra firma*. It was a moment of danger. The claim

---

* By this lane the British army marched from their ships when they
burned Fairfield.

of a holiday proved to be a blunder, or a story fabricated for the occasion; and the next day the matter was inquired into, and some punishments were inflicted; but I believe the boys of Holland Hill escaped what we all deserved. Indeed, I do not remember that the ferule was ever applied to my hand, or the rod to my back.

Of the situation of his mother after his father's death, he speaks as follows : —

That bereavement brought upon our mother a world of trouble ; and it was in that crisis that she was obliged to decide the question whether my brother and myself should receive a public education, — my age being eleven years wanting eighteen days, and my brother's thirteen years wanting three months and five days.

There was a very considerable property in land, with farming implements, carts, carriages, horses and cattle, — including cows, oxen, sheep, and swine ; but the establishment was unproductive without labor. I regret to record that there were slaves, — some slaves by purchase, others by descent, or slaves born under our roof. Our northern country was not then as fully enlightened as now regarding human freedom; there were house-slaves in the most respectable families, even in those of clergymen in the now free States; and those who fought for their country, of whom our father was one, did not appear to have felt their own inconsistency. Under our roof, or roofs, (for there was a distinct building for the black servants,) there were, at the time of my father's death, about a dozen negroes, young and old, including those who were occasionally there from their connection with ours. Among them were two married pairs, and their children swelled the list of consumers, but not of producers. The mothers served in the kitchen and the laundry, and the older girls and boys were waiters. Some of the older boys worked on the land. The principal man, Tego, (a corruption from Antigua, from which

island he came,) was an able man, but now having no master, he was bold and sometimes impudent to my mother.
His wife, Sue, was kind and faithful.

A sense of integrity alone induces me to record these
painful facts regarding the participation of our family
in the sin and shame of slavery. I trust that we have
been for many years cleared of these injuries to our fellow-men, and our nation is now settling an awful account
with heaven for the accumulated guilt of more than two
centuries, for which we are paying the heavy penalty of our
blood. . . . .

Domestic slavery was extensively diffused through these
colonies, in a mild form indeed, — the men working on the
farms, and the women generally in the house, more rarely
on the land, especially during harvest-time and haying.
The dairy was managed chiefly by the women, with occasional help from the men in milking. In general, the
treatment was not severe; the lash was rarely used on
human beings, and never on women. In general, the
slaves, especially on the farms, fared as to food as their
masters did. The in-door servants were often favorites
with the family, and especially with the children. In the
North, slaves rarely became fugitives, and were never
hunted by the gun and the blood-hound, and were never
loaded with the ball and chain, or with the iron collar;
nor, in general, were they overtasked with labor. England, from the planting of Virginia, forced slavery and the
slave-trade upon the colonies. On this subject, even the
Puritans, to a certain extent, followed the bad example
of the cavaliers of the South. The Quakers, however,
stood out as a noble exception, and are in general consistent opposers of slavery to this day. As regards my
paternal family, I am sure it was a wasteful institution, not
to mention its injustice. My father would have been
much better off with his legal business alone, than with
the horde of negro servants who consumed the products

of the farms, and were in general triflers, and some of them dishonest.

Mr. Silliman prepared for college under the tuition of his pastor, Rev. Andrew Eliot. During the occupation of Boston by the British, a number of families had left that place and taken refuge in Fairfield. Among them was the family of Rev. Andrew Eliot (Sen.), D. D., a patriotic and faithful minister, who himself remained in Boston in the discharge of his appropriate duties. Some of the persons who thus resorted to Fairfield found a permanent home there; and among them the younger Mr. Eliot, who became pastor of the church.

Mr. Eliot was a thorough scholar, and was so fully imbued with classical zeal that he was not always patient of our slow progress. He, however, devoted himself with great zeal and fidelity to our instruction in all good learning that was adapted to our age and destination, and carried us safely through. He was most faithful during the more than two years that we were his private pupils, — and his only pupils, except his own children. . . . . . Mr. Eliot took great delight in reading aloud to us from the Æneid. Being excited and animated both by the poetry and the story, he evidently enjoyed the subject, and would fain have imparted to us a portion of his own enthusiasm. Virgil's works were pleasant to me, even from this early period; and after I became sufficiently familiar with the language and the structure both of the grammar and the verse, they were to me an agreeable study.

We did not find the Orations of Cicero equally captivating as the epic verse of Virgil. Those beautiful allusions to natural scenery and physical facts and events, which abound in the writings of Virgil, had little place in forensic pleadings and popular appeals. It was also more difficult for boys at our age to resolve at a glance the sometimes long and elaborate and involved sentences and sections of the Orations of Cicero. Still, we diligently worked our way through them.

From a more extended sketch of society in Fairfield a few extracts follow.

There was also in Fairfield pleasant society. Thaddeus Burr, Esq., was a principal inhabitant, and a man of wealth, especially before his large mansion was burned and his property devastated by the British, in July, 1779. He then converted a store or warehouse into a dwelling, and it was a neat and commodious mansion. Mr. Burr was hospitable, and his wife was an accomplished lady. The place is memorable, having been a favorite resort of Dr. Dwight, afterward President of Yale College. He was then minister of Greenfield, and gave celebrity to that hill, both by the splendor of his talents and pulpit eloquence, and by the Academy for the instruction of the youth of both sexes, which he established and conducted for a series of years with great success. Dr. Dwight generally rode down two or three miles on horseback on Saturday afternoon, to pass those hours of relaxation, and take tea with his friends, Mr. and Mrs. Burr. He possessed rare colloquial talents. His mind was rich in intellectual stores, which he freely imparted in conversation, with a genial warmth of social feeling, and with the advantage of a noble person, a fine and powerful voice, and impressive features. His conversation was equally entertaining and instructive, a feast for both mind and heart.

Judge Jonathan Sturges, a noble gentleman, was an ornament to the town. He was a graduate of Yale, (in the class of 1759,) and although seven years later than my father's class of 1752, they were friends and contemporaries at the bar, at which both were eminent practitioners. Mr. Sturges was a member of the House of Representatives of the United States when convened in New York, in 1789, in the first year of the Presidency of General Washington, and the evening years of his life were devoted to the bench of the Superior Court of Connecticut.

With a fine person, he had the superior manners of that day, — dignity softened by a kind and winning courtesy, with the stamp of benevolence. He is pictured on my memory, and the reminiscence is very agreeable, — a recollection of my early youth. Judge Sturges had a large family, sons and daughters; the sons were gentlemen in sentiments and manners, and the daughters refined ladies, partaking of the blended traits of both parents. They were all amiable and intelligent and pleasant; some of them were beautiful. It was a delightful female circle. . . .

In my early days, much company resorted to Holland Hill, — not a few lodging guests; and it was a favorite excursion from Fairfield, especially with young people of both sexes, — and in Mr. Eliot's family there were sensible and agreeable daughters. The reverend gentleman was not forgotten by his Boston friends, even by the great. I remember that on one occasion the celebrated Gov. Hancock, President of Congress, drove up to Mr. Eliot's in his coach and four horses, and while he made his call, the coachman drove farther up the road to find a place wide enough to turn the horses and carriage.

Living in a situation perfectly rural, on elevated ground overlooking the country for many leagues; having before us Long Island Sound, a beautiful strait perhaps twenty miles in average breadth, — a strait often adorned by the white canvas of sailing vessels, occasionally fretted by winds and storms into waves which adorned the blue bosom of the deep with snowy crests and ridges, — in such a situation, we had only to open our eyes in a clear atmosphere to be charmed with the scenery of this beautiful world, as here presented to our view. A love of natural scenery thus took early possession of our young minds, and with it were associated all the attractions of the farm, of the forest, and the waters, — the beauty and melody of birds, and the activity and instinct of animals. In a word, we were by birth, by education, and choice, country boys; and we honored our rural origin by adopting the amusements and varieties of exercise which belong peculiarly to the country.

CHAPTER II.

A STUDENT IN YALE COLLEGE.

His Admission to College. — President Stiles. — President Dwight. — His Studies. — College Diary: His Anxiety to be cured of Faults; Inauguration of Dr. Dwight; Recitations under Dr. Dwight; Situation of College under the New President; His Reading; Dinner at Dr. Dana's; His Desire of Knowledge; Thoughts about a Profession.

MR. SILLIMAN entered Yale College in 1792, the youngest of his class save one. During the first three years of his college life the institution was under the presidency of Dr. Ezra Stiles. He was probably the most learned man of his time in America. In theology he was a diligent student of the Fathers and the Rabbies in the original tongues; but such was his avidity for all sorts of knowledge, that he made himself equally conversant with history, mathematics, and the physical sciences. Dr. Stiles was a liberal - minded man, was possessed of superior natural powers, and formed his opinions with independence. Yet his other qualities were in part hidden under the copious stream of erudition which seemed to pour out spontaneously whenever he opened his lips in public. Mr. Silliman being of the younger classes, seldom came into near contact with the President, and the chief impression which Dr. Stiles produced on him was that of awe for his station and for his uncommon acquirements. He retained a vivid recollection of occasionally walking through the long yard that fronted the President's house,* hat in hand, according to the old etiquette, (which Dr. Stiles strictly enforced,) to present an excuse, or obtain leave to be temporarily absent. Once, in his Freshman year, oblivious of the rule, he gave a kick to a stray football in the college yard, for which misdemeanor he was instantly fined a sixpence by the President, who happened to be an eye-witness, — a circumstance that drew upon him some banter from Mr. Eliot and his friends at home, who were much amused that " Sober Ben," as they were wont to style him, should be so unlucky as to fall into the hands of the law. This, it is believed, was the only instance in which he exposed himself to penalty or censure during his college course. Though only thirteen years old when he came to college, he was somewhat grave for his years, and his thoughtful temper disinclined him to coarse or mischievous sports. The purity of his character was sullied by no gross or unworthy act. The accession of Dr. Dwight to the presidency at the beginning of his Senior year made an epoch in Mr. Silliman's college career. This eminent man seems to have cast a spell over him from the first. The vigorous and animated discussions of Dr. Dwight, in the lecture-room and the pulpit, opened to his admiring pupil a new world of thought. Although Mr. Silliman, on account of a severe wound in the foot from an axe, which was unskilfully treated, was obliged to be absent during portions of his last year, he yet received a deep and lasting influence from the inspiring les-

* Which was on the lot where the College-Street Church now stands. — F.

sons of his preceptor. Through life, Dr. Dwight stood before his mind as a model of human greatness. Mr. Silliman exhibited in his college essays and debates, as well as in the letters written by him in that period, both a maturity of thought and a correctness of style hardly to be expected in one so young. He was fond of writing verses, and acquired no mean facility in versification. His closing piece at graduation was a poem, as was also the piece which he delivered afterwards on taking the master's degree. He does not appear to have shown an exclusive predilection for any one department of knowledge, but attained to a highly respectable proficiency in all. He speaks of himself as having been unusually fond of rhetorical and poetical studies, but as also taking delight in geometry, and being strongly interested in natural phenomena. His reading, as far as it went beyond the requirements of the curriculum, was chiefly in history and English literature, — especially in history.

Some extracts from a private journal, which he kept in the latter part of his college course, will show the tenor of his daily thoughts and occupations, at the same time that it affords glimpses of student life in Yale seventy years ago. These should be read with the recollection that they emanate from a youth of sixteen, on whom, as will be seen, they reflect no discredit. This diary shows that students then bore a close resemblance to students now.

1795; *Aug.* 13.—Rain in the forenoon, partly clear in the afternoon ; but it is still cloudy, and the weather appears to be unsettled. Studied in the forenoon, and wrote all the afternoon ; in the evening went to Brothers in Unity Society; returned to my room with Bishop, Robbins, and Tucker. We dressed Robbins in the *beau mode*, but making a little too much noise, Mr. Linsly came up to still us. Nevertheless, we finished the transformation of Robbins, and he strutted around college with considerable dignity. We raised the electrical kite this day, but the air was too near an equilibrium to afford any of the fluid. Mr. Day* called upon us in the forenoon on his return from Greenfield, and informed us that Dr. Dwight was dismissed, and that he (Mr. Day) was to take his school.

Aug. 15. — Fine, clear, wholesome air, — very cool. I studied in the forenoon, and came home in the afternoon determined to write, but as I felt in a poor mood for study, I went and danced in the hall; however, I might as well have kept to my books. I have been this evening at Bishop's room, when the conversation turned upon swearing, and a profane person who was present said that he was determined to break himself of swearing; but I fear that his promises are more easily made than kept. I have just now come to a resolution to write down every material error of my life in this journal, that by a retrospective view I may keep myself free from error. I hope I shall be enabled to do myself justice and not to be partial; but perhaps I shall sometimes express myself in ambiguous terms known only to myself, and I shall likewise write proper names, which I do not wish to have known, in a particular manner. I think of no material error of which I have this day been guilty, but in general I would observe that I am in some degree addicted to detraction, but I hope I shall be able to cure myself.

Aug. 17. — I have been this evening to the ΦBK. Selleck has been out in town and is not yet returned. I do not recollect that I have this day been guilty of any material error. I wish, however, to gain the ascendency over my irascibility, and to cultivate the heavenly virtue of affa-

---

* Afterwards President Day. — F.

bility and complacency to all, that so my life, whether short
or long, may be both more agreeable to myself and to
others. . . . . .

Aug. 22. — Somewhat cloudy, and very cool for the season of the year, but very good weather for study. I copied
compositions all the forenoon, and went to recitation at
eleven. The class recited about half round, and because
two of them missed and had not studied their recitations,
Mr. S—— jumped up in a pet and told the class to get
their recitations better, and to come prepared to recite the
same recitation on Monday, and went out of the chapel
with amazing velocity. In consequence of his intemperate
conduct, the class were very much offended, and declared
that they would not give him a present. I think that he
ought to have commanded his temper, although it must be
acknowledged that a man ought to have the patience of
Job to officiate as a tutor in the college . . . . .

. . . .

Sept. 8. — I stayed at Mrs. Hill's all the forenoon, copied
tunes, fluted, &c. Dr. Dwight was to have been inducted
into the office of President at ten A. M., but through some
misfortune was not, and it was postponed until six P. M.,
when I attended in the chapel, which was filled with clergymen, students, &c. The ceremony was begun by an anthem;
then a Latin oration and address to the President elect,
by Mr. Williams. The President then made a Latin oration and addresses to the corporation, and the whole was
concluded by an anthem called " The Heavenly Vision."
The first act of power exercised by the new President was —
" *cantatur anthema.*" I then went to supper and then to
college, to see the illumination and fireworks: the illumination was partial, as well as the fireworks, but the music
was very good. I walked the yard with Page, and feel
considerably fatigued, but hope to receive no material injury from my extraordinary exercise. There were very few
people in the yard, compared with some Commencements,

(I suppose) on account of the sickness and the rains which have hindered them from coming into town . . . . .

Oct. 29. — Thus after a long intermission of about seven weeks, I again begin to note down the occurrences of my life. I think that upon the whole I have never spent a vacation more agreeably than the last. I have been blessed with good health and good spirits, and no inconsiderable portion of my time was spent in the company of the ladies, which I think not an unprofitable employment, — which is a very happy circumstance, seeing it is so agreeable. I have attended four balls, or, more properly, one ball and three dances. I stayed for more than two weeks at Mr. Eliot's, while my mother was gone on a journey with my brother Selleck, and this I reckon among the most pleasant part of the vacation, as he has two very sprightly agreeable daughters. I have done nothing of any consequence this day, as I have been in town only two days, and am hardly settled in my studies. I board at present at Mrs. Hill's, but expect soon to live in commons. I have been this evening to the meeting of the Brother's Society, where I read a composition and returned, and am now sitting in my great chair, but hope soon to be in bed, — so good-night to you all. . . . . .

Oct. 31. — I studied as usual, and attended recitation. Our recitations are now becoming very interesting, by the useful and entertaining instruction which is communicated in them by the President. He is truly a great man, and it is very rare that so many excellent natural and acquired endowments are to be found in one person. When I hear him speak, it makes me feel like a very insignificant being, and almost prompts me to despair ; but I am reëncouraged when I reflect that he was once as ignorant as myself, and that learning is only to be acquired by long and assiduous application.

Nov. 1. — Clear and cold, but a very healthy air. I attended meeting all day in the chapel, and was well entertained with two excellent sermons from the President. One of them (the first) was upon the subject of indifference in the affairs of religion, which he thought to be a greater crime than direct opposition. The other was upon the authenticity of the account which the Evangelists have given of the death and resurrection of Jesus Christ, and the impossibility of the apostles being either deceived or deceivers. I remember to have heard the same sermon at Fairfield last summer, when I was at home. At a meeting in the afternoon I was attacked with a dizziness in my head, which rose to such a height that I was hardly able to sit erect, but it soon subsided to a degree, although it came on again in the evening, but was not so bad. In the evening Selleck went with Charles Denison to Dr. Gould's, and I spent a part of it at Prince's room, as I did not wish to be alone when I had that disagreeable feeling in my head. I returned and went to bed at a little past eight. . . . . .

Nov. 3. — My collegiate life now begins to draw toward a close, and I am perplexed to know in what manner I shall employ my time to the greatest advantage, but rather think that I ought to apply myself to history in the greatest part of the time which is not occupied by my classical pursuits and other necessary employments.

Nov. 4. — Clear and pleasant weather as usual. I have studied all day as usual, and nothing has occurred out of the common order of things which I now recollect. Mr. Meigs heard the class recite at noon, as Dr. Dwight is out of town.

Although Mr. Meigs is a very sensible man, and very well calculated for the office which (as Professor of Mathematics and Natural Philosophy) he now fills, still it is very easy to make a contrast between him and the President; but I am doubtful whether the comparison is not a false one, because the President is one of those characters which we very seldom meet with in the world, and who form its greatest ornaments. In the beginning of the evening I went with a member of my class to look at the planet Jupi-

ter through the large telescope from the Museum, which
with his four moons we very easily discovered. I returned
from the Museum, and had a call to go into Bacon's room,
to help despatch some wine; which I very readily obeyed,
and I presume acted my part faithfully. I then returned
to my own room, where I found Lynde; and soon after
Bishop came in, — who had been with me at Bacon's
room, — and soon after him Strong. We drank a few
glasses of wine, and had some sprightly conversation, &c.,
&c. They all returned about nine; and here am I at half-
past nine, sitting in my great chair, — Selleck reading the
History of Greece, and I writing what you now read. My
time passes very agreeably, and were it not for the cancer-
ous humor which I mentioned the other day, I should be
in perfect health ; but even this (at present) does not give
me much uneasiness, — it is only the future consequences
which I fear. I am now engaged in reading ancient history; and notwithstanding that Dr. Dwight talks very
pointedly against our reading much history while in college, still I must think that it is highly advantageous, if
read with judgment and attention.

Nov. 6. — . . . . I think that I have never seen college in
so regular a situation as at present. There are no disturb-
ances, and the students attend the exercises with punctuality. Vigorous preparations are making for commons, and
we shall enter the hall next week on Tuesday. I have just
now finished reading the first volume of ancient history,
and find a very pleasing, and I am apt to think a profitable,
study. The contest between those two powerful and
haughty republics, Carthage and Rome, affords a very interesting piece of history. How different was the state of
society — and particularly in the art of war — in those ages
from the present! And I cannot help concluding in favor
of the age in which I live, which has stripped war of half
its horrors.

Nov. 9. — . . . . I rose as early as usual, attended prayers,

and wrote in a part of the forenoon upon the question,
" Whether a minority can ever be justified in rebelling
against a majority." In the afternoon I read and wrote
upon the following question : " Whether the mental abilities
of the females are equal to those of the males," — of the
affirmative of which I am a strenuous advocate. I believe
that the difference in the appearance of the sexes (as to
their minds) is owing entirely to neglect of the education
of females, which is a shame to man, and ought to be rem-
edied. In the evening I went to the meeting of ΦBK;
returned and wrote upon the above question until half-
past ten. The wind is now N. W.; I think the possibility
is that it will be cold. It is so late that I must retire to
bed, and leave my observations.

Nov. 10. — Clear and pleasant, rather cooler than yesterday. I wrote all the forenoon in favor of the equality of
female abilities to those of the males. It was warmly con-
tested at the eleven o'clock recitation, and decided in favor
of the females, after a debate of more than two hours. I did
very little in the afternoon, as the boys were bringing up
wood into our chamber, and kept up a continual noise. . . .

Nov. 11.— . . . . I rose as early as usual, and attended
prayers ; then returned. I wrote poetry in the greater part
of the forenoon with tolerable success, and the same in the
afternoon, and likewise in the evening, until Marsh, a graduate, came in, and after him Tucker, Cantey, Bassett, &c.,
&c. We drank a few glasses of wine, and the conversation
ran upon politics in general, and particularly upon the corruption of some of our great men, the state of France, of
England, &c. Matters ran pretty high, as is generally the
case in politics. Many men who in private life are of the
most amiable and gentle dispositions, when they come to
converse upon politics are ravenous wolves. The company
did not break up until past ten. We invited Marsh to
stop at our room, which he did, and I slept with Prince at
his room.

Nov. 12.—. . . . In the afternoon I went to speaking, after which the Senior called up the Freshman class into the long gallery, and gave them some advice; after which I was appealed to as umpire between a Freshman and a Junior who had commanded the Freshman to go of an errand, and he refused. I decided conditionally in favor of the Freshman, and my judgment was afterwards confirmed by the opinions of my classmates. . . . .

Nov. 15.—. . . . I wrote poetry (or, perhaps more properly, rhyme) all the evening, in addition to a piece which I began some time since, and which I expect to exhibit before the Brothers' Society, in the form of an oration. It will be my first attempt in public; how I shall succeed I know not, but am prepared for the worst; so whether it should be acceptable or not, it cannot injure me.

Nov. 16.—. . . . At supper this evening Tutor S—— undertook to reprove the scholars for being too noisy, by telling a little story of President Clap. The effect was a universal laugh; thus his very reproof caused a repetition of the noise for which he was reproving them. But I must confess that I cannot tell whether they laughed most at the wit or folly of the story.

Nov. 17. — Cloudy. I rose early this morning, after a night of tolerable though not undisturbed repose. I wrote all the forenoon upon the question, " Whether the want of religious principles ought to exclude a man from a public office." Copied poetry in the afternoon. In the evening viewed the moon through a telescope, read the newspaper, &c., &c.

Nov. 23. —. . . . We (the Senior class) this day sent a petition to the steward, to change our sugar, &c. Nothing remarkable has occurred this day, but I could wish to find myself amended in several particulars. I find that I am very apt to be guilty of scandal, although I acquit myself of doing it through any malicious design. I desire to make it a rule from this time never to say anything concerning any person, (if I cannot speak in his favor,) unless it is absolutely necessary. . . . . .

I ought likewise to be more careful of speaking concerning myself. No person ought to speak of himself unless when it is absolutely necessary, and even then with the utmost modesty. For if you speak well of yourself, it argues vanity ; if ill, you will be called a hypocrite. I hope I shall observe these particulars, and any others which may tend to make one a Christian scholar and gentleman.

Nov. 27.—. . . I am every day more and more convinced of the importance of modesty in a young person ; it is his letter of recommendation. A bold and loquacious air may dazzle the thoughtless and ignorant, but modesty alone will procure the good-will of persons of real worth. If you wish to be noticed, say but very little of yourself, and that with the utmost modesty. Speak well of others ; make them pleased with themselves ; and there is no danger of their being displeased with you. Never strive to hurt the feelings of any person. Do not affect to despise others. Finally, put on modesty, and it will procure you a reception in all good company.

Nov. 28.— Clear and pleasant. I rose to prayers this morning by candle-light. I read ancient history, and Vincent's exposition of the catechism, in the forenoon, which we recited at eleven. Dr. Dwight disagreed with Mr. Vincent in some points. He does not believe that any of the attributes of Deity can be proved from the light of nature. He supposes that heathen nations have derived all their ideas of Deity from tradition, and that this tradition was originally founded upon the revelation given to Adam, &c. As he is a great man, I revere his opinions, but do not think myself bound implicitly to believe the word of any man, although I am rather inclined in favor of this doctrine.

Nov. 29.— Cloudy, and some small probability of snow. I rose this morning at half-past eight, and consequently did not attend prayers. The President preached in the forenoon upon the impossibility of forming an idea of the divine character from the works of nature. He thought that the bounty, power, and patience of the Deity might possibly be proved from his works, but none of his other attributes. The afternoon sermon was a continuation of the same subject, wherein he demonstrated the assertions which he made in the forenoon, from the total disagreement of the opinions of almost all the heathen philosophers, both ancient and modern. There were in Greece alone two hundred and eighty-eight opinions concerning the Chief Good, and three hundred concerning the Chief God. No two philosophers of any distinction agreed in their sentiments concerning the Deity, and each philosopher had his own peculiar standard of moral rectitude, and all indulged themselves in views of the most flagitious nature.—It began to rain this afternoon about three o'clock, with a strong wind from the east. I read Millot's Ancient History until eight in the evening, entertained company until half-past nine, and did not go to bed until after eleven. Some necessary business kept me up to the late hour which I mentioned. I do not mean to make it a practice to sit up late, because it always unhinges me for the next day.

Nov. 30. — . . . . I read Millot all the forenoon. In the afternoon I did the same. Athens and Sparta, although so much celebrated in later times, were nothing when compared with modern States, although it must be confessed that they were far advanced in civilization for the age in which they flourished. The pervading character of the Athenians appears to be fickleness,—always repenting of their errors, but never improving by their experience. They were likewise extremely jealous. . . . .

Dec. 4. — . . . . I have pursued my usual routine of employment, although not with very great vigor, as I have not been very well. I have read the news this evening. Paris appears to be in a state of open rebellion, and the Convention in danger. Unhappy country !—The President

has come in town with his family. There has been a fire
at New York which has consumed several houses, but was
fortunately extinguished. The weather is clear and very
moderate for the season. As I do not feel very well, I
believe that I must retire to bed. Good night! (half-past
eight.)

Dec. 8. — I have almost finished a piece which I expect
soon to exhibit before the Society. It is my first attempt
of the kind, and I am very diffident of success. After supper, as Selleck was absent with the keys of the room, I
went into Belden's room, where we had some conversation
upon the ladies, &c., a number of whom we toasted. I do
not conceive that they are very highly honored by it, but it
affords us amusement, and it is not probable that the affair
will ever come to their ears.

Dec. 24. — President Dwight gave us a very good discourse from this text: " Praise ye the Lord." Soon after
meeting, according to a previous invitation, I went with
my brother to dine at Dr. Dana's, where we were very
agreeably entertained with good company and good food.
After dinner, we employed our time in conversation upon
politics until prayer-time. Speaking of the division of
the German empire by the King of Prussia, Dr. Dana
observed that if such an event should take place, that
Prussia, Sweden, and Denmark would form a very good
barrier against that " Old She-bear of the North." He
appears, notwithstanding his misfortunes, to be almost as
cheerful as ever, and makes himself agreeable to his friends.
How much better is his conduct than that of many, who
sink under the weight of misfortune, and seem to think
that there is no other source of joy except that which they
have lost.

Dec. 28. — Clear and pleasant. I rose to prayers this
morning. My forenoon was principally employed in reading Paley. At the eleven-o'clock recitation, Dr. Dwight
gave us his ideas upon a number of bad habits to which

we are subject. Among them I remarked a few which I thought would very justly apply to myself. They were, whispering in the chapel, and sitting in uneasy postures, not only in my room, but in public. To these habits I am subject, particularly to the last; and before they are too deeply rooted, I will endeavor to eradicate them. In addition to these observations I would remark that I am apt to speak inconsiderately when in free conversation, and thus not unfrequently utter things for which I am afterwards very sorry. I am not sufficiently tender of the feelings of others, and thus (if I have not already done it) I may give offence. I studied spheric geometry in the afternoon; in the evening went to the Society meeting, returned about seven, and went to bed at half-past eight.

Dec. 30. — . . . . I rose to prayers and recitation, when I read the dispute which I wrote yesterday. I observe that young disputants (and myself among the rest) are generally very uncandid. If they find anything in favor of their own side, they impute everything to that simple cause, and allow no weight to anything which is advanced upon the opposite side. I will endeavor in future to canvass both sides, and allow everything its proper weight, and nothing more. We ought not to dispute for victory, but for the discovery of truth. I studied as usual until eleven, when the President gave us a most excellent discourse upon profaneness, ridicule, levity in matters of religion, &c. Just before dinner I took a walk to the shoemaker's. After dinner I went to Page's room, and he told me of an observation made by Miss ——, to this effect, that she liked the Messieurs Silliman very well, but Selleck the best. I suppose that I know the cause of her opinion; but if I do not, it gives me no trouble: I shall treat her in the same manner as usual. I mean to treat every person well; if I have failed to please in this instance, it is unfortunate, but cannot be helped. Whether her opinion arises from prejudice, from partiality, or from a little incident which happened the other evening, while I was in her company, I cannot tell. It is the lot of all mankind to be liked by some, and disliked by others; and she, among the rest, has a right to her opinion. These little incidents ought to prompt me to acquire something more durable for my harbinger into the world than the smiles of a woman; although I would wish, if possible, to live upon good terms with the whole sex; but, if the contrary is my lot, I will in silence kiss the rod.

In the afternoon I did little to effect, for while I was engaged in a number of things, nothing was finally done. Here, then, I may see the importance of seizing upon some one object, and there bending all my whole force. For, while the mind is engaged in a number of pursuits, none will be followed with assiduity, and thus, by aiming at too much, we often lose the whole. I just now begin, toward the last part of my college life, to discover that I am a mere infant in learning. It seems as if I had only obtained a sufficient degree of knowledge to discover my own ignorance. Then let me faithfully improve my time while it is still present.

1796; *Jan.* 1.— . . . . It was my intention to have attended a family ball this evening, but indisposition prevented, and I spent a great part of the evening at Prince's room. Returning to my room this afternoon, I observed a poor old beggar in the entry adjoining my room, and locked my door against him; but I was soon forced by the admonitions of that faithful monitor, conscience, to open it. Supposing this should ever be my lot, should I wish to have the door of the rich shut against me? Certainly I should esteem it a very great hardship! But nothing is more possible than that this may one day be my situation. Then let me no more lock my doors against the miserable whose wants very possibly I may relieve, or at least alleviate. How can I ask blessings from the Divine hand, which I refuse to confer upon a miserable fellow-mortal? I reprobate this action of mine, and would willingly efface it from my memory! As this poor old beggar was going down-stairs, one of my classmates threw a bowl of water in his face. My indignation rose to see gray hairs thus insulted by the levity of youth; but I very much doubt whether his deed was worse than my own. . . . . .

Jan. 3. — . . . . I rose this morning as early as usual. Read different books until the hour of public worship, when I attended meeting, but either was duller than usual, or the President did not preach with his usual pungency. I rather believe that there existed a little of both, for I could not tell what was his subject when I came home. . . . . .

. . . . . At prayers a very good sermon was read upon the text, " This year thou shalt die," — very applicable to the present Sabbath, as being the first after new-year. After supper I went with my brother to Dr. Gould's, where we spent the evening. There were a number of gentlemen present. Our conversation was not, I apprehend, of the most useful kind, for, as the company was large, none but the most frivolous subjects could be admitted. I shall not pretend to account for the phenomenon, but it is certainly a fact, that the conversation of the young ladies (at least as far as I have observed) is too prone to be confined to small and insignificant subjects. (*Query:* Is not this in some measure the fault of our sex, who very rarely introduce any other subjects ?)

.   .   .   .

Jan. 4. — I read in the forenoon as usual, and went to recitation at 11 A. M., where the President, in conjunction with our recitation, gave the democratic societies a severe and deserved trimming.

Jan. 6. — . . . . It was so dark by 4 P. M. that I could not study, and went to Prince and Bishop's room, where I enjoyed conversation until prayer-time, upon politics and smoking. I asserted that smoking was attended with nothing of a beneficial nature, and that it was a very bad habit. Bishop, on the contrary, (who, by the way, is an old smoker,) defended it with all the pathos of a person contending for his dearest rights; and the result of the whole was, that he should enjoy his opinions and I mine. He thought that I was wrong, but I knew that he was. Different persons will have different opinions, and, as long as this is the case, should learn to respect, although we cannot believe, the opinions of others. This is called, in one word, candor.

Jan. 7. — . . . . . After prayers I went to meeting; stayed until about seven, and went to Dutton's room, and then, according to a previous appointment, we, together with Page, went to Mrs. W——'s. Dutton introduced me with the usual ceremonies, and we took our seats. There were present Miss ——, two Misses ——, Miss ——, &c. We conversed upon — what? — ah! — what, sure enough, for I 'm sure I can't tell. Not a single useful observation have I heard this evening, but I have (I hope) made some. And the torture of etiquette! Stuck up like a wax figure, I must sit; first cross one leg, then the other; then thrust my hand into my jacket; then drag forth a studied observation, or hear one equally sensible; — such as, " Mr. —— is a fine dancer." " Did you attend the last assembly?" " Did you ever dance a cotillon? Mr. Silliman, do sing!" " Pray, excuse me, ma'am!" " O no, sir. Good singers always need urging." — Such is the conversation of great companies. I can see no pleasure in such conversation. The chimney-corner is the place for me.

Jan. 13. — . . . . . I arrived at home about noon. Found all friends well. I found my honored mother sitting alone in the parlor. Feeling very much fatigued, I lay down soon after I came home, and slept for a considerable time. I was much refreshed by my nap, and upon coming down found Mr. Day, whom I was very glad to see. He stayed until some time in the evening, and our conversation was principally upon the regulation of the interest of money by law.

Jan. 15. — . . . . . My time has this day been employed

upon a number of trifles, which have however whirled off
the time.   About the middle of the forenoon, (who will believe it?) Quixote-like, I assumed the character of a knight-
errant, viz., I literally went to the succor of a distressed
damsel, as all true knight-errants should do.   The damsel
had lost her horse, and I forthwith mounted Rosinante,
and with all speed went upon the pursuit, — ay! and with
success too, for I soon brought him back.—My brothers
William and Joseph took tea at our house this evening,
and we conversed upon the lawfulness of divorce; and this
subject was succeeded by one which more immediately concerned myself: it was that of choosing a profession.   Brother William and my mother would have, us preach; but
. . . . . I feel very little confidence in the idea that I shall
obtain a living by either of the learned professions.   I
won't be a doctor.   I am not good enough for a priest;
and lawyers are so plenty that they can hardly get a case
apiece.   What, then, shall I be?   Time only can answer
this question, to me so interesting.   In the evening I did
very little, my eyes being so weak that I could not read.
I fluted some, talked some, laughed some, and finally did
nothing at all.   So time goes.   If I were at college, and
spent my time as I now do, I think I should make these
pages look pretty black with self-reproach.   But it is vacation! and vacations were never made to study in.

.   .   .   .

Jan. 17. — . . . . . While I am reading the letters of
my deceased father, I cannot realize that he lives no more.
It seems as if he must still be alive.   A thousand little
circumstances, incidents, and modes of expression peculiar
to himself, set him afresh before my eyes, and make me
deeply sensible of the irreparable loss which I have sustained.   Why could he not have been spared a little longer?
But let me not complain: the hand of God has done it.

CHAPTER III.

His Labors on the Farm at Home. — Teaches School in Wethersfield. —
Becomes a Law-Student in New Haven, and Tutor in Yale College. —
Letters of Rev. Dr. Marsh and Rev. Dr. Porter. — His Early Friends. —
His Early Productions. — Early Letters. — His Religious Impressions.

THE year following his graduation Mr. Silliman
spent at the home of his mother, in Fairfield. His
father's business as a lawyer had been broken up by
the Revolutionary War; he had been obliged to neglect his farm; and as he was not in the continental
line, nor in active service at the time of his capture,
he was never reimbursed for the serious losses and
expenses incident to his protracted imprisonment.
His life terminated before he had extricated his affairs from embarrassment, and although his property
proved to be more than sufficient to meet the demands upon his estate, careful management was required. Mr. Silliman, on graduating, was still a sufferer from the effects of the hurt above mentioned,
and disabled for the most part from intellectual labor. For this reason, and moved by the stronger impulse of filial duty, he devoted himself to reclaiming
the farm-lands, which had run to waste. He went
into the field with the laborers, and had the satisfaction of conferring a substantial benefit upon his surviving parent. But during this period he was cut

off from the society of cultivated young men of his
own age. With the exception of an occasional in-
terchange of visits with former associates in New
Haven, he was almost bereft of companionship. In
this situation, uncertain as he was respecting his
career in the future, and oppressed with a nervous
infirmity, it is not strange that he became for a while
a prey to gloomy thoughts and apprehensions. His
letters manifest a dejection of spirits, occasionally a
despondency, which were naturally foreign to his
temperament. Yet perhaps in no part of his life
was the excellence of his character more manifest
than in the patient exertions which he made at this
time for the sake of his mother.

Another year brought with it an improved tone of
health; and this, together with the not less potent
influence of a change of scene, and a new, congenial
employment, soon restored his cheerfulness.

He accepted an invitation to take charge of a
select school in Wethersfield, where he resided during most of the year 1798. Here he was introduced
to a pleasant, genial circle. His fidelity and winning
manners gained the favor of his pupils, some of
whom were not far from his own age. His hopes
were revived, and he felt desirous of entering, as
soon as practicable, upon the study of law. He had
fixed his mind upon this profession, not from any
strong, controlling bias in favor of it, but from the
persuasion that he was better adapted to it than to
either of the other learned professions. And whatever his feeling in respect to the *practice* of law might
prove to be, his taste for the study of jurisprudence
needed no stimulant. In October, 1798, we find him

back in New Haven in the law office of Hon. Simeon Baldwin. It was necessary for him and his husband his pecuniary resources, and his correspondence shows that he was considering plans for abridging and providing for his expenses. His appointment the next year — in September, 1799, when he had just reached the age of twenty — to the office of tutor in college relieved him of apprehension as to the means of support.

He was now joined in his law studies by his brother, who had returned from South Carolina, where he had been engaged in teaching in a private family. Moot courts were held every week in the office of Hon. David Daggett. A considerable number of young men were preparing for the bar in different offices in town, and Mr. Silliman prosecuted his studies with zeal and pleasure. At the end of a year, with the full approbation of Judge Baldwin, — whom he held in the highest esteem for his disinterested character, — Mr. Silliman passed into the office of Hon. Charles Chauncey, late Judge of the Superior Court, where were assembled a larger number of students. At the expiration of his three-years' course he received ample testimonials from both these gentlemen, and, after the usual examination, was duly admitted to the Bar in 1802.

The two letters which follow are from venerable graduates of the College, who knew Mr. Silliman nearly seventy years ago. The first speaks of him more particularly as a teacher at Wethersfield; the second, as he appeared in the exercise of his tutorship.

BROOKLYN, N. Y., *March* 2, 1865.

SIR, — You are pleased to ask from me some reminiscences of our departed friend, Professor Silliman.   My
first acquaintance with him was in 1797, when I was nine
years of age.   That year he came to Wethersfield, Conn.,
the place of my birth, to teach our private, or, as it was
called, Grammar school.   My father, the pastor of the Congregational Church, anxious for the mental improvement of
the youth of his charge, had succeeded in establishing such
a school, placing in it as its first teacher the afterwards
famous Dr. Azel Backus.   At his graduation, Mr. Silliman
was recommended for the place, though his youthfulness
was considered a serious objection.   The school numbered
about forty, and some of the young ladies in it were already
highly cultivated and older than himself.   I was one of the
youngest in the school ; but being devoted, as most ministers' sons were, to a college life, I began with him my Latin
grammar and went nearly through it for the first time.   But
the next year I was transferred to the school of Dr. Backus,
at Bethlehem, where I remained two years ; when, under the
inspirations of two such teachers, I was able in September
1800, at the age of *twelve* (unfortunately), to tread the halls
of Yale.   During his residence and instructions at Wethersfield, Mr. Silliman was as marked for the elegance and
courteousness of his manners and his efficiency in all the
business that was committed to his trust, as at any period
of his life ; and it has ever been conceded that he did much
in perpetuating and even increasing among the young that
refinement of manners for which the place had ever been
signal.   Mr. Silliman was succeeded in the school by Professor Kingsley, a gentleman in most respects the opposite,
— so timid and bashful, that he could scarce appear in family circles or look a scholar in the face, and yet found to
be such a scholar himself as to inspire with fear all who

came to recite a lesson. He too was invaluable in his place.

On coming to New Haven, I found Mr. Silliman associated with Mr. (afterwards President) Day, Mr. Davis, Mr. Kingsley, and my brother, Ebenezer Grant Marsh, in the Tutor's office; (there were then no Professors but Mr. Meigs;) and rooming as I did with my brother, I often saw those lovely men there freely unbending amid the cares and labors of office; and never were there more congenial spirits, or men more worthy of their stations. No wonder that Dr. Dwight loved them, and conceived the thought of establishing them as Professors for life. When Mr. Silliman returned from his first winter in Philadelphia, and commenced lecturing on chemistry, our class rushed to the lecture-room with great eagerness to see and hear, and we considered ourselves as peculiarly fortunate in being born at so late a period, and as already wiser than all who had gone before us. What much impressed us, and made us feel that this was a new science, was to see Dr. Dwight, with whom we supposed was all wisdom and all knowledge, come regularly to the lectures, take a seat on the same floor with the scholars, (that he might see the experiments,) and drink in with great *gusto* all the truths which were developed.

Perhaps I have gone as far as you may wish, in these early remembrances of one whom from my boyhood I have known and loved, and who from his attachment to my father's family at Wethersfield, and to my brother who died in the Tutorship, and I may perhaps add to the cause of temperance, has ever admitted me to intimate friendship.

One thing which I may not fail to mention, and which endeared him to a large portion of the students, was his sympathy with the great revival of 1802. Had he turned from it in disgust, and become an infidel philosopher, what a blast he would have proved among scientific men. But he meekly bowed to the yoke of Christ. In August, 1802, I with sixteen others, — some of them proved eminent

men, — united with the College Church. At the next communion in September, to our great joy, Tutor Silliman and
others followed.   Yours truly,

                                          JOHN MARSH.

FROM REV. DR. NOAH PORTER (SENIOR).

FARMINGTON, *Dec.* 12, 1864.

MY DEAR SIR, — I had my first impressions of Mr. Silliman in the old chapel at the beginning of my Freshman
year, in the fall of 1799, — a fair and portly young man,
having his thick and long hair clubbed behind (*à la mode*
George Washington), closely following President Dwight
as they passed up the middle aisle for evening prayers,
and taking his seat in the large square pew at the right of
the pulpit. After prayers, the call from the President —
sedete omnes — brought us all upon our seats, when Mr.
Silliman, at a signal from the President, rose and read a
written formula declaring his assent to the Westminster
Catechism and the Saybrook Platform. So he was inducted
into the Tutorship. The other tutors that year were
Messrs. Day, Davis, Denison, and Marsh. Messrs. Silliman and Marsh were the tutors of the Freshmen, and the
division to which I belonged was assigned to the former,
and the entire course of instruction for the first three years
was given us by him alone ; for, although we were called
together with the rest of college, in a few instances, — Wednesday afternoon in the chapel, to hear a lecture by Professor Josiah Meigs in his department, — the latter was removed,
soon after I joined college, to the University in Georgia ;
and all our lessons, till we came under the instruction of
President Dwight, were recited to Mr. Silliman. I am,
perhaps, in consequence more indebted to him than to any
other man for such early education as I received ; and certainly there are few men for whom I have ever since entertained higher esteem or veneration. The class did not
consider him a profound scholar, but we admired him as an

accomplished gentleman; we respected him as a man of great sense and quick apprehension, and we exceedingly loved him as a teacher devotedly kind and faithful.   Having scarcely passed his boyhood when he entered college, he could not be supposed to have thoroughly mastered the whole course; and having never reviewed, as I suppose, in his mature years, he probably — as indeed some of us supposed at the time was the case — was obliged to devote almost as much time and labor to his preparation for the recitation room as his pupils themselves; but I do not remember that we ever found him wanting, or caught him stumbling, though my old friend Aaron Dutton sometimes said, " Benny blushed as he was trying to help —— floundering in the mire of a problem which he was unprepared to solve."

But the course of college learning at that time, — do you know how meagre it was?   As though we had come fresh from the common school, we were put back into our grammar, geography, and the common learning, and kept in them a great part of the first two years, so that at their close we had scarcely advanced farther than is now requisite for admission.   And then what poor barren things our grammars, lexicons, and text-books then were, compared with such as are now furnished!   And our teachers were as scantily furnished as our books, with stores of knowledge that are now prepared for the acquisition of the earnestly studious mind. I wonder that any of us came out men, or ever became such.   And yet we were fully employed, and on such things as were put into our hands we were kept hard at work. Though we were perhaps half a year on Morse's two huge volumes of geography, we were required to recite the whole of them, and our memories, if no other faculties, were severely tasked.   We were required to review our studies again and again, and to be very exact in our recitations. Every mistake was marked, and the account, we were told, was preserved.   And it may be less important, in the process of education, what is the subject of thought and study, than the thought itself, the habit of study, the power of concentrating the mind on whatever may come before it.

After leaving college, I was much delighted by Mr. Silliman's kind attentions. Particularly the winter following, on my way to the eastern shore of Maryland, I found him in Philadelphia, in attendance on a course of lectures on chemistry; and by his importunity was persuaded to remain over a day; — was conducted by him to points of interest, and brought to dine with him and a few other gentlemen of his circle. I was also favored with an epistolary correspondence with him for a year or two. Mr. Silliman was personally interested in the glorious revival at college in 1802. He was supposed to be a convert to Christianity at that time. He had been exemplary before, and his prayers in the chapel indicated thought and feeling on the great things of the Christian faith, though before the revival they were probably precomposed. Precious man, may we be prepared to follow him!

Some notice should be here given of the early friends of Professor Silliman. Among these, none stood nearer than his classmate Charles Denison. They were tutors together, and were admitted to the Bar at the same time. With the exception of his own brother, there was no one for whom Mr. Silliman cherished a warmer regard than for Denison. This gentleman became a lawyer of high respectability in New Haven, and died in 1825. Among his fellow-tutors were two with whom he was destined to be intimately associated for nearly the whole of a long life. These were Jeremiah Day and James L. Kingsley. Mr. Day was a year before him in college, and Mr. Kingsley three years after him. The three men were widely different from each other —

in some respects the complement of each other —
in their native characteristics; and during upwards
of half a century of daily association their mutual
confidence experienced no abatement. Of his other
contemporaries in the tutorship, Ebenezer Grant
Marsh died early; Henry Davis, who attracted the
strong esteem of his early colleagues, attained to the
Presidency, first of Middlebury, and then of Hamilton, College; Warren Dutton settled as a lawyer in
Boston; Bancroft Fowler became Professor of Sacred
Literature at Bangor; and Moses Stuart, after dis-
tinguishing himself as a preacher in the First Church
of New Haven, made himself still more eminent as
an author and theological professor at Andover. His
early letters of friendship are full of the exuberant
vivacity that characterized him through life. There
were other young men with whom Mr. Silliman
early established relations of friendship. Shubael
Bartlett, of the Class of 1800, who, in the decline of
practical religion in Yale College, which preceded
the Revival of 1802, was on one occasion the sole
communicant from the ranks of the students at the
Lord's Supper, and who remained after graduation
as a theological pupil of Dr. Dwight, was numbered
among his respected friends and correspondents.*
Mr. Stephen Twining, a contemporary in college,
and for many years the college steward, stood in the
same category. The most distinguished of his associates in the study of law was Seth P. Staples,
who rose to the first rank in his profession. But to

---

* This excellent minister, of simple and sincere piety, after he became an
old man, informed Rev. Dr. Bacon that he and his wife had together *sung
through* the Connecticut Collection of Hymns, which had not long before
been published.

none of those who have been named — not even to
Denison — was Mr. Silliman more warmly attached
than to the sons of his instructor, Charles and Elihu
Chauncey. They were his bosom-friends. Charles
Chauncey was admitted by examination to Yale
College when he was only ten years and one month
old, but was kept back by his father from entering
the institution until a year later. He received the
honors of the college in 1792, at the age of fifteen.
His younger brother, Elihu Chauncey, was a classmate of Mr. Silliman. Both the brothers were educated for the law, and established themselves in Philadelphia. The former, by his talents, probity, courtesy, and devotedness to professional duty, became
one of the foremost of American lawyers. The latter, if less distinguished, was nowise inferior to his
brother in intellectual ability. Early withdrawing
from his profession, he devoted his life principally to
financial studies and pursuits. When a young man,
he was one of the editors of the " United States
Gazette," an influential organ of the Federal party;
and in the political strife of that day he had occasion
to manifest in more than one way his characteristic energy and courage. Mr. Nathaniel Chauncey, a
still younger brother in the same family, was, it may
be remarked, at a later period, an esteemed friend
of Mr. Silliman. The latter sympathized with the
Chaunceys and the rest of his friends in political
sentiment. They were all stanch Federalists, holding the political theories of Jefferson in cordial de-
testation, and supporting with all their might the
party of Washington and Hamilton, of Jay and
Ellsworth. The warfare of politics was waged with

more zeal and more acrimony than have ever prevailed since in this country, — even during the late
Rebellion in the districts not the scene of actual
hostilities.

In his brother, his companion from childhood, Mr.
Silliman had a friend to whom he could pour out his
heart without reserve. That gentleman, after com-
pleting his law studies, took up his abode in Newport, Rhode Island, and was married to Miss Hepsa
Ely, daughter of the Rev. Dr. Ely, the minister of
Huntington, Connecticut. Had this lady been a
sister by the tie of consanguinity instead of by marriage, Mr. Silliman's fraternal love could not have
been stronger. In all the fortunes of his brother's
household he ever continued to feel the most affectionate interest.

Among the early productions of Mr. Silliman,
which have been preserved, are several of his college
compositions. One of them, which was written in
his junior year, when he was only sixteen years old,
is a dissertation, of about twenty pages in length, on
Natural History. It was read or delivered before the
Society of Brothers in Unity. It is a clearly and
concisely written survey of the three kingdoms of
nature in their fundamental peculiarities. It must
have been the fruit of careful study, and, when the
age of the writer is considered, discovers no ordinary
skill in composition. Mr. Silliman was early in life
an occasional contributor to the newspapers. A few
years after graduation he wrote for the New York
" Commercial Advertiser " — which had been established by Noah Webster — a series of essays, some of
them touching satirically on the follies of fashionable

society. The idea appears to have been suggested by Goldsmith's " Letters of a Chinese Philosopher." In one of these papers he descants upon the recent American poets, Dwight, Barlow, Trumbull, and Humphreys; and is bold enough to qualify his praise of the " Conquest of Canaan " — the youthful pro-duction of Dwight — by confessing that " his rhyme, from the length of the poem, produces an uniformity which is sometimes unpleasant." In 1802 Mr. Silli-man was honored with an invitation to deliver an address before the Society of Cincinnati, at Hart-ford. The theme of his oration was, " The Theories of Modern Philosophy in Religion, Government, and Morals, contrasted with the Practical System of New England." He attacks the Gallic theories of human rights, the notion that particular affections are to be supplanted by a general benevolence, and other pestilent heresies of that day. No small part of the discourse is levelled at Godwin's " Political Justice," which had made some stir in this country; and notice is taken of the work of Godwin's mis-tress and subsequent wife, — Miss Wolstonecraft's " Vindication of the Rights of Woman." The polit-ical bearing of the discourse was too obvious for it to be neglected by the democratic newspapers, which bestowed upon it their censure. But it was accept-able to the Federalists, and given to the press.

Allusion has already been made to Mr. Silliman's juvenile essays in poetry. His piece at graduation was a poetical sketch of the condition of the Euro-pean nations, in contrast with the comparatively happy lot of his own country. The closing passage is creditable to his feelings, and is at the same time a fair specimen of his verse : —

. . . .

"But who is this, sullen and sad amid
The joyful crowd, with downcast eyes, slow step,
And face of grief? While all around is life,
And ev'ry foot trips gayly on the ground,
He only drags a cumbrous weight of woe.
Ah! 't is the hapless African. No more
His sorrows wake surprise. Not for himself
He toils; nor for himself he lives. His life,
His labors, are another's wealth. For him
Life has no joys. The rising sun but brings
Another day of pain; and all the gay
Enchanting scenes of nature only serve
To mind him of his woe. Columbians brave!
While to your list'ning sons ye tell the deeds
Your sires achieved in freedom's cause, and teach
Their tongues to lisp the name of *Washington*, —
While in their tender minds ye plant the seeds
Of true, unblemished liberty, and teach
The feeling heart to mourn for all the ills
Which tyranny has brought on man, — then turn
Your eyes, behold the hapless negro toil,
And, moved by shame and pity, set him free!"

That he took a genuine interest in the theme of
this passage is shown by another poem which he
wrote not long after, and which appeared, after an
interval of several years, in the " Commercial Advertiser." It is entitled " The Negro," and embodies an
imaginary lament of a slave on the banks of the Potomac. The author explains in a prefatory note that
no imputation upon Washington is implied, since he
had given proof of his hostility to slavery; and he
appends to his verses the following remarks : —

" If the purchasers and holders of African slaves would
suffer their minds seriously to contemplate the miseries
produced by this accursed traffic, their hearts would certainly rise up in rebellion against a practice which outrages
every principle of natural right and of common humanity.
The wars, the carnage and desolation which this trade produces among the negro tribes of Africa ; the tearing asun-

der of those whose hearts are united by the tenderest relations, — husbands and wives, parents and children, brothers
and sisters; the confinement in irons, on board of crowded
ships, in the midst of darkness, pestilence, and death; the
second rending asunder of those whom mutual sufferings
have endeared to each other, when the promiscuous *vendue*
is made; and the stripes, the, labor, and the anguish of
mind which these unhappy beings endure through a life of
servitude, — certainly form a picture of horror from which
a Christian ought to turn with mingled emotions of sorrow,
pity, and indignation. A captain of an African ship, who
certainly could have no motive to exaggerate, as the facts
which he related made directly against himself, once told
me the following story : — ' We were sailing,' said he, ' on
the ocean, with a cargo of slaves, when, about midnight, the
moon shining clear, some of the stoutest and bravest rose
upon us and gained the deck. They had no fire-arms and
no weapons, except the loose articles which they could pick
up on deck. We therefore succeeded in driving them toward the stern of the ship. As I understood something of
their language, I stepped forward, and told them that they
might take their choice, — either to return peaceably into
the hold, or I would shoot the first man that refused through
the heart. A stout fellow, who appeared to be their leader,
instantly stepped out, offered his breast to my pistol, and
bade me shoot him for the *first*. I fired, and he fell
dead at my feet. A second and a third followed his example, and met the same fate. A fourth succeeded in their
place, — but the sight of the three men bleeding at my feet
was too much : I could proceed no further ; and I began to
feel also that I was diminishing the profits of my voyage.
By this time the survivors were so disheartened that they
surrendered at discretion, and we confined them in such a
manner as to prevent a repetition of the tragedy.'

" That the above relation was given to the writer, can be
satisfactorily proved, if necessary. This is only one *shade*

in the dreadful picture of the African slave-trade. How great must have been the anguish of mind, and how complete the despair of those unfortunate beings, to produce such a degree of desperate resolution and astonishing heroism! If this feeble attempt, in a country where so much is said about freedom and the *rights of man,* to turn the public attention to the real sufferings and inexpiable guilt arising from the slave-trade, should stimulate some American Wilberforce to advocate the cause of this degraded race with equal zeal, ability, perseverance, and success as have been exhibited by that great and good man, the writer would feel that pleasure from the consciousness of having contributed to the advancement of a good cause, which must ever form one of the highest pleasures of a real philanthropist."

The subject of Mr. Silliman's poem on taking his second degree, in 1799, was *Columbia,* — the sounding name by which the patriotic poets of that time generally apostrophized their country. The Indian aborigines, — the appearance of the country when the Europeans arrived, — the Revolution and its principal actors, — the subsequent prosperity of the country, are reviewed, — and then the author passes, like a true Federalist, to a dark picture of French intrigue, and its threatening consequences. This production still remains, with interlinear corrections of President Dwight, in his own handwriting; and the following extract, in which these are inserted, may not be unacceptable to the curious reader : —

> the same   successive
> " From ~~eastern~~ climes, ~~see gathering~~ numbers come,
>   howling
> To seek, 'mid ~~desert~~ wilds, a peaceful home.
>   The arms,
> ~~With them~~ the arts they bring of polished life,
> To till the ground, or kindle mental strife.
> Now, first, the axe resounded through the wood,

Where, thick and tall, the forest's monarchs stood, —

The ancient oak, whose ~~top~~ [head] for ages past

Had braved the lightning's blaze and winter's blast;

[Bows to the potent steel, and side by side]

~~The mountain pine, whose vertex pierced the sky,~~

The elm's broad shade, the pine's imperial pride.

~~With thund'ring noise came crushing from on high.~~

Where once the forest ~~stood with pierceless~~ [spread its unpierced] gloom,

See cornfields rise, and smiling orchards bloom;

See verdant mead~~ows skirt~~ [s embank] the river-side,

And rip'ning harvests wave their golden pride;

See verdure crown the rugged mountain-brow,

~~While~~ [And] crystal streams through spreading pastures flow.

See [cheerful] hamlets ~~rise with neatness o'er the~~ [gem the enamell'd] plain,

And future cities skirt the spreading main.

Lo! mighty rivers, ~~harbors~~ [havens,] straits, and seas,

Which long had useless rolled 'mid rocks and trees,

Beneath the weight of ships, indignant roar,

And crystal waters feel the dashing oar.

Wide o'er the land the spreading people roam,

And seek in unknown wilds their future home, —

~~In~~ [Full] many leagues along the ocean's strand,

~~In~~ [Full] many leagues amid the forest land,

Where'er they ~~go~~ [rove,] the strong, prolific soil

With ample ~~crops rewards~~ [harvest smiles beneath] their ~~hardy~~ toil."

This poem was published, with a complimentary
notice from the editor, in the "New England Palladium" of Boston. It is unnecessary to say more of
Mr. Silliman's efforts in poetry. He had too just an
idea of his own powers to aspire to fame in this
species of composition. Now and then, at later
periods in life, he wrote verses for the gratification
of friends, or as a natural expression of his own emotions on some occasion of particular interest. Many
years after these early productions were written, and
when he had become absorbed in scientific pursuits,
his friend Mrs. Sigourney, then Miss Huntley, in an

ode addressed to him, alluded to his former poetical
studies and compositions.   He responded (under
date of Sept. 18, 1816) in a sort of farewell to the
Muses, from which the following is an extract: —

1.

Many thanks to your Muse, and thanks to your lyre,
    For all the sweet numbers you sing;
Again they awaken the long dormant fire,
Anew fan the embers about to expire,
    And crown my cold winter with spring.

2.

For many a month and many a year,
    Old Time has rolled swiftly away,
Since I gave to the Muses a sigh or a tear,
Or felt for renown a hope or a fear,
    Or fashioned a rhyme or a lay.

3.

The Muses, if ever they deigned me a smile,
    Long since have they bid me adieu,
Nor did they consent to " tarry a while,"
Or list to the jargon of chemical style,
    'Mid odors and noises so new.

4.

No Muse waves her wings where furnaces blaze,
    And gases mephitic exhale;
Minerva, indignant, stops not to gaze,
Nor Apollo illumes with all-cheering rays
    The cell of the Alchemist pale.

To this, Mrs. Sigourney rejoined with an address
" to a Poet who had written a farewell to the Muses
in some very sweet stanzas."   A part of this humorous expostulation is here given: —

1.

Oh, bid not the train of Parnassus farewell!
    Or use not so gentle a strain;
For the sweet tones would summon each Muse from her cell,
From the murmuring fountain or slumbering dell,
    And bring them in legions again.

2.

So soft a dismission the musical throng
  Would mistake for a welcome as kind:
They would crowd to your mansion and beg for a song,
With ceaseless intrusion and visits so long,
  That no refuge or rest could you find.

3.

And should you complain, like the diligent clerk,
  That you have for such visits no time,
They 'll join in your toils, at your furnace they 'll work,
In the bills of the students mischievously lurk,
  And compel you to write them in rhyme.

From the early correspondence of Mr. Silliman
we select a few letters, most of which are addressed
to his brother. Two or three from his friends to him
are included. These letters serve to illustrate the
biographical statements which precede them in the
present chapter.

TO MR. G. S. SILLIMAN.

FAIRFIELD, *March* 11, 1797.

MY DEAR BROTHER, — Saturday evening brings me
home again to converse with one than whom none is dearer
to me ; for, believe me, in the last week I have hardly had
time to eat. Tired with murmuring at my situation, which
obliges me to stop short in a pursuit which is my delight,
and patiently to see my contemporaries outstrip me, I have
at length become quiet, and determined to submit where
resistance would be ineffectual. My last was from Wallingford. On my return home I stayed several days at
New Haven, which I spent in visiting my friends. . . . . .
I had the pleasure of seeing Miss Hepsa Ely at New
Haven, a lady whom I believe you have seen, although perhaps, at such a distance of time and place as that at which
you now are, you may not recollect her. Ever since my
return I have been assiduously employed in domestic
concerns, and have the satisfaction to find that my health

is slowly mending, and my mind recovering its accustomed tone.   Since my last, my mind has been greatly relieved by your welcome letters of the 19th, 20th, and 21st of January, in which I have the satisfaction to find that your situation is perfectly agreeable, and I am now easy concerning you as to everything but the climate.   But trusting in God and in your personal temperance and caution, I hope that you will escape. . . . . .

TO MR. G. S. SILLIMAN.

FAIRFIELD, *May* 9, 1797.

. . . . . I STILL continue at home, in the same employments which engaged my attention when last I wrote.   I endeavor, as much as possible, to lighten the cares and to cheer the spirits of that mother to whose anxious care and unwearied exertions we owe those superior advantages which it has been our lot to enjoy.   I have taken the whole care of the farm and its appendages, so that she has no further concern in the business than merely to give her advice.   It has been since the breaking up of winter, and still is, an object of constant attention to put every part of the farm into the best state of improvement of which it is capable.   The fences are all repaired; the lot which occasioned so much ill blood last year, and the lot before brother Noyes's door, are sowed with foxtail and clover seed, and next season I do not doubt that we shall have from them a plenty of the best of hay.   The orchard is to be ploughed and planted with corn in order to extirpate the elders which have overrun it, and the other lots are improving in some way or other.   We calculate that the productions of the farm will, this year at least, support the family, which you know was far from being the case last year.   My present employment is far from being one to which, at the present period of my life, I should wish to give my time.   But I have found by experience that it conduces to my health and to my interest, and therefore I think it is clearly my duty to pursue it until a return of health shall enable me to prosecute that employment to which I have been educated, and which is my delight. Think not, my brother, that I pay no attention to books. As often as leisure and health permit, I improve the opportunity in reading or writing, and not unfrequently in wooing the Muses. . . . . .

TO MR. STEPHEN TWINING.

FAIRFIELD, *May* 13, 1797.

. . . . . SINCE Commencement I have continued at home, and as the infirm state of my health would not permit me to pursue any business which requires much application, I have employed my time in attending to my mother's affairs. This employment I at first assumed merely to keep myself busy, not supposing that one half of my time would be occupied in it; but so astonishingly have cares of one kind and another increased upon me, that I find myself at the age of eighteen involved in all the business of active life, and in fact acting the part of a head of a family. But this constant occupation has answered a valuable purpose with respect to my health : it has kept me from thinking upon those gloomy subjects upon which I had been a long time accustomed to ponder, and has furnished me with abundance of bodily exercise. Upon the whole, I find myself much better in health and spirits than at Commencement, and hope, by perseverance in my present mode of life, before a long time, to be able to begin to make preparations for a permanent establishment in life. What this establishment will be, I do not yet know. If I find myself sufficiently firm in my health to pursue a literary employment, I think I shall pursue one of the learned professions. If not, I shall choose some other business which affords prospect of a decent support, — probably agriculture or trade. . . . . .

TO MR. G. S. SILLIMAN.

FAIRFIELD, *May* 19, 1797.

. . . . . WE are now separated, for life perhaps, perhaps only for a short period. God grant. that the last may eventually prove to be true. Oh, my brother, I wish I could at once lay open my heart to you without the trouble of writing. My mind is racked and torn by a thousand anxious cares, half of them perhaps imaginary; but whether real or imaginary, they have the effect of sinking my spirits. You will be curious to inquire the cause, and perhaps will first of all ask, whether it be *what sometimes makes the heart of a young man sad.* To this question I can confidently answer, No! My youth, my ill health, and consequent want of business, are sufficient motives to make me keep clear of all direct or implicit engagements of that kind, and I can assure you that my feelings upon that subject are at present quite calm. One great and constant source of uneasiness to my mind you are well acquainted with. It is the embarrassed situation of our affairs. I do everything in my power to render the remaining part of the estate as profitable as possible, but brothers are so much occupied with their own affairs, that they find very little time to attend to those of the estate. I hope, however, in the course of the summer, that this lengthy and perplexed business, which has already consumed almost seven years, will be brought to a close. But I have a still greater source of uneasiness than this. My health, although better than when you left us, is still so unconfirmed, that it would be folly for me to commence the pursuit of any business for life. In fine, I am in a state of perfect suspense with respect to my future prospects, and this alone is a cause sufficient to destroy the greater part of my peace. I know that you will tell me that I am still young, that I shall by-and-by regain my health, and that I ought to wait for providence. Of the truth of all this I am convinced, but this will not smother a ruling passion. . . . . But I will cease to complain. I deserve more than I suffer.

TO MR. G. S. SILLIMAN.

FAIRFIELD, *May* 27, 1797.

. . . . . BE not surprised at anything, nor be induced to believe that my feelings always run in so low a chan-nel. I experience for the greater part of the time a phil-osophic serenity, and it is only when I cast my thoughts upon the interesting subjects which I last spoke of that I experience a depression. But I see much ground to hope that my situation will by-and-by be better. Patience and fortitude are the best defence against adversity, and never does human nature appear more truly respectable than when calmly resisting misfortune. The public mind in this part of the Union has, in a short period past, undergone a great change with respect to France. Those who, before their depredations upon our commerce, were opposed to them, now cry out vehemently; those who were calm begin to bestir themselves, and their friends hold their tongues. A war with France is dreaded by all, but expected by many. . . . . .

TO MR. STEPHEN TWINING.

WETHERSFIELD, *March* 19, 1798.

. . . . . YOU no doubt have heard, from some one of those to whom I have written in New Haven, of the agree-ableness of my present situation. I am very happily dis-appointed in two respects. I was fearful that attention to business, after so long a season of relaxation, would cause a return of those disagreeable and dangerous companions, whose presence had obliged me to throw by my books. I presumed, too, that the employment of instruction would be tiresome and tedious. But I am happily disappointed in both these respects. I have not, in two years past, enjoyed five weeks of so great *mental* and *bodily* health as that which I have experienced during the five weeks in which I have resided here. . . . . .

NEW HAVEN, *July* 7, 1798.

. . . . . WE celebrated Independence here with great pomp and splendor. The morn was ushered in by the firing of cannon and the ringing of bells, — a cant expression, and it will be in every Boston paper for this month. At nine o'clock A. M. a procession was formed down in the new township, consisting of—1st, the Governor's guard ; 2d, the militia company ; 3d, the new-formed company of artillery, John P. Austin, captain ; 4th, mayor and aldermen of the city, the civil authority, the two orators Dr. Dwight and Noah Webster, Jr., Esq., sheriffs, deputies, clergymen, candidates, citizens, and students, and a military company of boys. Perhaps I have not got them exactly in their order. From the new township they moved up Chapel Street in procession till they came to the brick [church]; then the military opened on the right and left, and the procession walked through. After they were seated, the President delivered an excellent sermon, and Mr. Webster an oration equally good. After the exercise, formed again, and walked again in procession to the State House, where was prepared a public dinner with excellent liquors. After dinner, drank a number of very patriotic toasts, which you will probably see in your papers ; and a most ardent spirit of patriotism appeared to diffuse itself through every rank and grade of society. Many, before they left the tables, got very high. The ladies in town, to a very great number, took tea at Mix's, over in the new township. To give you an account of their manœuvres would exceed this letter. They drank toasts, sang songs, and appeared equally gay with the gentlemen.

FROM MR. ELIHU CHAUNCEY.

PHILADELPHIA, *Jan.* 30, 1801.

. . . . . . Politics here claim the attention of all, from the highest to the lowest, and my fondness for things of this kind will not suffer me to remain a calm spectator. A few weeks since, Bronson and myself attended a Democratic meeting, and amused ourselves among the mob for an hour or two. A scene of more complete riot and confusion I never witnessed; but, being unknown, we remained safe, though we were somewhat apprehensive that violence would be offered, in which case we should have come off poorly, notwithstanding we were well armed for our defence. But here they openly talked of settling the differences of party by the point of the bayonet, and their conduct and conversation evidently showed that they stood ready to cut our throats at the first signal. I thank you for your kind wishes for my prosperity; but, sir, such is the state of things in Pennsylvania, that I think no young man, whose principles are not fully Jacobin, can calculate upon an immediate rise in business. Such is the violence of the Democrats, that they deem no Federalist too insignificant for their exertions to obstruct his progress. They will use any means to accomplish their ends, and they are all-powerful in Pennsylvania. My brother [Charles] is doing tolerably well; but I have no doubt that, if he would turn Democrat, he would soon acquire a decent property, and gain political promotion. But I think he will yet prefer to subsist upon a few dollars, which he sometimes gets, than sacrifice his principles, though it should be attended with the first honors of the state. . . . . . .

TO MR. G. S. SILLIMAN.

NEW HAVEN, *Feb.* 13, 1800.

. . . . . I "HAVE resumed my change with alacrity," and shall make every exertion "to discharge my trust with fidelity," thankful at the same time "for all my mercies," although I do not yet know whether the tide of popularity runs against me or for me. Whichever is or may hereafter be the fact, no change will be effected in my governing principles.

I am resolved to do my duty with faithfulness, at the same time softening the tone of authority by affability and easiness of access. I should be in no hurry to leave my present situation, unless disagreeable circumstances should render it necessary.

TO HIS MOTHER.

NEW HAVEN, *June* 2, 1800.

. . . . . COLLEGE is in regular motion once more, and the wheels run very smoothly. I am as happy as I ever expect to be in this imperfect state. Indeed I cannot be too thankful for it. But I feel a constant aspiration after another and a better state. I hope, my dear mother, that while you are spared to bless your children, you will not spare those excellent counsels to which I owe almost everything which is good in me; and when you are gone to heaven, I sincerely pray that the bright image of your example may always be present to keep me from sin. I have found the excellent letter which you wrote last winter. I have read it with strong emotions of filial affection and reverence. . . . . .

TO MR. G. S. SILLIMAN.

NEW HAVEN, *June* 28, 1800.

. . . . . I AM resolved to free myself from all pecuniary embarrassment, which the regular returns of my salary will in a few months enable me to effect. After that, I shall certainly aim to lay by something every quarter, to assist me in the first months of professional life. My principal pecuniary weakness has been a *taste* for elegance, which in circumstances more eligible would have been perfectly proper, but in mine was certainly reprehensible. You justly remark, however, that our rank in society will not permit us to stoop to mean economy. It will not; but I am conscious that I have spent much money which I might have saved. Perhaps $200 would comprehend everything of this kind; but this sum, although small, is something in the support of a year. . . . . . President Adams arrived in town this afternoon, and we expect him at meeting to-morrow at the Chapel. I am very well; feel no bad effects from the summer's heat. . . . . . It is my turn to officiate this evening, and as the bell is now ringing, I must bid you adieu. . . . . .

The following letter describes a journey made on horseback from Newport, R. I., to Boston, and thence to New Haven, by the way of Worcester and Springfield.

TO MR. G. S. SILLIMAN.

NEW HAVEN, *June 5*, 1801.

DEAR SELLECK, — . . . . . . *Noon, Monday, May* 19. — After we parted with you and your charming companion, we rode on to the ferry, noticing in our progress the traces of war upon the surrounding hills. We passed the ferry safely; but from the extreme ill-nature and boorishness of the ferrymen, we were confident that they belonged to the lowest type of democracy. As we sailed, the seat of King Philip excited in my mind an interesting train of reflections upon the surprising declension of the Indian, and the rise of the Anglo-American, power in this country. The singular neatness and thrift of Bristol and Warren would have given me much more pleasure had they been produced by any other means than the misery of the Africans. Between two and three P. M. we dined at Cole's, and arrived in Providence a little before sunsetting. We put up at Aldrich's, took tea, dressed, &c.; but an unlucky rent which I gave one of my boots in drawing it on, lost for us half the evening before it could be repaired. I soon discovered that our hostess was a *lady of quality;* and, from our inquiring for Mrs. Bowman's, Pres. Maxcy's, &c., or from some strange defect in her optics, she took us for *gentlemen of style,* and in a very short time she actually pronounced us *Carolina gentlemen.* No attention was now enough for us; the good things of the house were brought forth, and the servants were all on tiptoe to await our commands. We were not anxious, you will readily believe, to undeceive our hostess; for, had we once informed her that we were from Connecticut, we should have dwindled to common travellers. What I anticipated respecting our bills we realized, for we were charged in proportion to our style. The time which we had allotted to spend at the President's and at Mr. Mumford's was now elapsed, and we found ourselves able to call only at Mrs. Bowman's. Unfortunately the whole family, except Miss Lynch and John, were abroad; with them, however, we spent an hour, left our respects for Mrs. B. and the family, and retired.

Tuesday, 20th, 6 A. M. — Notwithstanding the urgent solicitations of our hostess the evening before, and our partial promise that we would spend a few days in Providence, we left the town, not a little diverted that we had brought off our *quality* without discovering our Yankee extraction. The style of building in Providence is, I think, superior to that of any other town which I have seen. Pawtucket Falls attracted our attention as we passed the bridge. We passed on into the eastern part of Attleborough, where we found a most excellent breakfast at Holmes's, thirteen miles from Providence. The stage drove up full of sailors just discharged from the *George Washington.* They complained much of Captain Bainbridge, declaring that the Turks treated them with more humanity than he. We passed on through Wrentham and Walpole to Dedham, where we dined with the Judges of the County Court at

Gay's. They were plain, sensible men, but apparently of moderate information. All mouths at Dedham were full of the shocking murder committed the day before; and the perpetrator lay, groaning with his wounds, at a neighboring house. The appearance of the country had been very fine ever since we entered Massachusetts, but Dedham is a delightful spot, and Mr. Ames has the most charming seat in it. At three o'clock P. M. we started for Boston, and as we proceeded, the country grew more and more delightful. About four miles from Boston, my horse, which, in consequence of his being shod very badly at Providence, had frequently stumbled in the course of the day, when going upon a full trot, fell headlong with great violence, and pitched me over his head three or four yards. Owing to the great goodness of my Preserver, I was not in the least degree injured, but after leading my horse on for two miles I left him to be shod again in Roxbury, and I walked into Boston. We put up at Vose's, in School Street, — an excellent house. Dutton's and Denison's lodgings were only two doors off, but they being out, we spent the evening at the Columbian Museum. There we saw a great multitude of curious things, — wax figures, and particularly wax beauties in abundance; but I declare to you I am so little of a connoisseur, that these same wax figures freeze me; they have the coldness of death; — in truth, I had rather spend half an hour with Miss —— than a whole year with these wax beauties.

Wednesday, 21*st.* — After breakfast we went with Dutton and Denison into the Mall and Common, and ascended to the pinnacle of the new State House, where we were presented with a prospect which for extent and beauty exceeded anything I had ever seen. The limits of my paper will not allow me to give a description of Boston and its vicinity. But I will just remark that the country around Boston is really a terrestrial paradise. After descending from the State House, Ely and I mounted our horses and

rode over Charlestown Bridge to Breed's, usually called
Bunker's Hill. Here I spent half an hour with great emotion. Leaning against the monument of Warren, I surveyed
the scene of carnage, now a verdant, charming meadow.
Our lines of defence, however, are still visible. We descended the hill, and spent two hours with Doctor Morse.
He treated us with great politeness, and requested our
company to breakfast the next day. We returned to Boston, rode around the various parts of the town, and dined
at our lodgings. In the afternoon, Dutton, Denison, Ely,
and myself, with Mr. Wells, lately a tutor in Harvard, went
in a hack to Cambridge. Mr. Wells introduced us to the
gentlemen of college ; . . . . we were conducted into the
Library, Museum, &c., and took tea at Pres. Willard's. In
the mean time Mr. Ely and I called upon Mr. R——;
. . . . he received us very cordially, nor will I detract from
the goodness of his heart by hinting that the interesting
despatches of which I was the bearer might have added
some value in his view to the hand which presented them.
We drove back to Boston, and I spent the evening with
my companion at Captain Goodwin's. . . . .

Thursday, 22d. —We breakfasted with Dr. Morse, and he
waited upon us back to Boston. I then called upon Dr.
Eliot, brother of our Mr. Eliot. He showed me much
attention ; conducted me to the Historical Library and
Museum, introduced me to a number of respectable gentlemen, and showed me the house where Dr. Franklin was
born. The Doctor's mother, it seems, went to church in the
forenoon, became his mother in the intermission, and the
infant was baptized in the afternoon, —so that the Doctor
used humorously to say that he attended meeting the whole
of that day. I then called upon Eunice Eliot, and our
classmate Gurley. We dined with Dutton and a circle of
literati, ... where we enjoyed " the feast of reason, and
the flow of soul," until four P. M., when Mr. E. and I excused ourselves and retired. Mr. Eliot, of Fairfield, I

found at our lodgings; he had just arrived on a visit to his friends. At five P. M. we left Boston, and proceeded to Cambridge, where we were detained an hour by rain. We then proceeded through Watertown to Waltham, ten miles from Boston, where we put up for the night at Harrington's.

Friday, 23d. —We proceeded through East Sudbury and West Sudbury, where we breakfasted at Howe's; then on through Marlborough, Northborough, and Shrewsbury, to Worcester, where we arrived at one P. M., forty-seven miles from Boston. We dined at Barker's, and partook of a very animated dessert, administered by a democratic lawyer of the town who dined at our table. The subject of dispute was the right of the people to choose the electors of President. Unfortunately, the gentleman made me such concessions as ran him on shore at once, while our jolly landlord was laughing in his sleeve at the confusion of one who, I suppose, had hitherto ruled the roost in his house. Worcester is a beautiful inland town, and the country between it and Boston is generally very fine. At three, we proceeded through Leicester and Spencer, a hilly country, to East Brookfield, a delightful village in a fruitful vale, where one of my pupils — Reed — found us out, and conducted us to his father's, where we took tea. Major Reed lives in elegant country style. We proceeded to West Brookfield, where we put up at Draper's, fifty-seven miles from the place where we set out in the morning. This moment comes in your letter by Mr. Wales. I feel grateful to the persons who have expressed a wish to become acquainted with your brother, nor shall I ever forget the unmerited attentions which I received while in Newport, particularly from Major Lyman's family.

Saturday, 24th. —We mounted our horses at five P. M., designing to reach Hartford, if possible, fifty-six miles. We rode through a hilly country, but a pleasant one; the road was turnpiked; breakfasted at Bates's in Palmer, — a very contentious and ill-governed family. We proceeded for Springfield. In Wilbraham they showed us the pond where the six young people were drowned last summer. We arrived at Springfield about one P. M. The keeper of the Armory was absent, and we could not see the arms. We made no stop East, but crossed the river and dined in West Springfield. My horse was so much fatigued and stumbled in so alarming a manner, that we put up for the night at Suffield, although it was only four P. M., and of course there was sufficient time to have reached Hartford. Our landlord, Mr. Austin, was a warm, though weak, Democrat, and by drinking Jefferson's health with him we were soon in high credit.

Sabbath, 25th. — Before sunrise we proceeded for Hartford, but at Windsor my horse travelled so ill that I turned him adrift to follow Ely, and hired a chaise and boy to convey me to Hartford, where we arrived in good breakfast-time. Attended Mr. Strong's meeting; took tea with Dr. Fish; spent the evening all over town, as we fell in with a company of young ladies who were disposed to enjoy the fine evening in a walk, — and ladies, you know, when once in motion, are very erratic creatures.

Monday, 26th. — We breakfasted with Dr. Fish, and dined with Mills, Sherwood, and several other gentlemen of our acquaintance, at their lodgings. In the afternoon we proceeded to Wethersfield, where we remained until the next day, Tuesday, 27th, when Ely proceeded for New Haven (*via* Durham). I remained in Wethersfield a little longer; dined at Mr. Marsh's; took tea at Col. Chester's. After tea, I attended Misses Hannah and Mary Chester, with Hannah and Julia Mitchell, on a walk in the meadows by moonlight. We rambled about till nine.

TO MR. G. S. SILLIMAN.

NEW HAVEN, *Aug.* 29, 1801.

. . . . . You will learn with much pain that my good friend, Mr. Day, the tutor,* is, to all human appearance, fast

* Afterwards President. — F.

sliding into consumption. He relinquished all business several weeks since; has bled at the lungs frequently; is attended with an occasional fever, and grows poor and weak very fast. His misfortune was induced by preaching. Some chance remains for his recovery, but, although we do not entirely despair, we have no reason to hope. He is still in town. I passed the last night with him, and left him quite comfortable this morning. Chauncey Whittelsey of Middletown, a most respectable man, and an able and faithful officer, has been turned out, since my last, from the Collectorship of Middletown, and A—— W——, a known atheist, profligate, and bankrupt, appointed in his place. This is Jefferson's policy to heal national wounds; this is democratical sincerity. I am, my dear brother, not with *empty presidential* professions, your sincere friend and affectionate brother.

The annexed letter alludes to the separation of his brother's wife from her family consequent upon her marriage.

TO MR. G. S. SILLIMAN.

NEW HAVEN, *April* 3, 1802.

. . . . . I PITY her with all my heart when I think what a parting she must have had with the best of parents, and the most affectionate of brothers and sisters. Indeed, my dear brother, when I consider what sacrifices this dear friend is making to promote your happiness, I need not add anything to stimulate your exertions to supply, as far as possible, sources of happiness which shall in some measure compensate her for the loss she has sustained. I earnestly pray Heaven to bless you both, and to render the land in which you are settled as pleasant as that which you have left. I expect to receive letters from you by the middle of next week, but I shall endeavor to feel perfectly easy about you, since you are in the hands of a kind Providence, and every circumstance, so far as we can judge, is in your favor. I have not heard a word from any of our friends of either family since you left Connecticut. I must now say a word to Hepsa. . . . . .

DEAR HEPSA, — This is the first time that I ever sat down to write to you with my face eastward; but I think I shall now look upon the sun at his rising with additional pleasure, since he will shine upon two of my dearest friends before he illuminates New Haven. I have thought of you, my dear sister, often during this week, and I have felt for you sincerely when I considered that the ligaments which bound you to your family were so interwoven with the cords of your heart that they must bleed when torn asunder. But I will not enhance your grief by dwelling upon the subject. Think how happy you will be to return to the bosom of your family, and to welcome your friends to Newport. I trust that David and I shall be among the first from Connecticut who will enter your doors. . . . . . .

The effect of his oration at Hartford is thus stated in a letter to his brother: —

TO MR. G. S. SILLIMAN.

NEW HAVEN, *July* 24, 1802.

. . . . . THE oration was a systematical delineation of the doctrines of modern philosophy, as they affect religion, government, and the morals and habits of private life, and a comparison of them with the practical system of New England, with respect to these three great interests of society. It is hardly consistent with propriety, to detail in a letter what was said by the friends of the cause which I advocated. Suffice it to say, that their praises far exceeded the demands of justice. Babcock's paper, after a long piece upon the abuses of the society in permitting orators to write their own sentiments, pronounces Dwight's oration of last year one of the most execrable, malicious,

and libellous performances ; and declares *this* to be only a
continuation of *that*, with this difference only, — that the
abuse of the President and officers of government is
more *insidious* and *artful* in the latter, although it is evident that they both flowed from one pen, namely, Dr.
Dwight's. The *demos* were the more angry at me because
they supposed *I meant them*, although I did not say a word
about them. . . . . .

The foregoing pages have enabled the reader to
judge of the intellectual qualities of Mr. Silliman in
his youth, and of the culture which he attained. A
more particular notice of his religious views and impressions may properly conclude this chapter. Educated, as he was, at home, and being naturally sober
and reflective, he was never without reverence for
God, and a quick sense of moral obligations. His
frequent religious expressions — though an occasional
reference to religion was deemed to be a part of decorum in those days more than at present — are evidently spontaneous. He had been in the habit of
daily reading the Scriptures and offering up prayer.
Yet prior to the closing year of his tutorship, the
truths of the Gospel had not so vividly impressed
his feelings as to exert a full control over the purpose
and spirit of his life. A few months after graduation, in a letter to his brother, he indicates an intention to make Christianity a study.

TO MR. G. S. SILLIMAN.

FAIRFIELD, *April* 24, 1797.

. . . . . I AM well convinced of the importance of an
early and thorough examination of the evidence of the
Christian religion, and intend that it shall be one of the

first objects of my attention.   I am the more induced to
make this examination, as some of the doctrines contained
in the New Testament are apparently so contradictory to
each other, and so subversive of the conclusions drawn by
human reason, concerning the justice of the Deity in his
government of the world, and in the dispensation of future
rewards and punishments, that I expect to found my belief
of 'these doctrines solely upon the external evidence that
they came from God.   If I find sufficient evidence that
Jesus Christ so appeared, so lived, so taught, so died, and
so ascended into heaven, as in the Bible he is represented
to have done, to command my belief, then I must of consequence believe the doctrines which he taught.   I am
at present reading Bossuet's "Universal History," which
throws much light upon this subject by showing the connection of sacred and profane history. . . . . .

Three years after he writes in a similar strain.

TO MR. G. S. SILLIMAN.

NEW HAVEN, *Aug.* 22, 1800.

. . . . . I AM gratified with the seriousness which often
marks your letters, and which was particularly conspicuous
in your last.   It is indeed true that we must soon leave
"this vale of tears," and pass through the "dark valley of
the shadow of death" into that unknown world from which
there is no return.   The thought strikes me, I must confess, with terror, but still I am conscious that no object in
this world is capable of satisfying the desires of an immortal mind.   I am engaged in a serious examination of the
evidences of the Christian religion.   What I have already
perused would have staggered my mind had I been an
infidel.   I devote my Sabbaths to the pursuit, and mean to
continue it until I am able "to give a reason of the hope
that is in me."   The solicitude of our excellent mother is
so great respecting us both upon this subject, that I should

have engaged in the pursuit from duty alone, had other
motives been wanting. I have received a letter from her,
written upon the 8th instant, when you may remember I
completed my minority. It was full of every motherly and
excellent sentiment appropriate to the occasion.

In an earlier letter to his mother, after confessing
that his religious feelings had declined in strength,
though his determination to avoid all vice is un-
changed, he opens his heart without reserve.

TO HIS MOTHER.

NEW HAVEN, Dec. 15, 1798.

. . . . . I WILL tell you, my dear parent, what I esteem
to be the *strongest springs of action*, by which my mind is at
present impelled. By considering these, you will be better
able to determine the truth of my preceding remarks. I
find no propensity in my system stronger than a wish to be
highly *respectable* and *respected* in society. I must act in a
particular sphere, and that sphere which is assigned me is
the *Law.* This affords a boundless field for the display of
every great and good quality. In a country like ours this
profession is a staircase by which talents and industry
will conduct their possessor to the *very* pinnacle of usefulness and fame. This pinnacle is constantly in my eye. I
am not content (as I once thought it best) to walk ob-
scurely along through some *sequestered vale* of life. . . . . .
No, I must embark in the great business of life; and that
reputation and usefulness may attend me, my *present* time
must be devoted to laborious study. A lawyer ought to be
an *able counsellor* and an eloquent man. *Intense study* is
the only means by which he can attain the first character;
and practice, with unremitting attention to the great models
before his eyes, and a constant habit of elegance and accuracy of language, are the principal means for attaining the
second. This same thirst for respectability influences

likewise all my conduct. I wish to make myself the easy,
agreeable, and endearing man in society. With the grave,
I wish to be sententious; with the girls, easy, affable, and
polite, nay, sometimes moderately trifling ; but with the
friends of my *heart,* open and sincere. In short, I wish to
make myself " all things to all men," as far as decency,
morality, and religion will suffer me to go. Another strong
propensity is that which impels me to associate with females
of equal age and respectability, and from them to cull out
some guardian angel, some tutelary deity, who may be my
protectress and the object of my care. . . . . . Should I
meet a congenial soul I should be a *happy* man, but my
ardor may drive me to an improper connection, and then I
shall be truly miserable. These, my dear parent, I believe
to be the great traits of my present character. I could
enlarge upon them and trace them through all their various
ramifications, but I should tire you with egotism. Now, my
dear parent, is there anything in all this which is *unworthy?* I hear you answer, " No, my dear son ; but remember that *all* you have said respects the *little, very little,* space
of time comprehended within the limits of human life ; —
eternity succeeds, — prepare for that ! " I *feel* the full
force of the great truth, and sincerely pray God to assist
me, and to make me the good Christian as well as the
worthy man. . . . . .

Under a later date, he writes to his mother, de-
ploring his lack of vivid feeling in respect to the
objects of faith.

TO HIS MOTHER.

NEW HAVEN, *March* 15, 1800.

MY DEAR PARENT, — This evening brings us repose
from the fatigues of a four days' examination, and I sit
down with satisfaction to converse a little while with my
dear parent.

Your affectionate parental and instructive letter I have perused again and again. I wish, indeed, that I could give you an account of my religious concerns sufficiently pleasing to repay your exertions and to satisfy my own anxious feelings. I can say with truth that this great subject dwells in my mind when I am at liberty to think, " but shadows, clouds, and darkness rest upon it." Not that I doubt, but that I do not *feel,* although I readily assent to the proposition that these things are so. When I read that one of our frigates has fought a severe battle with a ship of superior force, I feel it at 'once. I trace every circumstance in my mind, and fancy that I hear the roaring cannon, the shouts of victory, and the groans of the dying. But — whether it is owing to some fatal cause, or merely to the triteness of the subject, I know not — when the awful truths of Christianity are announced from the desk, I do not always feel that interest which the subject ought to command. But I will reserve this subject until I see you. . . . . .

His letters to his brother at this time betray a like solicitude.

TO MR. G. S. SILLIMAN.

NEW HAVEN, *May* 14, 1800.

. . . . . WHY is it, since no fact not already accomplished is so clearly demonstrated as human mortality, and nothing is so uncertain as the time and manner of that event, that mankind treat the subject as an idle tale, the dream of superstition, and the bugbear of timorous minds? My dear brother, as we regard our eternal salvation, let us daily strive to run the Christian race, that in the end we may obtain a crown of glory which fadeth not away. . . . . .

In 1802, during the last year of Mr. Silliman's tutorship, a remarkable attentiveness to religion

sprung up in Yale College. In this Revival a large
number of persons became deeply interested, of
whom Mr. Silliman was one. During the progress
of the Revival he writes to his mother as follows: —

YALE, *June* 11, 1802.

. . . . . IT would delight your heart, my dear mother, to
see how the trophies of the Cross are multiplied in this Institution. Yale College is a little temple: prayer and praise
seem to be the delight of the greater part of the students,
while those who are still unfeeling are awed into respectful silence. Pray for me, my dear mother, that while I am
attempting to forward others in the journey to heaven, I
may not be myself a castaway. I send you one volume of
Pope's Letters, also a most excellent new publication. . . . .

On the 5th of September, 1802, he united with
the College Church. The following memorandum,
written on that day, is found among his papers, to
which is appended a record of a similar nature, made
a year later.

NEW HAVEN, *Sept.* 5, 1802.
Morning, 9 o'clock.

Sabbath and Communion Day. — This day I intend, with
the permission and assistance of the good Spirit of God, to
give myself up publicly in a perpetual covenant with God
as my Father, with Jesus Christ as my Saviour, and with
the Holy Ghost as my Sanctifier. O Thou Triune God,
my Creator, my Redeemer, and my Sanctifier, accept me
in the Covenant of Grace; dispose of me according to thy
own good pleasure; employ me in thy service; save me in
thy own way; and enable me to perform with sincerity the
solemn act of publicly committing my soul into thy hands.
Not because I am assured of my soul's health do I thus
resolve to profess and promise. I am not without hope

(although it is but faint and glimmering) that God has accepted of my soul, which was early given up to Him in baptism by my pious parents, one of whom I trust is now singing the song of Moses and the Lamb, and the other, I trust, is fast ripening for heaven ; nor can I entirely despair that the secret act of self-dedication which I have performed in my closet has been regarded by Him who searcheth the heart and trieth the reins. O my Redeemer, when this day for the first time I taste the bread, the sacred symbol of thy flesh, which was torn for my sins, and drink the wine, that sacred symbol of thy blood, which was shed for my sins, may I be melted with grief for my sins, warmed with gratitude for thy disinterested love, and elevated with hope by the remembrance that my Redeemer liveth, and that I shall stand before Him at the last day !

YALE COLLEGE, *Sept.* 11, 1803.

Sabbath and Communion Day. 4½ o'clock, P. M. — This day completes a year, reckoning by Sabbaths, since I did publicly and solemnly give up my soul to God the Father, Son, and Holy Ghost. On that day, for the first time, I sat down at his table, and commemorated his dying love. On that day I vowed not only to deny all sinful inclinations, but to resign friends and even life, should God call me so to do. I promised as far as possible to work out my own salvation, but with fear and trembling, humbly hoping for the blessing of God, without which I can do nothing. My life has been prolonged, my probation extended, and salvation may still be in store for me.

This year has been attended by mercies, — yes, innumerable and of incalculable value. I have enjoyed a state of health unexampled for many years, with great vigor of body and activity of mind. I have not been confined by sickness, nor detained more than two half-days from the house of God. My dear friends, in comfortable health and circumstances, have all been spared to me. I have received an appointment which will afford me a comfortable and honorable support through life, with the prospect of extensive usefulness to youth and to my country. My wants have all been supplied, and I am in health and comfort. This moment the funeral bell tolls for I know not whom, and I am alive; and is not this a great mercy!

But what have I done to show my gratitude to God? And have I received these blessings with humility, and with a sense of my entire dependence upon the Giver of all good? Have I striven to keep up a lively intercourse with Heaven by prayer, by reading, and meditation? Has my deportment before the world been so guarded that no reproach may be brought upon the Christian name; in short, have I striven to lead the life of a Christian? I must plead guilty, inasmuch as my obedience has been very imperfect, and sin has not always been excluded. Still I hope that God may have seen something good in me by his grace, and that I have not wholly neglected my religious duties while I have received innumerable blessings.

My devotions, although generally performed at stated intervals, have been sometimes omitted, or performed with coldness and constraint, and worldly thoughts have too often intruded in the hours of public worship, and opportunities of doing and obtaining good have not always been made use of as they should have been. My deportment has been too unguarded before the world, and I have been wanting in zeal, in love, and engagedness in the Christian life.

For all these things I desire to humble myself before God; and I ask his gracious aid to walk hereafter more worthily of my Christian profession.

This day I have again approached the table of the Lord, and I hope I may not have partaken unworthily of the sacred elements that represent the great sacrifice of our Lord and Saviour Jesus Christ.

God only knows whether another anniversary of this day will be granted to me, or whether I shall sooner be called to give up my account. O Heavenly Father, I implore thine aid through the Spirit of truth, should my life be spared another year, to enable me to live more agreeably to the character of a Christian; more agreeably to thy revealed will, and to my own solemn professions; and wilt Thou assist me this day to renew my covenant with Thee, and, having renewed it, to keep it inviolate.

Other proofs remain of the sincerity with which he entered upon the Christian life. Thenceforward, in all his plans, he had a conscious reference to the Divine will and to the realities of the invisible world. No one who peruses this memoir will find reason to doubt that he served God.

CHAPTER IV.

FROM this point we are able to avail ourselves of
Mr. Silliman's own *Reminiscences.* When he commenced this Record, he had chiefly in view that
department of instruction in Yale College with the
origin and growth of which he was so closely connected. He accordingly begins with a notice of his
relations to the College.

MY own membership in Yale College as an under-grad-
uate extended from September, 1792, to September, 1796;
Æt. 13 to 17. Its concerns continued to be known to me
during the two succeeding years, when I did not reside in
New Haven. In October, 1798, I resumed my residence
here, and was engaged in the study of the law. In September, 1799, I was appointed a tutor in Yale College,
(Æt. 20.) In October following I entered upon the duties

of that office, and remained in the instruction and government of the Institution until 1853, when I fully resigned,
having made an overture for a resignation in 1850, which
was not accepted. During this period, on two different
occasions, I passed nearly two years abroad. By invitation
of the Corporation and Faculty of the College, I continued
to give the chemical lectures to the termination of the
course of 1853, and the lectures on mineralogy and geology until the termination of the academic year of 1855.
My personal knowledge of Yale College has covered more
than sixty years, and therefore, as to historical facts, I may
be regarded as a competent witness during more than one
third of the period of its existence.

A primary object in the institution of the College was
the education of ministers of the Gospel. Classical learning was, therefore, the principal object of attention, and so
it continued to be until my time. To train young men to
write and to speak was the great effort of the instructors.
Theological, ethical, and metaphysical subjects were much
cultivated, and logic was also a prominent topic. The
mathematics were not forgotten, and their value was appreciated. The discoveries of Newton in the preceding century had given great dignity and attractiveness to astronomy and to physical dynamics, and there were always in
the College devotees to these sciences and to mathematics.
The Rev. President Clap — 1739 to 1766 — was an eminent mathematician and astronomer; and the Rev. President Stiles — 1777 to 1795 — in addition to a wide range
of knowledge on almost all subjects, was an ardent devotee to astronomy. It was said that he cherished the hope
that in the future life he would be permitted to visit the
planets, and to examine the rings of Saturn and the belts
and satellites of Jupiter. He continued to my time, having died in 1795, in the May vacation of my Junior year.

In the first century of Yale College, a single room was
appropriated to apparatus in physics. It was in the old

college, second loft, northeast corner, now No. 56.   It was papered on the walls; the floor was sanded, and the window-shutters were always kept closed except when visitors or students were introduced.   There was an air of mystery about the room, and we entered it with awe, increasing to admiration after we had seen something of the apparatus and the experiments.   There was an air-pump, an electrical machine of the cylinder form, a whirling table, a telescope of medium size, and some of smaller dimensions; a quadrant, a set of models for illustrating the mechanical powers, a condensing fountain with *jets d'eau*, a theodolite, and a magic lantern—the wonder of Freshmen. These were the principal instruments; they were of considerable value: they served to impart valuable information, and to enlarge the students' knowledge of the material world.   We should not now undervalue the mental culture, and certainly the discipline, of the first century in Yale College.   In relation to the early condition of the country, the means of education were commensurate with the demands of the community, and great and wise and good and useful men were trained in Yale College in those times, many of whom have left their mark on the passing age in which they lived.

During my novitiate, chemistry was scarcely ever named. I well remember when I received my earliest impressions in relation to chemistry.   Professor Josiah Meigs — 1794 to 1801 — delivered lectures on natural philosophy from the pulpit of the College Chapel.   He was a gentleman of great intelligence, and had read Chaptal, Lavoisier, and other chemical writers of the French school.   From these, and perhaps other sources, he occasionally introduced chemical facts and principles in common with those of natural philosophy.   I heard from him (Æt. 15 and 16) that water contains a great amount of heat which does not make the water any hotter to the touch or to the thermometer; that this heat comes out of the water when it freezes, and still the freezing water is not warmed by the escaping heat, except when the water has been cooled below the freezing-point before freezing; then, when it actually freezes, the temperature rises to 32°; and that all this heat must be reabsorbed by the ice when it melts, and then becomes latent, as if it were extinguished, but is again to escape when the ice melts anew. This appeared to me very surprising; and still more astonishing did it appear that boiling water cannot be made any hotter by urging the fire. My curiosity being awakened, I opened an encyclopedia, and there read that balloons were inflated by an inflammable gas obtained from water; and I looked with intense interest at the figures representing the apparatus, by means of which steam, made to pass through an ignited gun-barrel, came out inflammable gas at the other end of the tube. These and similar things created in my youthful mind a vivid curiosity to know more of the science to which they appertained. Little did I then imagine that Providence held this duty and pleasure in reserve for me.

President Dwight and his enlarged Views. — (1795 to 1817.) — This great man was the successor of the Rev. Dr. Stiles, who was both a living polyglot and a living encyclopedia. President Dwight, if his vigorous mind at the meridian age of forty-three was not overrunning, like that of Dr. Stiles, with every variety of curious lore, it included in his wide range of vision all the great branches of human knowledge. A divine, a poet, a rhetorician, a scholar, and a high-bred gentleman, he, when physical science did not sway the universal mind as now, still saw with a telescopic view both its intrinsic importance and its practical relations to the wants of man and to the progress of human society. Chemistry early attracted his attention, and although he had never been personally conversant with the science, it was apparent from his remarks that he understood its nature and its position among the physical sciences. I was, on an early occasion, much impressed with the correctness of his views, when I accidentally overheard him on the door-steps of the Laboratory replying to a lady, a stranger, who asked him, " Pray sir, what is chemistry ? " To her he correctly and forcibly enunciated its nature and object.

I have already mentioned that I returned to New Haven in 1798, (it was in October,) and that I then commenced the study of the law. This course of study, after my appointment as tutor in Yale College, I continued collaterally with my duties of instruction ; and having advanced nearly through the third year of my studies, I was favorably impressed by an overture for an establishment in a distant State. A proposal was made to me, through some of my college friends in Georgia, to take charge of the important and flourishing academy at Sunbury in Liberty County, not far from Savannah. As this county was settled by a Puritan population, — emigrants from the colony of Old Plymouth and Dorchester, — its people retained the institutions and habits of their Northern friends ; and those persons from Liberty County whom I had known contributed to confirm my favorable impressions. My Southern friends represented to me that a liberal income, enjoyed for a few years, would aid me in passing into the practice of law in Georgia, and thus I might obtain an establishment in a country where the profession commanded more ample rewards than at the North.

While I was deliberating upon this important subject, I met President Dwight, one very warm morning in July, 1801, under the shade of the grand trees in the street in front of the college buildings, when, after the usual salutations, we lingered, and conversation ensued. He had been a warm personal friend of my deceased father ; and their residences being but three miles apart, — Holland Hill and Greenfield Hill, both in Fairfield, — an active interest was maintained between them and their families. The President having ever, and particularly since his accession to the presidency in 1795, taken a parental interest in the welfare of my brother and myself, — my brother Gold. S. Silliman and myself were classmates, — I felt it to be both a privilege and a duty to ask his advice on this occasion. After I had stated the case to him, he promptly replied, and with his usual decision said : " I advise you not to go to Georgia. I would not voluntarily, unless under the influence of some commanding moral duty, go to live in a country where slavery is established ; you must encounter, moreover, the dangers of the climate, and may die of a fever within two years. I have still other reasons which I will now proceed to state to you." He then proceeded to say that the corporation of the College had, several years before, at his recommendation, passed a vote or resolution to establish a Professorship of Chemistry and Natural History as soon as the funds would admit of it. The time, he said, had now arrived when the College could safely carry the resolution into effect. He said, however, that it was at present impossible to find among us a man properly qualified to discharge the duties of the office. He remarked, moreover, that a foreigner, with his peculiar habits and prejudices, would not feel and act in unison with us, and that however able he might be in point of science, he would not understand our college system, and might therefore not act in harmony with his colleagues.

He saw no way but to select a young man worthy of confidence, and allow him time, opportunity, and pecuniary aid to enable him to acquire the requisite science and skill, and wait for him until he should be prepared to begin. He decidedly preferred one of our own young men born and trained among us, and possessed of our habits and sympathies.

The President then did me the honor to propose that I should consent to have my name presented to the Cor-

poration, giving me at the same time the assurance of his
cordial support, and of his belief that the appointment
would be made.   I was then approaching twenty-two years
of age, — still a youth, or only entering on early manhood.
I was startled and almost oppressed by the proposal.   A
profession, — that of the law, — in the study of which I was
already far advanced, was to be abandoned, and a new profession was to be acquired, preceded by a course of study
and of preparation too, in a direction in which in Connecticut there was no precedent.

The good President perceived both my surprise and my
embarrassment, and with his usual kindness and resource
proceeded to remark to this effect : — " I could not propose
to you a course of life and of effort which would promise
more usefulness or more reputation.   The profession of
law does not need you ; it is already full, and many eminent
men adorn our courts of justice ; you may also be obliged
to cherish a hope long deferred, before success would crown
your efforts in that profession, although, if successful, you
may become richer by the law than you can by science.
In the profession which I proffer to you there will be no
rival here.   The field will be all your own.   The study
will be full of interest and gratification, and the presenta-
tion which you will be able to make of it to the college
classes and the public will afford much instruction and
delight.   Our country, as regards the physical sciences, is
rich in unexplored treasures, and by aiding in their development you will perform an important public service, and
connect your name with the rising reputation of our native
land.   Time will be allowed to make every necessary preparation ; and when you enter upon your duties, you will
speak to those to whom the subject will be new.   You will
advance in the knowledge of your profession more rapidly
than your pupils can follow you, and will be always ahead
of your audience."

Thus encouraged by remarks so forcibly put and so

kindly suggested, I expressed my earnest and most respectful thanks for the honor and advantages so unexpectedly
offered to me, and asked for a few weeks for consideration
and for consultation with my nearest friends. We then
emerged from under the shade of those noble elms, and I
retired, thoughtful and pensive, to my chamber. The confidence reposed in me by President Dwight, and thus tendered in advance, increased my sense of responsibility in
view of a highly important and arduous undertaking. I
felt it, however, to be a relief to escape from the practice
of the law, which never appeared to me desirable. There
are indeed bright spots in a career at the Bar: right may
sometimes be vindicated against wrong, and injured innocence protected; but the temptation would often be strong
— especially when backed by wealth — to contend against
justice, and by force of talent and address to make the
worse appear the better cause, and to screen the guilty from
punishment, the fraudulent from the payment that is justly
due. If one could always be engaged in a good cause, and
could be at liberty to follow the promptings of his conscience, without suppression or perversion of truth, or con-
cealment or palliation of wrong, then indeed the practice
of law would appear most desirable and honorable; and
with requisite talent and learning, and the impulses of a
generous temperament, a career at the Bar might be truly
noble; but having been a diligent and attentive listener in
the courts of law during my course of study of the profession, I had seen that the *beau-ideal* sketch was too often
merely a picture of the imagination. The associations
which the practice of the law creates are often highly
undesirable. Often the most unworthy part of mankind
throng the courts of justice, or are compelled to appear
there by the mandate of law, and the practising lawyer is
obliged to consort with the weak and the wicked, as well
as with the wise and good. Such were some of the thoughts
which occurred to me on the first view of the question of

changing professions. On the other hand, the study of
Nature appeared very attractive. In her works there is no
falsehood, although there are mysteries to unveil, which is
a very interesting achievement. Everything in Nature is
straightforward and consistent. There are no polluting
influences; all the associations with these pursuits are elevated and virtuous, and point towards the infinite Creator.
My taste also led me in this direction, and I anticipated no
sacrifice of feeling in relinquishing the prospect of practice
at the Bar, although I had no occasion to regret that I had
spent much time in the study of the noble science of the
law, founded as it is in sound reason and ethics, and sacred
to the best interests of mankind.

Consultation with Friends. — Prominent among them was
a wise and good mother, standing in the place of an excellent father, whom death had removed when I had attained
but half of my then present age. To her and to a higher
Tribunal I had chief reference, and I found the impression
gaining strength in my mind in favor of the pursuits of
science. I therefore decided to accept the proffered nomination of the President, and to take my chance of appointment by the corporation. As I was, however, drawing near
to the close of my term of legal study, I resolved to continue my efforts in that direction, and secure an admission
to the Bar as a retreat in case of disaster to the College
from the violence of party spirit. President Dwight was
an ardent Federalist of the Washington School, and his
eloquent appeals excited the hostility of the rising Democracy. I stood my examination successfully, as conducted
by the Hon. David Daggett on the 19th and 20th of
March, 1802. I was admitted, with the usual oath, to the
Bar of Connecticut, in company with my friends and fellow-
students, Charles Denison and Myron Holley. President
Dwight kindly consented to remain, for the present, silent,
and I continued to act and teach as a tutor, until the devel-

opment took place which is announced in the following paragraphs.

President Dwight had been in office but three years be-fore he procured the passage of the following resolution, which is taken from the record of the doings of the President and Fellows of Yale College at their regular meeting, Sept. 12, 1798 : —

" *Voted*, That a Professorship of Chemistry and Natural History be instituted in this College as soon as the funds shall be sufficiently productive to support it."

From the doings of the same, Sept. 7, 1802, four years later : —

Whereas, in Sept. 1798, it was voted by this Board that a Professorship of Chemistry and Natural History be insti-tuted in this College as soon as the funds shall be suffi-ciently productive to support it ; and it now appearing that the funds are adequate to the object, —

" *Voted*, That a Professorship of Chemistry and Natural History be, and it is hereby, instituted in this College.

" *Voted*, That it is expedient to elect, for a Professor of Chemistry and Natural History, some person of competent talents, giving him such time to give his answer whether he will accept such appointment or not, as he may desire, and as may be agreed on between him and the Corporation.

" The Corporation being led to the choice of a Professor of Chemistry and Natural History in this College, on the provisions of the foregoing vote,

BENJAMIN SILLIMAN, ESQ.,

was declared chosen."

The secret had been faithfully kept by President Dwight and the small number of friends to whom it had been con-fided. The appointment was, of course, a cause of wonder to all, and of cavil to political enemies of the College. Al-though I persevered in my legal studies, as already mentioned, I, soon after the confidential communication of President Dwight, obtained a few books on chemistry, and kept them secluded in my secretary, occasionally reading in them privately. This reading did not profit me much. Some general principles were intelligible, but it became at once obvious to me that to see and perform experiments, and become familiar with many substances, was indispensable to any progress in chemistry, and of course I must resort to Philadelphia, which presented more advantages in science than any other place in our country. As to my appointment, when ignorant of the science I was appointed to teach, it was easily explained and vindicated to all reasonable people by such suggestions made by President Dwight himself as are recorded above. I was not elated by the appointment; but having youth, health, zeal, energy, and perseverance on my side, I did not, with God's blessing, despair of success.

FIRST RESIDENCE IN PHILADELPHIA.

(*Nov.* 1802 *to March* 1803.) — Absent from New Haven from Oct. 26th to March 17th, — four months and twenty-one days. I was all the time, except six days, in Philadelphia. I arrived in Philadelphia at the close of a season of yellow fever, having never been there before. The city was comparatively deserted; the streets were quiet, and an air of anxiety was visible in the aspect of the remaining citizens. Still, as cool weather had commenced, no serious danger was apprehended, and by the recommendation of my friends, Charles and Elihu Chauncey, I engaged lodgings with them at Mrs. Smith's, corner of Dock and Walnut streets. Dock Street runs diagonally from the river, crossing Walnut Street at an acute angle, and there a wedge-shaped house had been erected which was now to be my home for four months, both in this year and the next.

This house attracted a select class of gentlemen. The Connecticut members of Congress resorted to it, I believe, while the government was in Philadelphia; and after its removal, as they were passing to and from Washington, it was a temporary resting-place. Other gentlemen of intelligence were among its inmates, and several of them, being men of great promise, were then rising into the early stages of that eminence which they attained in subsequent years. Among them were Horace Binney, Charles Chauncey, Elihu Chauncey, Robert Hare, John Wallace and his brother; and as frequent visitors, John Sargeant and George Vaux. There were occasionally other gentlemen, but those I have named were our stars. Alas! of the eight whom I have named only two remain; and if I add myself,—then an almost unknown young man, — the circle of names will be nine, and the survivors three, — Horace Binney, Robert Hare, and B. Silliman.* Horace Binney, Charles Chauncey, and John Sargeant rose to the head of the Philadelphia Bar, and John Sargeant was afterwards a member of Congress, and, I believe, of the Senate of the United States. Robert Hare took the first rank as a chemist and philosopher; Elihu Chauncey was an eminent banker and financier, and the Wallaces and Vaux were most agreeable gentlemen, — Vaux, a Quaker, but warm-hearted and of easy, polished manners. Enos Bronson, of Connecticut and Yale College, was also of our number. He edited the " United States Gazette" with much talent.

The gentlemen whom I have named, with the friends and visitors that were by them attracted to the house, formed a brilliant circle of high conversational powers. They were educated men, of elevated position in society, and their manners were in harmony with their training. Rarely in my progress in life have I met with a circle of gentlemen who surpassed them in courteous manners, in brilliant intelligence, sparkling sallies of wit and pleasantry, and cordial greeting both among themselves and with friends and strangers who were occasionally introduced. Our hostess, Mrs. Smith, a high-spirited and efficient woman,

* Dr. Hare died May 15th, 1858.

was liberal almost to a fault, and furnished her table even luxuriously. Our habits were, indeed, in other respects far from those of teetotalers. No person of that description was in our circle. On the contrary, agreeably to the custom which prevailed in the boarding-houses of our cities half a century ago, every gentleman furnished himself with a decanter of wine, — usually a metallic or other label being attached to the neck, and bearing the name of the owner. Healths were drunk, especially if stranger guests were present, and a glass or two was not considered excessive, — sometimes two or three, according to circumstances. Porter or other strong beer was used at table as a beverage. As Robert Hare was a brewer of porter and was one of our number, his porter was in high request, and indeed it was of an excellent quality. I do not remember any water-drinker at our table or in the house, for total abstinence was not there thought of except, perhaps, by some wise and far-seeing Franklin.

Accustomed to a simple diet in New Haven, without wine or porter, and perhaps with only cider at dinner, the new life to which I was now introduced did not agree well with my health. Occasionally, vertigo disturbed my head, and the nervous system was affected. At the end of both seasons in Philadelphia I had made some progress towards incipient gout. On my knuckles, what appeared to be chalky concretions began to form, which however went away after my return to New Haven and to my usual mode of living. In the upper classes of society in Philadelphia, the habits of living were then very luxurious and the spirit worldly. In my case, the effects of luxurious living were to a degree counteracted by vigorous exercise. Often I walked with my friend Charles Chauncey, even in severe weather and before breakfast, to the river Schuylkill, two to two and a half miles, and of course four to five miles' out and back; and Robert Hare's brewery, one and a half mile up town, often gave the occasion of useful exercise:

he became a warm friend to me. There were no outward
manifestations of religion in our boarding-house. Grace
was, I believe, never said at table, nor did I ever hear a
prayer in the house. I trust that private personal prayers
ascended from some hearts and lips, in a house where so
many were amiable and worthy, although without a religious garb. On the Sabbath, some of our gentlemen resorted to the churches, and some dined out on that day.
For myself I attended, almost without exception, the
church of the Rev. Dr. Ashbel Green. He was an excellent preacher, and I was favored with his kind regard.
Rev. Dr. Janeway was his colleague, and preached with
ability. My friend Charles Chauncey was generally my
companion at Dr. Green's church in Arch Street. Mrs.
Smith and her daughter Elizabeth also attended in this
church, — they held Dr. Green in high reverence, and respected religion. He was afterwards and for many years
President of Princeton College.

My Opportunities for Professional Improvement. — The
lectures on chemistry by Dr. James Woodhouse formed a
part of the course of medical instruction in the Medical
School of Philadelphia. These were given in a small
building in South Fourth Street, opposite to the State-
House Yard. Above, over the laboratory, was the Anatomical Hall. Neither of these establishments was equal to
the dignity and importance of the Medical School, and the
accommodations in both were limited: the lecture-rooms
were not capacious enough for more than one hundred or
one hundred and twenty pupils, and there was a great deficiency of extra room for the work, which was limited to
a few closets. The chemical lectures were important to
me, who had as yet seen few chemical experiments. Those
performed by Dr. Woodhouse were valuable, because every
fact, with its proof, was an acquisition to me. The apparatus was humble, but it answered to exhibit some of the

most important facts in the science ; and our instructor delighted, although he did not excel, in the performance of experiments. He had no proper assistant, and the work was imperfectly done ; but still it was a treasure to me. Our Professor had not the gift of a lucid mind, nor of high reasoning powers, nor of a fluent diction ; still, we could understand him, and I soon began to interpret phenomena for myself and to anticipate the explanations. Dr. Woodhouse was wanting in personal dignity, and was, out of lecture - hours, sometimes jocose with the students. He appeared, when lecturing, as if not quite at his ease, as if a little fearful that he was not highly appreciated, — as indeed he was not very highly.

In his person he was short, with a florid face. He was always dressed with care ; generally he wore a blue broadcloth coat with metal buttons ; his hair was powdered, and his appearance was gentlemanly. His lectures were quite free from any moral bearing, nor, as far as I remember, did he ever make use of any of the facts revealed by chemistry, to illustrate the character of the Creator as seen in his works. At the commencement of the course he treated with levity and ridicule the idea that the visitations of the yellow fever might be visitations of God for the sins of the people. He imputed them to the material agencies and physical causes, — forgetting that physical causes may be the moral agents of the Almighty. His treatment of myself was courteous. I dined with him in his snug little bachelor's establishment, — for he had no family, and a matron housekeeper superintended his small establishment. I should add respecting his lectures that they were brief. He generally occupied a fourth or a third of the hour in recapitulating the subject of the preceding lecture, and thus he advanced at the rate of about forty or forty-five minutes in a day.

At the commencement of my first course with him, in 1802, he had just returned from London, where he had been with Davy and other eminent men. He brought with him a galvanic battery of Cruickshank's construction, — the first that I had ever seen, — but as it contained only fifty pairs of plates, it produced little effect. Dr. Woodhouse attempted to exhibit the exciting effects of Davy's nitrous oxide, but failed for want of a sufficient quantity of gas, and the tubes were too narrow for comfortable respiration. He did not advert to these facts, but was inclined to treat the supposed discovery as an illusion. I had afterwards, at New Haven, an opportunity to prove that there was no mistake, and that Davy had not overrated the exhilarating effects of the gas when respired conveniently and in proper quantities, — three or four quarts to a person of medium size, inhaled through a wide tube. An amusing occurrence happened one day in the laboratory. Hydrogen gas was the subject, and its relation to life. It was stated that an animal confined in it would die; and a living hen was, for the experiment, immersed in the hydrogen gas, with which a bell-glass was filled. The hen gasped, kicked, and lay still. "There, gentlemen," said the Professor, "you see she is dead;" but no sooner had the words passed his lips, than the hen with a struggle overturned the bell-glass, and with a loud scream flew across the room, flapping the heads of the students with her wings, while they were convulsed with laughter. The same thing might have occurred to any one who had incautiously omitted to state that this gas is not poisonous, like carbonic acid, but kills, like water, by suffocation.

The death of Dr. Woodhouse took place in 1815, I suppose from apoplexy. He was found dead in his bed. He had a short neck, and was of a full sanguineous habit. The chemistry of that period — that of my attendance on the lectures of Dr. Woodhouse, more than half a century ago — had not attained the precision which it now has. The modern doctrine of definite proportions or equivalent proportions was then only beginning to be understood; the combining proportions of bodies were generally given in centesimal numbers, and thus the memory was burdened, and with little satisfaction. The modern analysis of organic bodies was then hardly begun. Galvanism had indeed awakened Europe, and progress had been made towards those interesting developments which have filled the world with astonishment; but their era was several years later. We may not, therefore, impute to a professor of that period the deficiencies which belonged to that stage of this science.

I had not reason to regret that I attended on the lectures of Dr. Woodhouse. He supplied the first stepping-stones by which I was enabled at no distant day to mount higher.

The deficiencies of Dr. Woodhouse's courses were, in a considerable degree, made up in a manner which I could not have anticipated. I have already mentioned that Robert Hare was a fellow-boarder and companion at Mrs. Smith's. He was a genial, kind-hearted man, one year younger than myself, and was already a proficient in chemistry upon the scale of that period; and being informed of my object in coming to Philadelphia, he kindly entered into my views and extended to me his friendship and assistance. A small working laboratory was conceded to us by the indulgence of our hostess, Mrs. Smith, and we made use of a spare cellar-kitchen, in which we worked together in our hours of leisure from other pursuits. Mr. Hare had, one year before, perfected his beautiful invention of the oxy-hydrogen blow-pipe, and had presented the instrument to the Chemical Society of Philadelphia. His mind was much occupied with the subject, and he enlisted me into his service. We worked much in making oxygen and hydrogen gases, burning them at a common orifice to produce the intense heat of the instrument. Hare was desirous of making it still more intense by deriving a pure oxygen from chlorate of potassa, then called oxy-muriate of potassa. Chemists were then ignorant of the fact that, by mixing a little oxide of manganese with the chlorate, the oxygen can be evolved by the heat of a lamp applied to a glass retort. Hare thought it necessary to use stone retorts with a furnace-heat; the retorts were purchased by me at a dollar each, and, as they were usually broken in the experiment, the research was rather costly; but my friend furnished experience, and, as I was daily acquiring it, I was rewarded, both for labor and expense, by the brilliant results of our experiments. Hare's apparatus was ingenious, but unsafe as regards the storage of the gases. Novice as I was, I ventured to suggest to my more experienced friend that by some accident or blunder the gases — near neighbors as they were in their contiguous apartments — might become mingled, when, on lighting them at the orifice, an explosion would follow. I was afterwards informed, although not by Hare, that this accident actually happened to him, although with no other mischief than a copious shower-bath from the expulsion of the water. Many years afterwards, Professor Hitchcock at Amherst, from the same cause, met with an explosion which gave him a great shock, and for a time greatly impaired his hearing.

After my return to New Haven, I contrived a mode of separating these gases so effectually that they could not become mixed. Eventually I employed separate gasometers, one to contain the oxygen and the other the hydrogen, and during forty years that they were in use no accident ever happened. On this subject I may remark again farther on. During the second course in Philadelphia (winter of 1803–4) I commenced writing lectures on heat and other general topics of chemistry, with reference to the commencement of my labors of instruction in Yale College. I enjoyed the important assistance of the lectures of the distinguished Dr. Black of Edinburgh, then recently published by his pupil and friend, Dr. Robison. This book was to me a mine of riches. The first edition of Thomson's Chemistry, in four volumes, had then just appeared, and I took hold of it with avidity and with profit.

The temptation was strong to attend other courses of
lectures, and I attempted it; but soon found that I must
confine my attention mainly to my own pursuits, and therefore I relinquished all, except two extraneous courses, which
I will presently name.

I attended an introductory lecture of Dr. Benjamin
Rush, and had the satisfaction of identifying his person
and manner, and I occasionally met him in society. His
voice was musical, his person and features pleasing, and
his diction clear and emphatic. Alluding to the use of the
lancet in yellow fever, he called it in his lecture, that
"*magnum donum Dei.*"

Dr. Barton was a learned professor of *materia medica*
and Botany, and his name is perpetuated in several valuable works. He was also a proficient in natural history
generally, and he offered a private course — I think — on
zoölogy. This I attended in the evening, and was entertained and instructed. After the course had advanced far
enough to make illustrations from specimens instructive,
our Professor one evening remarked to us, that it would
be desirable to visit Peale's Museum, which was rich in
preserved specimens of animals, birds, reptiles, &c. The
week being filled with lectures, Dr. Barton proposed that
we should go, by special permission of Mr. Peale, on Sunday, as that was a day of leisure, and then we should
not be interfered with by the usual visiting company. The
proposition was no sooner made than it was adopted by
general silent consent. With some hesitancy I rose, and
in the most respectful terms stated that I regretted to interfere with the wishes or convenience of the Professor and
the class, but that for myself I had other occupations on
the day proposed, and if that were to be the time, I must
lose the instruction. After a moment's pause, the Professor named Saturday afternoon, which was adopted. A
few days after, when passing down Market Street, I met a
Dr. Parish, a young Quaker physician, who caught me by

the hand, and said : " Friend Silliman, I was glad to hear that thee had objected to visiting Peale's Museum on first day, when it was proposed by Dr. Barton." First day is not sacred time with the Quakers, but they generally hold meetings on that day, and partake, to a degree, of the general reverence for the Sabbath entertained in most Christian countries.

The lectures on anatomy and surgery by Dr. Caspar Wistar enjoyed a high reputation, and I was not willing to resist the temptation to attend them, especially as I expected eventually to be connected with a medical school in New Haven ; and chemistry, moreover, sustains important relations to anatomy. The lectures of Dr. Wistar were highly instructive and interesting. He combined perfect dignity with deep feeling and enthusiasm, which enabled him to throw a charm over his subject, revolting as many of its demonstrations appear to an unprofessional novice. So great was his command of his class, that no levity was manifested by them on occasions when it would have been with difficulty repressed by a professor of an opposite character. He had an able demonstrator, by whom the recent subjects were skilfully prepared. The structure of our wonderful frame was most ably demonstrated in all its parts. Their combination and use were fully explained, and the reasons that must have influenced the Creator in the adaptation of every part to every other were made manifest. Dr. Wistar's treatment of his classes was paternal and kind, and he took a deep interest in their improvement. On one occasion he was demonstrating the structure and functions of the eye and the theory of vision, when a student left the theatre. The Professor made an abrupt pause, and, with evident and strong emotion, added : " Gentlemen, this is the first time I ever knew a student to go away during the demonstration of this most interesting organ." Many of these things have remained for half a century so deeply impressed on my mind, that they now appear vividly, almost as if I had heard them recently. I should mention that Dr. Wistar, when returning from Europe in his early manhood, having finished his professional studies abroad, landed at Boston, and in his journey to Philadelphia, stopped at New Haven, visited Yale College, and had an interesting interview with President Stiles. He admired exceedingly his various and curious erudition, his enthusiasm and eloquence, and the winning courtesy of his manners. He seemed fond of returning to the theme, which was of course pleasing to me as a son of Yale, who passed almost three years under the Presidency of Dr. Stiles.

Dr. Wistar treated me with marked consideration, and I was invited twice to dine at his hospitable table, which was supplied with an elegant and tasteful liberality, but without ostentation. I enjoyed these occasions exceedingly. Dr. Wistar was childless; but his wife seemed to be actuated by the same spirit of hospitality.

Meeting with Dr. Joseph Priestley. — This celebrated gentleman was also a guest on one of these occasions, when I dined at Dr. Wistar's. As a very young man, (of twenty-three or twenty-four years,) I felt it an honor and advantage to be introduced to so celebrated an author and philosopher. He had become obnoxious in his native country on account of political and religious opinions, as he was a friend of civil liberty, and his religious creed was Arian, or Unitarian. At that time, during the early part of the French revolution, there was a strong excitement in England against revolutionary sentiments and movements. Dr. Priestley then resided at Birmingham, and during an anniversary commemoration of the destruction of the Bastile, although he was not then in the city, the mob proceeded to his house, which they burned, with his library, apparatus, and manuscripts. All were lost; and the outrage was said to have been countenanced by persons of consideration both lay and clerical. In 1794 he fled from persecution, and took refuge with his family at Northumberland, Pennsylvania, on the Susquehanna River. Here he resumed his philosophical pursuits, and made occasional visits to Philadelphia. It was on one of these occasions that I was invited to meet him at Dr. Wistar's table, and the interview was to me very gratifying. In person he was small and slender, and in general outline of person not unlike the late President Stiles. His age was then about seventy. His dress was clerical and perfectly plain. His manners were mild, modest, and conciliatory; so that, although in controversy a sturdy combatant, he always won kind regard and favor in his personal intercourse. At the dinner, Dr. Priestley was, of course, the honored guest, and there was no other except one gentleman and myself.

Some of Dr. Priestley's remarks I remember. Speaking of his chemical discoveries, which were very numerous, he said: — " When I had made a discovery, I did not wait to perfect it by a more elaborate research, but at once threw it out to the world, that I might establish my claim before I was anticipated." He remarked upon those passages in the Epistle of John which relate to the Trinity, that they were modern interpolations, not being found in the most ancient manuscripts.* He spoke much of Newton and his discoveries, and the beauty and simplicity of his character; and I think that he claimed him as thinking in religion as he himself did. He mentioned being present at a dinner in Paris given by the Count de Vergennes during the American Revolution, and the seat next to him was occupied by a French nobleman. At another part of the table were two gentlemen dressed in canonicals. When, said Dr. Priestley, I inquired of the nobleman the names of those two gentlemen, he replied: " One of them is Bishop So-and-so, and the other Bishop So-and-so; but they are very clever fellows; and, although they are bishops, they don't believe anything more of this mummery of Chris-

* Dr. Priestley doubtless referred to 1 John v. 7. — F.

tianity than you or I do." " Speak for yourself, sir," I replied ; " for, although I am accounted a heretic in England,
I do believe what you call ' this mummery of Christianity.'"
Dr. Priestley, whom I saw on various occasions, when invited to dine, accepted the invitation, but took out his
memorandum-book and noted the engagement, remarking
that he had now only an artificial memory. He died in his
seventy-first year, at Northumberland, February 6th, 1804.
After rejecting the doctrine of Phlogiston in early years,
he resumed it at a later period of life ; and it was reported
at Philadelphia that he was occupied on his death-bed in
correcting the proof of a new pamphlet on that subject.
He died from inanition, being unable to take any food, —
his digestive powers being gone.

Summer of 1803, *at New Haven.* — On my return to New
Haven in March, 1803, I resumed the instruction of a class
in the ordinary routine of college studies. I had previously, in conjunction with my respected colleague and
friend, Rev. Ebenezer Grant Marsh, carried a class through
the three years from 1799 to 1802. In the fourth year
the class passed into the hands of the President, and was
graduated in 1803. I ought to have been released from all
other duties of instruction, that I might devote my time
entirely to professional study; but the College was poor,
and it was necessary to economize in the labor of the officers, as well as in all other ways. Still, I found time to
perform some experiments, and to construct apparatus
which would be available in my future labors. I devoted
as much time as possible to scientific studies, and was thus
the better prepared to resume my residence in Philadelphia during the next winter.

Brief Residence in Princeton. — At this celebrated seat of
learning, an eminent gentleman, Dr. John Maclean, resided
as the Professor of Chemistry, &c. I early attained an

introduction to him by correspondence, and he favored me
with a list of books for the promotion of my studies.
Among these were Chaptal's, Lavoisier's, and Fourcroy's
Chemistry, Scheel's Essays, Bergman's Works, Kirwan's
Mineralogy, &c. I also passed a few days with Dr. Maclean in my different transits to and from Philadelphia, and
obtained from him a general insight into my future occupation ; inspected his library and apparatus, and obtained
his advice regarding many things.' Dr. Maclean was a man
of brilliant mind, with all the acumen of his native Scotland ; and a sprinkling of wit gave variety to his conversation. I regard him as my earliest master of chemistry, and
Princeton as my first starting-point in that pursuit ; although I had not an opportunity to attend any lectures
there. Mrs. Maclean was a lovely woman, and made my
visits at the house very pleasant to me. She was a sister of
Commodore Bainbridge, afterwards signalized by the capture of the British frigate *Java*, in the war of 1812–15.
Mrs. Maclean gave me an introduction to the family of
Commodore Bainbridge in Philadelphia, in which I was
an occasional visitor. Dr. Maclean, the President of
Princeton College at this time and for some years past, is
the worthy son of Professor Maclean, and does honor to
his father and to the institution over which he ably presides. President Samuel Stanhope Smith was the head of
the college during my early acquaintance with Princeton,
and I had the honor of an introduction to him, and of dining in his family. Mrs. Smith, a grave, taciturn lady, was
a daughter of the celebrated Dr. Witherspoon, of Revolutionary memory, a member of the Congress which declared the independence of the Colonies, to which instrument he added his signature. The personal presence of
President Smith was noble and commanding ; but there
was a stately gravity about him which did not encourage
freedom, and I felt much constraint in his society. He was
a powerful writer and an eloquent speaker.

My Second Winter in Philadelphia. (Nov. 5, 1803, to March 25, 1804.) — There was little to distinguish this from the preceding winter. I attended, as before, the course of chemistry and anatomy, and resumed my private labors with Robert Hare. The familiarity which I had acquired in the preceding year with men and things, enabled me to derive additional advantage, and made me feel more at home. My circle of acquaintance was more extended, quite as much as was consistent with my studies. I was admitted hospitably or socially to some of the most estimable families, — that of Judge Wilson, son of him of the Revolution; to Bishop White's, Dr. Strong's, Col. Biddle's, where there were beautiful daughters, (afterwards Mrs. Dr. Chapman and Mrs. Cadwallader.) I have mentioned the Wistars, Bainbridges, and Greens. At Judge Peters's, also, I was acquainted, and at Mrs. Bradford's. I visited also the public institutions, — the Hospital, the Mint, the Navy Yard, the Water Works, the libraries, manufactories, &c. Philadelphia had then seventy-five or eighty thousand inhabitants; now it has more than half a million. The present beautiful Washington Square was a Potter's Field, and all was country between it and the Hospital. About this time I was elected a member of the Philosophical Society founded by Franklin, and of course had free access to its library, and to its very intelligent and kind librarian, Mr. John Vaughan, a man of large benevolence. I continued the writing of my lectures, and began to collect apparatus, although on a humble scale.

In March, 1804, after passing a few days in Princeton, I returned to New Haven, and devoted my time to writing lectures.

To Mr. Silliman's reminiscences, written after the lapse of many years, may be added brief passages from his correspondence during the period covered by the foregoing chapter.

TO MR. STEPHEN TWINING.

PHILADELPHIA, *November* 21, 1802.

. . . . . THIS is truly a great town, and presents many objects worthy the attention of a stranger. If I live to return to Connecticut, I will describe them to you. But I have seen one which I cannot refrain from mentioning. Governor McK—— is so popular among tavern-haunters that the owners of public-houses are very fond of hoisting up a picture of his Excellency over the doors. Two men in Dock Street, brothers, one a Demo and the other a Fed, being joint-owners of a house, — but the Fed possessing rather the most wit, and consciously the superior influence, — differed concerning a new sign which they thought of putting up. The Demo plead for his Excellency, and the Fed finally consented, but gave the printer private orders to represent the Republican magistrate in the attitude in which he generally appears at four o'clock P. M. The governor accordingly stands forth, or rather staggers forth, on the sign, a solemn memento to the lovers of brandy and Democracy. . . . . .

TO MR. G. S. SILLIMAN.

No. 46 Walnut St., PHILADELPHIA.
November 19, 1803.

MY DEAR BROTHER, — . . . . . The honorable confidence tendered to me *in advance* by the Corporation, the hopes of many friends, and the envy of a few ambitious contemporaries, — the extent and importance of the sciences I am to teach, and the responsibility for their advantageous introduction into the College and State to which I belong, — are motives sufficient to excite my most active and unremitted exertions. Since the Chair has been offered to me, I have not therefore considered myself as at liberty to indulge in recreation, or even in the common relations and most interesting pleasures of friendship. My vacations, in common with the rest of the year, have been devoted to the study or practice of my profession, and I have the satisfaction to find that I have made progress.

With these considerations before you, you will acquiesce in my conduct, although like me you will regret that it should have prevented us from an intercourse which, next to that with a reconciled God, affords the truest, the most heartfelt delight. Indeed, I bless Heaven that I have such a brother, and that he has allied me to such a sister; and I trust that more of those elevated pleasures which I have experienced in their society are still in store for me. . . . .

Pray, my dear brother, write to me soon; detail the *minutiæ* of your welfare; tell me something about my dear little niece. — *My dear Hepsa*, write something with your own hand; let me know how you are sustained under God's chastenings, — whether religion or time bring you any consolation, and at all alleviate your grief; and above all, whether you have reason to hope that the present affliction, though it seem not joyous but grievous, will in the end work for your good. And now, my dear Selleck and Hepsa, with the tenderest affection and the sincerest prayers for your welfare, I commit you to the care of Heaven.

Your very affectionate
friend and brother,
BENJ. SILLIMAN.

FROM TUTOR J. L. KINGSLEY.

February 18, 1802.

THE President called upon me this morning and wished me to write you a request from him to pay some attention, if possible, before you return, to the analyzing of stones. You may possibly recollect that we some time ago received some of the basalts from the Giant's Causeway. The President supposes there is stone in the neighborhood of this town of a similar nature, and wishes to ascertain the fact.

December 5, 1802.

. . . . . I HAVE lately heard from Mr. Day. He is no better, but rather worse, than when he left us. . . . . . Dr. Dwight told me, a short time since, that he had given over the expectation of ever seeing Mr. Day in the professor's chair. What a loss to the Institution! A character so near perfection is not often found in this wicked world. Indeed, I know but few who are his equals, and I never saw his superior. That such a man should be cut off in the very blossom of life is to the human eye dark and mysterious.* We must, however, submit to Him who seeth not as man seeth. . . . . .

The following are passages from a humorous letter of one of his colleagues in the tutorship. In the treatment of these light topics, the reader will detect traits of style which reappear in the erudite essays and commentaries of the author's later years. The "Gazette" was a document composed by the tutors for the entertainment of their absent associate.

YALE COLLEGE, *December 21, 1802.*

DEAR SIR, — So much time has elapsed since the publication of our last "Gazette," that it becomes pleasing, and in a degree necessary, to give you further information respecting the "gestion" of our affairs. To be very brief, Mr. —— has been rusticated, (for rolling barrels down my stairs,) for the term of two months. Sophomore —— has received the darts of Dr. Dwight's quiver, until they were exhausted, for cutting bell-ropes and blasphemy, but without any harm; he yet stands unhurt "amidst the war, &c." Freshman —— has been suspended for crimes

---

* Mr. Day is now (October 1865) living, at the age of *ninety-two*. — F.

of almost every name. Many others stand trembling in "*fearful looking for of fiery indignation.*" In short, there appear to be more devils in college at present than were cast out of Mary Magdalene. I have been honored by a broadside at one of my windows, which popped off without ceremony six squares of glass. No matter; you were honored in the same way. I congratulate myself on having obtained the honor. "*Fiat justitia ruat cœlum,*" is my maxim. But the devil does not extend his dominion over students alone. The august body of tutors have occasionally acknowledged his power. Last evening they met at the "*Luxembourg*" to read "*Dialogues*" for the January exhibition.

The letter proceeds to detail, in the same sportive vein, the particulars of a harmless frolic such as young men, even though clothed with tutorial dignity, sometimes indulge in, and in which a wrongly directed missile — "*miserabile dictu,*" to quote the writer's phrase — shivered into a thousand pieces a large mirror belonging to Mr. Silliman.

This was the catastrophe: "*Valete, Plaudite.*" The only observation I have to make on the above is: I hope the students will not discover it. "*Dulce est desipere in loco,*" is a sentiment we feel to be true, and I have only to regret that you were not present to heighten and partake of our festivity, hilarity, puerility, madness, pleasure, or whatever name it may deserve. You will probably be occupied at least two weeks in deciphering our "Gazette." I am desired by our brethren to excuse our not sending it on sooner. The reason was, we waited to send it by Morse, the printer, who finally failed of going to Philadelphia as he intended.

Since I have been here, I have been paying some attention to Italian, but I am not able to procure suitable books.

If in some of your rambles you would call at some of the Philadelphia bookstores, and inquire for an Italian grammar, dictionary,—Tasso, Dante, Ariosto, Metastasio, or any other Italian writer, if it even be a novelist,—I would thank you. If any or all of these can be found, you would oblige me by giving information soon, that I may take the proper means of procuring them. Especially, I want Dante, Ariosto, and Tasso. . . . . .

Yours forever,

B. SILLIMAN, Esq.   MOSES STUART.

A second letter from the same vivacious writer announced the reception of the Italian books, and remarked further on the state of the College.

YALE COLLEGE, February 6, 1803.

DEAR SIR, — I have received my "Italian Library," and am much obliged to you for the pains you took in procuring it. I could wish you had not purchased *Metastasio*, as the edition is somewhat incorrect and very badly printed; but since it is come, I acquiesce in the purchase. My intention was to have you write me a catalogue of some Italian books which could be purchased at Philadelphia, and not to make the purchase before I had calculated what I could afford to spare from my " liberal wages," in making a purchase of this kind. I presume, however, that I did not express myself in my letter to you according to this intention, and therefore am content with my " library." . . . . . We are all anticipating your return, and expect to be taught where we may find, or rather how we may compose, the " *philosopher's stone.*" For my own part, I am so grossly ignorant respecting chemistry, that I hardly know what it cannot effect. This business of *analyzing* sometimes makes bad work. If you confine yourself to the laboratory of Woodhouse, and do not happen to get analyzed in the laboratory of some Philadelphia ladies, you will do well. But

I fear the particles of which you are composed, and those of some fine ladies there, are sufficiently homogeneous to possess in a great degree the attraction of affinity. If so, I am convinced that on near approach they would cause such a fermentation as would produce a composition. . . . . As to College affairs, they go on much in the old way. We had many convulsions last quarter, many furious " spasms of infuriated " Sophomores and Freshmen. . . . . . Mr. Fowler's door almost split to pieces with stones; my windows broken; Freshman —— publicly dismissed; Sophomores —— and —— sent home; T——, Sophomore, rusticated three months; and W——, Freshman, sent off. Nothing but wars and rumors of wars. This term there appears to be some disposition to enter into a treaty of peace; at least, a cessation of hostilities is agreed upon.

The time of your return is now so near that we begin to anticipate much pleasure from a relation of some of your chemical experiments. Wishing you a safe return, without leaving your heart in any *laboratory* in Philadelphia,

I am, sir,
Yours with esteem,
· MOSES STUART.

FROM PROFESSOR DAY.

YALE COLLEGE, *January* 7, 1804.

. . . . . I AM much obliged to you for your plan of lectures, so far as you have already arranged them. As for myself, instead of having written my fifth lecture, I have not written my first, and probably shall not this long time. My present course of instruction occupies all the attention which my health will allow me to pay to the subject. My principal object at present is to collect and arrange the most important materials in a course of philosophy. I so contrive the business as to communicate the substance of these, in my recitations, to the Senior class, and at the same time preserve them for future use. I take the several branches nearly in the order in which they are arranged in Enfield's Philosophy. I consult the various authors on the subject, select what is particularly interesting from each, and if my own noddle suggests anything beside, I put all upon paper and throw it into a form somewhat like the *skeleton of a lecture*. This I carry to recitation, and, with such enlargements as occur on the occasion, retail it to the class. In addition to these recitations, I propose frequently problems in philosophy which require a mathematical solution. The answers which are handed in by the members of the class, I examine and correct. This, little as it may seem, is *all* that I am doing at present. As to what I intend to do hereafter, I can say very little. I intend to do what I can ; but my health is such that I form no very distant and extensive projects. The course which I have begun I shall probably continue through next term. The summer will be partly or wholly occupied with experiments. After Commencement, it is possible I may begin to read lectures in the chapel. . . . . . I have anticipated with much pleasure your return to this place in March. But if you are to hold a talk of three weeks with your *great brother* in Princeton,* I see plainly my expectations will be frustrated. Pray bring home with you a specimen of the strings of wampum exchanged on the occasion. . . . . . My dear friend, I daily long for your return to this place. Though I am surrounded with excellent friends' and companions, yet, for one reason and another, there is no one to whom I *unbosom my full soul*. I could do it to Mr. Davis, if he were in health ; but his situation is such at present that it is desirable that his mind should be kept as free as possible from all painful or turbulent emotions. You already know my feelings on *one subject* of immense importance. When I see you again, perhaps I may, and perhaps I may not, disclose to you some *other* anxious thoughts which contribute at times to disturb the serenity of my mind. . . . . .

* *I. e.*, the Chemical Professor in Princeton College. — F.

FROM MR. CHARLES DENISON.

NEW HAVEN, *February* 8, 1804.

. . . . . I READILY recognize not only your handwriting, but *your very self*, in your very acceptable letter. You are still Ben Silliman, notwithstanding the *mysterious* addition to your name of " Chem. & Hist. Nat. Prof." I don't mean, my dear Ben, that this learned addition to your former simple title of Esq. does not perfectly becloud you with dignity, so that those who view you at a distance must exceedingly fear and quake. Yet you must excuse me, to whom you deign the honor of a near approach to your chemical majesty, if I should be more familiar than properly becomes one whose highest honors reach no higher than once to have been grand-juror and lister for the town of New Haven. . . . . .

The following letter was addressed to an esteemed pupil who was engaged in teaching in the State of Maryland.

TO MR. [*now* REV. DR.] N. PORTER.

YALE COLLEGE, *October* 14, 1804.

. . . . . I AM glad that experience enables you *practically* to realize the feelings of an instructor towards a pupil, of which you were before but an incompetent judge. An amiable, worthy, and industrious pupil makes advances in the affections of his instructor, of which he has but little conception. I am gratified that you find your situation in so many important points agreeable. . . . . . In my opinion you are, on the whole, employing your time very profitably; the rust which gathers on your learning you will soon brush off again. In the mean time you are gaining a species of knowledge without which the other would be of little use, — I mean a knowledge of mankind. And in my opinion, gentlemanlike manners are worth some time and attention ; they are a perpetual letter of introduction, wherever you go. On this point you cannot fail to improve, and I am sure you have too much good sense to reject the instruction. I cannot be understood by you to exalt good manners and a knowledge of the world beyond their real value; for without good sense, good 'principles, useful employment, and intellectual improvement, they are the mere tinsel gilding on a wooden ball. I am happy to hear that you intend to return as soon as January. I hope you will make New Haven the scene of your professional studies. You will find your friends Dutton and Whittlesey are here, and I shall be happy to have you an inmate of our society. I have lately received a letter from your classmate Chiffelle. Poor fellow! his spirits are much depressed by the conflict between his religious feelings and principles and the habits of Carolina, to which he seems to submit with the utmost reluctance.

CHAPTER V.

His First Lectures in College (1804). — Construction of the Subterranean
   Laboratory. — Its Alteration. — Lectures to the Class of 1804–5 (in the
   Fall of 1804). — His Apparatus. — Suggestions of Dr. Priestley. —
   Plan for Visiting Europe. — Interview with President Dwight. — Prep-
   arations for Departure. — Letter from Rev. John Pierpont. — Letters of
   Professor Silliman to his Brother.

MY FIRST LECTURE. *April* 4, 1804. — In a public room,
hired for college purposes, in Mr. Tuttle's building on
Chapel Street, nearly opposite to the South College, I met
the Senior class, and read to them an introductory lecture
on the history and progress, nature and objects, of chemistry. I was then twenty-four years old, and in August of
that year I was twenty-five. I continued to lecture, and I
believe in the same room, until the Senior class retired in
July, preparatory to their Commencement in September.
My first efforts were received with favor, and the class
which I then addressed contained men who were afterwards
distinguished in life. Among them were John C. Calhoun,
S. C.; Rev. John Chester; Rev. Ezra Stiles Ely; Bishop
Gadsden; John Preston, Hampton, Miss.; Judge Hinman,
Conn.; Dr. Lansing, N. Y.; Rev. Dr. M°Ewen; Rev. John
Marsh; Rev. John Pierpont, poet; Rev. Dr. Tyler, and
others. On the 4th of April, 1804, I commenced a course
of duty as a lecturer and professor, in which I was sustained during fifty-one years; and now, by God's blessing,
I am still in good health and power, sixty-five and a half
years from my entrance into Yale College; sixty-one and
a half years from graduating; fifty-eight and a half years

from being appointed tutor; and fifty-six and a half years from my appointment as Professor.

In 1802 the Corporation of Yale College erected the building which has ever since been known as the Lyceum. Its position is between the old South Middle and the North Middle College. I understood that a deep excavation under the west end of the building was intended for a laboratory. This building was erected before my appointment, and soon after President Dwight had confidentially offered the Professorship of Chemistry to me. I could, therefore, before my appointment, only look on with suppressed curiosity as to the structure and progress and destination of the edifice, as I was not at liberty to speak. It was understood that the main object was for a library-room, and for suitable apartments for the recitations of the classes, and for study-rooms for two of the professors. I was not consulted as to the laboratory, nor could I have been, openly, before my appointment, nor afterwards with advantage, until I had acquired some knowledge of chemistry. Still, after the prospect of my appointment had been opened to me by President Dwight, I cast anxious glances into that deep excavation, not exactly comprehending how it could be rendered available for the purposes of science; but my lips were as yet sealed in silence.

An English architect, Mr. Bonner, had established himself in New Haven, and had acquired a deserved reputation for knowledge, talent, and taste in his profession. He was charged with the erection of the Lyceum; but, having no particular knowledge of a laboratory, he placed it almost under ground. On my return from Philadelphia, in the spring of 1803, I found that a groined arch of boards had been constructed over the entire subterranean room. It rose from stone pillars of nearly half of the height of the room, erected in each of the four corners and on the middle of the opposite sides. The effect was, therefore, by the curves of the arches, to cut off the light, more or less, from all the windows, — one third, or half, and even two thirds in some of them. At once I saw that it would never answer, and I made my appeal to the Corporation at their next meeting. I invited them to visit the room, to which there was no practicable access except through a hole or scuttle in the roof of the arch. A ladder was therefore raised from below, or let down from above, and, Crusoe-like, the grave and reverend gentlemen of the Corporation descended, as Robinson did into his den, and arrived safely on the floor. President Dwight, Rev. Dr. Ely, Hon. James Hillhouse, and his venerable father, then fourscore or more, and others, — members of the College Senate, — found themselves in a gloomy cavern, fifteen or sixteen feet below the surface of the ground, into which, especially as there was as yet no trench excavated around the outside of the building, little more light glimmered than just enough to make the darkness visible.

To see was to be convinced. I had no difficulty in persuading the gentlemen that the model arch of boards must be entirely knocked away, the stone pillars removed, and the space opened freely to the roof of the room, which should be finished square up to the ceiling, like any other large room. It was indeed to be regretted that several hundred dollars had been worse than thrown away upon the preposterous arch. How did it happen? I suppose that Mr. Bonner, an able civil architect, as I have already said, had received only some vague impressions of chemistry, — perhaps a confused and terrific dream of alchemy, with its black arts, its explosions, and its weird-like mysteries. He appears, therefore, to have imagined, that the deeper down in mother earth the dangerous chemists could be buried, so much the better; and perhaps he thought that a strong arch would keep the detonations under, although, as an architect and engineer, he would of course know that the arch, when pressed from above, grows stronger until it is crushed; but, struck from below, its resistance is feeble, and it may more easily collapse with a crash.

I lost no time in having the model arch removed, and the room finished as if there had been no arch. I caused also a wide trench to be excavated outside, all around the room, and the earth-banks to be sustained by the masonry of stone walls whitened, so that a cheerful light was thus reflected into a large and lofty room, whose windows were now free to the external radiance of the atmosphere and the solar beams from the west.

Still the place was a very unfortunate one, to which, had I been seasonably informed, I should have objected decidedly. When I stood on the floor of the room, my head was still six feet below the surface of the ground, and of course the room was very damp: all articles of iron were rapidly rusted, and all preparations that attracted water became moist or even deliquesced.

I devoted the spring and early weeks of the summer to the finishing and arrangement of my half subterranean working and lecture room. There was no remedy; the College was not able to construct another, and I was afraid of alarming them with the prospect of expenses which I was well aware must be considerable, and would be annual and always recurring. There was therefore no way but to make the best of a faulty location. The room was now paved with flag-stones; a false floor of boards was constructed, rising from the lowest level as high as the ground-sill of the outer door, and thus affording an elevation — an inclined plane — sufficient to prevent the vision of the rear from being obstructed by the front rows of hearers. A gallery was erected on the side of the room opposite to the windows, access being made from the front of the tower or steeple through the intervening cellar, over a paved walk. Tables were established on the floor of the laboratory, in a line with a large hydro-pneumatic cistern or gas-tub, and a marble cistern for a mercurial bath. The small collection of apparatus which I had got together was duly arranged, and things began to look like work. Arrangements were made for furnaces, and for the introduction of water from a neighboring well. The tables were covered with green cloth ; the stone floor was sprinkled with white beach-sand ; the walls and ceiling were whitewashed ; the backs and writing-tables of the benches, and the front and end of the gallery, were painted of a light lead color ; and the glass of the windows being washed clean, the laboratory now made a very decent and rather inviting appearance, like the offices, store-rooms, and kitchens that are seen almost underground in cities.

During fifteen of the best years of my life, from the age of twenty-five to forty, I was a diligent worker in this deep-seated laboratory, and I will mention further on how I finally emerged. This room had the advantage of a more agreeable temperature than if it had been on the surface of the ground.

In October, 1804, the new laboratory received the class that were to graduate in September, 1805. Here, again, were those who in after-life became men of renown. Among them were Thomas Hopkins Gallaudet, friend of the deaf mutes ; Edward Hooker, an able classical instructor; Rev. Heman Humphrey, D. D. ; Rev. Samuel F. Jarvis, D. D. ; Dr. J. M. Scott McKnight, S. C. ; Rev. Gardiner Spring, D. D. ; &c. The very limited apparatus was somewhat extended and embellished by several chemical instruments which I found in a closet in the old philosophical chamber, and which, as I understood, had been brought out from London, in the time of President Stiles, by the late President Ebenezer Fitch. This gentleman was graduated in Yale College in 1777 ; was a tutor in it from 1780 to 1783 ; went into trade with Henry Daggett, Esq., in New Haven, and their concerns led him to England, where he obtained the apparatus named above. There were several very beautiful gas-flasks, with sigmoid tubes ground into them. There was also a Nooth's machine for impregnating water with carbonic acid gas, and a collection of glass tubes. I used also some of the glass bells from the philosophical apparatus; and, as my audience were novices, probably the appearance of the apparatus was respectable. I recollected, also, a remark which I heard Dr. Priestley make, namely, that with Florence flasks (cleaned by sand and ashes) and plenty of glass tubes, vials, bottles, and corks, a tapering iron rod to be heated and used as a cork-borer, and a few live coals with which to bend the tubes, a good variety of apparatus might be fitted up. Some gun-barrels also, he said, would be of much service; and I had brought from Philadelphia an old blacksmith's furnace, which served for the heating of the iron tubes. He said, moreover, that sand and bran, (coarse Indian meal is better,) with soap, would make the hands clean, and that there was no sin in dirt.

At that time there were very few chemical instruments of glass to be obtained in this country. I had picked up a few glass retorts in Philadelphia, and I made application to Mr. Mather, a manufacturer of glass in East Hartford, a few years later, to make some for me. On stating my wish, he said he had never seen a retort, but if I would send him one as a pattern, he did not doubt he could make them. I had a retort the neck or tube of which was broken off near the ball,— but as no portion was missing, and the two parts exactly fitted each other, I sent this retort and its neck in a box, never dreaming that there could be any blunder. In due time, however, my dozen of green glass retorts, of East Hartford manufacture, arrived, carefully boxed and all sound, except that they were all cracked off in the neck exactly where the pattern was fractured; and broken neck and ball lay in state like decapitated kings in their coffins. This more than Chinese imitation affords a curious illustration of the state of the manufacture of chemical glass at that time in this country, or rather in Connecticut; the same blunder would probably not have been made in Philadelphia or Boston.

As far as I could judge, the impression on my pupils of the institution and on the public was favorable. The experiments were prepared with great care, and a failure was a very rare occurrence. Although manuscripts fully written out lay before me, I soon began to speak without reading, and found my own feeling freer and easier, and the audience more interested. I always, however, prepared the matter of the lecture thoroughly, and therefore avoided embarrassment in the delivery. Even with my immature and limited acquirements I was encouraged to proceed by recollecting other remarks which I heard from Dr. Priestley. Being complimented upon his numerous discoveries, he replied to this effect : — " I subjected whatever came to hand to the action of fire or various chemical agents, and the result was often fortunate in presenting some new discovery. In teaching I have always found that the best way to learn is to teach, when you will be sure to study your subject well, and I could always keep ahead of my pupils. Thus while I was teacher, I was still more a learner."

In September 1804, at a meeting of the President and Fellows of Yale College, it was voted to expend ten thousand dollars in Europe during the ensuing year, in the purchase of books for the library, and in the purchase of philosophical and chemical apparatus. Symptoms of dysentery were ·coming upon me during the examination that preceded the Commencement, and I was hardly able to perform my duty. The disease made such progress that I was entirely unable to attend the public exercises of Commencement week, but was confined to my bed at Mrs. Twining's under medical treatment by Dr. Eli Ives. There I accidentally heard of the vote of the corporation, and, immediately I believe, a project occurred to me which I resolved to disclose as soon as I should be sufficiently recovered to walk abroad ; fearful in the mean time that I might be anticipated.

President Dwight was at that time fifty-two years of age, and was in the full splendor of his exalted powers, physical and mental.

I called upon him at his house, and found him at leisure in the front parlor, and in a state of mind to receive my suggestions favorably. After ascertaining from him that the report which I had heard of the appropriation of ten thousand dollars was true, I inquired in what manner the business would be transacted. He replied, probably through the house of Isaac Beers & Howe, the college booksellers, and by the agency of their correspondents in London. I then inquired on what terms. He replied, by paying them a commission of perhaps five per cent. I then added, " Why not, sir, send me to transact the business, allowing me the percentage, and continuing my salary, which, if I were absent but six or eight months, would probably pay my expenses, and I should in the mean time have opportunity to improve in my profession." The plan was afterwards altered, and the time allotted was double of that originally proposed..

To this proposal he instantly replied with his characteristic decision and frankness, and spoke as follows: — " I am very glad you have made the suggestion ; the thought had never occurred to me ; this will be the best possible arrangement, and it shall have my decided support; but the corporation of the college have adjourned and cannot now be consulted without calling a special meeting, which I think will not be necessary, as the Prudential Committee* can arrange the business, and I have no doubt they will be willing to assume the responsibility. Step into a carriage, therefore, and drive to Repton " (now Huntington, fourteen miles from New Haven), " and consult the Rev. David Ely, D. D., a member of the corporation and of the Prudential Committee, Then go to Farmington, twenty-eight miles, and submit the matter to Gov. Treadwell, who is an *ex-officio* member of both boards. You will thus have consulted the Committee, and Rev. James Dana, D. D., the other member of the Prudential Committee, is here in town, and can be readily seen.

The proposal of President Dwight was immediately adopted and carried into effect. I was too much interested to make any delay, and hastened to those excellent patrons and guardians of the college, explained to them the proposed plan, and had the happiness to find that it met their cordial approbation. I had now a prospect of gratifying the cherished desire of visiting Europe, and under auspices that would insure my favorable reception. This arrangement was adopted, it is to be observed, in the autumnal vacation. I entered, therefore, upon the labors of my course of chemistry already referred to, with a fresh stimulus for exertion, and was cheered through the winter with prospects brightening on my view as the spring drew near. As yet the plan was not spoken of except to a few friends; but I was making my arrangements to carry into execution the proposed undertaking.

The lectures were given at the rate of four in a week, which furnished a course of sufficient length, — sixty lectures or more, including some notices of mineralogy. By the middle of March I had accomplished all that I proposed to do in that season, and was now ready to finish my final arrangements and to take my departure, which was fixed for the 22d of March, from New Haven for New York and Philadelphia, to obtain additional letters of introduction, to select a ship, and engage my passage for Liverpool, not expecting to return again to New Haven before sailing. Four years and eight months had elapsed from the time when President Dwight gave me the first confidential intimation of his views and plan, and three years and a half since my appointment. Chemistry was a favorite with Dr. Dwight, and he looked forward to its establishment with the connected sciences with a high and evident interest, which increased in strength as the department advanced towards active efficiency. The present was an epoch in my life. In my old expense-book under the date of March 22, 1805, I find the following remark : — " Here close my accounts in this town (New Haven), having paid every de-mand, — being about to depart in the evening for Europe." If I had never returned, no one would have been a loser by me.

A survivor of the Class of 1804, and a hearer of Mr. Silliman's first lectures, himself distinguished in the walks of literature, writes as follows : —

REV. JOHN PIERPONT TO G. P. FISHER.

WASHINGTON, D. C., *March* 6, 1865.

. . . . . My first sight of Mr. Silliman was, when the day before Commencement 1800, I, with other candidates for admission to college, with a very turbulent heart, took my seat in the old dining-hall, for examination. I felt that it was — and very probably it was — the most eventful day of my life. The Examiners were then the now venerable and saintly Ex-President Day, and Mr. Silliman, who, I then thought, was the *handsomest* man that I had ever seen.

I was never in a class — academical — that enjoyed the advantage of Mr. Silliman's immediate instruction ; he, if I remember aright, being connected with the Junior, when I was of the Freshman class.

As you remark, sir, I was of the class that first heard his lectures on chemistry, in the preparation of which he had spent some time. I do not recollect whether or not I went to his first lecture prepared to take notes of it. But I think I remember the introductory sentence of it, *defining* the science that was to be the subject of his course ; — " Chemistry is the science that treats of the changes that are effected in material bodies or substances by light, heat, and mixture."

My impression now is, that he did not read his lectures ;

so that his instructions were not etymologically lectures or readings, but free, fluent talks, prepared for evidently with care, and delivered in a style, as some would say, rather ornate for a strictly scientific discourse. Severe and sensitive critics might go so far as to say that there was in his style of lecturing a slight affectation of the exquisite ; while others would say " nay, but a very natural elegance."

In his demonstrative experiments he was always successful, and in all his manipulations there was uniformly a grace and nicety that was pleasant to those of us whose *ideality* had begun to be developed.

His elocution was distinct, sometimes rather too rapid for those of us who were slow of apprehension, but it seemed to go so fast because he feared there would n't be time enough for it all to get out — there was so much of it — before the clock would strike and shut the laggards in.

It was, I think, in 1829, that, at the request of the first association for a course of popular lectures in Boston, I called upon Mr. Silliman to solicit from him a course of lectures in that city. As to his manner in that course, I could see in it but little change. It seemed almost identical with what it was when I first heard him. His style of rhetoric was perhaps rather more severe, but his experiments were equally graceful, and, as of old, equally and always successful. What, under certain combinations and mixtures, he said would come to pass, always did come to pass. He was as a lecturer a true prophet, showing a full knowledge of his subject, and because of that knowledge able to predict the phenomena that would result from stated conditions.

Mr. Silliman's chemical lectures in Boston were eminently successful. In regard to his *manner* of lecturing when I just compared it with what it was when I first heard him, if I speak as I have done, of its almost perfect identity, thereby implying that he had not improved much between those periods, you, sir, ought not to be greatly surprised; for what great improvement could be rationally expected in 1829, in what was so nearly perfect a quarter of a century before?

I fear, my dear sir, that you will be able to make little, if any, use of what I have here given you, but as the poor best that I can do for you, I beg you to accept it.

With respects of

Your obdt. servant,

JNO. PIERPONT.

The annexed letters were written after his plan for visiting Europe was formed, and prior to his departure.

TO MRS. G. S. SILLIMAN.

YALE COLLEGE, *January* 12, 1805.

. . . . . A WEEK to-morrow evening I wrote to your husband and gave him reason to believe that it would be impossible for me to visit you before my embarkation. My heart knows how much I regret this. I love you both more than I can express, and I know not any earthly wish that I should sooner pray to have gratified than that which would place you both where I could see you and converse with you every day. I love your society; it not only agrees with every sentiment of duty derived from family alliance, but it suits my taste exactly. With all the delights of science and varied society, I have a sad vacuum; I have, I trust, about me many well-wishers and more than one cordial friend, but *mother* is not here, *Selleck and Hepsa* are not here, and I must smother in my own bosom much which would make my tongue eloquent had I such ears as yours and theirs to lay my mouth to; but I must grow concise and proceed to other topics. . . . . . My chemical lectures were most of them written carelessly as to the handwriting, because I expected to copy them; but this I have given up. But I will make no excuses; and although I believe they will afford Selleck but little entertainment, because they all go upon the supposition that the experiments elucidating the principles are exhibited at the same time, I will, nevertheless, send them; they with the *Spectacle de la Nature* will just fill a small trunk, which I will forward. The lectures must be returned as soon as I return next fall, that I may have them to begin my course with.

The feeling and eloquent, though too flattering, manner in which you urge me to leave behind a copy of my face, as a sad remembrance, should I never return, took strong hold of my feelings, and drew tears from eyes very little prone to weep. I felt the request to be reasonable, and I will not be so fastidiously delicate as to doubt that a faithful copy of my face would be to my friends a dear memorial of one whom they loved living, and would lament if dead. . . . . .

I intended to tell you how I am delighted with the details which maternal tenderness, and not weakness, has led you to give me of those dear babes ; if you insist that it is weakness, continue to be weak whenever you write. Your pencil is so successful that I see them both now in my mind's eye. Kiss them six times apiece for me, and tell them Uncle Ben dearly loves his little " pappoose " and his little " bow-wow." On Monday evening my friend Day is to be married. I stand bridesman. The connection promises mutual happiness on the most rational grounds. I assure you I feel very much disposed to go and do likewise, but at least six thousand miles of water lie between me and any glimpse of matrimony. . . . . .

TO MR. G. S. SILLIMAN.

Rye, (State of New York,)
January 24, 1805.

Dear Selleck, — . . . . . I left New Haven on Wednesday morning of last week with Dr. Dwight, and proceeded to New York, which we reached on Thursday at eleven o'clock A. M. We left it to-day at twelve o'clock.

Our stay was therefore one week. This period I have spent very usefully and agreeably. I have met with very polite and friendly attention from people of the first respectability. I have secured letters of introduction to Scotland, England, Holland, and France; from Samuel M. Hopkins, Dr. Mason, the house of Murray and Son, Oliver Wolcott, Dr. Perkins, Col. Trumbull, and Mr. King. All these gentlemen offer me every information and assistance in their power. Mr. King will introduce me to Sir Joseph Banks, President of the Royal Society, to Sir Charles Blagden, late Secretary of it, &c. Col. Trumbull, in addition to letters, will give me in writing directions for travelling to advantage,— particularly to enable me to make a respectable appearance with the least possible expense; for he remarked that he had visited Europe in circumstances very similar to mine, and therefore knew how to direct me. In company with Dr. Dwight and Mr. Rogers, I spent two hours one morning at Mr. King's. I was gratified to find in a man who had been so long conversant with Courts, and who had so long enjoyed the admiration of Europe and America, the utmost affability and a total freedom from formality and that repulsiveness so commonly mistaken for dignity. . . . .

While in New York I dined with Moses Rogers, in company with James Watson, Dr. Mason, Mr. Hopkins, Mr. Gracie, Oliver Wolcott, &c. I dined also with Wm. Woolsey, Lynde Catlin, Mr. Winthrop; breakfasted with Peter Radcliff, Mr. Hopkins, and Mr. Rogers, &c., &c. I must stop to-morrow night with brother John, and reach New Haven on Saturday evening. On Monday I shall go to Middletown to spend a day or two with Hon$^{d\cdot}$ Mother, and this will close the vacation. I must then give an assiduous application to the duties of my professorship and to my preparations, till my departure. . . . . .

A voyage to Europe sixty years ago was a far more serious undertaking than now; and the farewells exchanged were proportionately serious.

TO MR. G. S. SILLIMAN.

YALE COLLEGE, *February* 21, 1805.

. . . . . THE solemn trust which you so tenderly commit to me in case of an event, — which may God of his infinite mercy avert, — I with all seriousness and sincerity accept. As you do not doubt the strength of my affection for you, our dear Hepsa, and the lovely babes, so you cannot hesitate to believe that my affections would be seconded by my principles and exertions. So long, then, as I have life or ability, you may rest assured that any relicts of a brother, whom I love as I do my own life, would share my last farthing, and the little ones would command all my vigilance and wisdom to form their hearts to piety and their understandings to knowledge. Do not, I beseech you, lay it to heart that I cannot visit you. We should be obliged to part even then; and would it not be more painful than to make up our minds to it now? I trust firmly, cheerfully, and confidently in Heaven, that *we shall meet again.* I have not *one gloomy foreboding, one desponding thought* or *doubtful apprehension.* Do not think I want feeling. Most sensibly do I feel the idea that I must be separated for more than a year from those I love; but I will not give way to such feelings; my mind is made up, and I go, resolutely and cheerfully, to meet whatever is before me. I have also a firm confidence, under God, that I shall not be influenced by the infidelity or the splendid pleasures and gilded fopperies of the Old World. *Spare me not,* when I return, if you find that I have made a fool of myself. My mind is bent on acquiring professional science, a knowledge of mankind, that general information which shall give me pleasing resources for reflection and conversation, those polished manners which shall prove a perpetual letter of introduction, and that easy, elegant, and chastened style of speech which shall give a garnish to all the rest. I have not the vanity to believe I shall accomplish all this; but such are my objects. . . . . .

CHAPTER VI.

Residence in Europe. — Mr. John Taylor. — Dr. William Henry. — Dr. Dalton's Lecture and Conversation. — Arrival in London. — Mr. William Nicholson. — Frederic Accum, the German Chemist. — Dr. George Pearson and his Lectures. — Illumination by Gas. — Scientific Societies. — Davy. — Sir Joseph Banks. — Visit to Cornwall. — Dr. Ryland and Mr. Winterbotham. — Military Preparations on the English Coast. — Back to London. — At the House of Benjamin West: Joel Barlow, Robert Fulton, and Earl Stanhope. — Interview with Davy. — Professor William Allen's Lecture and Conversation. — At Cambridge: Professor Farish. — Visit to Lindley Murray.

THE year which Mr. Silliman spent abroad was crowded with profitable and agreeable employments. In Liverpool, where he landed and first saw the English on their own island, he had the good fortune to form the acquaintance of Mr. Roscoe. After a visit to Manchester, he resorted to the Derbyshire mines, which he diligently explored. At Coventry he witnessed the confusion and riot of an English election. Pursuing his way to London, he took up his abode in that metropolis for several months, executing the commission with which he was charged by the College, prosecuting his scientific studies, and making himself acquainted with things and persons of note. In society he met the leading scientific men of the day, including Watt, and our countryman, Robert Fulton. In Parliament he had the opportunity to hear the celebrated statesmen Pitt, Castlereagh, Windham, Fox, and Sheridan. He saw Lord Nelson on the Strand, with a crowd at his heels, and afterwards witnessed his embarkation at Portsmouth, with the glittering decorations on his breast which soon after proved a mark for the fatal shot on the deck of the *Victory;* and he witnessed the mingled exultation and grief of the English people at the news of Trafalgar. He made an excursion to Cornwall, and a laborious examination of the mining operations in that region, besides excursions to Bath, Bristol, and other places in England. Passing over to Holland, he encountered the only serious disappointment attending his tour. It was during the period after the rupture of the Peace of Amiens, when the tide of Napoleon's wrath against England was at the highest point, and when the great army which soon after achieved the capitulation at Ulm and the victory of Austerlitz had suddenly marched from the northern coast of France, where they had long menaced the opposite shores with invasion. At Antwerp, Mr. Silliman and his travelling companion were stopped by the French police on suspicion of being spies, — no other proof being alleged than the fact that they had come from England. To come from England, whatever might be the nationality of the traveller, was at that time considered an offence meriting the imperial displeasure. Though deprived of the privilege of seeing Paris and its men of science, Mr. Silliman embraced the opportunity to visit several of the principal cities of Holland. Returning to London, he saw Mrs. Siddons in the Covent Garden Theatre, in one of her favorite parts, the Grecian Daughter; he received the hospitalities of Mr. Thornton, member of parliament and friend of Wilberforce, and by that gentleman was introduced to the illustrious statesman, with whom he spent several hours most agreeably; and he was brought into personal intercourse with the distinguished scientific professors, Davy and Allen. Taking the University of Cambridge on his way, and passing through York and Newcastle, he arrived in Edinburgh in the latter part of November, 1805. He found everything to delight him in this ancient and beautiful city, and in the University, where he found the ablest instructors in the departments of study to which he was devoted. Here he remained until the following spring, when he set sail from Greenock, and reached New York on the 27th of May.

In his Reminiscences, Mr. Silliman has presented fresh and lively details of this early sojourn in Europe, and especially of the winter at Edinburgh. To no part of his long life does he seem to revert with more pleasure than to this. The following passages embrace but a part of what he has written : —

My travels and residence in Europe in 1805–6, although undertaken chiefly for the interests of Yale College and of science, did not preclude observations of popular subjects along with notices of science and the arts. These observations were preserved in a Journal which was published in 1810, and two other editions followed.

The ride from Liverpool made me acquainted with a gentleman, Mr. John Taylor, who proved to me an invaluable friend through a long life. He died Dec. 9, 1857, aged 78. (For a fuller notice of him see the 8vo. edition of my first travels published in 1810, Vol. I. p. 70 ; also Vol. I. pp. 17 and 20 of the visit to Europe in 1851.) My relations with him were most agreeable and useful to me, but had no particular reference to science. He was, however, ever ready to serve me, and did, many years after, perform an important service in the line of my studies, by sending me large specimen slates from the sandstone quarry of Storeton, near Liverpool, containing fine copies, in relief, of the feet of the Chirotherium ; they are now in the Cabinet of Yale College.

Two gentlemen eminent in science, resided at Manchester. I sought them under the guidance of Mr. Taylor, but did not find Dr. William Henry, an eminent author on chemistry, of whose excellent "Elements" I published, a few years after, three American editions with notes. I sustained an occasional correspondence with him, and sent him a rather copious table of errata in his work, which he received courteously and even gratefully.

I found Mr. Dalton, who was a Quaker, with the plain dress and address of his sect. He was apparently from thirty-five to forty years old. I attended an evening lecture by him on Electricity. The audience was popular, and ladies formed a part of it. The lecture was beautifully illustrated by experiments, and among them, in a darkened room, the electrical discharge was conveyed around the cornices of the room by means of an interrupted wire, cut at short intervals ; and as the discharge passed, there was a brilliant light at each interruption, and without any appreciable succession in time. Mr. Dalton had already distinguished himself by his researches on heat and vapor and evaporation and the law of diffusion of mixed gases. His great achievement, however, was the establishment of the doctrine of definite or equivalent proportions, including the volumes of gases. Gay Lussac in Paris had also brought forward similar views and proofs, before there was any communication between them, or knowledge of each other's researches. The morning after the lecture, Mr. Dalton gave me an hour or two in a conversational explanation of his views, and in showing me his apparatus and mode of experimenting. I had, in after years, occasion often to quote his discourses. He lived to an honored old age, and his name, as well as that of his (then to him unknown) co-worker, Gay Lussac, is deeply engraven on the monumental column dedicated to men eminent in science. Mr. Dalton was the first scientific man whom I saw in England. I had seen Mr. Roscoe equally eminent in literature.

Dr. Henry was a great favorite with the scientific public, and by the aid of chemical manufactures had secured wealth, and his labors in science had won for him a high and deserved reputation. But a mysterious Providence removed him from life. He had recently returned from a meeting of the British Association at Bristol, when, as is believed, in a fit of derangement, he shot himself in a domestic chapel in his own garden.

On Monday, May 20th, I arrived in London, last from Oxford, and obtained a home at No. 13 Margaret Street, Cavendish Square, which had been the abode of a friend of mine, Dr. Archibald Bruce of New York. By him I was introduced to the worthy lady of the house, Mrs. Brooke ; and this was my residence for nearly six months. It was every way comfortable and desirable. The vote of the President and Fellows of Yale College, of Sept. 7th, 1802, included Natural History along with Chemistry in the Professorship. So wide a range of research was very startling to me. I was, however, willing to look at the subject and see what could be done. The orders which were committed to me for the purchase of books and apparatus required a residence in London during the summer ; and I was desirous to discover what sources of information were accessible in the metropolis. My first object was, however, to make arrangements for obtaining the books for the library, and the apparatus for the philosophical and chemical departments. I had already arranged my money concerns with the great American banker of that day, Samuel Williams, Esq., of Finsbury Square, a nephew of Col. Timothy Pickering, by whom I was responsibly introduced ; and the funds which I brought were deposited with him, a well-known, exact, and reliable man, of few words, but of many good deeds of kind service.

A stranger in London, and a novice in its business affairs, I did not feel safe in proceeding without mature and wise counsel. For this purpose I obtained an introduction to William Nicholson, a veteran in science, and an author and journalist of high reputation. I called on him at his residence in Soho Square, and was personally introduced by a friend. My calls were repeated several times, and I was present at one of his *conversazioni*. Nicholson was an instrument-maker. I found this distinguished man very affable and kind ; and having explained to him my object in coming to London, he entered into my views with great readiness, and would not permit me to apologize for the call. He said, on the contrary, that he had always made it a principle to aid, as far as possible, every worthy effort, and to impart to inquirers all the information in his power. In this course he said, moreover, that he had received his reward in the great readiness which he found in others to aid him in turn. Such liberal sentiments relieved any embarrassment which I might have felt, and I hope his sentiments have not been lost upon me, as an example. Mr. Nicholson survived these interviews about fifteen years, and the world was a loser when he died. In my published journal of travels in England, I have recorded that he bore a strong resemblance to the late President Dwight, both in person and in the features of his mind. In his communications he was, like him, copious, flowing, lucid, and courteous, bearing upon the given topic with great energy and scope of thought, ready on almost every subject, and pouring a full stream from a fountain so much more full and ample that it was never exhausted.

I early made the acquaintance of a celebrated practical chemist, Frederick Accum, a German, but fully established in London, and speaking the English language very intelligibly. After frequenting his establishment near Soho Square daily for many weeks, for purposes to be mentioned hereafter, I became satisfied that I could employ him advantageously to obtain for me the desired chemical apparatus. He was well acquainted with practical chemistry, and was much resorted to to make chemical analyses and examinations of many things ; — he was to the Londoners a pet chemist. He was a most obliging and kind-hearted man ; and in ways which I will hereafter mention, as well as in relation to apparatus and preparations, he was always prompt to serve me, and would for that purpose go to the end of London, if not to the end of the earth. He had been, moreover, the operative assistant of Davy, in the Royal Institution, and in that way had become familiar with the requirements of philosophical chemistry and class instruction, as well as with the wants of the arts and economics. In his house he kept a considerable variety of apparatus ; and his extensive acquaintance with all dealers and manufacturers of instruments enabled him to obtain all that I wanted, better than I could do it myself in the immense world of London, then (the summer of 1805) containing a million of people, now, I suppose, two and a half millions.

Before coming to England I had made myself familiar, in a good degree, with popular chemistry, and having a natural tact for manipulations, I was already a pretty expert experimenter. I wished, however, to become acquainted with difficult processes, and I therefore engaged Mr. Accum to give me private instructions, and to devote some hour or hours to me daily in his working laboratory. He then requested me to name the subjects with which I was least acquainted, or not acquainted at all, and to them we devoted our time and efforts. Among the subjects were the analysis of ores, the formation of the crystallized vegetable acids, the arsenical compounds, &c. We operated upon arsenious acid, white arsenic, by nitrate of potassa in a hot crucible, for the purpose of turning it into arsenical acid. Mr. Accum did not caution me against inhaling the fumes which were floating about the room, and, indeed, without a caution from him, I ought to have been on my guard, as I very well knew these fumes to be poisonous ; but our minds were so much engaged that we neglected our safety.   We both suffered serious inconvenience for some days in prostrated muscular power, and in debility and derangement of the digestive organs. The time passed in this manner with Mr. Accum was, in general, profitably spent ; sometimes we were engaged together a whole morning. He would receive no compensation for his time, his re-agents, and his services,— the only instance of the kind that I met with anywhere, at home or abroad, during my novitiate.

Eventually, however, Mr. Accum received compensation indirectly by the very considerable order, already named, which he executed for Yale College. . . . . . Coming to the laboratory one day, I found Accum laughing and in high glee on account of a good bargain he had made with Mr. Pitt, the Prime Minister, for government. Mr. Pitt, he said, had ordered a large quantity of chemical apparatus for a place in my country. "Ah," I replied, " what is the name of the place ? " " Pondicherry," he replied. " Pondicherry, indeed !   That is not in my country : it is in India, at our antipodes ; and, moreover, Mr. Pitt would not send apparatus to my country." " But no matter," he said, " I have taken this opportunity to sweep my garrets of all my old apparatus and odds and ends that had been accumulating for years, and have turned everything over to government."   Well, thought I, Mr. Pitt is not here to look after his apparatus, and if he were present he would probably not be a very good judge ; but I am here, and shall keep a sharp lookout for my own concerns.

On my passage out from New York, I copied into my

journal all my documents and letters of introduction. Among the latter was one from the late Benjamin Douglass Perkins to Dr. George Pearson. Mr. Perkins passed several years in London, occupied in diffusing the knowledge of the once celebrated metallic tractors, first applied to use by his father, the late Dr. Perkins of Plainfield, Connecticut. Dr. Pearson favored the efforts of B. D. Perkins, and thus a personal interest was cherished between them. In the introduction to Dr. Pearson, he (Perkins) wrote thus : — " Visiting your country with such views, [explained in the preceding part of the letter,] to whom could I with more propriety address him than to the oldest lecturer and the greatest chemist in England ? " There were then — it being summer — no other chemical lectures going on in London, except, perhaps, at the hospitals, and as I wished to make the best use of my time, in obtaining professional knowledge, and to hear moreover in what manner eminent men in Europe lecture, it appeared to me fortunate that I could listen to " the oldest lecturer and the greatest chemist in England." I therefore took Dr. Pearson's tickets. He gave lectures on three different subjects — Chemistry, Materia Medica, and Therapeutics — in immediate succession. He began in the office connected with his house, at eight o'clock A. M., and lectured forty-five minutes on Chemistry ; next on Materia Medica for the same time ; and last on Therapeutics forty-five minutes ; finishing at fifteen minutes past ten. There was no interval for breathing or for a gentle transition to a new subject. This mental repletion was not favorable to intellectual digestion. I attended the lecture on Chemistry and that on Materia Medica. A learned man Dr. Pearson certainly was, but I was disappointed in the great advantage which I had expected. The lecture-room was ill furnished, and the appearance of it was shabby and even mean. The apparatus was quite limited, and the experiments not numerous nor well performed. The class was composed of

young men, seemingly very raw, and not appearing like
cultivated and intelligent youth. Dr. Pearson usually came
into the lecture-room quite in dishabille — but half dressed,
and the air of things was not up to the dignity of a lecture-
room. I felt that I was out of place, and in company to
which I did not belong. Some of Dr. Pearson's own discoveries were interesting to me ; for example, the composition
of James's powder, and the decomposition of carbonic acid
by boiling phosphorus with carbonate of soda. The greater
part of the things said and done were familiar to me, and
some I thought I had done better at home. On the whole,
I did not feel that these lectures returned me an equivalent
for my time and money. Had I not paid for my tickets, and
— a stronger reason still — had I not been personally introduced and received civilities from Dr. Pearson, I should
have given up these courses. I breakfasted with Dr. Pearson and family, and he had taken me in a coach down to
Woolwich, — a government military station, eight miles below London ; and I looked about while he visited a patient.
His personal deportment towards me was courteous, and he
even commended me to a friend as having made " astonishing progress while attending his lectures." Of this progress I was not myself sensible, nor could I feel how he
could have discovered my improvement, as there were no
scientific communications between us, except that I occasionally made an inquiry.

. . . . . The first illumination by gas in London took
place in the summer of 1805, and it was my good fortune
to see this exhibition on the evening of July 4th of that
year. Returning with a companion from Hyde Park,
through Piccadilly, we stopped at the shop of a chemist
and apothecary, near Albany House. This shop — it being
evening — was surrounded by a large crowd of people who
were attracted by the brilliant exhibition of gas-light. It
sufficed not only to illuminate the premises, which it did
very splendidly, but the doors and windows being open, it

made noonday in the streets. As I had never seen anything of the kind before, beyond the small experiments of
the scientific laboratory, I asked permission of the head of
the establishment to see his apparatus. At first he refused,
but when I assured him that I had no manufacturing or
trade interests to serve, but only those of science, he consented and accompanied me into the cellar. There was
nothing in the arrangement different from those now in
use, except that they were less perfect. The upper apartment being open to the breeze, the numerous long and
pointed jets of flame of great brilliancy, waving with every
breath of air, seemed as if endowed with animation, and
produced an effect almost magical. Fifty years have produced a great change. Now, illumination by gas prevails
throughout the civilized world, and its advantages are too
obvious to require any illustration. I suppose that the gas-
tubes of London — those in the houses included — must
extend several hundred miles.

Among the advantages which I enjoyed in London, I
must not omit the learned societies, — The Royal Society,
the Antiquarian Society, the Academy of Painting and
Sculpture, the Exhibition of Paintings (annual) in Somerset House, the Royal Institution, Sir Joseph Banks's *conversazioni* at his house, and the British Museum. From all
these, some rays of light would shine into the mind of a
young stranger seeking knowledge. At the Royal Institution I saw and conversed with Davy in an informal interview in his working laboratory. At Sir Joseph Banks's I
saw many of the most eminent men of the day. I had
daily freedom of access, so far as my time would allow, at
Sir Joseph's, where there was always a public breakfast in
addition to the *soirée*. At Sir Joseph's, beside himself
and his learned secretary Dr. Solander, I saw Mr. Watt,
Major Rennell, Dr. Wollaston, Dr. Tooke, Lord Macartney
the ambassador to China, Mr. Cavendish, Dalrymple the
marine geographer, Windham the parliamentary orator,

and many others. I heard William Allen lecture at the Royal Institution, and dined with Mr. Greville, of Paddington Green, son of the Earl of Warwick, whose collection of minerals was one of the first in Europe.

In the course of his journey to the mines of Cornwall, he tarried at Bristol.

The Rev. Dr. Ryland, head of the Baptist College in Bristol, and his colleague the Rev. Mr. Page, showed us much kindness while here. They by their influence obtained access for us to several important manufactures: that of pins, that of brass, and that of glass bottles, for all of which Bristol was famous. They showed us also many Oriental idols, and other objects connected with the early Baptist Mission in India, in promoting which these gentlemen and their friends had been actively engaged.

Mr. Winterbotham, a clergyman, an author of a voluminous work on American geography, met us at Dr. Ryland's. He had been captivated, as many worthy people were, by the French revolution, and becoming obnoxious to the British government, he was shut up in Newgate Prison, where he produced his large work. While in prison he became acquainted with the detestable principles of some of his political associates, one of whom declared to him, that if his party should prevail, not a teacher of religion should be left alive in the land. Winterbotham replied : — "I am a preacher, and the moment I am liberated from prison, I will preach again." "Then," said his companion, "I will be the first to plunge a dagger into your bosom." Mr. Winterbotham deserted this violent party and made amends for his error; and indeed his parishioners, the people of his flock, believed that government had dealt too harshly with him.

. . . . . Rev. President Ryland kindly volunteered to give me a general introduction to his friends in the region which I was about to visit. His letter was truly a catholic epistle, not indeed to the churches, but to the ministers of his denomination in the provincial places on my intended route to Cornwall and back to London.

After stating my character as it was made known to him by President Dwight, and my object in travelling, he recommends me to a long column of clergymen with their places of residence annexed ; and finally, " to any one else who knows John Ryland." . . . . .

As I travelled along the coast of the English Channel, I saw piles of combustibles which had been placed on the hills, to be seen as burning signals in case the French should invade England. Before I left London I was informed that every volunteer was warned to be ready, and not to leave his place even for a short time, without leaving a notice where he might be found at a moment's warning. My book-merchant, Ogilby, showed me such a government notice. All the vehicles of the country, including farmwagons, were numbered and registered, that they might be employed in transporting troops ; and the people were in a state of constant anxiety. When I crossed the Channel I found that the fears of the English had not been without cause. An immense array was assembled at Boulogne, ready to embark. Troops were actually embarked in Holland, and were ready to embark from other ports, when the new war in Germany called for the troops to be marched in that direction, and the campaign which ended in the battle of Austerlitz, diverted Napoleon from his purpose of invading England.

. . . . . Returning to London, at the house of Mr. West, the distinguished American artist, I met our celebrated countryman Joel Barlow, recently from the Continent. He was a Fairfield-County man, was acquainted at my father's, and was a class-mate with my oldest half-brother, Joseph Noyes, in Yale College. He received me with great cordiality, and furnished me with letters to eminent men of science

in Paris and Lyons, which my repulse at Antwerp prevented
me from delivering.   Although his own field of fame had
been in poetry and *belles-lettres*, he appreciated science, and
kindly invited me to pass an evening at his lodgings in
Swallow Street, to meet Earl Stanhope and Robert Fulton,
two scientific stars.   I went accordingly, but there is little
to record, except the pleasure of meeting men of renown.
The conversation turned chiefly on scientific subjects and
those connected with the arts.   Mr. Fulton was silent
respecting his reputed projects for submarine explosions
in war for the destruction of an enemy's ships or flotillas.
There was, at. that time, much conversation in London
regarding Mr. Fulton and his reputed invention, called
" kata maran " (beneath the sea), and no small amount of
asperity and ridicule was vented on the occasion.   In table
talk, I heard it said that neither the French nor the English government favored the propositions of Mr. Fulton, to
explode the marine armaments of their respective enemies.
However this may have been, and whether true or not, it
was fortunate for mankind and for the fame of Mr. Fulton,
that his inventive mind, perhaps from disappointment, received another direction, which resulted in placing the
Chancellor Livingston steamer triumphantly upon the Hudson, within two years after the time when I saw him.   The
world is his debtor, and his country is preëminently so ; but
that country has been shamefully parsimonious to his family,
while untold millions alone can adequately represent the
amount of her gains, resulting from the only successful application of steam to navigation.   As to Earl Stanhope, —
omitting his gloomy political auguries, (for he was in the
opposition), — I will mention only a very ingenious, but not
very important, invention which he named to me.   There
was with the Earl at Mr. Barlow's, a German lady, possessing both musical genius and musical taste and tact in so
high a degree, that upon the piano she would often throw
off extempore, from the ends of her fingers, the most de-

lightful airs, which she herself could not afterwards recall. In order to arrest this fugitive harmony, the Earl contrived an apparatus to be connected with the keys of the instrument and to be actuated by their movement, so that the music was dotted down as it was played, and thus recorded on the tablet which was placed to receive and preserve it.

Mr. Barlow inquired with much interest concerning his native State and his Alma Mater. He expressed satisfaction that chemistry and the associated sciences were being introduced into Yale College, and added, that he would have sent out a chemical apparatus and preparations had he not supposed that, coming from him, the college authorities would make a bonfire of them in the college yard. I could, in reply to this bitter remark, add nothing more than the assurance that such a gift would have been highly acceptable, and that the articles would have been carefully preserved. Mr. Barlow had been a minister of the gospel, had preached and prayed publicly, and written sacred hymns in elevated strains, both of poetry and devotion, some of which are still preserved in our Congregational collection of sacred poetry. He espoused the French revolution with great warmth, even in its most bloody periods, and even wrote a song in praise of the guillotine ; and one sentiment in it was, that under the axe " Great George's head would roll." In his poem on the " Hasty Pudding," he apostrophizes the cow, and says : —

> ———" Sure it is to me,
> Were I to leave my God, I 'd worship thee."

His early friends regarded him as an apostate from Christianity. As an ambassador to Napoleon, he sought him in Poland, and fell a victim to the severity of winter at Wilna in 1815–16.

. . . . . Just before leaving London, in November 1805, I visited again the Royal Institution under the introduction of Mr. Accum, who had formerly been assistant operator to

Professor Davy. My principal object was to see that celebrated man, whom we found in his laboratory in the basement of the building (in Albemarle Street), beneath the
lecture-room.   He received me with ease and affability, his
manners being perfectly polite and unassuming.   In person
he was above the middle size, with a genteel figure and an
open countenance.   In our brief interview, we conversed
on chemical topics and upon his late tour in Ireland, from
which he had only recently returned, having been absent
through the summer.   He showed me an ingenious article
of apparatus which he had lately invented.   His appearance at the age of twenty-six (nearly my own age) was
even more youthful than the years indicate.   He inquired
about Dr. Woodhouse, who was here in 1802.   I have
already mentioned that the obscure town of Penzance, in
Cornwall, was his birthplace, and, although without social
position or university education, he had by his own efforts
and talents, arisen to his present eminence among the most
distinguished philosophers of Europe.   I wrote at the time
about him, thus : — " He is now very much caressed by the
great men of London, and by the fashionable world ; and it
is certainly no small proof of his merit that he has so early
attained such favor and can bear it without intoxication."
It is not agreeable therefore to add, that after his elevation
to the title and rank of an English baronet, and to the
Presidency of the Royal Society, he became haughty, and
his biographer and eulogist, Dr. Paris, records that he bore
himself so loftily during a visit in Paris, as to repel the
advances of the Parisian philosophers, who were themselves so distinguished for unassuming courtesy of manners.   I have been credibly informed, also, as I believe, by
the late Dr. Mantell of London, that when Faraday, then
Davy's assistant, was with him in Paris, he was repressed
by him, who was unwilling that he should appear in French
society as his companion and equal, although he then gave
promise of equalling if not surpassing the attainments,

merit, and fame of his patron. Alas for human weakness! When, in July 1851, I stood by the grave of Davy in the public cemetery of Geneva, I forgot his follies, and remembered only his virtues and his brilliant success and service to mankind. He was cut off at fifty-one and a half years of age, a little past the meridian of life. "What shadows we are and what shadows we pursue!"

..... Prof. William Allen belonged to the Society of Friends. I first met him at dinner at Mr. William Vaughan's, and was interested by his intelligence and agreeable manners, — the manners of a gentleman, joined to those of a Quaker, — simple, but without stiffness or any unnecessary deviation from customary forms of speech. I was indeed happy in hearing a lecture from him in the Royal Institution, which I felt to be some compensation for missing Prof. Davy, who would not lecture until after I should have left London. The lecture-room of the Royal Institution accommodates an audience of one thousand persons. The room is sky-lighted, and a movable screen with the aid of a pully enables the lecturer to cut off the daylight and thus to darken the room in the daytime. In this way Davy was able to exhibit the wonderful illuminating power of the gigantic battery of the Royal Institution, of two thousand pairs of plates, and Faraday has successfully followed his steps with results still more astonishing. At Mr. Allen's lecture, the audience was of all ages and of both sexes; and about half were young ladies with some matrons. Thus one of the great objects of the Institution is answered by affording rational entertainment and instruction for the vacant aristocracy of London, as well as for those who are in earnest in seeking mental improvement. Prof. Allen gave a very interesting and instructive lecture on the general properties of matter;—his style was lucid, his illustrations were appropriate and satisfactory, as were his conclusions. It was my privilege again to hear a lecture in the Royal Institution, but it was after an interval of forty-six years.

On his way to Edinburgh, he stopped for a short time at Cambridge.

Arriving at evening, I had drawn my boots off, and with pen in hand was just beginning to write, by a comfortable fire in my chamber in the hotel, when I received a call from one of the Fellows, to whom I forwarded a letter of introduction from London. He insisted upon my going over to his apartments to sup with him, and the invitation was so kindly pressed that I complied, and enjoyed a very pleasant interview with a most agreeable and polished gentleman, the Rev. Mr. Cunningham. The next day, by the introduction of another Fellow, Rev. Mr. Currie, I dined with a large circle of University men, Heads of Colleges, Professors, Fellows, &c., and thus I was made to feel at home.

Elementary Chemistry, in 1805, was taught in the University by Prof. Wollaston. Prof. Farish was the founder of a new course of chemistry and mechanics, applied to the arts. I called on this gentleman, to whom I had letters of introduction, and was received with great courtesy and kindness. He took me to the laboratory and showed me his extensive apparatus. Prof. Farish made it his leading object to demonstrate the most important applications of chemistry and mechanics to the arts of life, and particularly to the manufactures of Great Britain, many of the establishments of which he had in person visited for the sake of inspecting their processes. He had a complete set of models and machines, and of apparatus for the purpose of carrying his designs into effect. A small steam-engine served to illustrate the nature of that instrument, and the moving power thus obtained was then applied to work the rest of the machinery.

. . . . . Lindley Murray, a man equally distinguished in a different line,— that of English grammar and philosophy,— resided near York at the time of my visit here in November 1805.   At evening I rode out on horseback to his residence at Holgate, a suburban village.   I passed out under a Roman arched gateway.   This eminent man, early in life, removed from New York to old York, on account of a muscular weakness in his limbs, hoping for relief from the climate of England ; and in this country he found a permanent home, although he did not obtain the desired relief. His grammar of the English language was the best that had been written, and he published several other works. " In the chaste, perspicuous, and polished style of his writings, and in the pure and dignified moral sentiments which they contain, one may discern proofs of the character of the man.   Both he and Mrs. Murray retained the simplicity of Quaker manners, while they were refined and polished people.   I was fortunate in finding him able to converse, for at times he cannot utter even a whisper, and is compelled to decline even seeing his friends."

CHAPTER VII.

, His Residence in Edinburgh. — His Associates, Mr. Codman and Mr. Gorham. — Introduction to Dr. Thomas Hope. — Dr. Gregory. — Dr. Hope's Lectures.— Dr. John Murray and His Lectures.— Dr. Hope and Dr. Murray on Geology. — Controversy of the Huttonians and Wernerians. — The Progress of his own Geological Views. — Dr. John Barclay's Lectures on Anatomy. — Narrow Escape on Salisbury Craig.

MR. SILLIMAN came to Edinburgh well provided with letters of introduction to persons whom he would wish to know. Some of these had been furnished by Mr. Thornton ; and the interest which this gentleman had taken in forwarding the plans of the young American is indicated by the following note, which he doubtless sent to Mr. Silliman after the arrival of the latter in Scotland.

HENRY BROUGHAM, ESQ., (*now* LORD BROUGHAM,) TO MR. THORNTON.

1, TANFIELD COURT, *January* 4.

DEAR SIR, — I have only to-day received a letter from Edinburgh, with one enclosed from you, in which you do me the favor of introducing me to Prof. Silliman. He does not appear to have arrived at Edinburgh previous to my departure, — at least he never called on me before that time. I therefore have to regret that I had no opportunity of making his acquaintance. But I have to-day written a letter to some of my friends at Edinburgh, whom I conceive Prof. S. would like to know, as they will immediately introduce him to the best literary circles of the place. I have particularly requested the person alluded to, to introduce Mr. Silliman to a club composed of the most select part of the professors and other eminent men in Edinburgh, which is one of the greatest resources in point of good society that the place has.

I am, however, a little afraid that it may be difficult to find Mr. S.'s address, as he left none when he called at my father's house. If you know it and can send it to me, you will greatly oblige,

Dear sir,

Your obliged and faithful servant,

HENRY BROUGHAM.

Mr. Silliman was the bearer of a letter from President Dwight to Dr. John Robison, Professor of Natural Philosophy at Edinburgh. In addition to scientific writings of importance, he had published in 1797 a book against the *Illuminati*, entitled, " Proofs of a Conspiracy against all the Religions and Governments of Europe." This brought upon him both praise and odium. He died before the arrival of Mr. Silliman in Edinburgh ; and the letter of Dr. Dwight, for the intrinsic interest that belongs to it, is here subjoined.

NEW HAVEN, March 20, 1805.

DEAR SIR, — This letter will be handed to you by Benjamin Silliman, Esq., Professor of Chemistry in Yale College. He goes to Europe on business of this Seminary, and to further his own acquaintance with his science and scientifical men. I beg leave to introduce him to you, as a young gentleman of the best character and hopes. He is ambitious of an acquaintance with persons of literary distinction, and particularly desirous of seeing *you*. The ambition is worthy of him, and merits every aid which I can furnish ; and the particular wish which he indulges of knowing Prof. Robison is highly agreeable to me. When you have become acquainted with him, I am confident that this introduction will need no further apology.

The letter which you were so good as to direct to me, in answer to one from me to our good friend Doctor Erskine, was by some means or other left in the Custom-House, whither it was carried by some accident, and did not come to hand until six or seven months after I received Doctor Erskine's answer. I had given it up for lost when it arrived. The controversy which it respected was given up by your enemies, — if those may be called such who opposed you because you opposed vice and falsehood, and opposed you without even a disadvantageous thought of your real character. The reason why they gave it up was their inability to maintain it against the continually accumulating evidence of the unstained respectability of your character, and of the substantial foundations of your book. Multitudes of my countrymen, and among them the wisest and best, feel deeply indebted to you for your efforts in the cause of truth and righteousness, — efforts, in their opinion, able, upright, and indispensably demanded by the time. I have the satisfaction to inform you that beyond all doubt, you have contributed largely and effectually to the erection of an immovable standard against the miserable scheme of profligacy formed by Weishaupt, and then spreading through this country as well as through Europe. Around this standard a great number of wise and good men have rallied, and have presented a body of opposers too formidable to be hopefully resisted. I am sure this information will give you pleasure. It is to be deeply regretted that mathematical philosophy and chemistry, so honorable to the present age, and so calculated to advance our views of the divine wisdom, should be prostrated to the miserable purpose of dishonoring God and corrupting man. We cannot, however, be surprised at such an event when we remember that Revelation itself has been thus abused. I have been looking for the publication of the books announced by your letter, but have hitherto learned nothing concerning this subject. Should they appear, particularly the *formidable one*, which the French philosopher has prepared for the final overthrow of theism, I hope your health and your business will permit you to answer it. I have not a fear that any effort of this kind will stand the test of fair examination, but I dread the immediate effect of all such efforts on the votaries of both pleasure and the world. Truth will ultimately prevail, even in this wicked world; but the ravages of falsehood will, whenever it comes out in a specious and imposing garb, be great and lamentable. Would my poor eyes permit, I would willingly write more on this subject than your time or patience would suffer you to read. But I am obliged to desist. My best wishes attend you. I am, with the most respectful sentiments,

Dear sir,

Your very obedient friend and servant,

TIMOTHY DWIGHT.

PROF. ROBISON.

Of Edinburgh and his residence in that city, Mr. Silliman writes : —

My Domestic Establishment. — My banker and friend, Mr. Samuel Williams, of Finsbury Square, London, gave me an introduction to two very worthy gentlemen from Boston, U. S., — Mr. John Codman and Dr. John Gorham. With them I became associated. We occupied the square apartment of a house in Fyfe Street in the old town, and near to the University. Our repasts were provided for us by Mrs. Herriott, the head of the house : the breakfast was in one of our three parlors, the dinner in another, and the tea in the third. We paid the net cost of the articles of con-

sumption, with a gratuity to our faithful female servant.*
Every Saturday night we cancelled the bill, and Mrs. Herriott's gain was in the rent of her apartments.   My associates were, except myself, the only men from New England
in the University, and as we were congenial, we formed a
happy domestic society.   There were attending the lectures
more than thirty Americans, chiefly from the South.   My
companions became distinguished in after-life, — Dr. Gorham as a Professor in the Medical College of Cambridge
and Boston, and Mr. (afterwards Dr.) Codman, as an
eminent Congregational minister at Dorchester, Mass., and
as a very influential man in the religious concerns of the
country.   Dr. Gorham died before attaining the meridian
of life.   Dr. Codman enjoyed a long life of usefulness.

. . . . . My earliest introduction among men of science
was to Dr. Thomas Hope, Professor of Chemistry, &c. in
the University of Edinburgh.   I found him at his house in
the New Town, and received a very kind and courteous
welcome.   Dr. Hope was a polished gentleman, but a little
stately and formal withal.   After reading the letter of introduction, he turned to me and said, " I perceive that I
am addressing a brother Professor."   I bowed, a little
abashed ; a very young man, as I still was, (at the age of 26,)
thus to be recognized as the peer of a renowned veteran in
science, the able successor, as he had been the associate, of
the distinguished Dr. Black.   He proceeded, — " Now sir,
from long experience, I will give you one piece of advice, —
that is, never to attempt to give a lecture until you are
entirely possessed of your subject, and never to venture on
an experiment of whose success you are doubtful."   I bowed
respectfully my assent, adding at the same time that I was
happy to find that I had begun right, for I had hitherto

* We each of us gave good Margaret a shilling on Saturday evening, in-
tending the gratuity both as a reward for her fidelity and as a comfortable
addition to her small wages ; but we were sorry and displeased to learn late
in the season that she was compelled to pay this money over to her mistress,
while the poor girl was going barefoot in the winter.

endeavored to adopt the very course which he had presented, and which I should endeavor still to follow. I thought I perceived that something in his manner indicated that he would have been quite as well pleased if I had not in some measure anticipated his experience. He proved himself a model professor, and fully entitled to act as a mentor.

The professorship of chemistry was, at the time of my Edinburgh residence, very lucrative. The chair was so ably filled, and the science so fully illustrated by experiments, that the course drew a large audience, which, at three guineas a ticket, probably gave him an income of four thousand dollars or more, — some said, five thousand. He, with his brother, kept bachelor's hall in a handsome house on Princes Street, in the New Town. In this house I was received with hospitality, being one of a party of invited guests, — I believe students of the University, and others, older gentlemen. Dr. Hope dressed and appeared like other gentlemen, and his conversation was easy and polite. No lady appeared in the parlor or at the table; it was exclusively a party of men, — and such parties are never equally agreeable with those of which ladies form a part. The famous Dr. Black, the predecessor of Dr. Hope, was also a bachelor, and there was unfortunately among gentlemen in this country too great a tendency towards celibacy. An establishment must of course be maintained at an expense approaching that demanded by a family, but without its solaces and home-felt joys. — At Dr. Hope's, this evening, (Dec. 18th), I met a son of the celebrated Dr. Darwin, and a brother of the no less celebrated Maria Edgeworth. As neither of the gentlemen conversed at all, I had no opportunity to judge of their talents and attainments. Mr. (or Dr.) Darwin was a man of large and massy frame. At Dr. Hope's I was somewhat annoyed by the frequent mention of my title. I should much rather have preferred to pass simply as *Mr.*, being sufficiently conscious that my years — not to say my attainments — hardly justified the appellation of Professor. It is true that Professor Humphrey Davy of London was a man of my own age, and was equally youthful in appearance; but he had already distinguished himself by important researches and discoveries. To Dr. Hope I was indebted for other civilities, — particularly in walking with me to Leith, to use his personal influence in obtaining for me some articles of glass apparatus, especially some instruments like those which I had seen successfully used in his own experiments. He was too liberal to allow any little jealousy of a pupil to restrain him from a kind and useful action. The father of Dr. Hope was Professor of Botany in the University. In a walk with Mr. Codman to Leith, we entered the Botanical Garden, which was beautiful, although it was winter. A monument has been erected in the garden by the late Botanical Professor to the memory of Linnæus. It bears the simple inscription — *Linnæo posuit C. Hope.*

Expecting from the first to be ultimately connected with a medical school in Yale College, I attended the course of anatomy in Philadelphia, and here in Edinburgh I selected several courses of which mention will be made hereafter. That of Dr. Gregory had great celebrity, and I took his ticket among the first. An amusing circumstance occurred when I called at his office. It was evening, and I found him in a basement room impatiently listening to a long story of ailments, and he evidently wished to be rid of his long-winded patient. I waited quietly until the man rose to depart, evidently very much to the Professor's relief, and the departing invalid had only cleared the door, when Dr. Gregory threw it back with a thundering noise, and then turning to me abruptly, exclaimed, "A dyspeptic man, — never get well and never die, — plague one to death!" I contented myself with taking the Professor's ticket and paying for it, (£3 5s.,) but as I did not make myself known, I had no occasion to complain of want of liberality. The courtesy of a free ticket was never in any similar case extended to me, at home or abroad. I have myself generally given free tickets to professors and to those who are preparing to be professors. When, however, they have gone through the practical drill of instruction by daily labors in the experimental laboratory, I have generally charged the institutions with which they were connected. It has been my practice to give free tickets to clergymen, and to their daughters, when, as pupils in the female schools in New Haven, they have attended my lectures. — But to return to Dr. Gregory. As the son of an eminent father, the author of " A Father's Legacy to his Daughters," he enjoyed a prestige of enviable fame. But there was no occasion to build on his father's foundation. Being a man of distinguished talents, of large stores of knowledge, and a fervid, rapid eloquence, his lecture-hall was crowded with an attentive and gratified audience. His lectures were very informal, although not immethodical; if they were written out, he made no use of notes, but began without exordium, and poured out the rich treasures of his ardent mind with such crowding rapidity of diction that it was not always easy to apprehend fully his thoughts, because we could not distinctly hear all his words. He had many historical and personal anecdotes, some of which have remained with me during the fifty-two years that have passed since I heard them.

Dr. Gregory sometimes indulged in sarcastic wit. He was not on good terms with Dr. Hope, who was reputed to be very conservative of money; and Dr. Gregory was reported to have said, that no sooner did a golden guinea touch the palm of his colleague's hand, than it produced a convulsive movement of the flexor muscles which locked fast the precious coin.

Dr. Gregory's mind kindled so much with his subject, that he was not ready to stop when the bell told that the hour was gone, and the students rushed for the door that

they might reach the best seats in the hall of the professor
who was to lecture next.   But the zealous teacher did not
give over with the ebbing tide of his pupils, but continued,
with an elevated voice and excited action, to pursue the retiring crowd until they had cleared the door and he could
be heard no more. . . . . . I never lost one of Dr. Hope's
lectures, although I was absent from one, — I believe on
the occasion of going to breakfast with Dr. Anderson,
April 2, 1806, with my friend Mr. Codman, to meet the
Earl of Buchan and a literary circle ; but my kind friend,
Rev. David Dickson, took full notes for me.   I took notes
myself always ; and in my rough way, without graphic
skill, I made such sketches of apparatus, when there was
anything peculiar, that I could afterwards recall the structure and arrangement.   I still have my note-book of Dr.
Hope's lectures, and they were of material service to me
both in the composition of my own lectures, and in the experimental preparation and delivery after my return. . . . .
I have paused for a few moments to look them up, and
have them now before me, numbered " Hope's Lectures, I.
II. III."   They were hastily written, chiefly in the lecture-
room, and although fifty-two and fifty-three years old, they
are still quite legible, and the figures, rude indeed, are intelligible.   There is a pensive interest in looking them
over.   I believe all who were concerned in them with me,
and at Dr. Anderson's breakfast, are dead.   Dr. Codman,
Dr. Gorham, the learned Professor Hope himself, Rev. Dr.
Dickson, who wrote the notes in my stead, Dr. Anderson,
and his guest the Earl of Buchan, and probably most, if
not all, of those assembled at that literary breakfast, are
now in the other world, and perhaps I may be the only survivor, at the age of almost seventy-nine.   On looking at
my notes and journal, I find that I lost no time.   I arrived
in Edinburgh at midnight, November 22d, 1805, on Friday.
Saturday, November 23d, I settled myself in lodgings ; the
24th was the Sabbath, and on Monday, the 25th, the ear-

liest day possible, I attended the lectures of Dr. Gregory, Dr. Hope, and Professor Dugald Stewart. I find in my note-book the very leaves which were neatly and accurately written out in full by the excellent Rev. Dr. Dickson. The subject was Copper, and I pinned the lectures in their proper place among my own notes: there they are, as legible as print, and afford me a touching remembrance of my departed friend Dickson. The very pin which holds them was put in at Edinburgh, and has never been moved. These preliminary recollections have interested me, although it is like wandering among funeral monuments, like Old Mortality; and I now turn to the lectures of Dr. Hope, — still following, however, the record of the dead.

Dr. Hope's lectures formed a strong contrast to the course which I attended in Leicester Square in London. They were not only learned, posting up the history of discovery, and giving the facts clearly and fully, but the experiments were prepared on a liberal scale. They were apposite and beautiful, and so neatly and skilfully performed, that rarely was even a drop spilled upon the table. No experiment failed, except that in two instances glass vessels were broken by the heat evolved in the experiment: in one case, by burning phosphorus, and in another, by sulphur and iron filings combining with incandescence when gently heated; — but in these cases there was no fault in the experimenter; the experiment was hazardous to the vessels, and in such cases, if the lecturer states the fact beforehand, he will save his credit, even if the glass should be shattered. Dr. Hope lectured in full dress, without any protection for his clothes; he held a white handkerchief in his hand, and performed all his experiments upon a high table, himself standing on an elevated platform, and surrounded on all sides and behind by his pupils. It was an indifferent room for a laboratory, and the furnace conveniences were very limited. He, however, overcame the difficulties by ingenious contrivances. . . . . . The lectures were all written out, but very rarely read. He generally spoke, doubtless casting his eyes upon his MS. to observe and follow the order of his subject. He was very methodical, and filled out his themes without omission, repletion, or confusion. He was not, like Dr. Gregory, fluent and impetuous; he was cool and lucid, but sometimes rising above his MS., he essayed a flight of eloquence. In these cases he was not very successful, and we regretted that so able a man should provoke a smile when he looked for admiration. I thought he once caught me with a smile upon my face, which might have appeared equivocal, unless self-love might have preferred to regard the expression as one of approbation rather than of mirthfulness. After this, I was more on my guard, especially as a friend who attended the lectures informed me that, as I generally sat very near the Professor, he kept an eye on his " brother Professor," and once remarked to my informant that he believed I lost nothing of the lectures, and did not permit anything to escape my attention; and I supposed that he might have descried some of my *pen sketches*, which might well have provoked a smile in turn. I was early a faithful and delighted student of the lectures of Dr. Black, as published by his surviving pupil and friend, Professor Robison, from notes taken by himself and others. This work, being very familiar to me, I was forcibly struck with the great resemblance of Dr. Hope's lectures, in style, substance, and illustrations, to those of his great master. As his pupil, admirer, and assistant, it is not extraordinary that he should have formed himself upon that excellent model. Dr. Black's lectures, in two volumes quarto, were so instructive and attractive too, that I studied them with equal pleasure and profit. Dr. Hope had enjoyed also the advantage of knowing and studying under another great master. He informed me that he was associated with, and was instructed by, the illustrious Lavoisier, the Newton of Chemistry, as he has been called. He was made familiar

with his apparatus and experiments, and with the operations of his great mind; and as my conversation regarding
Lavoisier was only eleven and a half years after his death,
Dr. Hope's recollections of him were doubtless correct.
Lavoisier was guillotined May 8th, 1794, by the Revolutionary Tribunal, on the frivolous pretext that he had adulter-
ated tobacco; and they even refused him a respite of a few
days, to enable him to complete some experiments then in
progress.   The report in his case declared that the Republic had no need of chemists.   Bloody and execrable despotism, — infamous through all time!   Dr. Hope's admirable course finished my educational training in chemistry.
I understood, realized, and retained every part of it.   To
me it was worth a voyage across the Atlantic.

Dr. John Murray — called then Mr. Murray — was a
private lecturer, not connected with the University; but his
high reputation for talents and learning secured him a
class respectable for numbers and character.   He had also
distinguished himself by an excellent elementary work on
chemistry, and by a system of *materia medica* which was
of the first authority among the treatises on that subject.
He was a very agreeable lecturer, with a pleasant intonation, and a voice of sufficient strength.   He spoke with
perfect ease, in a style lucid, terse, and flowing, but without
diffuseness.   His manner and action were graceful, and his
treatment of the class polite and friendly; so that he secured their good-will, and was able to maintain good order
in his lecture-room, which was an apartment in his house,
not capable of containing more than thirty-five or forty
persons.

Dr. Murray, when I was his pupil, was threatened with
consumption, and died not many years after I left Edinburgh.   He wrote to me a year or two after my return, and
informed me that he was about going to the south of England to revive his health.   A son who bore his name, re-

published his father's elementary work on chemistry, posting it up to the time. The principal advantage which I derived from Dr. Murray's course of chemistry was from his perspicuous and highly philosophical views of the science, as such. His experiments were few and simple, and not very remarkable for tact and beauty in the performance. . . . . . . His mind was of a highly philosophical cast. The flow both of his language and the thoughts of his mind was like that of a deep river, smooth on the surface, transparent to the very bottom, and whose evenness, free from rocks and eddies, presented no impediment to the equable current. Dr. Murray's course was a valuable adjunct to that of Dr. Hope, and, both united, gave a finish and completeness which was all I could desire to enable me to resume my course of instruction at home.

Dr. Hope and Dr. Murray on Geology. — There was no distinct course of geology in Edinburgh in 1805-6. Some dissatisfaction was indeed expressed regarding Professor Jameson, — who had then recently returned from Werner's celebrated school of geology at Freiburg, in Saxony, and who was fully imbued with the doctrines of his great master, — that he did not commence his course of instruction. He had, however, an able substitute in Dr. Murray, who was a well-instructed and zealous advocate of the Wernerian theory on the agency of water ; while Dr. Hope, on the other hand, was an ardent and powerful supporter of the Huttonian or igneous theory. The discussions on these subjects were held in the midst of the chemical lectures, being introduced in connection with the elementary and proximate constitution of rocks and minerals. My geological notions were crude and unsettled when I left home ; I had not enjoyed any opportunities of geological instruction, and was slowly climbing up the ladder of mineralogy, when I took my departure for England. Both subjects began to be unfolded in the mines and mineral districts of England,

and both in those regions, and in others marked by diversity of structure, I had received the elements of geological and mineralogical instruction ; and I was in the condition of a hopeful pupil, who already understands enough, both to enable and dispose him to know more ; keenly alive to see, and prompt to understand, everything that was presented to my view, — industrious, persevering, and hopeful. My Edinburgh life was one of constant effort, and my exertions, while in that city, pressed hard upon my health, so that I was compelled occasionally to relax my labors, and both to take additional exercise and to indulge in the recreations of social intercourse in society which was enlivened by female conversation. No five months of my life were ever spent more profitably ; and this residence laid the top stones of my early professional education, which extended nearly through four years. Not, however, that I considered the work as even then done. As a teacher, I was still more of a learner than my pupils, and I found my own pupilage to be coextensive with my professional life of fifty years ; for I have never ceased to learn, especially as the progress of discovery in science unfolded new facts and modified or substantiated old views. The discussions of Dr. Hope and Dr. Murray afforded me a rich entertainment, and a wide range of instruction. Dr. Murray would solve most geological phenomena by the agency of water. Even granite, and of course the members of that family, were a crystalline deposit from the primeval chaotic ocean ; and this being granted, the Wernerians would fain give an aqueous origin even to porphyry and basalt and all the traps. As far as I had any leaning, it was towards the Wernerian system. Water is always active upon the surface of the earth, and it flows also from its interior ; and atmospheric waters are ever descending upon the earth in rain, snow, and hail, as well as in the gentle dews, not only to refresh the surface and to sustain life, in all its various forms, but to replenish the fountains themselves. Then again it reascends by

evaporation to form the clouds, those exhaustless store-
houses of rain, snow, and hail. But in the progress of this
endless circulation, it is everywhere obvious that water
produces extensive and highly important geological results,
in the transportation and deposition of solid as well as of
dissolved materials, in the formation and disintegration of
strata, and especially in the ceaseless wear of rivers and
torrents, and in the never-ending motions of the oceans
and seas in tidal waves and storm billows and currents. It
is not wonderful, then, that the powerful mind of Werner
should appreciate, and even exaggerate, these agencies.
He had not travelled far away from his own (geologically)
peaceful Saxony, and knew little from personal observations
of the agencies of internal fire. He founded his system,
therefore, upon a partial and imperfect view of evidence ;
but his zeal and eloquence captivated his numerous pupils,
whose delight it was to blazon the system of their great
teacher ; and for many years few were bold enough to
question its entire truth. But a change of opinion had
been for some years going on. The philosophy of fire as
regards its agencies in the earth — not entirely new indeed — had been revived and greatly extended by the researches of Dr. Hutton of Edinburgh, aided by his enthu-
siastic followers, Playfair, Hall, Hope, Seymour and others.
The followers of Hutton were now organized into a geological phalanx, and my residence in Edinburgh occurred at
the fortunate crisis, when the combatants on both sides
were in the field ; and I, although a non-combatant, was
within the wind of battle, and prepared, like victory, to join
the strongest side. When Dr. Hope came out with his
array of facts in support of the Huttonian theory, I was in
a state of mind to yield to evidence. Being a young man,
uncommitted to either theory, I was a deeply interested
listener to the discussions of both the Wernerian and Huttonian hypothesis. From the fierce central heat of the
philosophers of fire, and its destructive heavings and irrup-

tions and overflows, I went to bathe in the cool ocean of Werner; and as both views were ably and eloquently sustained, the exercise was to me a delightful recreation and a most instructive study. I found time, also, to read Playfair's illustrations of the Huttonian theory, and Murray's comparative view of both the conflicting theories; and I was not long in coming to the conclusion that both theories were founded in truth, and that the crust of the earth had been formed and greatly modified by the combined, or sometimes antagonistic and conflicting powers of fire and water. The two theories occupied to a considerable extent a common ground as to the agency of water, but fire came in to modify, or entirely transform, the materials which water had deposited. The stratified rocks, the igneous theory still conceded to the dominion of water; but porphyry and all the trap family, and even granite, it claimed as the products of fire. The strong analogy existing between the porphyries and traps and lithoid lava, both in physical characters and composition, and frequently in position, left no reasonable doubt that both are igneous. The dykes and intrusive veins in rocks, go to the same account. I felt greatly relieved when I was excused from attempting to compel myself to believe that porphyry, trap in all its varieties, and even granite, had ever been dissolved in water. I became, therefore, to a certain extent, a Huttonian, and abating that part of the rocks which the igneous theory reclaims as the production of fire, I remained as much of a Wernerian as ever. But I held myself aloof from entire committal to either theory, or to any theory except one derived directly from the facts. Up to the time of my leaving New Haven for England, (March 20, 1805,) I only supposed that the east and west rocks of New Haven were of the basaltic family, agreeably to a suggestion reported from an English traveller many years before. Now I felt assured of their igneous origin. New Haven resembled Edinburgh, having trap rocks in its immediate vicinity.

Salisbury Craig is situated in relation to Edinburgh, almost exactly as the East Rock is in reference to New Haven, and the two are not unlike in form. I have already mentioned the Castle Rock as trap or basalt. Arthur's Seat, also very near to Edinburgh, is nearly eight hundred feet high, and in elevation and form is not unlike our Mount Carmel; and between the old town of Edinburgh and the new, or rather on the borders of the new, rises the Calton Hill of porphyry, — the hill which is consecrated to monuments, — those of Hume, Sir Walter Scott, and others. I now felt that my geological difficulties were vanishing, and I began to repose, in great confidence, upon the double action of fire and water. After my return home it was a great pleasure to me to view all the trap ranges of Connecticut and Massachusetts and New Jersey, as belonging to the same category with Scottish trap, or whinstone, as it is called in Scotland. I became convinced, also, that the basalt of the Giant's Causeway belonged to the same family; and that compact lava and trap basalt and porphyry, are merely modes of one and the same operation. Many years afterwards, (May 1851,) on Mount Etna, I saw true basaltic columns that had been formed in a lava current. (See Visit to Europe in 1851, Vol. II. p. 26). Extended observations in different countries, and comparison with Vesuvius and Etna, by a visit to those mountains, have given my mind entire satisfaction on the subject of igneous agency. Seventeen years after my return from Scotland Cordier's little book appeared, assuming to prove, as he did prove, that the heat increases regularly in all countries as we descend into the earth, after passing below the effects of atmospheric variations; and the average rate of increase is about one degree for every fifty feet of descent. Of course, if the ratio, or any ratio of increase, continues, we must eventually arrive at ignited and even melted rocks. The deductions of Cordier have been since confirmed by observations made in many countries, particularly in deep

mines and artesian wells, whose water, if derived from
deep sources, always rises to an elevated temperature, and
in many countries hot and even boiling springs spout from
the ground.   I was greatly satisfied with the result of my
geological studies in Scotland, and felt that, on account of
that subject as well as chemistry, it would have been worth
a voyage across the Atlantic.

Remark. — In April, 1851, I saw Cordier in Paris, still
vigorous, active, and cheerful, at the age of eighty-five, and
full sixty years after he with others went to Egypt in the
train of Napoleon, as a member of the corps of learned
men, artists, &c. which that extraordinary man took along
with him.   In war Napoleon did not forget the arts of
peace and the interests of science.

I was desirous to add anatomy to my list of studies, and,
of course, my mind was at first directed to the Anatomical
Hall of the University.   I did attend a single lecture there
under Professor Monroe, the third of the name and family,
— father, son, and grandson having occupied that chair.
More, certainly, from the reports of students and others
who had attended on him than from the slight experience
of a single lecture, I decided not to attend on that course,
and to prefer that of Dr. John Barclay, a private lecturer,
to whom many of the medical students resorted, to take
advantage of his high talents and accurate knowledge, not
only of human, but of comparative anatomy.   The students
took the Monroe ticket because it was necessary to enable
them to graduate, and often they took Dr. Barclay's ticket also
for the sake of the valuable knowledge which was imparted
by that course.   I had not occasion to regret my decision.
I found Dr. Barclay to be a man of vigorous mind and
great enthusiasm.   As to his subject, or rather subjects, he
was *totus in illis*.   He was not satisfied with human anatomy only ; he illustrated it in a very instructive and interesting manner by comparative anatomy, ranging through

the creation, and bringing monkeys, or the quadrumana, the cetacea, the carnivora, the amphibia, the rodentia, and pachydermata alongside of man, to illustrate their comparative corporeal structure, and, so to speak, mental powers also, and the perfection of their respective organizations. A statue of the Venus de Medici stood elevated on a pedestal to illustrate the *beau ideal* of the human figure; while the head of a crocodile was placed side by side with a human cranium, the frontal orb of the latter rising in intellectual grandeur, the same portion of the skull of the former being very shallow and depressed, leaving little room for brain and intellect. Thus he followed the intellectual gradation of animals from its lowest to its highest development; and in fact he showed himself the master of human and comparative anatomy and of physiology, in both brutes and men; while the whole range of natural history afforded him ample and happy illustrations. One of his most favorite topics was muscular action and its laws. On this subject he was great; and his thoughts and illustrations were afterwards published in a work which, I believe, has a high reputation among anatomists. He was himself a striking example of powerful muscular organization. His figure was short and very robust, with powerful limbs; a massy figure constructed for strength and not for speed; and, indeed, judging from his energetic, decisive manner, he could hardly regret that he was not made for flight, for I believe he would not have fled in battle. Although more than half a century has passed away since I heard his voice, I can see him now, with his iron frame and firm features, enforcing his lucubrations by the gestures of his brawny arm, and earnestly enforcing the truths he taught, with his broad Scotch dialect and intonations, not softened, as in the case of the professors whom I have named, — in them deprived in a great measure of national peculiarities by southern cultivation in England and even by foreign travel. While writing these reminiscences of Edinburgh chiefly

from recollection, I have been surprised by the fidelity.
with which that faithful prompter, memory, summons up
scenes and thoughts that have apparently long since passed
into oblivion, and have faded away from our minds. Association is, however, the strongest cord which, woven into
a moral and intellectual network, yields to our soliciting
force expended upon it, and produces a rich result, as a
seine in the sea draws in a multitude, a whole school, when
we might have thought that there were only a few strag-
glers, and they scarcely worthy of the capture.

Salisbury Craig. — Among the visits which I made to
this celebrated mountain, that of March 5, 1806, came very
near being made memorable. As it was a very fine morning, I passed several hours in examining the Craig, in pursuit of its minerals. The columns appeared to be from
seventy to one hundred and twenty feet high, and immediately at their feet commenced a sloping descent, so nearly
vertical, that one could walk only with great care, making
his way over it with watchful eyes. The mass is composed
of the ruins of the cliffs, brought down, through ages, by
frost, rains, wind, and gravity. The accumulation forms a
slope of two hundred to three hundred feet. My course
lay along at the top of the slope and at the foot of the cliffs ;
immediately over my head were the impending cliffs, and
at my feet a giddy descent to the bottom of the mountain.
Stopping every few minutes to examine the rocks, and
freighting my pockets with minerals, I pursued my course
at leisure, not without some solicitude lest a false step or
a faithless fragment, treacherous to my weight, should pre-
cipitate me to the bottom. Coasting along the front of the
mountain, I had nearly reached its western extremity, when
I was induced by a place that looked very promising,
to clamber up over a great mass of loose stones to the
very foot of the precipice, and was busily occupied beneath the ragged and ruinous cliffs, which seemed ready

for a movement, — and indeed they occasionally gave a premonition by the fall of a fragment of stone, but not large enough to excite alarm. Soon, however, on looking up, I saw with consternation a large mass of rock at that instant separating to commence its fall. A little below me a column of some magnitude, an avalanche from an earlier convulsion, lay in its bed, firmly projecting, prominent from the mass of ruins. It was but a glance upward and then downward, when I saw my asylum, and, quick as thought, with a desperate effort, I leaped over the stones and was sheltered by the friendly column ; had I delayed, even the few beats of the pulse, while the ruin was beginning its fall, it might have been too late. Thank Heaven! I was securely sheltered *while the desolation was passing by.* One mass of rock as large as a barrel struck about twenty feet above where I had stood, and, rebounding, flew with great velocity down the mountain, passing in the line of my former position, at about the height of a man's breast, and of course might have been fatal to me had I remained where I was. In my flight I had left behind me my collected minerals, and my cane, which stuck fast in the crevices of the rock. Thinking that the avalanche was past, I was, with some hesitation, stepping forward to recover my relics, when another mass, which must have weighed twenty tons, broke off from the cliff, and came thundering down with a loud crash, filling the air with flying rocks and fragments and dust, and covering all that tract of the mountain where I had been exploring, and to which I was returning, with ruins and desolation. Had the fall been delayed for only one minute, I should have been in the midst of the space which it swept, and a more brief narrative by some other hand would have related the result. Such was the noise produced by this avulsion, that the people living in the vicinity and in the Palace of Holyrood came running out to learn the cause.

CHAPTER VIII.

My time was so much engrossed by my professional studies and the engagements connected with them, that I had little leisure, when residing in Edinburgh, to become acquainted with its celebrated men. Several of them I have, however, already mentioned at some length, — Hope, Gregory, Murray, Barclay, the Monroes, &c. To Professor Dugald Stewart, I was indebted for very courteous attentions, but unfortunately I missed him, both when I called at his house and when he returned my calls. I missed him always in both places, and indeed I thought it very condescending in a man of double my age and of his high reputation, to reiterate his calls at my lodgings. At last, however, we met at an informal *soirée*. This was held at the house of the distinguished professor, and there was present an interesting group of persons of both sexes. Their manners were easy and polite, and the more so as the refreshments were all served upon several tables in different parts of a large room, — a cold collation with a warm reception ; and the guests walked freely about enjoying conversation or refreshments as they chose. "Professor Stewart is the pride and ornament of the University, and of Scotland. With a countenance strongly marked by the lines of intellect; with an expression of thought amounting almost to severity, but in conversation softened by great benignity, and with manners uniting everything of dignity and ease, he, even at first sight, impressed a stranger forcibly with an idea of his superiority." "When he speaks, either in his lecture-room or in conversation, he draws forth the resources of a highly enriched and polished mind ; he charms the hearer by the beauty of his language and the fine cadence of his voice, while he arrests his attention by the energy and fulness of his eloquence." (Published Travels of the author.) Professor Stewart conversed with me upon American topics. Soon after the American war, he had known Dr. Franklin in Paris, and he spoke of him in terms of the highest respect. On topics of American literature, he expressed himself in polite and delicate terms, although it was evident that our literature was not highly appreciated by him. When our poems were inquired for, it was evident that the distinguished men around me had not heard even the names of our poets, Dwight, Trumbull, Barlow, Humphreys, and others. Before I had met him, I went with my friend, Mr. Codman, to hear one of Professor Stewart's lectures. It was equal to his high reputation, and served to identify his person and manner. He was very sensitive as regards inattention and levity in his lecture-room. Mr. Codman told me that the Professor was much incensed one day by the improper conduct of a pupil; he made a solemn pause, and, with a stern voice and a keen glance, required the offending youth to call and receive his money back, surrender his ticket, and never to appear in that lecture-room again.

Professor Leslie was of our party at Professor Stewart's; he had honored me by calling upon me, and I was already in some degree acquainted with him. He had not the quiet, polished dignity of his friend Stewart; his manners had a blunt frankness which, however, inspired confidence in his sincerity. His person was large. He was distinguished by an ingenious and original volume containing researches on heat. The differential thermometer was described in that volume, and many curious results on the radiation of heat were obtained by means of this instrument. (The originality of the discovery of the differential thermometer was afterwards denied in the Edinburgh Journals.) Professor Leslie had travelled on the Continent, and in his researches on heat there were occasionally poetical and picturesque allusions to scenery. He visited the United States soon after the peace of 1783, at the close of the American Revolution. He said that he found the country poor, and the people discontented, — and no wonder, considering the immense expenditure of money and blood by which the conflict had been sustained during eight years of suffering. The election of Professor Leslie was attended by a severe conflict between the Orthodox party which sustained him, and the Arminian party which opposed him. The latter charged him with infidelity, and the former vindicated him. A war of pamphlets was carried on during the winter, and in one of them which I saw, the clergy were, by name, arranged in two columns. The Orthodox column was headed by *Clean*, and the Arminian *Unclean*, — " *Tantæne animis celestibus iræ ?* " The column of the *Clean* was headed by the name of the President of the University, Dr. Baird ; but it should be remembered that it was not placed there by himself, but by the invidious rivalry of party. Professor Leslie was regarded as well worthy to fill the place of his illustrious predecessor, Dr. Robison.

I was never introduced to that eminent writer, Dr. Thomas

Thomson, whose chemistry, as I have already mentioned, was among my very early studies. It is always interesting to see the persons and to observe the manner of eminent men, and with this view I resorted to the lecture-room of Dr. Thomson. In person he was not above the middle height, his complexion was dark, and the impression of his entire appearance was not prepossessing. His manner as a lecturer — judging from a single lecture — was formal and precise, not flowing and easy, like that of Murray. It seemed to be in harmony with the excellent method of his published works.

Dr. (now Sir David) Brewster, was present at the *soirée* of Prof. Stewart, and should have been mentioned in that connection. Although I saw him only on that occasion, I retain a very distinct impression of his personal appearance. He was of about the middle stature, complexion bright and slightly florid, form rotund but not corpulent; manners affable and pleasing, simple, direct, and unaffected. I did not suppose I had made a lodgment in his memory, but an editorial sympathy brought us together in subsequent years. In 1819 a joint-editorship of the "Edinburgh Philosophical Journal," by Dr. David Brewster and Prof. Jameson, (1819–1823,) was established, and ten volumes were published. Then followed a distinct work, (the editors having dissolved their partnership,) Brewster's "Edinburgh Journal of Science," (1824–1829,) also in ten volumes. Prof. Jameson then instituted still another journal, — the "Edinburgh Philosophical Journal." (1824–1826 ; four volumes). Then Prof. Jameson published still another journal under the same title, — the "Edinburgh Philosophical Journal" (1826–1838 ; eighteen volumes). A degree of rivalry seems to have been cherished between these eminent men. Dr. Brewster established still another journal, — "Brewster's Edinburgh Journal of Science," (1829–1832; five volumes). These works are now in my library. From the dates last mentioned to the present time, Edinburgh has never been without a journal of science. That of Prof. Jameson was continued until his death, a few years since; and able successors have followed in the same line of labor.

A mutual sympathy was sustained between Sir David Brewster and myself, not only by editorial services and courtesies, but by his numerous memoirs. Being desirous that they should appear in the "American Journal," he sent them to me from time to time, in detached printed forms or " brochures," as the French call them; and each memoir was usually accompanied by a letter from the author. If I live to revise my files of letters, and to select those that are to be preserved, I shall leave a small file of Dr. Brewster's. Dr. Brewster still lives, and is almost alone among my Edinburgh contemporaries. He has led a highly useful life, and must, I should think, have now reached fourscore. He is not only a man eminent in science, he is a man of decided religious principles, and, I trust, of piety.

At Prof. Dugald Stewart's I met Lord Webb Seymour. I know little of his history. He was, however, a compeer with Playfair, Hope, Leslie, Sir James Hall, and other men eminent in physical science, especially in mineralogy and geology. It was a pleasure to me to meet him, not because he was a nobleman, but because, being a nobleman, he was exempt from pride and bore himself with perfect courtesy and affability. I had an agreeable conversation with him, and to me it was instructive also. IIe appeared to be well acquainted with chemistry, and named several processes in the arts in which there was great loss from an ignorance of chemical principles. In person, he was tall and rather slender; his dress was that of a genteel man, or, in other words, that of a gentleman, as without his title he would have been a noble man. His age appeared to be about thirty-five.

I am not certain whether I met Dr. Thomas Brown first at Prof. Dugald Stewart's; he called on me at my lodg-

ings, and when returning his call I found him living with
a widowed mother. His intellectual and metaphysical
works are well known in this country. He gave me a small
Latin treatise of his own composition ; I think it was entitled "*De somniis.*" His appearance was that of an amiable man, of modest and conciliating manners. His person
was genteel, his countenance mild and pleasing ; and his
age might have been thirty-two or thirty-three.

I have mentioned a literary breakfast at the house of a
celebrated gentleman,— Dr. Anderson, the well-known editor of the British Poets. I met there an agreeable circle of
gentlemen, and the conversation was more or less literary.
American literature, of course, comes in for a share of attention on such occasions. Dr. Anderson conceded to us
much talent and keenness, especially in debate,— what the
English call cleverness, — with a fair amount of information,
but he said we had not yet attained to taste. Our literary
productions being "often tumid and bombastical," (but
hardly more so than a sermon which I heard, on the occasion of the National Thanksgiving, by Dr. Baird, President
of the University of Edinburgh). If such remarks are
annoying, I could not but admit, tacitly, that they were
but too well founded. I parried Dr. Anderson's censure,
however, by adding, that there was much talent and taste
in my country, the results of which did not reach Europe.
Dr. Anderson was a gentleman, I should suppose, then
turned of fifty. His person and presence were both commanding and affable, but his costume was negligent, his
apparel old and worn, and was hardly worthy of himself or
his guests ; but I was led to believe that his circumstances
were far from affluence, — a fact not uncommon in Edinburgh.

That eccentric nobleman, the Earl of Buchan, was one
of the guests at Dr. Anderson's. He appeared to be sixty
or sixty-five years old. I was no sooner announced to him
as an American, than he singled me out as a subject of

attention. This arose from his political position. He was
a decided friend to the Americans in their Revolutionary
struggle, and remained an ardent admirer of Washington.
He had, as most persons will remember, transmitted to
General Washington a box made from the wood of the tree
which sheltered Sir William Wallace. It was accompanied
by a request that General Washington would designate
a successor, one whom he would regard as most worthy
to possess the box after he should have done with it.
That great man declined the invidious office, and in his
will directed that the box should be returned to the Earl
of Buchan. On the present occasion he was full of Washington, condemning his own government not only in their
treatment of the colonies, but for entering upon one unnecessary war after another, thus involving the nation in debt
and wasting human life. Had things been ordered as his
friend, Mr. Fox, and the party which he led, himself included, had wished, all these evils would, he said, have been
avoided. As the Earl was short-sighted, he came so near
to me that I was within the limit of his distinct vision,
and when I retreated to gain a little more offing, he followed me so perseveringly that I brought up against the
mantle and was rather inconveniently pressed between the
fire and his nobility. Without preface or apology he gave
me the history of his agricultural proceedings for the season, and especially in the culture of the turnip; and he
continued to pour forth an uninterrupted effusion on agriculture, John Bull, Mr. Pitt, General Washington, and
twenty other topics, and I could find space only for an
occasional interjection of admiration or wonder. From the
embarrassing effort to preserve the gravity of my muscles,
I was occasionally relieved by flashes of wit or humor which
now and then broke forth from the Earl, and the relief was
complete when a hearty laugh exploded between us. When
seated at the table, the garrulous old nobleman resumed
the same strain of talk, — the most extraordinary specimen

of incongruities and eccentricities that I have ever met with. This, it is said, was always the character of his mind, and that it had been excited almost to a happy delirium by the recent success of his party. In person, the Earl of Buchan was not much above the middle size, and there was very little of dignity in his appearance. His dress was coarse and negligently worn, so that he might have been mistaken for a very common man. Indeed, my friend Codman told me that the Earl was conducted into the kitchen, while the house-servant went to inform the Rev. Charles Lowell of Boston, that a man wished to see him; and of course an apology was made for the blunder.

The Earl of Moira, olim *Lord Rawdon.* — This distinguished nobleman and commander was probably acquainted with no other science than that of war. It was that distinction which created a strong interest in my mind to see a man who inflicted much suffering on my country, especially in the Southern States, where, as the daring and impetuous Lord Rawdon, he combated our ablest generals: but a stain remains permanently attached to his character on account of the military execution of Col. Isaac Hayne, in Charleston, in August, 1781. This act of severity, alike cruel and unnecessary, brought so much odium upon Lord Rawdon (then only twenty-seven years old) and his coadjutor, Col. Balfour, that Lord Rawdon in 1813, thirty-four years after the event, wrote an elaborate defence, which was not published until 1824. This defence, with all the most important historical documents relating to the tragedy, is ably analyzed in the "Southern Review," (Vol. I., Art. III.,) for February, 1828. A careful perusal of the article has not served to change my opinion. To say the least, it was a case in which clemency was demanded, and it would have promoted the royal cause far more than the merciless severity which was exercised. But it was in harmony with the spirit which prevailed in the British coun-

sels — the counsels of the king and the ministry, not of
the people of England, — and armies, during that bloody
and barbarous crusade against the colonies. The occasion
when I saw Earl Moira was at a military review (January
18, 1806), both of the regulars and the volunteers. I encountered it accidentally in a morning walk, in Princes
Street, in the new town. I chose a position very near to
his lordship, who was on horseback in the full British uniform of the commander-in-chief of the forces in Scotland.
The housing of his saddle was a leopard skin, the holsters
were covered, as is usual, with bear-skin, and he wore the
three-cornered military hat. He was a noble-looking veteran. Although only fifty years old, care, fatigue, and danger had given him the aspect of sixty years. His face was
furrowed and marked by anxiety. I studied him intently,
and thought to myself, "then you are the man who, as an
active and brave young officer, associated with Col. Tarle-
ton, and both, acting under Lord Cornwallis, desolated
South Carolina, and hanged one of its most estimable citizens." I was so near that I could have heard every word,
had he spoken, but he was entirely silent. It was a mere
reconnoissance of troops, exercising and passing before him
in review by hundreds and thousands, — a grand and beautiful spectacle; with all the pomp and apparatus of war
it gave a spectator a vivid impression of the reality of
those sanguinary scenes, so falsely called the fields of
glory. The mute artillery, with burnished brass cannon,
attended by their gunners and matrosses with their cais-
sons, and all their machinery, passed quietly along, a harmless pageant, but ready to wake the thunders of war.

The Earl of Moira appears not to have lost his dislike
to the Americans, even when the contest was finished.
Col. Trumbull told me that when one of his historical pictures — I believe it was Bunker Hill — was being exhibited
in Somerset House, and was visited by the young army officers, Earl Moira caused them to be informed that the visit-

ing of the pictures of that artist would be regarded as a proof of want of loyalty, and of course the visits ceased. This was very narrow and illiberal, and of a piece with the execution of Col. Hayne. From 1812 to 1822, he was Governor-General of India. In 1824 he was appointed Governor of Malta, and resided there until 1825, when he died on board of the British ship-of-war *Revenge* in the bay of Baiæ, near Naples. It is mentioned to his honor, that his "profuse liberality and generous hospitality," particularly to the French emigrant *noblesse,* clouded the later years of his life. His country-seat was near Edinburgh, and Holyrood House was occupied by the Count D'Artois and his friends of the Bourbon family; and again it became an asylum for French exiles after the fall of Charles X. in 1830. . . . . .

Among the celebrities of Edinburgh, Mr. Liston (afterwards Sir Robert Liston) must not be forgotten. Probably he had no more to do with science than the Earl of Moira; for, unlike him, he had passed a public life, not in the field, but accredited as a minister to most of the cabinets of Europe, and to that of the United States. He had had, therefore, an opportunity to study the science of government. From Henry Thornton, Esq., M. P., I had brought a letter of introduction to a venerable friend of his in Edinburgh, Mr. R. S. Moncrieff; and he was on terms of intimacy with Mr. Liston. Mr. Moncrieff, learning from me that I bore a letter from Col. Pickering to Mr. Liston, proposed that we should ride out together on horseback to Mr. Liston's residence at Melbourne, five miles from Edinburgh, in season for breakfast. We were received by Mrs. Liston with great politeness, and then by her husband, who was called in from the field, where he was directing the agricultural operations of spring. During the administration of General Washington, Mr. Liston had been long resident minister of Great Britain at the American court, which was then held in Philadelphia. They (Mr. and Mrs.

Liston) both retained the kindest recollections of their American residence, and Mrs. Liston cherished a small American garden devoted to our trees, shrubs, and plants; and into this garden she admitted nothing that was not of transatlantic origin. I looked with peculiar interest to these natives of my country. We found these interesting people living in all the simplicity and retirement of rural life. Their house, a neat stone cottage, was of one story, with a thatched roof, and had a few handsome rooms. It was situated in the midst of a farm which Mr. Liston cultivated, not without personal toil. His person was tall and dignified, his manners presented a model of graceful simplicity, and his conversation was highly intelligent, instructive, and agreeable. We took breakfast in a small octagonal apartment resembling a ship's cabin, and lighted from above. Mrs. Liston did the honors of the occasion with much dignity and affability. Their sentiments on the United States and its affairs, its government, and the prospect of the permanency of its institutions, were highly favorable. Mr. Liston was now in retirement, and appeared to be past sixty years of age. A revolution of parties having recently taken place, and the party of Mr. Fox having come into power, allusion was made to that fact, and to the probability that he, Mr. Liston, would soon be called again into public life, when he replied, — " If they want me, they know where to find me ; " and I believe he was soon after sent on some foreign mission. Mr. Liston, while residing in Philadelphia as minister from the Court of London, was constantly assailed by " The Aurora," the leading Democratical paper of that day. At breakfast he remarked to us pleasantly, that finding one morning that his name did not appear in " The Aurora " sheet as usual, he was led to inquire whether he had done any base act that day or recently to entitle him to favor from " The Aurora." He remarked that the editor, Duane, was a renegade Englishman, and Callender was another base instrument also, — an

Englishman who was set up on purpose to assail General Washington and his administration. At this day, as for many years, a Scotchman in New York edits a paper notorious for falsehood and slander. It is thus that foreigners disgrace us.

Sir Harry Moncrieff Wellwood, an excellent baronet, deserves to be commemorated among the eminent men of Scotland of my time. He was an established minister of the West Kirk at the foot of the Castle Rock, Parish of St. Cuthbert's, and although a titled man, he was a fervent minister of the gospel. Cowper mentions, as a wonder, the Earl of Dartmouth, who " wears a coronet and prays." I often attended the preaching of the Rev. Sir Henry M. Wellwood, who retained his aristocratic title, and was rarely called Reverend. He exhibited every appearance of a sound and excellent mind, and every proof of rational, although ardent piety. He appeared to be about sixty; but his physical frame was robust, and he seemed to have the stamina of a long life.

Rev. David Dickson was an intimate friend of my associate, Mr. Codman, and he honored me with his friendship and confidence. I was also kindly received in the family of his father, the Rev. Mr. Dickson, senior. I occasionally heard the father preach, and often listened to the son in the West Kirk, near which Mr. Dickson resided in a bachelor's home, with an intelligent and agreeable sister to do the honors of his house. His hospitality we often enjoyed, and the most valued part of the entertainment was derived from his own bright intelligence, joyous spirits, sparkling wit, and warm welcome. He was a man of talents and learning. In the pulpit, he was solemn, earnest, and affectionate; his sermons were lucid, and their tendency was eminently practical. He had read the writings of our principal New-England divines, — Edwards, Hopkins, Bellamy, and others, — and he remarked to me once that he thought our preachers indulged too much in metaphysics. " We here," added he, "take the doctrines for granted, and appeal directly to the hearts of our people and make our teachings bear upon their lives." Still the preaching of the Evangelical clergy in Edinburgh often involved doctrines with their warm exhortations. On my leaving Edinburgh, in April, 1806, he gave me as a remembrancer a volume, elegantly bound, of the published sermons of Sir Henry Moncrieff Wellwood, and on a blank leaf he wrote, —

"TO B. SILLIMAN, Esq.,

from a friend.

Etsi corpore absens, spiritu tamen præsens.

Edin. April 26, 1806."

The inscription was in his most beautiful chirography, and the sentiment was so perfectly printed by his pen in an imitation of the impress of type, that even now, more than fifty-two years after the time, I find it difficult to convince a friend that it is not really printing.

Rev. Mr. Black, an excellent man, was a devout and earnest preacher of the gospel. He was not reckoned among the stars of Edinburgh, but he was greatly respected, and he drew very large and attentive congregations. We were occasionally in his church, and every seat was occupied. The people filled the alleys, and hung around the door in dense masses, like bees clustering around a hive in cold weather. The spirit of John Knox had not died out in Scotland, and seemed to animate many of the preachers and no small portion of the people. We enjoyed occasionally the hospitality of Rev. Mr. Black, and met there intelligent and interesting people. The standing topic of American literature being introduced with the usual intimations of its inferiority, I ventured to suggest that an American, Lindley Murray, had given to Britain as well as America the best grammar of the English language which had been published. Mr. Black then with playful retaliation replied, that Mr. Murray, by long residence in this country, had learned the language. Alas, the winter was not passed before Mr. Black was called away! Hearing that he was sick, we sent our servant-girl daily to inquire as to his condition. At last she returned one morning and said, "*Sir, he has gone to his rest,*" — a beautiful annunciation of his death.

The fame of our American Dr. John Mitchell Mason was widely extended in Scotland, and especially in Edinburgh where he was educated. Although they were proud of his talents and eloquence, adorned as they were by a noble person and a commanding voice and manner, he was not permitted to preach in the churches of the Establishment, because his family, which was from Scotland, belonged to the Seceders. They regarded him, moreover, as too ornate in his style; and in London he was censured for eulogizing Colonel Hamilton, who in July, 1804, had fallen in a duel with Colonel Burr.

"*Edinburgh Review.*" — A curiosity, natural on my part, to know something more of the organization and history of this Review, was gratified by the hospitality of our bookseller, Mr. Ross. This kind friend, as he ever proved himself to be, invited me to meet at dinner at his house a party of gentlemen, and among them Messrs. Constable and Hunter, the publishers and proprietors of the Edinburgh Journal. These gentlemen, with great frankness and liberality, communicated to me those facts respecting the origin and plan and execution of this journal which I have published in my early travels. . . . . . At dinner, at Mr. Hunter's, the next day, I found in him not only hospitality but great intelligence, with an extended knowledge of books, especially those that are rare and valuable, of which Mr. Hunter was a great collector. I mentioned Mather's "Magnalia," of which I wished to obtain a copy for a friend at home. It was sometime after procured at an expense of seven dollars, but unfortunately was lost from the stage between Edinburgh and Liverpool. Mr. Hun-

·ter's house had then in the press for Walter Scott, "Marmion." His sun was at that time in the ascendant, but it did not culminate in full splendor until years after my return home. I believe, however, that the "Minstrelsy of the Scottish Border," and his "History of the Scottish Border," had been published.

Sir John Stirling and Lady. — In my childhood, an itinerant mechanic, an artist in metals, travelled from place to place, bearing his tools on his back, and he was occasionally at my father's house to repair the utensils of the kitchen. My brother and myself, both below our teens, were delighted with the visits of the old man, — listening to the clatter of his hammer as it was applied to the sounding brass, and entertained more still by his legendary lore. Among other tales, he was wont to enlarge upon the high condition of a daughter, married, as he said, to a Laird in Scotland, the possessor of a great estate, and of flocks of sheep and herds of cattle, with their herdsmen and shepherds. The story sounded like romance ; but it was stated in proof of its truth, that the daughter, still filial in feeling, although exalted in condition, did not forget her family, and proved her fidelity by sending out annually presents of valuable things to her humble sire and mother. Such was the story of old Fulsome (Folsom), as he was called ; and the tale went through Stratford and Fairfield that, before the American Revolution, a young Scotch Laird stopped over the Sabbath at Stratford, either voluntarily or constrained by the strictness of Puritanical laws which forbade travelling on that day ; and what could he do better than go to church ? And to church he went, seeking edification, as we might charitably hope, but finding, at least, occupation, and finding, moreover, a boon little expected. The legend relates that a beautiful girl among the singers caught the eye of the young traveller, and, more than the minister, fixed and engaged his attention.

Inquiry discovered her humble condition, but did not abate the virtuous feelings which she had excited, and doubtless they were confirmed by personal interviews. She was in due time favored with educational training, and having native dignity and good sense, it may be presumed that she honored her station not less than it honored her. Many years passed away; the tales of childhood faded into glimmering recollections; and this story would doubtless have been remembered no more, had it not been revived by an accidental occurrence. Being invited to dine at the house of one of our friends, a clergyman, I was informed that I should there meet an American lady. I accepted the invitation, and was introduced to Sir John Stirling and lady and daughter. They were sensible and agreeable people, intelligent and courteous, and, withal, dignified without formality. Sir John might have been fifty-six, and his wife fifty-three. Conversation, of course, turned on America, and Lady Stirling and myself were drawn a little nearer in interest, as we could speak of a common country. The course of conversation soon discovered that New England and Connecticut was our native land, and I avowed myself Connecticut born. It appeared that the lady had left the land of her nativity thirty years or more ago; and when I took the liberty to inquire still farther for her native town, she named Stratford, and I responded that it was also my native town, although that portion of it where I was born now bore the name of Trumbull. The next town, Fairfield, was the abode of my family, but my mother was driven into exile by the British invasion along our coast, and I was born away from home. In an instant the tales of childhood were summoned afresh from their long repose in my memory, and I felt no doubt that the once young and beautiful Miss Folsom was now before me as Lady Stirling, — a grave matron, — and the ardent and gallant young Scotchman was the veritable Sir John Stirling, — a grave knight. I pursued my inquiries no further;

and as the lady did not name her family, I remained silent, except to my two Boston friends, the companions of my domestic retirement. I thought that perhaps she would not care to advert to her own early history; and I saw them no more.*

Among the Edinburgh friends whose hospitality and kindness Professor Silliman always remembered with pleasure, was the family of Mr. Ebenezer Mason, a respectable merchant, an uncle of Dr. Mason of New York. After many years he had the satisfaction of renewing his acquaintance with members of Mr. Mason's family, who emigrated to this country.

The recollections of his Edinburgh life conclude as follows : —

A supper at nine o'clock, ample although frugal, and got up in good taste, frequently afforded a scene of pleasant intercourse in Edinburgh families. Social intercourse was easy, and in a high degree friendly. The time went away rapidly, and brought us sometimes to the midnight hour, when a hearty good-night followed, not unfrequently animated by a farewell song. Scotch social feelings needed physical excitement; it is, however, not to be denied that they were often intensified by libations of the mountain dew, — the favorite name of " Highland whiskey." A large bowl, reeking with hot whiskey-toddy, sometimes found a place in the centre of the supper-table ; a ladle served to transfer portions of the cheering fluid from the central reservoir to the glasses of the guests, who sipped it from time to time, by means of small ladles, one in each glass ; and it was not difficult to discover the effect on the

* In Dod's *Book of Peerage*, &c., 1856, Sir Samuel Stirling is described as the " son of the sixth baronet by his marriage with Miss Folson [an error for Folsom] of Stratford, North America." — (F.

sociability and colloquial powers of the company. However gratifying at the moment, the tendency was no doubt bad, and we presume that the jovial beginnings had sometimes a melancholy end. Entertainments were not always, however, so frugal. I dined on one occasion with a Scotch bachelor, who for a few guests spread a sumptuous table, which he told me of his own accord cost twelve pounds, or sixty dollars. It was less agreeable than the frugal suppers, and was not recommended by the free habits and sentiments of our host as developed by himself. In family parties in Edinburgh, music, both vocal and instrumental, was a favorite entertainment. Native airs and native songs or poems exerted a fascinating power, and it often happened that the music of the piano was the signal for Scotch reels on the parlor carpet, ending at the usual hour of family retirement. To these few notices of social manners in Edinburgh, I add a paragraph from my published travels. "The Scotch are a noble people; and, poor and narrow as is the tract of earth allotted to them, cut up by friths, enfiladed by mountains, and girded by a belt of stormy islands, Scotland may still proudly challenge the nations whom the Creator has placed in more favored climes, to produce higher examples of all that adorns and ennobles the human character."

RESULT OF MY RESIDENCE IN EUROPE IN RELATION TO THE OBJECTS OF MY MISSION. — I. *In Relation to Business.* — I was fortunate in my engagements in London for the purchase of books and apparatus. I met with faithful men in all the departments, who executed the orders with zeal, punctuality, and fidelity. All the books, and every article of apparatus, except a few unimportant pieces of glass, arrived in safety, and met the full approbation of my patrons. After examining all my accounts, and those of the artists and booksellers, with the vouchers, and my own account of personal expenditures, I received a full discharge of my pecuniary responsibility and a vote of approbation. It was. signed by the Prudential Committee of Yale College, namely, — Timothy Dwight, President; John Treadwell, Governor of Connecticut; Rev. James Dana, D. D.; and Rev. David Ely, D. D. The two latter were members of the Corporation of Yale College, and Dr. Ely was Secretary.

I was charged also with various private commissions, all of which were executed with fidelity, and the money duly accounted for, and I made no charge for services. I have on my files the book which contained the account of all my personal expenses, and entries of the concerns of other persons. I left home for Europe, and Europe for home, without leaving any unsatisfied demand; in a word, with a healthy conscience and an unsullied character; a name, I trust, without reproach, — and, for the satisfaction of my children, may it ever so remain ! As regards my personal expenditures, I not only kept an account of every disbursement, but I footed up always on Saturday night, and noted the ratio of my expenditure compared with my means. Thus I was able to keep myself within the limits of safety. I neither borrowed money nor loaned my funds, and therefore my resources proved sufficient; but there was no excess. I had no money left; but I had not anticipated my salary, and therefore my small means began again to grow.

II. *In Relation to Professional Improvement, Intellectual Culture, Enlargement of Mind, and Social Advancement.* — My first duty and highest obligation were, to dispose of the funds of Yale College which had been confided to me with fidelity, and, as far as possible, with good judgment, so as to effect the objects in view. Ten thousand dollars was a considerable sum more than fifty years ago, and a few hundred more were remitted afterwards, in addition to the bills of exchange which I carried with me, and of which, for safety, duplicates were forwarded by the usual channels. I have already stated that I received a full discharge from my pecuniary responsibility. This document I still hold, with the signatures of the great and good men who are long since removed from life. I hold also another document, an honorary and honorable testimonial of entire satisfaction on the part of my patrons, as regards the use of all the means, opportunities, and time that were placed at my disposal. This document has the signatures of a majority of the Board, — the Prudential Committee of Yale College. It is in my recollection that two of the gentlemen were absent from the meeting, and that I neglected afterwards to obtain their signatures, which would have been given at any time. In relation to professional improvement, I trust it has been already rendered evident that a much higher standard of excellence than I had before seen was presented to me, especially in Edinburgh. Upon that scale I endeavored to form my professional character, to imitate what I saw and heard, and afterwards to introduce such improvements as I might be able to hit upon or invent. It is obvious that, had I rested content with the Philadelphia standard, except what I learned from my early friend, Robert Hare, the chemistry of Yale College would have been comparatively an humble affair. In mineralogy, my opportunities at home had been very limited. As to geology, the science did not exist among us, except in the minds of a very few individuals, and instruction was not attainable in any public institution. In Edinburgh there were learned and eloquent geologists and lecturers, and ardent and successful explorers; and in that city the great geological conflict between the Wernerian and Huttonian schools elicited a high order of talent and rich resources both in theory and facts. Here my mind was enlightened, interested, and excited to efforts which, through half a century, were sustained and increased. Had I remained at home, I should probably never have reached a high standard of attainment in geology, nor given whatever impulse has emanated from New Haven as one of the centres of scientific labor and influence. Intellectual culture and enlargement of mind resulted, of course, from the opportunities which I enjoyed. I went abroad at a period of life when the ardor of youth was associated with the maturity of manhood. Having no proclivities to wrong courses, my time, money, efforts, were all enlisted in the enlargement not only of professional, but of general knowledge. I had vigorous health ; and, except a few days of debility and derangement arising from the inhalation of arsenical fumes in London, and from the influence of the stagnant waters of Holland, — producing, however, no intermission of labor, — I was, during my entire European noviciate, capable of strenuous exertion. I found it a source of enjoyment as well as of improvement; and the acquisitions of that period, with the habits then formed, proved to be an available capital, even forty-six years afterward, when Europe was the theatre of mature observation in the evening of life. That some enlargement of mind and social culture in the survey of human society and institutions, as well as in physical observations, resulted from my European residence, has, I hope, appeared in some degree in my earlier as well as more recent published volumes of travels. They have proved, at least, that I was not an idler nor a devotee of pleasure, and that I made the best use of my time and opportunities of which I was capable. I believe I may, without vanity or presumption, repose upon the verdict of approval which has been pronounced upon those works by the public in all their numerous editions. Thus I conclude my review of an important portion of my life, and with grateful acknowledgment to a kind Providence, which, as with an unseen hand, guided me in a path which I had not known, and having kept me in safety and prospered my efforts, brought me back in peace to my native land. I arrived in New

York May 27, 1806, being then twenty-six years and nine months old.

On Thursday the 29th, I breakfasted with Oliver Wolcott, Esq., who arranged the business concerns of my mission, and with whom I corresponded. Mr. Wolcott was successor to Gen. Alexander Hamilton as Secretary of the Treasury of the United States under President Washington. Mr. Wolcott was a highly dignified and intelligent gentleman, and was now a merchant of high position and connections in New York. With him I called on Col. John Trumbull, who had acted as my patron and friend in England. I dined with my old friend, Mr. Zachariah Lewis. Although Mr. Wolcott had lost his wife, who is remembered as a lady of great excellence and loveliness, he, notwithstanding the derangement of his family, held at his house a *soirée* of some of the most eminent men of the city, among whom were Mr. Hoffman, Mr. William W. Woolsey, Col. Trumbull, Archibald Gracie, Judge Radcliffe, and many more. Probably not an individual of them is now living. The gentlemen thus assembled were members of a social club, and this was one of their meetings. On looking into my journal written at the time, I find that I was admitted in courtesy. The meeting was social, easy, and agreeable, and was characterized by good sense, intelligence, and politeness. I received of course many warm greetings from the friends whom I met on this occasion. On Friday, May 30, I breakfasted with Mr. Samuel Miles Hopkins, a delightful man with a polished and intelligent wife (Miss Rogers, daughter of Moses Rogers, an eminent New York merchant). I dined with Mr. Codman, uncle of my Edinburgh friend, and like him, an agreeable and friendly gentleman.

Steamboats and railroads were in those days unknown, and stage-coaches were slow. Dr. Gorham and myself prepared to take our chance in a New-Haven packet, the *Maria*, Capt. Bradley, in which we embarked at four o'clock P. M., on Friday. With a continuance of the fair wind with which we set sail, we should have been in New Haven the next morning, as we confidently expected. We were however becalmed, and wore away both our Saturday and the Sabbath in listless inaction; but we were not unmindful of the holy day, and occupied some of its hours with reading sermons and singing hymns, — this being the only instance in which I had witnessed such observances on shipboard on the Sabbath. The day had been passed off Stratford Point, within twenty miles of home; but at last a favoring breeze arose, which wafted us safely into the harbor. At four o'clock P. M., Sabbath evening, June 1, 1806, I stepped upon the long wharf, and was first welcomed by my early friend, Charles Denison. The public services of the day were over, but I resorted to the evening prayers at the college chapel. President Dwight, my great and good friend, led the services; when they were finished he gave me a warm, paternal welcome, inviting both Dr. Gorham and myself home to tea; and we had a very interesting evening. I then realized that I was indeed at home again, and safe once more in my own town and institution. My excellent friend, Professor Day, came to President Dwight's, and we accepted his invitation to find our beds at his house, which had become a house of mourning by the death of his estimable wife (Miss Sherman, daughter of the eminent patriot, Roger Sherman). Instances of death among my friends and acquaintance had been painfully numerous during my absence of fourteen months and ten days; but I had been protected and preserved in every vicissitude on the ocean and on the land, and excepting some political jealousy at Antwerp, I had been treated everywhere with confidence and kindness. I had therefore only to thank my great Preserver, and to address myself to perform with zeal and energy the arduous and interesting duties appertaining to my professorship.

During his absence from home and country, Mr.

Silliman was not forgetful of his friends. The selections which follow from his correspondence afford pleasant glimpses of his relations to them.

NEW HAVEN, *May* 7, 1805.

DEAR SIR, — I regret, that having so good an opportunity, it is out of my power to write you more. My eyes have been miserably worried for some time past, and are now very troublesome.

All whom you love are as well in this neighborhood as when you left us. Two pamphlets for Doctor Ryland accompany this, and a certificate of your church-membership.

Governor Strong is elected by a majority of somewhat more than two thousand votes; and Governor Trumbull by the usual majority. Democracy appears plainly to decline here. The Livingstons and Clintons are entirely separated, at least for the present. The Pennsylvania fever is not yet come to a crisis. Mr. Porter, of Hadley, is sensibly better; and will, I think, soon recover a sound state.

We have had many fears concerning you on account of the islands of ice, and they are not yet over.

I am, very affectionately, your friend,

TIMOTHY DWIGHT.

BENJ. SILLIMAN, Esq.

LONDON, *June* 3, 1805.

. . . . . My letters of introduction are beginning to take effect, and I am daily receiving civilities; but a letter of introduction to an Englishman is generally little more in effect than an order to this purpose: "Sir, — Please to give the bearer a dinner and charge the same to yours, &c." But among the numerous letters which I have delivered here, I shall secure, no doubt, some friends whose attentions and civilities will be both interesting and useful. I

already find this in an eminent degree in Mr. Williams, a
most excellent man, formerly our consul here. I begin to
look out for letters from America, and you must not be
negligent in writing. Tell me everything; how do the
sweet babies? kiss them for me, and tell them there are no
such lovely ones in England. . . . . .

TO PROFESSOR J. DAY.

LONDON, *July* 9, 1805.

. . . . . THE death of Mr. Heart is a striking instance
of the vanity of human hopes. God grant that the destroying angel may not be suffered to enter the houses of
any of my friends! Present me affectionately to our good
friends, Mr. and Mrs. Davis. I am glad to hear even of a
little amelioration in his health, and hope that his journey
has proved useful to him, — never forget him in your letters. That the State and College still keep on in the good
old way gives me great pleasure, as you say the March
Devil has kept far to *leeward.* I hope he will be joined
with the political devils, and that all will drift away, I care
not whither.

As to myself you will learn how I am spending my time
from my letter to Dr. Dwight. In my domestic situation I
am very fortunate; my good landlady treats me with the
kindness of a mother; but there are hours which neither
study, business, nor amusement can occupy, and then I
very much want a friend *intra mœnia et parietes.* This is
the only serious drawback on my enjoyment. I have seen
a considerable number of the distinguished literati, politi-
cians, and philosophers of this country. I have heard Pitt,
Fox, Sheridan, and Windham in the House of Commons.
I have conversed with Sir Joseph Banks, Sir Charles Blagden, Dr. Tooke, Major Rennel, Mr. Watt, &c.; have been
in company with Cavendish, Wollaston, Lord Macartney,
&c.; have attended a meeting of the Royal Society, and
seen their Majesties and the Royal family. My own coun-

try has risen in my estimation by a comparison with this. We are in the rear, but not so far as I had imagined before I came to England. I have it in contemplation to go to the Continent for a few weeks in the coming autumn, but I cannot speak decisively. I want a good companion who speaks French well. Those whom I remember with affection in New Haven are so numerous that I cannot mention them all; I therefore give you a general commission to remember me as you know I wish to be remembered. Pray write often, and remember that you are surrounded by friends and the dearest relations of domestic life, but that I am a stranger in a strange land, and therefore need the consolations of friendship. I am, my dear friend, very affectionately yours. . . . . .

TO MR. AND MRS. G. S. SILLIMAN.

LONDON, *July* 14, 1805.

. . . . . DEAR HEPSA, — Give me credit a little, if you please. I have not lost my heart since I arrived in England. The worst thing I have done in this way is to fall in love with a portrait of a young lady in a gallery of pictures in London. I have been several times to see this lovely picture, and have ranted about it terribly in my journal, but that's all; the lady I believe is dead, — so no harm done.

How are you both? Do you ever talk about your brother? Have the sweet babes forgotten me? how do they do? kiss them both a hundred times. As I said before, there are no babes in England like them. Has our venerable mother visited you this summer? . . . . . Now that I am so far away, I realize, more than I ever did, her almost saint-like excellence. There are very few such mothers (or such women) as, dear Hepsa, your mother was and mine is. I doubt not that the one *will go* to heaven, and the other *is there*. There is no news, my dear friends; only invasion is still talked of, and the English are expecting every day to hear that Lord Nelson has destroyed the French and Spanish fleets. . . . . .

TO TUTOR J. L. KINGSLEY.

LONDON, *July* 26, 1805.
16 Margaret Street, Cavendish Square.

. . . . . You judge correctly that a multitude of interesting objects now crowd upon me on every side. It is so indeed. I am very industrious in exploring the metropolis, but it is such a world of men and things that the most a stranger can expect to do is to make a judicious selection from a whole wilderness of curiosities. I have already seen much, and am now so familiar with London that I go everywhere by night or by day, and generally without embarrassment. You may rely upon it, I shall take great pleasure in satisfying the curiosity which you express, as far as it is in my power. My only fear is that my information will not be equal to your expectations. I have it in contemplation to go on to the Continent early in the month of September. I want a good companion who speaks French well, and this I have some prospect of obtaining. I shall probably return to England by the beginning of November, and then fix down for the winter, either in London or Edinburgh. I still speak with uncertainty.

I do not think it worth while to fill my letters with my views of England; they are recorded every day in my journal, and if I am so happy as to return in safety, *I will talk you to death if you wish it*. I could say very little in the compass of a letter if I were to attempt a description of anything. I will just say, however, that I went the other day to see the garret where Goldsmith in his days of poetry and poverty used to live. It is small and low, and lighted through the roof with one window, set with the old-fashioned diamond glass in lead frames.

Remember me particularly to our friend Mr. Stuart, and tell him for me, that should he be settled according to the prospects held out in the letters which I have received, I should think it a very fortunate circumstance to have him added to our circle of friends in New Haven.

There is no news. The invasion is still talked of, but it does not come, although immense preparations are said to be going forward. We wait impatiently to hear the event of Lord Nelson's interview with the French and Spanish fleets. With sentiments of great esteem, and the best wishes for your happiness, I remain, truly your

Affectionate friend, &c.

TO PROFESSOR J. DAY.

LONDON, August 22, 1805.

. . . . . AND now, my dear friend, having given a *complete*, I fear a *tedious*, statement of our concerns, I must say a word to you in your character of a friend. I have literally been *longing* for letters these many weeks. Had I been in love and been expecting letters from my *charmer* so long without obtaining any, I should long ago have gone mad and jumped over London Bridge into the Thames. But as it is not the fashion to kill one's self for *friendship*, I have thought it best since I am not in love, to take the matter more coolly and wait a few weeks longer. . . . . .

Your Commencement approaches. I shall think of you on that day; write me anything interesting concerning it. I hope you will grant a degree of *Master of Arts* to Bonaparte, for he certainly has discovered himself to be a master of arts in the management of his fleets this summer.

There is no news of much importance. Before this arrives you will have heard of the action between the combined fleets and Admiral Calder. The English are much chagrined at the result.

The alarm of invasion has been very active here for two or three weeks, and the whole country has been on tiptoe looking towards France; but I think the sensation is subsiding, although the danger and probability of invasion are certainly as great as they ever were.

Farewell, my dear friend; I wish you health and happiness, and remain, with every sentiment of esteem and emotion of friendship, truly yours.

TO MR. CHARLES DENISON.

BRISTOL, *September* 1, 1805.

..... WE received every attention from Miss Herschel, so celebrated for the discovery of some of the satellites of the new planet; she obligingly explained to us the arrangement of the machinery, and left little for us to wish but the sight of the Doctor himself. This telescope is indeed a wonder. His Majesty has walked through it, stooping however, I presume; but *Bony*, I am confident, might go through it erect, with hat and feather standing. I will thank you to tell Mr. Kingsley that the beautiful young lady whom his ardent imagination had painted as star-gazing through her father's magnificent tube, and discovering moons with eyes which might well have slain lovers, *is an ancient maiden lady, hard on threescore, and the sister, not the daughter, of the great astronomer.*

FROM PROFESSOR DAY.

NEW HAVEN, *September* 30, 1805.

..... OUR good friend, Mr. Davis, has declined accepting his appointment at College. His health appears to be slowly mending. He will probably spend the winter in New Haven, boarding and instructing young gentlemen and ladies. He has not yet fixed upon any business for life. It may be merchandise, but more probably instruction. Dr. Dwight is elected Professor of Divinity with a compensation of five hundred dollars for himself and an amanuensis. I know it will do you good to hear that Mr. Kingsley is elected Professor of Languages and Ecclesiastical History. You will ask what are to be his duties; and how is he to be supported? There is no vote concerning either. But I understand something like this, — that he is to have charge of one division of the Junior Class; that he is to instruct in Hebrew, and be Librarian. Whether he or the senior tutor is to matriculate is yet a controverted point. His salary I suppose is to be made up much in the same way: one hundred pounds instead of a tutor's salary; thirty-six for Hebrew instruction; something for keeping the library; and fifty pounds taken from the salary of Professor of Divinity, will make up the two hundred pounds; which, it would seem, is to be the whole Professor's compensation. I was surprised to hear Dr. Dana say the other day, that he should strongly oppose the idea of giving houses to professors. It seems, then, we have calculated too much upon the premium matrimonial. We must learn a little of Mr. Jefferson's republican economy, to support families upon six hundred and seventy dollars a year. Mr. Kingsley, when he left town, requested me to inform you that he regretted extremely that he was unable to write to you; that he had several times taken his pen, but was obliged to drop it. He was so unwell during commencement week as to be unable to attend to any business. We hear he is better since he has been in the country. He left the following list of books, which he has obtained the President's approbation to have forwarded for the library, and which you will add to your catalogue: — Bingham's "Ecclesiastical Antiquities," Jortin's "Remarks on Ecclesiastical History," with the continuations, Father Paul on "Ecclesiastical Benefices," Bowers' "History of the Popes," — the first two volumes are now in the library; the other volumes are much wanted. . . . . . I wrote in my last for a few mathematical books. The principal were Hutton's "Mathematical Recreations," and the works of *Donna Maria Gatona Agnesi*, female professor at Bologna, translated by Colson. This is for *de curiosity of de ting.* As for myself, I am as happy as I ever expect to be in this world. My health, I think, has not been so good these four years as it is now. I am the same steady, silent, slow-moulded jogger that I always was; and as affectionately yours as ever.

J. DAY.

NEW HAVEN, *November* 16, 1805.

. . . . . WE have been in much commotion in our society through the past summer and until now, with Doctor Dana. The ground of the difficulty has been an irreconcilable hostility in the Doctor to the settlement of Mr. Stuart in the society, and a very general attachment of the members of the society to him. The present week, a compromise has been effected between the society and the Doctor, by which the Doctor unites with the society in asking a dissolution of the pastoral relation between them. I expect an Ecclesiastical Council will meet to dismiss the Doctor about the first Tuesday in December, and that an invitation of Mr. Stuart to settle will immediately succeed it. There is some talk here of war between this country and Spain. In Pennsylvania, McKean's party, with the help of the Federalists, have prevailed over Duane and his party, the Snyderites, by a majority of about five thousand votes for McKean. The State of Delaware holds to its Federalism. New Jersey has been considerably agitated by the revolutionists; but the Quids and Federalists have a large majority. The legislature of this State had more Federalists in it than it has had for several years. . . . . .

EDINBURGH, *December* 28, 1805.

MY DEAR FRIEND, — . . . . . Brother Davis* will not doubt that I am deeply grieved at the part which he has found it necessary to act with respect to his office. We must submit to God's will, believing that all is 'for the best. I hope, however, that our brother (for so we must still call him) will be able to find a proper avocation in New Haven, so that we may still enjoy his society and conversation. My love to him and Mrs. D. Dr. Dwight, it seems,

* Afterwards President Davis.—F.

is *rising;* he may live to be a tutor yet if he goes on at this rate.* I need not tell you how well I am pleased that since we are thwarted with respect to Mr. Davis, we may still sit under his [Dr. Dwight's] preaching. To the *new-born* Professor of Languages and Ecclesiastical History,† you will, in the first place, in an *official* capacity, make my *most profound salutations,* and then assure him it is with real pleasure I learn that there is a probability of his being permanently connected with us, for the books which he sends for seem to indicate that he will accept.

I am not at all pleased with the remarks which you quote from ——. I cannot believe, however, that a majority of the corporation are of the same opinion. I should certainly consider it as severe and unjust treatment. So far from being diminished, the compensation of the professors must be increased, or they cannot live with families, and will be compelled to resort to some other employment. I thank you for various articles of intelligence, which I cannot now particularly notice. The death of my venerable friend, Mr. Eliot, gives me pain. He has, however, left a most worthy son to bear up his name and usefulness. . . . . .

TO MR. CHARLES DENISON.

EDINBURGH, *January* 6, 1806.

. . . . . On the 22d of November I crossed the Tweed, and at midnight arrived in Edinburgh. I live most agreeably. Mr. Codman, a student in divinity, and Mr. Gorham, a student in medicine, (the only Yankees here besides myself,) both from Boston, men of correct habits, congenial sentiments, and the most amiable manners, are my companions ; for we three occupy a house and have our meals at a common table ; our landlady provides whatever

---

* An allusion to President Dwight's acceptance of the Professorship of Divinity, which Mr. Davis was obliged to decline. — F.

† Professor Kingsley. — F.

we order, and we have separate apartments. This mode of living unites retirement, independence, comfort, and economy; in short, it is just what Mr. Day, you and I should have realized, if he had not deserted.* I am in the midst of professors, lecturers, apparatus, and books, and wholly devoted to my studies. . . . . . I am much satisfied with my advantages here. I can tell you no news except what you will learn from the papers. Peace and security reign in this island, while human blood is flowing in carnage almost unexampled on the Continent. I pray God to preserve you, my dear Charles. . . . . .

TO PROFESSOR J. L. KINGSLEY.

EDINBURGH, *January* 29, 1806.

YOUR favors of November 18 and 19 are before me; they arrived on the 10th inst., accompanied by others from Mr. Twining, Dr. Dwight, Mr. Whittelsey, Mr. Day, &c. These letters afforded me a degree of pleasure of which *you*, in the midst of your country and friends, can have no adequate conception. There was a period of five or six months in the past summer and autumn, when I was almost without a letter. I had fretted myself *quiet*, and began to find some consolation in despair; when a flood of letters burst in upon me, and has continued since to flow in a regular stream, so that for a month past I have bathed in epistolary pleasures. I answered Mr. Twining's letter three days ago. I wrote to Mr. Day and Mr. Denison on the 6th inst., before their last letters arrived, and shall delay writing to them again till the next ship, especially as I cannot give Mr. Day satisfactory information concerning his apparatus, as my returns from London are behindhand. You will remember me to these gentlemen, to the academic board, and to all my friends, with every expression of remembrance. And now as to your letters,—there is no doubt that they are genuine; never did compositions

* A reference to his marriage.—F.

contain stronger internal evidence ; there are *Kingsleyisms* in every sentence, and this is only saying that they are replete with what makes letters interesting to one in a foreign country.   I would gladly notice every particular that gives me pleasure, but I must set bounds to my garrulity, or I shall swell your postage unreasonably.   I hope your health and that of our little Mantua is by this time restored ; it gives me concern that either should have been impaired. If Mr. Davis is still with you give my love to him and his lady.   I wish he would settle in New Haven that we may have him near us.   The prosperity of our College, the general health of our friends, the increasing number of hymeneal devotees, the happiness of those who have so recently surrendered their liberties, — all afford me pleasure.   With these general acknowledgments I must pass to a few articles of business.   The books which you and Mr. Day and Dr. Dwight have written for are all ordered. I trust you have by this time received Reiske's "Greek Orators," with a great many other classical books which I bought in Rotterdam ; they were shipped in the *Diana*, Captain French, from Amsterdam.   The other classical works will be sent from London.   I sent you poorer editions of the French and Italian classics than I could wish to have done, because, as they were not ordered by the Committee, and as there is a prepossession especially against French writings, I did not feel myself authorized to expend much money upon them.   A copy of Aristotle's works went with the rest.   As to the books which remain, we are waiting only to receive answers to the queries which we sent out to the Committee, when the business can be closed in a few days. . . . . .

. Since I am disappointed in not having "The Gazette," * I beg that you will preserve it till my return, for it will afford a " sentimental history " of your circle.   Now, then,

* The humorous production of the young college officers, for private circulation. — F.

for a few words about myself, and then I will fill the rest
of my letter with anything which may amuse you. I left
London about the middle of November, and went first to
Cambridge. I had letters to the gentlemen of the University, and was constantly 'among them, — dining, supping,
walking, &c., for two days. I was a kind of phenomenon, — *an American Professor* is a kind of personage not
often on this side the water, and of course I was not a
little stared at. How little my external man came up to
the gravity and *vastitude* of those associations which the
European world connect with a *Professor*, (not to mention
more important matters,) I leave you to judge. I cannot
now say much of Cambridge, for want of space and time;
but I will fully satisfy you if we live to meet again. I was
however gratified and instructed, and on the whole, I was
treated with great kindness. The University gentlemen
of England are rather more convivial than we are in our
American colleges. They push the bottle briskly, and I
was urged to take a rubber at whist with a party composed
of Masters and Professors. At York I saw Lindley Murray, and was greatly gratified with the interview. He was
pleased at hearing that his grammar is a text-book with
us. I am finely situated for study in Edinburgh. The
medical professors are able men, and Dr. Hope gives us
chemistry in high style. I have heard Dugald Stewart
lecture. He is the first man in the University, and is
really a fine example of a highly enriched and polished
mind, with manly and impressive eloquence. I sup with
him on Friday evening. At last I have realized our old
project of keeping bachelor's hall. Dr. Gorham and Mr.
Codman, two fine young men, from Boston, with myself,
occupy a house, and live in all the comfort, independence,
economy, and quiet which can be imagined. Our landlady does everything that we say; we have everything in
good order, and I never lived more comfortably. Query —
If I should live to return, and you should remain unmar-

ried, what then ? Now for the "tender and pathetic.", I have been through Holyrood House, and have seen Queen Mary's apartments; they remain precisely as in her time. There are her bed and sofa, wrought by her own hands; her toilet, with all its female ornaments and appendages. I saw the apartment in which she sat at supper when Darnley and the conspirators entered; and there is the stain of Rizzio's blood on the floor. I have seen the apartment in the Castle where James I. of England, and VI. of Scotland was born. His mother retired there for safety after the assassination of Rizzio; it is a little room, not larger than one of your college studies. I have been to see David Hume's mausoleum. It is a large cylindrical stone monument, and records only his name and the time of his birth and death.

I have seen the house where the sweet pastoral bard, Allan Ramsay, used to live. It is a neat little octagonal lodge, well suited to the moderate wishes, and still more moderate means of a poet. I am happy to inform you that Robert Burns's favorite dog is living in good health. I have not seen him, but hope to be introduced to his *dog-ship* among other distinguished personages.

I have been to see the ruins of Roslin Castle, about seven miles from town. Every lover has heard of Roslin Castle, and it is very happy that this celebrated ruin is not near New Haven; for some of your remarkable young Strephons, in the delirium of success or the paroxysms of despair, might be induced to throw themselves down from the giddy height on which it stands. I am much engrossed by my studies, but am occasionally in Scotch society, where I am treated with much cordiality. I know some of the pretty Scotch lassies and am not a little diverted with their "dinna kens" and other Scotch phrases. Conversing the other day with a young lady. on the subject, I lamented my ignorance of the beauties of the Scotch language and begged her to instruct me. She consented, and began by saying, — "Qua canta colin pre my moo." (I only give you the sounds, probably not the orthography.) Now what do you think this means? I puzzled myself to no purpose, till a grave matron, sitting by, gave me the interpretation: "Come my smart laddie and give me a kiss." But as I had not made the discovery myself, I was not entitled to the benefits of it. I begged the young lady to repeat it that I might get the pronunciation more perfectly, but she was too wary for me. I trust you have now enough of the "tender and the pathetic," and remain sincerely your friend. . . . . .

TO MR. CHARLES DENISON.

EDINBURGH, *February* 27, 1806.

. . . . . AND now, Charles, as to your hypothetical and paradoxical statements of, — *it may be and it may not be,* — that *you are* and *you are not* — that *you expect to be* — and that *you do not expect to be.* I know what it all means ; as Falstaff says, I know you, — I know you, Hal! Well; as the old ladies say, *I thought it would come to this.* I conclude, then, my dear fellow, that *your die* is cast, at least by this time. Well, I will not be selfish. It will give me the most heartfelt satisfaction to see you as happy as our friend Jere * is, and you do not deserve to be any happier, deserving as you are. By the by, Charles, I am afraid you will work up this play so fast, that *the catastrophe* will happen before my return. If you *must* put on fetters, like the rest of the world, I should like to stand by and see them riveted, as I did last winter when Jere was married. . . . . .

* Professor Day. — F.

CHAPTER IX.

Visit to his Mother. — Reaction from Excitement and the Benefit of Occupation. — Lectures to the Class of 1806. — Introduction to the Cabinet
of Col. Gibbs at Newport. — Miss Ruth Gibbs. — The Collection of Minerals in Yale College. — Origin of Geology in Yale College. — Geological
Excursions about New Haven. — Dr. Noah Webster. — Lectures in
1806-7. — Intercourse with Col. George Gibbs. — Visit to Boston and
Cambridge. — Kindness of the Gibbs Family. — Purchase of the Perkins
Cabinet. — Visit of Gov. Trumbull to the Cabinet. — Republication of
Henry's Chemistry. — The Weston Meteor. — Correspondence.

My last duty on leaving my country for Europe, in March
1805, was to bid farewell to my mother and the excellent
family in which she had formerly resided; so my first duty
after my return, was to resort again to Wallingford — she
had been married in the spring of 1804 to Dr. John Dickinson; her home was now at Middletown, but our interviews were at Wallingford — to present myself to her, by
God's blessing, safe and sound. At seventy years of age,
her faculties were still in full vigor, and her affections fresh
as in earlier years. This filial duty being discharged, professional claims commanded my attention next. I attended
to the opening of the chemical apparatus and preparations.
This occupation was both a duty and a relief. It was a
duty as an indispensable preliminary to the renewal of my
professional labors, and it was a relief from mental collapse.
I had been between fourteen and fifteen months in a state
of high excitement, and while in Europe I was constantly
engaged in efforts which called into action both my intellectual and physical powers.

After the warm welcome of friends had subsided, and the enthusiasm of travelling had ceased, a mental collapse ensued. I felt a sinking of spirits, and *ennui*, which was foreign from my natural character, began to make its approaches. What remedy should I seek, and what substitute should I find, for the exciting and engrossing scenes in which I had been so long engaged, — for I had then no home, " sweet home," of my own. Occupation was my only resource, and this, happily for me, was demanded immediately in the line of my profession. The boxes of apparatus and preparations had arrived, and it had been requested in my letter that the opening of them might be reserved for myself. Accordingly, without wasting time, I took hammer and chisel in hand, and with some assistance removed the covers and explored the treasures that had been packed in London.

At the period of my arrival from England, June 1, 1806, the summer term was already begun, and but five weeks remained for the then senior class before their final examination. I therefore commenced lecturing without loss of time, and carried the subject of chemistry as far as possible in the short period at my command. In this class, also, there were distinguished men, among whom were Gov. Bissell, Judge Carlton of Louisiana, Nathaniel Chauncey, Isaac M. Ely, Alfred Hennen of New Orleans, Jabez W. Huntington, Henry Strong, Dr. Wm. Tully, *et alii*.

Introduction to the Cabinet of Col. George Gibbs. — This gentleman, as I was informed, had in 1805, brought over from Europe a splendid collection of minerals, augmented from time to time by magnificent additions, only a part of which had as yet been opened. He himself had again gone abroad, and was still absent. My brother, through a common friend, obtained for me an introduction to Miss Ruth Gibbs, a sister of Col. Gibbs, who very kindly permitted me to inspect and examine such minerals belonging to her brother's collection, as were open and accessible.

They were stored chiefly in the chamber of a warehouse in the Main Street [in Newport] contiguous to the family mansion. In this room, Miss Gibbs was so obliging as to meet me several times, and to remain while I examined the minerals. Her intelligence, courtesy, and benignity made these interviews extremely agreeable to me. If I was fearful of intruding upon her time and engagements, she made everything easy to me, and I was even more delighted with the lady than with the minerals, although the latter were very instructive and gratifying, and gave me exalted ideas of what the entire collection probably contained. Important results grew out of these interviews, as I shall have occasion to mention farther on. Miss Ruth Gibbs married her cousin, Wm. E. Channing, afterwards, and for a long life, the admired and honored Rev. Dr. Channing of Boston, whose exalted talents, attainments, and virtues made him well worthy of so noble a woman. He was removed by death a number of years ago, but she remains his honored widow, and has not participated in the decays which commonly attend the evening of life. Dr. Channing gave me strong proofs of esteem and confidence during the years when I knew him in Boston, and Mrs. Channing has recently spoken with interest to a common friend in Boston, (Miss D. L. Dix,) of those early interviews over her brother's minerals.

I had not been negligent of the few minerals which I found in the drawers of the old Museum of Yale College. I have often mentioned that I carried them in a small box to Philadelphia, and that Dr. Adam Seybert kindly named them for me. They were chiefly metallic ores, among which lead and iron were the most remarkable ; there was a splendid specimen of irised oxide of iron, from Elba. My brother had then recently purchased for Yale College a very small collection of minerals brought out from England by Dr. Senter, who afterwards fell in a duel with John Rutledge at Savannah—"*femina teterrima causa.*" Among them there were some beautiful specimens, particularly in the lime family. They were regarded by me us an interesting acquisition. My own collections in the mines of Derbyshire and Cornwall, in England, — not numerous, indeed, but valuable, — with a beautiful suite of Italian polished marbles purchased in Edinburgh, and some local specimens obtained in my rambles among the trap-rocks of the Scottish capital, — all these things, when arranged, labelled, and described in illustration of the mineral portion of the chemical lectures, served to awaken an interest in the subject of mineralogy, and to produce both aspirations and hopes, looking towards a collection which should by-and-by deserve the name of a cabinet. Our own localities in the vicinity of New Haven, containing agates, chalcedonies, phrenite, zeolites, marble, and serpentines, were, in the progress of research, not neglected, and the discovery of them in due time excited zeal and afforded pleasure-

Origin of Geology in Yale College. — It has been already remarked that when I left New Haven, in March, 1805, on my way to England, I was quite in the dark regarding the nature of the rocks that surrounded me at home, and I have already stated how light broke in upon me in Edinburgh. It was, therefore, natural that I should, early after my return, attempt to ascertain whether the geological analogies, which I thought I had discovered between New Haven and Edinburgh, were well founded. Accordingly, as soon as academical duties would permit, I commenced the examination of the mineral structure of our plains, hills, and mountains. In these excursions, generally made on horseback, because an extensive area and circuit of country were to be examined, I was attended by several friends who felt an interest in the subject, and who, both from personal and scientific feeling, sympathized with the youthful explorer. I mention with pleasure, that the distinguished philologist, Dr. Noah Webster, then in the me-

ridian of life, was among the most zealous of my companions, and with activity and perseverance he dismounted
with me to examine every feature of the country which was
not intelligible when viewed from the saddle. His large
mind admitted every species of knowledge, and the fruits
of his untiring industry in the prosecution of truth are
garnered in his admirable Dictionary.

I arrived in New Haven from Scotland on the first of
June, 1806, and on the first day of September I read to
the Connecticut Academy of Arts and Sciences a report
on the mineral structure of the environs of New Haven,
which was printed in the first volume of the transactions
of the Academy. This report occupies fourteen pages,
and having been published more than fifty-two years ago, —
when I was twenty-seven years of age, — I have been gratified to find that an attentive re-perusal yesterday, (January
6, 1859,) — after I know not how many years of oblivion, —
suggested very few alterations, and I have not discovered
any important errors. As regards the trap-rocks, and their
relation to the associated sandstone and conglomerate rocks,
the analogy is fully sustained between Edinburgh and New
Haven. The coal formation, and the fossiliferous lime-
stones and fossil trees of Edinburgh, are not found here ;
but the relation of the trap and sandstone formations to
the primary slates, now called metamorphic, is here immediate and accessible, and thus affords the geological student
an interesting field of observation and instruction. On the
whole, I do not see any reason to be ashamed of my youthful effort in geology, nor do I think that half a century has
materially improved my style of writing. In a literary
point of view, I could not do the work any better now than
I did it then.

In the autumn of 1806, I found myself, four years after
my appointment, in a condition to attempt a full course.
Through that winter and spring, and through half of the

summer, I labored with zeal and untiring industry to impart instruction in chemistry, including also mineralogy and geology, as far as I had means of illustrating them. I gave three and four lectures in a week, and the mineralogy and geology were interspersed among the chemical lectures, wherever there were mutual relations.

This course of lectures in 1806–7 was more satisfactory to myself than either of the more imperfect courses which I had given. Among the members of this class were some men of note: Thaddeus Betts, Lieutenant - Governor of Connecticut and Senator in Congress; J. P. Cushman, member of Congress; William Dubose, Lieutenant-Governor of South Carolina; Thomas Smith Grimke, of Charleston, an eminent jurist and scholar; William Jay, judge, and son of the distinguished John Jay; Dr. Alexander H. Stevens, of New York, an eminent surgeon; James Sutherland, judge, &c. in the State of New York; Dr. Nathaniel W. Taylor, an eminent divine and theological professor; Jonathan George Washington Trumbull, an amiable and excellent man, but never in public life.

Colonel George Gibbs having returned from Europe, I was introduced to him in Newport, where, after the lectures were finished, I passed many weeks in the summer and autumn of 1807. He was a courteous gentleman, and a zealous promoter of physical science, especially of mineralogy and geology. Having been made acquainted with my pursuits he warmly espoused my cause, and made me at home in his house and in the family of his mother and sisters. He was a bachelor, but he maintained a distinct establishment in a mansion on the hill opposite to the old stone tower, (doubtless once the foundation of a wind-mill, although some assigned to it a fabulous origin and antiquity). In this house, Colonel Gibbs — Colonel Gibbs, although he cherished a martial spirit, had never seen service; the title of Colonel is given by courtesy to an aid of the commander, who in this case was Governor Fenner of Rhode Island —

had established himself with a portion of his library, and more of his cabinet of minerals than I had before seen was here opened, while numerous boxes, filled with minerals, remained in the warehouses, unopened. What I now saw, and had before seen, excited in my mind a strong interest to see and examine the whole. My daily visits to the Gibbs house, which was always accessible to me, made me familiar with its contents, and placed me on terms of easy intercourse with its liberal-minded proprietor. An intelligent colored servant, Scipio, was always ready to admit me.

I had now acquired a scientific friend and a professional instructor and guide, much to my satisfaction, and he appeared equally pleased to find a companion in his scientific sympathies and pursuits, especially in a young man full of zeal, and both willing and desirous to work. There were in Newport no other men that were devotees of science, and therefore we, as regards these pursuits, became intimately associated, and were not long in planning excursions on this picturesque and beautiful island, whose physical features of course depend upon its geological structure.

Soon after our return from an excursion to Cumberland we visited Boston, and returned to Newport October 3, 1807. This visit introduced me to some persons having a taste for science. Among them was the Hon. John Davis, Judge of the District Court under the General Government. Judge Davis showed me much kindness; I enjoyed his friendship to the end of his long life; and his brother, Mr. Isaac P. Davis, was also my friend.

There was not at that period — fifty years ago — much of a spirit of science in Boston. Literature was cultivated and flourished. In my visits to Cambridge, I saw their small but beautiful collection of minerals, given them by the French Republic, which was followed by a similar donation from Dr. Letsome of London. But mineralogy seems not then to have taken root at Cambridge; and neither mineralogy or geology entered into the plans of education in any of our seminaries. Salem presented a very interesting and instructive collection in its East India Museum. This remarkable institution was founded by the illustrious Dr. Nathaniel Bowditch.

I made three journeys to Newport in the season of 1807, and there and in the environs, including Boston, passed all the time which was at my command. The summer was a very profitable one for me in a professional view, and, as will appear farther on, drew after it important results.

Among the families to which I was indebted for a kind hospitality, I must not omit to mention, more specially than I have done, the families of Gibbs and Channing. Their social position was elevated, and their means being ample they of course stood first in the rank of society; and although I did not feel particularly flattered on that account, their kindness and favor, shown in hospitable and other useful and agreeable manifestations, formed a pleasant and sustaining indorsement of the adoption of me already made by their son and brother. The mother of Col. Gibbs was a dignified and estimable matron, and the daughters cultivated, refined, and agreeable ladies.

The second full course of lectures in my department was given in 1807–8. I had now tried my powers and my acquirements so far successfully, that I felt very much relieved from anxiety in regard to my ultimate success. A warm interest had been excited in the College and in the public mind, and it was my earnest wish to increase in every way in my power the means and the value of instruction in my departments.

About this time, the Corporation were persuaded by Mr. Silliman to purchase the cabinet of minerals belonging to Mr. Benjamin D. Perkins of New York. This had been collected during the residence of Mr. Perkins in England, and was of considerable value.

The price paid for it by the College was one thousand dollars. It was transferred to Mr. Silliman's chamber, and was the starting-point for more extensive collections added afterwards.

Soon the news of the arrival of this cabinet was spread abroad, and my chamber was visited by many persons, — ladies and gentlemen. Some were intelligent, and appreciated the cabinet in relation to science, and all were curious to see beautiful things. On one occasion the late Governor of Connecticut, Jonathan Trumbull, Esq., honored the room with a visit, and I had much pleasure in displaying and explaining the specimens. He was very cautious and reserved as to handling them, and when I presented to him the beautiful silky amianthus, at the same time handling its delicate threads and offering it to his own fingers, he declined, saying that he would obey the general *noli me tangere* rule of cabinets. I assented, adding, however, that the rule was for the many, but as there was only one governor in the State, the precedent could not be followed, and therefore he might handle. The remark was received with his usual courteous smile of acquiescence. I was then twenty-eight years old, and confess I was not a little gratified that the devotion of five years to my profession at home and abroad had been so far successful.

B. D. Perkins, of whom the cabinet was purchased, had become, with a partner, Mr. Collins, a publisher of books; and to that firm I intrusted the republication of "Henry's Chemistry" with my additions. The work was in progress in their hands, and the proofs were arriving for my correction, when the Weston Meteor made its appearance. As soon as the news reached New Haven I broke off every other engagement, and immediately resorted to the scene of this remarkable event. On my return, after an absence of some days, I found an accumulation of proofs from friend Perkins, not without some *reproofs*, as pointed as a Quaker, and a newly converted one, would presume to indite, — the dampened sheets being ready for the press: but the re-proofs were cancelled when the cause of my absence was made known, and the Weston Meteor furnished an inter-esting subject for future annotations. I may as well men-tion in this place, that my edition of " Henry," with notes and other addenda, met with so much favor, that two other editions under my hand followed, and these editions were generally adopted in the schools.

I have introduced a digression in my narrative, as there was a digression of events. In Europe I had become ac-quainted with meteorites and the phenomena that usually attend their fall, and several specimens had come under my notice. I did not dream of being favored by an event of this kind in my own vicinity, and occurring on a scale truly magnificent. The event happened on December 14th, 1807. In the morning of that day, at early dawn, (6½ o'clock,) a grand fire-ball passed over the town of Weston in the county of Fairfield, apparently two thirds as large as the moon. Its motion was mainly from the N. to S., rising rapidly towards the zenith, with a vermicular or serpentine motion. Several loud explosions took place near the zenith, like heavy cannon, with intermediate and subsequent dis-charges like those of musketry. There were three princi-pal explosions, during which the fire-ball travelled about ten miles, and at each of those explosions stones fell to the earth, — some of them very large, — twelve, twenty, and even thirty-six pounds in weight. One mass that was split to pieces upon a rock and ploughed its way into the earth, might have weighed a hundred or two hundred pounds. It made a hole in the ground of five feet long, four and a half broad, and almost deep enough for a grave. It was ascertained that stones fell at six places, and probably at many more, as the report of falling bodies was heard in various directions, several of which were examined, both with and without success. The report of these events did not reach New Haven until two or three days had passed, when my friend and colleague, Professor Kingsley, accompanied me to Weston, which is about twenty-five miles west from New Haven. We visited all the places where stones were reported to have fallen ; we examined most of the witnesses as well as the attendant circumstances, and brought away a considerable number of specimens. We published an account of the facts in the "Connecticut Herald," of New Haven, which was extensively copied into other papers. I afterwards made a chemical examination of the masses, and in the course of the season a revised account, with the chemical analysis, was communicated to the Philosophical Society of Philadelphia, which was published in their transactions, and afterwards republished in the memoirs of the Connecticut Academy of Arts and Sciences. The case was deemed so interesting and important that the published account was read aloud in the Philosophical Society of London, and in the Academy of Sciences of Paris. It was admitted to be one of the most extensive and best attested occurrences of the kind that has happened, and of which a record has been preserved.

The exciting effect produced on his own mind, as well as on the minds of others, by the investigation of the Weston Meteor, may be gathered from the subjoined letter which Mr. Silliman wrote from Philadelphia to his friend, Mr. Kingsley.

TO PROFESSOR KINGSLEY.

PHILADELPHIA, *January* 23, 1808.
Saturday Morning.

DEAR KINGSLEY, — I am by no means ripe for an ultimate account of everything, yet, knowing your keenness for letters, I now begin a few memoranda. We arrived on Wednesday morning, after riding all night through New

Jersey. The night was very cold, and we suffered much, but as Miss W—— was very solicitous to get forward, I would not hang back. Anecdotes of the journey will come better orally, — there were, however, none of any moment, — but I hasten to Philadelphia. I attended Woodhouse's lecture the day after I arrived. He received me politely, but made no allusion to the offensive part of his letter. He showed me his laboratory, which is a very fine one indeed. I dined with him yesterday and met a large party of *savans*. I cannot stay to relate many particulars. (Monday 25.) The meteor is immediately brought forward in every circle where I go. It was so at Woodhouse's. He was very modest, and even ridiculed the lunar theory which he advocated in his letter. There was a Dr. C. present, who, with an air of ridicule and of self-importance, began questioning me, and intimated incredulity on several chemical and astronomical points; but I met him with a decision and severity which I would not often indulge in society, and the Doctor being really as ignorant as he was vain and impertinent, I found no difficulty in laying him on his back. N. B. — Through the remainder of the evening he treated me with fawning civility. Both Mitchell's and Coxe's "Journal" are out, so that our piece cannot appear under two or three months in either of them. Perkins told me in New York that the first piece would undoubtedly be reprinted in the "Medical Repository." I am uncertain what I shall do. They are very solicitous here to obtain the communication for the Philadelphia transactions, which are now on the point of appearing. I would give it to them, if they would at the same time permit us to send it abroad; this, however, would be considered as invading their priority. I shall, nevertheless, make the proposition to the secretary, and if he refuses, as I expect he will, I shall bring it home that we may revise it, copy the printed part, and forward it to London and Paris. Our account has been reprinted in most or all of the papers of this city, and has been the subject of universal conversation. I have had occasion many times to detail and illustrate President Clapp's theory, and it has generally been considered as better than any other; the lunar philosophers are humorously called *lunatics.* I am told that at a public dinner here the meteor was the subject of conversation, and a gentleman present exclaimed, — somewhat impiously perhaps, but very pithily, — " Well, I must believe it because of the testimony, and I do believe it, but before God it is impossible ! " (Ten o'clock at night). — I have dined with Bronson since writing the above and he has thrown new light on our subject, — or, to make my figure more consistent with fact, — he proposes to throw a little money into our purses. I am quite serious in what I am now saying. Bronson says, that if we will immediately revise the whole subject, collect all well-authenticated instances of similar events, arrange and illustrate them, relate our own case with the analysis, and the result of the analytical examination of the rest, state all the theories and refute them, bring forward the Yalensian theory with the ample illustrations of which it is susceptible, and, in short, *make a book*, which shall be worth a dollar, that there can be no doubt that it will give us a handsome remuneration. He says he will bear and risk all the expenses of publication, and will remunerate us in any way that we can agree upon. He even went so far as to say, that he had no doubt it would bring us a sum equal to a *year's salary.* Besides, he urges that this is a favorable time to come before the public and to write ourselves into reputation and into bread ; that we ought not to lose the benefit of the labor which we have already expended, and that if the work is throughout as well executed as what we have already published, he will insure its success. Much more passed, and Elihu Chauncey, who was present, is of the same opinion. Both these men know the whole book-selling concern from beginning to end, and are therefore qualified to judge. I confess myself an entire convert to their opinion. You will remember I mentioned this thing before we parted, although not with a view of profit. Now I think the thing perfectly practicable. You must collect all the historical evidence. I will do everything connected with mineralogy and chemistry, and together, and with the occasional aid of brother Day, we will state and refute the prevalent theories and *magnify our own* and *make it honorable*. I am confident the thing may be done *in high style*. With this view I have determined not to leave our communication with any of them, especially as it contains all my original chemical matter, and this is capable of much amplification and illustration. Dr. Seybert is the only man here who has perused it. He gives it full credit and says that my views of the effects of heat, connected with the experiments, are demonstrative. I have not communicated the piece to ——, nor said anything to him about it. I am convinced, from what he has told me, that his own analysis was altogether loose and not to be depended on, nor am I at all afraid of any publication of his. Seybert advised me not to trust him; said he would play me some trick, — for instance, purloin and publish it as his own; and averred that he did not know how to analyze a stone, and that he had not a single sure test or agent of any kind to do it with.

——'s reputation is *up*, both here and at New York, for unfair dealing and in matters affecting scientific reputation. I leave this place on Wednesday morning for Princeton, and shall be in New York on the succeeding Monday; there let a letter meet and tell me that you have been employed every leisure moment in attending to this business. It will be very important that the work come out soon. We shall not lose reputation, and some money we shall certainly gain. Now don't trifle with it; close in with the proposition; the bones of the business are already together. If you do not undertake it, I shall do it without you. Elihu Chauncey says, — " Publish the journal by all means ; one

edition can be sold good or bad, and if popular, it will
be a permanent source of profit." *   You see, matters look
up. . . . . . Direct to me at 86 William Street, New York,
care of David Ely.   Remember me to all friends.   Show
this letter to nobody but brother Day, and lose no time in
going to work on our new book.   I will return as speedily
as possible ; will repeat the analysis and analyze every
separate part.   You don't know how keen the world this
way are for meteors.   Perkins told me that the publication was received with great favor in New York, and that
no occurrence had, in his recollection, excited such general
interest.   It is late, so good-night.

Yours affectionately,

DIOPETES.

The annexed letter makes mention of his mode of
living and of the labors in which he was engaged.

TO MR. G. S. SILLIMAN.

YALE COLLEGE, *December* 5, 1807.

. . . . . I HAVE a complete equipment of every article
requisite for breakfast and tea, arranged in a large new
closet in one of my studies, and it is now four weeks that I
have taken my breakfast and tea in my own chamber, with
more economy of time, addition of comfort, and independence, than I can describe, and with very little additional
trouble or expense.   My little writing-desk lies open on
a stand on the right of the fire, and on the right of
that is a table for my books in immediate use. - I have
now the accommodations and respectable establishment of
a genteel, literary man, and I have no thoughts at present
of leaving my state of celibacy.   The publication of the
chemical text-book, of my journal, the completion of my
lectures, an admission after some previous study to the
faculty of medicine, now become very necessary by my

* The reference is probably to his manuscript journal of travels. — F.

being about to become permanently one of the Board who will instruct and license the physicians of this State; an increase of salary which is, I trust, no very distant event, and an increase of revenue from the chemical tickets, seem to be necessary preliminaries to a matrimonial settlement. . . . . . Dr. Dwight and all the Faculty of College have at various times taken tea with me, and occasionally other friends. . . . . .

TO MR. G. S. SILLIMAN.

YALE COLLEGE, December 10, 1807.

. . . . . MR. DAGGETT * and family have lately perused my journal with eagerness, if I may judge from the rapidity with which they called for the volumes. I met Mr. D. in the street the other day while he was perusing the work. He stopped me, and, after requesting the remaining volumes, added: "I observe you describe the manner of rapping in London. I wish you would rap *four* or *five times* at my door." This rap, you will remember, is the gentleman visitor's rap. When he had finished the work, he delivered the last volume with a flattering note, thanking me for the pleasure I had afforded him, saying that he had accompanied me with great satisfaction through every part of my journey, and had learned many new and interesting facts. The approbation of such a man is highly encouraging and gratifying. I cannot, however, even commence any great labor for some weeks, till the text-book is finished. The ladies affect to consider me as gone over to irremediable celibacy; but I do not perceive that they are less polite than before. You see I egotize as much as ever. I only wish I could do it by word of mouth. I remember with great satisfaction our many happy hours last summer and fall, and do not entirely despair of their return. . . . . . But, at any rate, let us write frequently; and, for my part, I promise to write as much folly as I would

* Hon. David Daggett. —F.

talk. . . . . . Dear Hepsa, kiss the pretty children for me . . . . . My dear brother and sister, I bear you affectionately on my heart, and long again for your endeared society. . . . . .

His sympathetic feeling when any danger impended over those whom he loved, may be seen in the following letter

TO MR. AND MRS. G. S. SILLIMAN.

YALE COLLEGE, *March* 16, 1808.

MY DEAR FRIENDS, — I sympathize with you in your distress, and have waited with trembling solicitude to hear how it was to fare with the dear little lamb.* I did not answer your first letter because I was in hopes of receiving another immediately. That letter came to-day, and I could hardly muster resolution enough to break the seal, till I saw that it was not a black one. You must pardon me for not having forwarded your first letter to Huntington, because I really did expect better news, and thought that in the worst event I could but send it as preliminary. I shall now commit both letters to David's care (he is in town). I am writing in the midst of company and conversation, and must beg you to pardon my hurried letter. Most frequently do I beseech Almighty God to spare the life of our darling. She is very dear to me, for she is a very lovely child ; but if she is to be removed, may God of his infinite mercy grant that you may be sustained and comforted, and that the affliction may redound to our good. My dear friends, I feel most sensibly for you, and am anxious that every passing hour should bring me news on this most anxious subject. Write a line by *every mail, — yes, by every mail, without omitting one,* — till our dear little lamb is out of danger, for I trust that she will be soon, notwithstanding her distressed state. I mention no other topic, except that

* Mary, afterwards Mrs. Jones. — F.

I go this week to meet our mother at Wallingford.   She is now there, but no better.   Dr. Dana lies dangerously ill, and I am to watch with him to-night.   Commending you both, but especially our lovely little friend, to the care of Him who doeth for us, and will deal justly and mercifully with us, even in His present dispensations, I remain, my dearly beloved brother and sister, .

Most affectionately your sympathizing
                                          Friend and Brother.

CHAPTER X.

AN important event in the life of Mr. Silliman
occurred about three years after his return from
Europe. This was his marriage to Miss Harriet
Trumbull, daughter of the second Governor Trumbull. Jonathan Trumbull, the elder, a graduate of
Harvard College, had distinguished himself by re-
fusing to join a part of his colleagues on the Council in administering to Governor Fitch the oath to
execute the stamp-act, and being chosen Lieutenant-
Governor, he had himself likewise refused to take the
oath to carry out the oppressive measures of Parliament. Chosen Governor in 1769, he was reëlected
for fourteen consecutive terms, — the only Colonial
Governor who retained his office after the beginning
of the Revolutionary war. He stood very high, as
is well known, in the esteem of Washington, who
pronounced him "one of the first of patriots," and
whom he sustained with resolute, unfailing patriotism to the end of the great struggle. A sedate

Puritan, deeply imbued with the spirit of religion, and fearless in the discharge of every duty, he stands among the heroic figures in our national history.*

His son, the second Governor, and the father of Mrs. Silliman, was worthy of such a parent. After filling various important offices, which will be mentioned hereafter, he was made Governor of Connecticut in 1798, and held this station until his death in 1809.

In one respect, Mr. Silliman's marriage had more than the ordinary influence resulting from such a connection. The Revolutionary character and services of the family to which he was now allied strongly moved his feelings, and contributed to establish him in the political ideas, as well as patriotic sentiments, in which he had been educated. He has recorded, in a separate manuscript volume, notices of Governor Trumbull and his family; and a portion of these, independently of their bearing on his own personal history, will be interesting to all who would know New England as it was in the past.†

JONATHAN TRUMBULL was the second of that name who held the office of Governor of Connecticut. In stature he could not have exceeded five feet and eight inches. In form he was slender, erect, well proportioned; in movement alert, but with an air of energy and decision. The impression which he made on an observer who was a stranger to him, would lead him to conclude that he was

---

* A life of the first Governor Trumbull has been written by Isaac Stuart.

† Important letters of General Washington, and a letter of Martha Washington, addressed to Governor Trumbull, the father of Mrs. Silliman, are printed in the Appendix to this Memoir.

no common man. Dignity without formality, hung about him like an every-day robe, worn easily and naturally as his common costume. His manners were those of a well-bred, polished gentleman, combining in a high degree dignity with a finished courtesy and affability. His benevolence shed a charm over his intercourse; it animated his features, prompted and enlivened his conversation, and shone like a living soul in his interviews with society. The most humble people were so kindly received by him; and, without descending to undue familiarity, so well did he adapt his conversation to their intelligence and circumstances that they left him with friendly and grateful feelings. His versatility of manners fitted him equally for the society of the most elevated and refined individuals, and for that of the small farmers and mechanics around his rural abode, who, not unfrequently, called to pass an evening hour at his house. Still, this was the same man who had been the associate and confidential friend of Washington, his private secretary, and the intimate of his marquee.

His conversation was very attractive; it was full of intelligence, uniting perspicuity and vivacity, with occasional sallies of humor. The existing portraits of him (the best is at Ex-Governor Trumbull's, at Hartford,) convey no adequate idea of the animation and expression of his face, in which both the mind and the heart shone forth, although correct in the form of the features and head.

His voice was very remarkable. It was strong, clear, and melodious, with a fine musical cadence and intonation. His reading of the Scriptures in the family worship was very impressive, being distinct, deliberate, and solemn. Not a word was lost, and the hearer felt that he received a more forcible impression of the meaning than ever before. With his diction, the Prophet Isaiah appeared doubly majestic. His manners in his family were delightful. His cheerfulness, his cordiality, his hopeful temperament, his ample store of materials for conversation, and his unwavering kindness shed a charm over the domestic circle and made his house a happy home. It was a beautiful rural residence. The house was not an architectural structure according to the rules of art. It had indeed a colonnade with square pillars, in imitation of Mount Vernon. There were noble trees, and ample fields and out-houses, and an office detached from the mansion. A wide court-yard separated the house from the office. A long gate, or pair of gates, for the admission of carriages, seemed to swing, almost voluntarily, on the hinges, and arriving friends drove in, with full confidence of a kind and hospitable reception.

Many friends were there received. The hospitality of the house was well known, and besides relations and family friends and associates, few strangers of distinction passed through Lebanon without calling to pay their respects to him who had been Paymaster of the Northern Army, Private Secretary of Washington, Speaker of the second Congress under the Constitution at Philadelphia, when Washington was President; Senator of the same august body, and finally Governor of his native State of Connecticut, in which office he remained until death. The interior of the house was a model of chastened elegance. It made, indeed, no pretensions to splendor; but everything was in the highest degree neat and comfortable, and in the best taste. Mrs. Trumbull * had admirable administrative talents. She united great energy with excellent judgment, and the power of influencing and moving her servants and all who owed her deference. Her daughters † were lovely and accomplished women, and being trained also in habits of useful industry, they both aided their mother efficiently, and were the bright and polished ornaments of a family circle, than which none was more attractive.

* Eunice Backus, of Norwich.
† Mrs. Daniel Wadsworth, Mrs. Henry Hudson, Mrs. Benj. Silliman.

The house at Lebanon had ample literary resources. A large library in the office, and a smaller select collection in the house afforded abundant means of entertainment and instruction, especially in the long winter evenings, and in the many days of the same season when cold and snow gave almost undisturbed quiet in a country village of sparse population, and whose principal street was in fact a wide common across which it was not always easy to pass. It used to be said, sportively, that the people on the opposite sides of the street had so little intercourse that they spoke different languages.

The physical comforts of the family were also abundant. The apartments had a cheerful, hospitable air; the table was spread with the best food, prepared with skill and taste; the table furniture was in keeping with the dignity of the house, and Mrs. Trumbull, by her provident care and energy, managed to obtain the more rare articles of food, and even the treasures of the seas.

Kindness to the poor and the humble was a bright trait of this family. Not only was charity extended to the needy and suffering, but plain and obscure neighbors were received with a gentle welcome, and made to feel happy in the society of those whose social position was so much superior to their own. Some persons of this description, perhaps coming from a more distant home, were received as visiting friends, and remained for several weeks at a time in the family, but they were always distinguished for personal worth.

With the dignity of elevation there was no family pride. A sense of religious duty, and the mild but prevailing effect of Christian feeling, shed a happy influence over the domestic scenes; and family worship, always attended with seriousness and punctuality, seemed both a fair exponent and a happy result of the living religion of the house.

It was usual to anticipate the arrival of the Governor,

when attending the Legislature at New Haven or at Hartford, by a cavalcade of honor composed of large numbers of citizens, both in carriages and on horseback, who met the Governor some miles from town at some designated place, — I believe Woodbridge's tavern in East Hartford, ten miles from Hartford, and Eastman's tavern in North Haven, eight miles from New Haven. Salutations were interchanged, some refreshments taken, and the procession returning was received with the ringing of bells and other demonstrations of joy. I remember, long before my marriage, coming in from Eastman's, on one occasion, in Governor Trumbull's retinue, when we were wrapt in a cloud of dust so dense that we were all in uniform. I should mention that the Governor usually entered the town on horseback. Governor Trumbull told me the following anecdote of a little occurence near Hartford. The cavalcade had arrived at the ferry in East Hartford, opposite to the city, and there being at that time no bridge, they were waiting for the flat-boat to carry them over, when an old salt — a short, thick-set little man — was pressing his way among the crowd to obtain a sight of the Governor; but not finding, like Zaccheus of old, a friendly tree, he rose on his toes and eagerly asked, "Which is the Governor?" Some one pointed out a small, genteel man mounted conspicuously on a fine horse, when the sailor exclaimed, — "That the Governor, — why, he is not bigger than a cob!" He had associated official dignity with physical volume of person. The Governor was much amused by Jack's surprise, the expression of which he overheard.

While the Legislature was in session he always, when he appeared abroad, wore a three-cornered cocked hat, such as was worn by officers in the Revolutionary army. There was mounted upon it a handsome cockade, made of black satin ribbon, elegantly and tastefully arranged, probably by the hand of a daughter. He wore breeches and long boots with white tops, and he always retained the sword as a badge of office. Although not above middle size in person, and in other respects dressed like a citizen, the costume that I have named on a gentleman of a decidedly military air corresponded well with the dignity of his station as Governor of the State.

The Governor was *ex-officio* President of the Council (or Senate), and being present at all their deliberations his opinions had deservedly great weight. When there was a public hearing, the House of Representatives came in a body to the Senate Chamber. The Governor's speech or address at the opening of the session was delivered in presence of the entire Legislature. I was present on one of those occasions, and I well remember Governor Trumbull's highly dignified and impressive manner. His powerful and musical voice filled the room; his enunciation was perfect, and, being very deliberate, not a word was lost. His sword and cocked hat lay on the table before him, and his graceful and elevated manner gave the best possible effect to his communications. Never before or since have I listened to such a speaker.

I believe I must have seen Governor Trumbull first in some of those public gatherings to which I have alluded. As he was Governor from 1798 to 1809, and was *ex-officio* a member of the College Corporation, he always attended the Commencements and united in the deliberations. He appeared on these occasions in the costume which I have described,— the sword, perhaps, excepted,— and was seated on the stage, in the place of the highest honor. He may have been present when my class took their first degree, in September 1796, but he was then Lieutenant-Governor. When, in 1799, I became a tutor in Yale College, in common with the other members of the faculty I was introduced to the Governor and to the other members of the corporation. Dr. Dwight established the custom of a friendly meeting, at dinner of the faculty and corporation, on the day before the Commencement, and this afforded a pleasant opportunity of recognition. In 1802, having been appointed Professor of Chemistry, &c., I passed the next two winters in pursuing my studies in Philadelphia, and was of course, by my appointment, known to the Governor. I was present at the College Commencements, and he as a member of the corporation knew my position. In the autumn of 1804, it was determined that I should proceed to England in the ensuing spring of 1805. A few weeks before my departure from New Haven, which was March 20th, I addressed a letter to Governor Trumbull at Lebanon, informing him of my projected journey, and requesting from him, as chief magistrate of my native State, an official document certifying my citizenship and my collegiate and social position. To this request he promptly acceded. I have his letters respecting this matter, but I believe that the paper was left in Europe, — perhaps with Mr. Monroe, then our minister in London. When the Governor met the Legislature in New Haven in the October following my return, the College was remembered in his speech, and he did me the honor to mention emphatically the new department of chemistry, and to recommend it and me as its head to the favor of the Government. The terms in which he mentioned me were such as to gratify and encourage a young man of twenty-seven years of age, and the impression on his mind was only that of an increased sense of obligation to perform his duty in the best manner possible. The confidence of this distinguished magistrate thus bestowed on me in advance, was followed by an invitation, warmly expressed, that I would call on him at his house in Lebanon, and I did not forget the invitation. In the summer of 1807, Mr. Daniel Wadsworth of Hartford, the husband of the Governor's eldest daughter Faith, came to New Haven, — prompted by an interest excited in his mind by the perusal of the MS. volumes of my "Travels in England, Holland, and Scotland." On this occasion he made my acquaintance, proffered me his personal friendship, and tendered me the hospitality of his house. Early in the autumn, I was most kindly received there as a guest, and there became acquainted with that most estimable lady, Mrs. Wadsworth. I remained a day or two, and took my departure for Newport, *via* Lebanon and Norwich. Mrs. Wadsworth volunteered a letter by me to her sister, Miss Harriet Trumbull, which was made introductory by my name upon the outside. I availed myself of the short stop which the stage made at the post-office in Lebanon, to run forward half a mile, and thus I gained time to deliver the letter. The family were at dinner, but I was promptly admitted, most kindly received by the Governor, and with courtesy by Miss Trumbull. A chair was placed for me at the table, and I yielded to the hospitable invitation to occupy it even for the few minutes that were at my disposal. The occasion, apparently fortuitous, was fruitful of the most important results, and a series of providential events brought that noble and lovely lady, whom I then saw for the first time, to this house, which she blessed during forty years. . . . . .

The confidence reposed in me by the good man [Governor Trumbull], was truly paternal, and I had full opportunity to scan and understand the character and circumstances which in the preceding pages I have endeavored faithfully to unfold. My visits were, of course, frequent, and Hartford afforded an interesting and convenient middle ground. During several weeks of suffering that preceded his death, I remained constantly in the family, and participated in the final scene. . . . . . I ought not to omit to mention an action of Governor Trumbull's public life, very near the close of his career, which was regarded as very important. The American Democracy had long been seeking an occasion to quarrel with England, and the leaders at Washington were not only preparing the public mind for that result, but were meditating on the means of carrying it into effect. It was therefore deemed of primary importance to

obtain the control of the militia, and especially of that of
New England and New York, with particular reference to
the invasion of Canada. With this view the experiment was
made, first upon Governor Trumbull, whose courtesy of
manners and kindness of temper might have induced them
to believe that he would not oppose the wishes of the administration. General Dearborn was then Secretary of War,
and Mr. Madison, President. In the spring of 1809, I happened to be at Lebanon, when the letter of the Secretary
was received. He appeared to be aware that he was tread-
ing on delicate ground, and therefore his letter was written
in the most deferential terms. The object in view was to
obtain the Governor's approbation to the placing of the
militia under the command of military officers of the United
States, in which case they might be marched out of the
State into Canada or anywhere else. It was requested by
the Secretary that in communicating the order to the militia and in the selection for service the utmost kindness and
even delicacy might be used. The administration had mistaken their man. Governor Trumbull did not hesitate to
refuse compliance ; and in firm but respectful terms, informed the administration that he did not discover either
in the Constitution of the United States, or in the laws of
his own State, any power to surrender the command of the
militia, which were reserved for local defence and to repel
actual invasion. He communicated the correspondence to
me and requested me to criticize his reply with severity,
adding that the step he was taking would make a great
deal of noise and be trumpeted as incipient rebellion. So it
proved, but the decision was warmly welcomed by the opposite party and by the Governor's personal friends. I was
present at an evening's conversation at Dr. Dana's, when
Judge Daggett, alluding to this decision, said that Governor
Trumbull had not a weak nerve in him, and Samuel W.
Dana, Dr. Dana's brilliant son, said that if the hot men of
the South should come, as they threatened, to fight Con-

necticut, their coffins would be a necessary part of their baggage.

How the acquaintance with Miss Trumbull ripened into an intimacy and resulted in their union, is detailed in the " Reminiscences," to which we now revert. It may be remarked that the course of lectures to persons outside of College, of which he speaks, was an event of no little importance in his career as a teacher of science.

First Course of Popular Lectures in Yale College, May 1808. *Personal Events.* — My mother some two years before had fallen on the ice and inflicted a severe injury upon the wrist of her left arm, which had been unskilfully set, so that the arm remained useless, and was even an encumbrance. A journey of business in the month of May 1808, took me to Norwich and through Lebanon, where I received such decisive evidence of the skill of the elder Dr. Sweet in breaking up and setting anew injured members, that after an interview with him I induced my mother to come on with me and place herself under this self-taught surgeon. The effort in which I participated as an assistant was successful. A delicate lady of seventy-two submitted to the severe torture, supported solely by her own firmness, without stimulants or sedatives, and the injured arm, although not rendered perfect, was eventually restored to usefulness and comfort, and served for ten years more until her death. My frequent journeys to Lebanon to attend on my mother's case during several anxious weeks, produced an interesting social intercourse with my mother's early friends, the family of Governor Jonathan Trumbull. Before I left New Haven a course of popular chemistry for ladies and gentlemen had been proposed by Mr. Timothy Dwight, Jr., the eldest son of President Dwight; and the proposal having been sanctioned by him and consented to by me, the class, to the number of about forty-five, had been secured without any effort on my part. The proposition was pleasing to me, as it placed me professionally in a new position, responsible indeed, but promising to secure additional favor for the science then so new in Yale College, and almost new indeed in this country. Having been before accredited in my public character by Governor Trumbull, and invited by him to his house, I learned with pleasure that his daughter, Miss Harriet Trumbull, would soon go to New Haven, and pass some weeks with the ladies of the family of the Hon. James Hillhouse. I thought it not intrusive, therefore, to invite her to attend on the professional course of lectures with the young ladies of the Hillhouse family; and having been before received into the confidence and friendship of Mr. Daniel Wadsworth, of Hartford, Miss Trumbull's brother-in-law, I ventured still further as his friend, to offer myself to show her those civilities which might be useful and agreeable during her stay in New Haven. This statement would hardly be appropriate to scientific reminiscence, were it not that the proposed course had, in New Haven, turned on female hinges, and as I had occasion afterwards to know, sentiment lubricated the joints. It was my province in the proposed course to explain the affinities of matter, and I had not advanced far in my pleasing duties before I discovered that moral affinities, also moving without my intervention, were playing an important part. To this I could not object, and it was certainly the most gratifying result of my labors that several happy unions grew incidentally out of those bright evening meetings. The happy parties enjoyed many genial years, although death has now broken all those harmonious bands asunder. This being my first attempt to explain science to a popular audience I endeavored to study simplicity and perspicuity; simplicity in the absence of all unnecessary technicality, and perspicuity by the choice of good Saxon words and by explaining all that would not be obviously intelligible to a good mind. The lectures, I have said, were given in the evening, and as the course was begun in the spring vacation, ladies were not embarrassed in coming to the college laboratory; and the precedent being once established, was easily continued into the summer term. The lectures were fully illustrated by experiments which were carefully prepared and successfully performed. On the whole, the course itself was a decided success, and I had no reason to regret that I had undertaken it. I have before had occasion to observe that Providence often leads us in ways that we know not, and to results which we are not aware of. This course was the opening of a series of labors performed many years afterwards, with popular audiences, often in large assemblies, and sometimes in distant cities, — as I shall in due time have occasion to relate. It is also with grateful, although pensive recollections, that I mark this course as one of the most important crises of my life, — important to my professional reputation, and fruitful of the most signal blessings extending through many years, and I trust, connecting earth with heaven.

The hint on the preceding page will prevent surprise, and the conclusion will have been already anticipated. I was drawn again to Lebanon, but on a more agreeable errand than in May; and the courtesies of hospitality which I then received were now most agreeably ripened into the confidence of an assured friendship, without other desired limits than that of life itself; and so, by God's blessing, it proved. Visits of reasonable frequency shed a cheering influence over the time as it passed, and I could discern that earlier events, then not understood, had providentially guided me in a way that I then knew not, until I perceived at last whither the path led. My early travels in Europe — the travels addressed to my brother — which were sent out in MS. volumes, and, by some liberty in loaning, came under the eye of Mr. and Mrs. Wadsworth and her sister, two or three years before they were published, had silently pleaded my cause; they made Mr. Wadsworth my friend. The influence was, however, not confined to him; and my mother's severe casualty placed me in the most favorable circumstances for observation and influence. Ten months passed rapidly away, and the sun during all that period shone upon me without a cloud. But the halcyon days were about to be overcast by domestic afflictions, and the happy family at Lebanon were soon to be called to mourn. In the early part of the summer, their loved and venerated head began to experience alarming symptoms, which created solicitude, and produced fruitless efforts for relief by travelling; but the succeeding days and weeks brought only increased anxiety.

After the middle of July, I was at liberty as regards college engagements; my letters had prepared me to expect unfavorable tidings; and accordingly I was summoned, about July 15th, to the bedside of the sufferer. The stages were circuitous and slow, and I therefore took a spirited horse, with a chair-sulky without a top, and crossing the Connecticut, made as straight a course as possible; and, in an all-day tempest of wind and rain, holding an umbrella with one hand and driving with the other, I arrived at Lebanon by daylight, and found the revered patient still living. . . . . . He died August 7, 1809, having attained the age of seventy the preceding April. Thus passed away the wise and good man, the faithful husband and affectionate father and friend, the tried patriot and governor, the confidential secretary, companion, and friend of Washington, who loved him as a father loves a devoted son, and corresponded with him to the end of his life. The people of the State were sincere mourners, and his loss was felt throughout the United States.

My Marriage, September 17, 1809. — This event, so happy for me, — happy, I may say, for both parties, — took place at Lebanon, September 17, 1809, — six weeks, wanting one day, after the death of Governor Trumbull, whose approbation and blessing rested upon us. After a journey to Newport, to visit my brother and family, and calls upon other friends, we returned to the now solitary mansion at Lebanon. After a few days of repose, the bereaved mother, with Christian firmness, resigned the only remaining solace of her home, and we with mixed emotions bade farewell. At Hartford we were cheered by a brief visit with Mr. and Mrs. Wadsworth ; and a Sabbath at Wallingford formed a tranquillizing transition to our own home at New Haven, where our house was in readiness to receive us. October 16, 1809, is to me a memorable day, for we then for the first time crossed the threshold of our own door and found a home, — " a sweet home," — over which, as I have already written, the lady who now honored me by adopting my name presided most happily for forty years, — presided, too, with dignity, wisdom, kindness, and hospitality. She died January 18, 1850, aged sixty-six years, four months, and fourteen days, having been born September 3, 1783. Now, at the time of my writing, January 14, 1859, I am still an inhabitant of the same house, and if I live and remain here until October 16 of this year, I shall have inhabited the same house fifty years.

Mrs. Trumbull maintained her independent establishment in Lebanon until 1814, when she came to this house as a home, visiting at Mr. Wadsworth's, as she had done at both Hartford and New Haven before, — passing months at a time in either place, as she found it convenient.

In a letter to his brother, dated May 9, 1809, he describes the house which was his place of abode for the remainder of his life.

. . . . . I have been so fortunate as to obtain a charming new stone house, completely and genteelly finished from cellar to the very ridge, with an acre of ground: rooms: — parlor, dining-room, bed-room, and five lodging chambers, besides a finished garret, two kitchens, and cellars paved, and little accommodations in abundance. The house was built by Mr. Hillhouse, and stands in that beautiful avenue near his house, — rent, $175. No house except this could be obtained in the town under $200, except half-houses, and they were from $130 to $150. . . . .

A day or two subsequent to his marriage, he wrote to Professor Kingsley as follows: —

LEBANON, September 19, 1809.

DEAR KINGSLEY, — My story is a very short one, and, fortunately, as pleasant as it is short. I arrived here on Saturday at five o'clock, and found my friends well. Mr. and Mrs. Wadsworth had arrived the day before from Hartford.

On Sunday the intention was duly announced. *We* attended meeting all day; but Mr. Ely stole the march upon us by reading the publishment at the commencement of the afternoon session, and before —— and I had arrived. As we were, however, entirely ignorant of the circumstance, we had the *pleasure* of expecting it through the afternoon, and of being disappointed at last by having our friends whisper to us that the thing had been done already. We had, however, the advantage of going into meeting in the afternoon with the utmost composure. On the Sabbath evening, between seven and eight o'clock, the ceremony was performed by Mr. Ely, and in a very impressive and proper manner. Miss Sebor was the only person present not belonging to the family, except Jonathan G. W. Trumbull and Mr. and Mrs. Wm. Williams, who came in in the evening.

To-morrow we set out for Newport, and expect to return here within a fortnight.

Tell Mr. Denison that on Thursday he may expect a wagon from Lebanon with furniture. I shall direct the man to drive at once to the house; but I wish Mr. Denison would walk up and see that everything is safely put away. I attended freemen's meeting here yesterday, and voted for the nomination; thus you see that in the midst of private felicity, I did not forget my duty to the State.

I cannot say more, and I am not disposed to say less than that everything has been as happy as I could wish; and although I am now actually wearing those badges of subjection which some consider as iron chains, and some as silken bands, I am conscious of no diminution of liberty, nor of any irksome weight of obligation.

You will give *proper* publicity to the thing; and, as a name and a fee are now demanded at the " Herald " office for such publication, you will be so good as to furnish both.

Remember me affectionately to Denison and Day; and I have only to add that I hope you will all *go and do likewise.*   Your affectionate friend.

CHAPTER XI.

Publication of his Journal of Travels. — Reception of the Work. — Letter
of Chancellor Kent. — Letter from Mr. Wilberforce. — Accident in the
Laboratory. — Transfer of Colonel Gibbs's Cabinet to New Haven. —
Impression made by the new Cabinet. — War with Great Britain. — The
Medical Institution of Yale College: its Origin and Organization. — Pro-
visions for the Defence of New Haven against the British. — Birth of a
Son. — News of the Conclusion of Peace. — Destructive Gale of 1815. —
Death of President Dwight. — Letters of Judge Desaussure, Professor
Cleaveland, and Judge Daggett. — Letter from Dr. John Murray.

In the year next following his marriage, he gave
to the press his "Journal of Travels in England,
Holland, and Scotland," which passed through three
editions. He had been advised by Dr. Dwight and
other friends to publish this work, but the circumstance which determined him to comply with their
wish was the unsolicited offer of Mr. Daniel Wadsworth to assume the pecuniary risk of the publication. The manuscript journal had been circulated
among his personal friends, and, as narrated above,
had found its way into the family of Mr. Wadsworth,
and won for the author their respect and regard.
Probably no book of European travel, by an American, has been so much read or so generally admired.
A great many persons derived from it their first distinct impressions of England and English society.
Not a few, who still live, preserve a fresh recollection

of the delight with which, in their youthful days, they hung over its pages. It was well received by the critics, at home and abroad; and was favorably noticed in the " Quarterly Review," a journal not disposed to flatter American writers. The Reviewer (in the number for July, 1816) says : — " The American traveller brought with him such feelings as become a man of letters and a member of that commonwealth in which all distinctions of country should be forgotten, or remembered only when principles and paramount interests are at stake. His Journal represents England to the Americans as it is, and exhibits to the English a fair specimen of the real American character." " Mr. Silliman is a good representative of the best American character." " England is to them what Italy and Greece are to the classical scholar, what Rome is to the Catholic, and Jerusalem to the Christian world. Almost every hamlet, says Mr. Silliman, has been the scene of some memorable action, or the birthplace of some distinguished person. It is interesting to observe this feeling, and trace its manifestation in a writer who makes no ostentation of his feelings, and who never disfigures his plain and faithful Journal by any affectation of eloquence or of sentiment." More pleasing to Mr. Silliman than even this praise was a compliment which came to him from a much humbler quarter. Professor Olmsted, on a certain occasion, stopped at a toll-gate and found the toll-keeper, who was also a shoemaker, with Silliman's Travels open before him as he labored on his bench, — the most interesting book, he said, that he had ever read.

This publication served to bring the author into

an acquaintance with the distinguished jurist, Chancellor Kent, from whom he received a complimentary letter.

FROM CHANCELLOR KENT.

ALBANY, *April* 11, 1810.

DEAR SIR, — This is the first letter I have ever written to a stranger with no other motive than to gratify the wishes of my heart. We all owe a debt of gratitude to an author when he has pleased and instructed us. I have just finished your "Journal of Travels," and I feel a propensity too strong to be resisted of making known to you the pleasure I have received from the perusal, and the lively impression of respect and esteem which it has given me for your character. The volumes were read by me with minute attention and unceasing interest. By the aid of excellent maps I followed your steps over every part of the town and the country, and I feel proud that an American, and more so that a professor of the College to which I once belonged and for which I still feel a filial veneration, should have given to the world one of the most instructive and interesting views of England that any single traveller has ever presented.

It would not be proper here to enlarge on this subject. I will only add that your work has one feature not always to be met with in books of that description. It has preserved "virtue in its dignity and taught innocence not to be ashamed." If ever you should be led to visit this part of the country I hope you will give me the pleasure of seeing you, and perhaps my duties would not intervene to prevent me from attending you to any interesting objects or scenery in this State to which your taste or scientific researches might direct you.

I am, with much respect,

Yours, &c.

JAMES KENT.

PROFESSOR SILLIMAN TO CHANCELLOR KENT.

NEW HAVEN, *April* 30, 1810.

DEAR SIR, — I have the pleasure of acknowledging your favor of the 11th inst., and you will do me the justice to believe that uncommon occupation and not insensibility to your kindness has alone prevented me from thanking you before for an honor which was as unexpected as gratifying. Although I have not been so happy as to enjoy your acquaintance I am not ignorant of the character which you have long sustained, nor of the enhanced value attached to a spontaneous commendation flowing from such a source. There is something in the manner of a kindness which is often as important as the substance, and you will allow me to say, sir, that no mark of approbation could have been communicated in a way more delicate and generous, or have been more grateful to my feelings. Although I was supported by the opinions of friends whose judgment I respected, I dismissed the Journal with unfeigned diffidence, and endeavored to prepare myself for the sneers of fastidious criticism, if not for the condemning sentence of the candid and discerning. But when you, sir, assure me that you have found my book "one of the most instructive and interesting views of England that any single traveller has ever presented," and, more than all, that "it has preserved virtue in its dignity, and taught innocence not to be ashamed," I confess I feel my courage so much fortified that I can look forward with composure to treatment of a different character. Should I ever visit Albany again, it will give me great pleasure to avail myself of your kindness, and I shall take as much pleasure in receiving the polite and useful attentions which you offer as I should in returning or advancing them should you visit New Haven, or should circumstances ever allow me the pleasure of meeting you at another place. Whatever may be the general voice respecting the *Journal,* it can never be worthless in my eyes, since it affords me an opportunity of subscribing myself, with sentiments of gratitude and respect,

Your obliged, humble servant,

B. SILLIMAN.

Mr. Silliman received the following letter from the eminent statesman and philanthropist whom he had met in England, and to whom he had sent a copy of the "Journal of Travels."

FROM MR. WILBERFORCE.

(Near) LONDON, *January* 23, 1811.

SIR, — I fear I may appear chargeable with the imputation of making a very unfriendly return for the kindness which obtained for me the obliging marks of your remembrance with which I was favored about three weeks since, 'in delaying for so long a time to make my acknowledgments; but I can truly assure you that my dilatoriness has not arisen from my having been insensible to your obliging conduct towards me; but I have been, and indeed I still am, exceedingly occupied both with public, and, as it happens, with private business, and being thus circumstanced, I have naturally put off sitting down to a letter which I conceived might probably wait in the post-office a week or more before it would depart. But in justice to myself, I must no longer remain silent, though I can now do little more than thank you for the kind recollections which prompted you to send me a proof of your regard. I shall avail myself of some of my first leisure intervals for perusing your book, convinced that the remarks of an intelligent writer (I do not like to call a subject of the United States, stranger or even foreigner, though a member of a different community) who lives in a circle different from our own, may afford both profit and pleasure. I should have been happy to introduce you to Mrs. H. More, whom, besides respecting her as one of the most elegant writers and useful characters of our age, I have the pleasure, and indeed honor, to number among my personal friends. The praise due to her for her writings is scarcely less than that which she has justly earned by her humane and judicious labors, carried on now for many years, in educating and improving the lower orders of a populous country, which she found in a very rude and ignorant state. I cannot lay down my pen, though forced to draw towards a conclusion, without expressing my most earnest hopes, that instead of mutual jealousy and recrimination, much more, instead of an actual rupture between our two countries, they may be long united together by the bonds of reciprocal esteem, confidence, and affection. It cannot be that the well-being of each is inconsistent, rather let me say is not identical, with that of the other. To admit the contrary supposition, would almost deserve the name of blasphemy against the great Creator of us both, and surely we can never so well fulfil His purposes, or provide for our common happiness, as by striving to maintain between us unbroken peace and harmony. This may include in special cases a disposition to forego *on either side* some temporary gain, but again to be far more than compensated by a greater and more durable benefit. I have no time to dilate, explain, or qualify; but trusting these effusions of the heart to your candor, and may I not also hope, to your fellow-feeling,

I remain, sir,

Your faithful servant,

W. WILBERFORCE.

P. S. — I am chiefly occupied (*inter alia*) in considering how best to enforce the act for abolishing the slave-trade, which, I grieve to say, is shamefully evaded. I must add, by none so much as by your countrymen; I should, however, say, by individuals among them, for the government of America has shown an eager disposition to enforce your own laws against that wicked traffic; but the aid of individuals may be more useful in this case, by obtaining intelligence, especially legal evidences of breaches of the act, and assisting prosecutions, &c., &c. I am persuaded I need not apologize for this hint.

Mr. Silliman persevered in zealous attention to his professional pursuits. While engaged in his laboratory, in the preparation of fulminating silver, the materials exploded in the vessel over which he was bending. The accident is described in the Reminiscences.

My own experience in chemistry had hitherto been very successful. I devoted myself laboriously and zealously to the duties of the laboratory, and had now acquired a good degree of confidence in my own experience, — too much indeed, as the sequel will prove. I had still to a degree the characteristics of youth, and was just advancing into mature manhood.

After detailing the process of the experiment, he adds : —

My face and eyes being directly over the dish, they received the full force of a violent explosion, which threw me back upon the wall behind, and produced intense pain both from the concussion and from the corrosive materials, — alcohol, nitric acid, and lunar caustic, — blown forcibly into my eyes. I was stunned, but not deprived of my consciousness, and I fully comprehended my perilous condition. I was entirely alone ; my assistant, Lyman Foot, having gone away on an errand. I made my way, in the horror of deep darkness, — for my eyes were involuntarily shut, — I groped my way to the pneumatic cistern, the only water that I could hope to reach. It was covered with drawers full of minerals, but I managed to throw some of them aside, and thus reached the water with which I washed my face, and especially my eyes abundantly. My first anxiety was to ascertain whether fragments of the porcelain dish had hit and penetrated the balls of the eyes. With intense anxiety I passed my fingers carefully over the blind orbs, and to my inexpressible relief, ascertained that the eyes were there and not lacerated. I then pulled the lids apart, one after the other on both eyes, and to my great and grateful satisfaction, found that the objects in the room could be dimly discerned as if through a thick and yellow haze. I had now done everything for myself that I could possibly do alone, and sat down to await the arrival of my assistant. Happily he came at the critical moment. The carriage of my friend and family physician, Dr. Eli Ives, was at hand, and I was borne to my own house, distressed, even more than by the injury, because I must inflict severe mental suffering upon my devoted and affectionate wife. Her firmness was, however, equal to her kindness, and no heroine of romance or of the battle-field could have behaved better.

It was an hour of dismay when I was carried, a blind and suffering man, to my before happy home, — perhaps, like Milton in that one particular, to behold no more the loved faces of my excellent wife, my sweet daughter of one year and one month,* and of many loving and loved friends. As I passed along from the College, I prayed mentally that I might not thus be consigned to darkness, so early after I had begun my professional career, and in the bright morning of my domestic happiness. I was then nearly through my thirty-second year, and had been but five years fully established in my professorship. But it pleased God to give me in time perfect restoration. My eyes gradually recovered their strength ; and now, forty-seven and a half years after the accident, and when I am almost

* His eldest child, Maria, now Mrs. John B. Church, of New York, was born June 16, 1810. The birth of this child, writes Mr. Silliman, "sent joy to many hearts and grateful thanks to Heaven. With this new theme of gratulation came a new motive for exertion and a novel source of happiness, — which, blessed be God, still remains." — F.

half way through my eightieth year, I am writing without
glasses, my eye is not dim by reason of age, nor is my natural force abated; and I bless my great Preserver that I
am so exempt from infirmities incident to the evening of
life, that I am passing comfortably and hopefully through
my evening twilight, and looking forward to the glorious
morning light, which will break forth beyond the dark
valley.   •

About the time of this accident, Mr. Silliman received a noble accession to the means of illustrating
one of his favorite sciences.

In the winter of 1809–10, Colonel Gibbs, on a journey,
called on me in the evening, and, as usual when we met,
the conversation turned on the cabinet, and I inquired:
" Have you yet determined where you will open your collection ? "   To my great surprise he immediately replied:
" I will open it here in Yale College, if you will fit up
rooms for its reception." I rejoined: "Are you in earnest?"
and he instantly responded: " I am." ·· May I then consult President Dwight and the college authorities on the
subject ? "   " You may, as soon as you please."

I was thus suddenly called upon to think of and propose some feasible plan for the accommodation of this
large cabinet. There was no building on the college
ground fitted for its reception. I lost no time, however, in
laying the subject before President Dwight. His enlarged
mind warmly espoused the design, and, without hesitation,
acceded to the plan which I suggested. . The alleys or entries of the college halls divide them crosswise or trans-
versely; and two rooms, with their bedchambers and
closets, occupy the breadth of the building. I proposed to
knock down all these divisions in the second floor, north
end of South Middle, throw the entire space into one room,
and thus establish a mineral gallery, lighted at both ends
by two windows. The dimensions of the room thus pre-

pared would be forty by eighteen feet. Colonel Gibbs having observed the premises, approved of the plan, and no time was lost in taking steps to carry it into effect. . . . . . While the work was in progress, the Rev. Dr. Ely, one of the most active and efficient members of the College Corporation and of the Prudential Committee, said to me, on inspecting the work : "Why, Domine," (his usual style in college matters,) "Domine, is there not danger that with these physical attractions you will overtop the Latin and the Greek ?" I replied: "Sir, let the literary gentlemen push and sustain their departments. It is my duty to give full effect to the sciences committed to my care." . . . . . Nothing had been before seen in this country which could, as regards mineralogy, be compared with this cabinet. It kindled the enthusiasm of the students, and excited the admiration of intelligent strangers. It was visited by many travellers, and New Haven was then a focus of travel between North and South. Railroads were unknown, and navigation by steam had hardly begun. The comparatively slow-moving coaches conveyed the passengers, who were generally willing to pass a little time in New Haven; and the cabinet of Colonel Gibbs afforded a powerful attraction, while it afforded also a high gratification. The liberal proprietor of the cabinet was himself highly gratified, both by the brilliant appearance of the collection, and by the admiration of the country, and especially by that of such men as the Hon. Josiah Quincy, the Hon. Harrison Gray Otis, Hon. Daniel Webster, Col. David Humphreys, and other eminent individuals who were among the visitors. Trains of ladies graced this hall of science ; and thus mute and animated nature acted in unison, in making the cabinet a delightful resort.

Before his new treasures had been deposited on their shelves, Mr. Silliman had been disturbed in his work by the alarms of war.

June, 1812, is rendered memorable by events associated
in my mind. Mr. Mills Day, a tutor in Yale College, and
brother of Professor (afterwards President) Day, lay dead
at his brother's house on the corner of Orange and Crown
Streets. Mr. and Mrs. Daniel Wadsworth were in my
house on a visit ; and Colonel Gibbs was in town, ready to
proceed with the opening of the cabinet, when, on a Sabbath morning in June, the tidings came of the declaration
of war with England. A thrill of painful excitement — an
electrical stroke — vibrated through the Continent. It
was a thrill of horror to all good minds that were not par-
alyzed by party ; for fraternal blood, after a peace of almost
thirty years, was now to be shed again ; and it did flow in
torrents. This war of less than three years, — indeed, only
two years and eight months, — sent probably 50,000 men
on both sides to premature graves, while nothing was
gained on either side but military and naval renown, —
dearly bought. A spirit of justice and mutual conciliation
would have prevented the conflict. On our side we gained
not one of the points for which we had contended. In the
treaty of peace concluded at Ghent in December, 1814,
the principal alleged causes of the war — the right of
search for the property of an enemy, and the impressment
of American seamen — are not even mentioned. But I
forbear. The painful topic was, however, not without an
important bearing upon the peaceful pursuits of science.
The question of course arose in our minds : Shall we proceed to open more treasures in a maritime town, — treasures which we cannot remove, and which may be destroyed
by the vicissitudes of war? We concluded, however, to
trust in God and proceed with our work.

Colonel Gibbs devoted himself with great zeal to our
pleasant labor, and he was quite satisfied to remain quietly
in New Haven, for he had brought with him a treasure
more valuable than his gems. Miss Laura Wolcott,
daughter of the distinguished statesman and patriot, the

Hon. Oliver Wolcott, now appeared here as Mrs. Gibbs, and cheered our labors by her agreeable society and assistance. The work went on cheerfully, and by mid-summer we had occupied the new cases, and the entire circuit presented a rich and beautiful sight. The fame of this cabinet was now blazoned through the land, and at-tracted increasing numbers of visitors. This collection doubtless exerted its influence upon the public mind in attracting students to the College, and was regarded as a very valuable as well as brilliant acquisition. The collec-tions were all (I am not aware of any general catalogue of the Russian Collection *) furnished with catalogues, scientific and popular; and it could not happen that the opening and examining of ten thousand specimens, with a frequent refer-ence to the descriptive catalogues, could fail to give greater extension and precision to my knowledge of the subject. I had become a zealous student of mineralogy and geology, and now felt that the time had come to present them with more strength and fulness than in former years.

Hitherto the public instructions in mineralogy and geol-ogy — I mean those which were intended for the entire classes — had been given, as I have already stated, in the laboratory in connection with the chemical courses. The lectures to the private class on the Perkins cabinet had been given in my chamber. Being now furnished with ample means of illustration, I separated the lectures on mineralogy and geology from the chemical course. The Perkins cabinet was brought over to the newly prepared rooms, that thus all the resources in the department might be in one place. The requisite fixtures of table and seats were also introduced; and as soon as practicable, I began to lecture in the new rooms, but I believe not fully, until the next year, 1813. Thus the department became fully inaugurated, and I had the pleasure of seeing the progress from the small box of unlabelled minerals, carried to Phil-

* The "Russian Collection" formed a part of Col. Gibbs's cabinet. — F.

adelphia to be named by Dr. Seybert in 1802–3, — the triumphant progress from this humble beginning to the splendid cabinet of twelve thousand specimens by which I was now surrounded ; and many more were contained in closets and in drawers.

The Medical Institution of Yale College. — It is not my purpose to give a history of this department, but I must make some mention of it on account of my own connection with it. Rev. Dr. Nathan Strong of Hartford, then a member of the Corporation of the College, introduced, in 1806, a resolution for establishing a Medical Professor — such is the language of the resolution ; doubtless it was intended as the leading step towards a Medical School, which actually took its origin from that resolution — in the College ; and I had the honor of being named with him as a committee to examine and report, and to devise means for effecting the object. There was a general Medical Society for the State, and there were local societies for the counties, and to the last named belonged the duty of examining and licensing candidates for practice. At first there was jealousy of the College, and it was necessary to conciliate. I omit the mention of many intermediate steps, and come at once to the important measure, — the appointment of a committee of conference and consultation, — an equal number being appointed by the Medical Society and by the Corporation of the College. President Dwight was at the head of the college committee, of which I was a member. Dr. Woodward, the elder, led the medical committee, of which Dr. Eli Ives was a member. The joint committee met in my chamber in the Lyceum. The prejudices with which some of the medical men appeared to have come to the meeting, were removed, and harmonious action ensued. . . . . I pass over the various enactments of the Legislature, of the Corporation of the College, and of the Medical Society, which were necessary to authorize and organize the medical institution and to carry it into effect. In the end everything was harmoniously effected. A new stone building, erected by the Hon. James Hillhouse, was rented to accommodate the lectures, and after some years it was purchased. . . . . . . The medical students attended the lectures in the college laboratory along with academical students, but with separate seats. The laboratory was enlarged for their accommodation. I gave them also distinct instruction on their own subjects, both by lectures and recitation. . . . . . . The institution has been decidedly successful, as regards valuable instruction and the elevation of the medical profession in the State. As regards the number of students, it has been only moderately successful.

When the subject of the organization of the Medical College was under discussion in the Corporation, I was present and heard from the Hon. Chauncey Goodrich the following observations, succeeded by a distinct proposition. "The medical class," he remarked, "having a building devoted to their use, and many of them having their rooms there, they constitute in fact a peculiar family, and they ought to have a family constitution. There must, therefore, be prayers, as in the College proper." The proposition was accepted with little discussion, and without inquiring for my opinion. Not being a member of the Corporation, I could not volunteer in the discussion. I did not, however, believe it to be a wise measure, although proposed by a very wise and good man. A transient collection of students, most of them without previous discipline, afforded but a small prospect of a reverent and attentive audience; but the attempt succeeded better than I expected, and some special religious meetings were held in the Medical College on Sabbath evenings. Commons were also instituted in the Medical College as a family; but the experiment was unfortunate. . . . . . Neither did the inhabiting of the building by the students produce a happy result. They were, in their habits, too familiar, sometimes noisy and rude, and of course the studious individuals were annoyed by their more restless companions. By degrees the entire building, except the wing, was relinquished in favor of the public purposes of the institution, and the attempt at sustaining a family condition was tacitly relinquished.

The decisive and sanguinary battle of 1814 on Lake Champlain between the American commander McDonough, and the British commodore Downie, — fatal to the latter, — followed the not less bloody and equally decisive conflict of 1813, on Lake Erie, between the commanders Perry and Barclay. I should hardly allude to these events, had not the same state of things placed us in peril upon the seaboard, and caused us to hesitate, even in our quiet and peaceful walks of science. British cruisers and squadrons occupied Long Island Sound and Gardiner's Bay. Our local commerce by water was suspended, and heavy land-wagons laden with flour and other objects of traffic, and drawn by teams of four and six horses, constantly traversed the roads between New York and Boston. Some hesitating scruples we had indeed felt while unpacking and arranging our minerals, lest the chances of war should reach and destroy them ; and we were hardly settled in our enjoyment of these treasures, when increased strength was given to our apprehensions by British depredations on Connecticut River, and by the appearance of a British squadron at anchor near Guilford, only sixteen miles from New Haven. Two hours of favoring winds might place them at the mouth of our harbor ; their spars were distinctly visible from our heights, and we could make out a ship of the line, a frigate, and a sloop of war.

The citizens of New Haven had, for some weeks, been alarmed, and the bombardment of Stonington had shown the probability that New Haven might be assailed in the same manner, although the want of depth of water in the harbor might afford protection against large ships, but not against bomb-ketches. Money was contributed by the citizens, and personal labor also was contributed to strengthen the old fort of the Revolution on Prospect Hill, east of the harbor. Officers of the College and their pupils entered zealously into the plans of defence, and quotas of the students, say fifty at a time, led by their officers, worked in relief-parties along with the citizens. Professor Day and myself were among the laborers ; we worked in earnest, as our blistered hands might prove. Engineering skill was also employed ; a substantial bomb-proof was constructed to contain the powder ; the old breastwork in the form of a regular redoubt was raised, and a triangular outwork to protect the gate on the land side. Some heavy cannon were drawn up from Fort Hale, — a low and indefensible water-battery but little above the waves. There were no soldiers, however, to man our main fort, but the citizens and military companies volunteered. On the day when the British squadron were descried near Guilford, the companies paraded. I saw Mr. James A. Hillhouse, the scholar and poet, in the ranks, marching with shouldered musket as a volunteer, emulating the example of his noble father, when this city was invaded by the British forces, July 3, 1779, during the American Revolution. Happily our alarms died away and no hostile aggression was made. On one occasion there was a report that a small British cruiser was in the Sound, and forthwith an artillery company, commanded by Captain Philos Blake, volunteered to go out to attack the enemy. I saw them embark on board a sloop at the end of the long wharf, with their pieces of field artillery mounted as for long service. I saw it with regret, for it was obvious that they stood no chance against ship-guns, and that their only hope would be the forlorn one of boarding. · Happily they did not sail, and Captain Blake remains my neighbor to this day.*

* Captain Blake states that Major Thomas Sherman had the chief command, and that they sailed for some distance out into the harbor before they were led to abandon this imprudent enterprise. — F.

The most interesting domestic event of this year (1814), was the birth of a son. Jonathan·Trumbull Silliman was born August 24, 1814, in the midst of the alarms of war, on the very day on which the city of Washington was destroyed by a British army. The Government was disgraced by permitting this capture; and the British disgraced themselves, not by burning the ships and the munitions of naval warfare at the navy-yard, — for that was within the rules of war, — but by destroying by fire the National Capitol, the Presidential Palace, the National Library, and Public Offices. It was indeed said in palliation, that General Dearborn's army had committed similar atrocities at Little York, on Lake Ontario, now Toronto. If so, they also disgraced themselves. The little stranger, unconscious of these events, brought joy to the hearts of his parents during the almost five years of his short life, and deep sorrow when his beautiful form was laid in a premature grave, June 27, 1819.

But of this severe bereavement I may say somewhat more, when in these annals that day arrives,—dark, indeed, in parental grief, but bright in the full assurance that the lovely boy, who, while with us, won all hearts, became in a better world like an angel of light. The sanguinary and decisive battle of New Orleans had been fought and won on the 8th of January, 1815. Many other victories had been obtained by land and by sea; but still the war was very distressing, and tidings were eagerly desired from our Commissioners, who were in conference with the British Commissioners at Ghent. As we were going to the chapel service in the afternoon of an early Sabbath in February, we met Mr. Wm. M'Crackan, who informed us that an express had just passed through town from Boston, bearing the joyful news of peace. I suppose that the news had not been made known, and it was announced by President Dwight from the pulpit by reading the following very appropriate hymn : —

" Great Ruler of the earth and skies,
    A word of thy almighty breath
Can sink the world or bid it rise :
    Thy smile is life, thy frown is death.

When angry nations rush to arms,
    And rage and noise and tumult reign,
And war resounds its dire alarms,
    And slaughter spreads the hostile plains; —

Thy sovereign eye looks calmly down,
    And marks their course and bounds their power;
Thy word the angry nations own,
    And noise and war are heard no more."

The audience were thrilled with joy. The impressive manner of the President, with a touch of pathos, as he was himself deeply affected, and the following prayer, — grateful, fervent, and eloquent, — produced a powerful effect. The city was illuminated on Monday night, and the people manifested their joy by congratulations and many sportive exhibitions.

The summer of 1815 found the cabinet fully arranged, and the lectures of that department well systematized and established. I gave elementary mineralogy in a course, generally twelve or fifteen lectures. They were given in the spring, and the geology followed. The private course was also continued, parallel with the public course. The lectures on geology were delivered in the summer, and the lectures relating to both mineralogy and geology were given in the cabinet, which had now become the grand repository of all the specimens in these departments.

President Dwight, who, from the first, took a deep interest in the lectures on these subjects, was now more interested than ever, and was generally present, particularly at the lectures on geology.

My early friend, Robert Hare, who, ten or twelve years before, led me in chemistry, was now content to follow me in geology, which he had not studied. Having formed a happy alliance with a superior and lovely lady, Miss Harriet Clark of Providence, he came to pass the summer in New Haven, and was daily with me in the cabinet, and in attendance on the lectures. He became well informed in geology, and made valuable observations, as he travelled, during subsequent years.

In the autumn of 1815 a fever prevailed in New Haven, and I removed Mrs. Silliman and the children to Wallingford. I remained most of the time in town, going out frequently to my family, until the malady had subsided. In September there was a very destructive gale which devastated the coast of New England. It blew from the southeast, and the saline spray was blown far into the interior of the country. There was a saline incrustation upon the front windows of my house, and the fruit-trees that were not protected by the buildings were killed. The twigs and leaves were said to be salted as far inland as Worcester, Mass. The town of Providence presented an appalling scene of devastation. My friend, Mr. Wadsworth, proposed to me to go with him to see it. We travelled in his phaeton, and saw with painful interest the records of the tempest, in ships on shore, high and dry in the streets, or on high sandbanks, and in ruined warehouses and dwellings. Mr. Wadsworth made a pen-and-ink sketch of the scene as it appeared from an upper room in our hotel; and this drawing, bold, graphic, and effective, I have preserved to this day. We returned to his beautiful villa at Monte Video, ten miles from Hartford, where the family were staying.

Mr. Silliman, recording only the events which were most noteworthy, passes to the death of his illustrious friend, Dr. Dwight.

This great and good man was called home, January 11, 1817. His physical frame had been growing more and more infirm for two or three years, but his mental powers remained almost to the last. His disease was ascertained to be of the prostate gland, — which in popular language is usually called a cancer of that organ. His sufferings were very severe, and surgical instruments were necessary for his daily, almost hourly, relief. His instructions were continued until within a few days of his death ; but towards the last, his mind wandered, and he sometimes spoke incoherently, but he always preserved his courtesy. He appeared not to be fully aware of his approaching end. I read aloud to him the 14th, 15th, and 16th chapters of St. John, which appeared to command his earnest attention. When I parted with him the evening before his death, he bade me good-night, and added : " My best respects to the ladies." By invitation of the Corporation, I delivered in the Centre Church a eulogy upon his talents and character ; and to this I refer for my views.

The state of public feeling during the latter part of the war with Great Britain is indicated in the letters which follow. The first is from the Hon. Henry W. Desaussure, the distinguished jurist and scholar of South Carolina. The writer of the second, Professor Parker Cleaveland, of Bowdoin College, was at that time preparing his meritorious work upon mineralogy, a department in which he acquired deserved honor. Judge Daggett, the author of the third letter, was then United States Senator from Connecticut.

FROM JUDGE DESAUSSURE.

COLUMBIA, S. C., July 5, 1814.

DEAR SIR, — I avail myself of the opportunity furnished by my worthy friend Mr. Hooker, who has the pleasure of a personal acquaintance with you, to inquire after your health, and to transmit you catalogues of the officers, graduates,

and students of the College established at this place under
the State authority.   You will perceive that something has
been done since the work commenced, and I doubt not that
the College will succeed, and will be of very great utility to
the country.   You will, I dare say, be struck with the few
deaths marked or starred in the catalogue; and you may
be induced to think that this is not so dying a climate as
you northern gentlemen usually think it is.   The truth is
that the country from about the falls of the river which are
generally at one hundred and twenty miles from the sea,
(by the road.) is a very sickly country.   But from thence
to the mountains it is remarkably healthy.   I am inclined
to think that this part of the two or three southern States
is the healthiest part of the United States, being equally
free from the bilious diseases of the flat, swampy sea-coast,
and the consumptions, rheumatisms, and pleurisies of the
eastern and northern States, and being absolutely clear of
the spotted and other malignant fevers of every species.
. . . . . I am thus particular in my communication to you,
because I am persuaded that you take a deep interest in
the success of all literary institutions.   Indeed, it seems to
me that upon their success depends, not only a large portion of happiness in considerable numbers of the community, but the duration of our free institutions and of the
Union of the Republic.   For no people can remain long in
the enjoyment of so much freedom, so little regulated, without abusing it to its destruction, unless enlightened to a
very high degree.   I have, however, trespassed too long on
your time already.   Allow me only to add my grief at the
present deplorable state of our country.   If the same wise
and overruling Providence which has so recently prostrated
usurpation and tyranny in Europe, and tranquillized the nations, almost against all hope or expectation, does not save
us and give us peace, I fear we are doomed to great suffering, and, what is of infinitely more importance, I fear
your discontents in the East will drive you to the desperate

measure of a dissolution of the Union, which would seal the ruin of our country. I am, dear sir, with very sincere esteem,

Your obedient servant,

HENRY W. DESAUSSURE.

BRUNSWICK, *September* 20, 1814.

MY DEAR SIR, — I have long been wishing to write you, and among other things, to thank you for the politeness, &c., of your last favor. I need not attempt to describe to *you* the state of alarm in which we have lived during a great proportion of the last summer; for I perceive you must have participated in similar troubles. There is now one army of nearly two thousand men within seven miles of my house — another of nearly three thousand at the distance of eighteen miles, — and another, this larger, about twenty-six miles west of us. It has been supposed, that *Brunswick* is in very considerable danger of an attack, as we have two large manufacturing establishments, and two iron furnaces, one of which is constantly bringing forth the *means of annoyance,* — as Mr. Madison calls them, — that is, cannon-balls; and more especially, as we are so easily accessible from the sea. I have not, perhaps, felt so much consternation as many of my neighbors, because I have ever believed that college-ground would be held *sacred.* I have, however, found it difficult to avoid entirely the *contagion of alarms,* and have for some time kept my most valuable papers, &c., in trunks, ready to decamp when I see contiguous buildings in flames. So much, — and all to gratify the cursed democracy of this country. Can brother Day keep *cool,* even when breathing the sober atmosphere of mathematics? I confess I cannot, — and, when I reflect on the present state of our native country, and perceive " *Troja fuit* " written on all our greatness, my only relief is to sally forth with my hammer, and vent my feelings in the demolition of some rugged cliff of granite that rise on the banks of the Androscoggin. But I have insensibly gotten into the mineral kingdom, and will now endeavor to feel a little calmer, notwithstanding these turbulent times. I still go on, and suffer no day to pass *without a page or two.* For several reasons, however, the work cannot appear before the winter. Indeed, were I this day ready for the press, I should doubt the expediency of proceeding instantly, such is the universal state of excitation and alarm throughout our country. I am yet to receive considerable assistance from two or three gentlemen in Baltimore, which must, of course, be delayed by recent events in that vicinity.

FROM HON. DAVID DAGGETT.

WASHINGTON, *November* 28, 1814.

DEAR SIR, — Your letter of the 24th instant, concerning a twenty-dollar note of one of the banks of this district, is received. I will readily do all I can in the case. It can scarcely be credited in Connecticut, but so the fact is, that the Treasury of the United States cannot pay this nor any other sum in any other than a depressed currency. Our wages we must spend here, or fund, or loan to individuals. A dollar cannot be raised here in any paper east of Baltimore. Silver and gold are literally banished. You might as well hunt for foxes or deer on our green as for a dollar in Washington. I need not tell you how deplorable is our condition as a nation. I see no prospect of a *favorable* change. If the war shall continue a year, the government must cease to operate. It cannot — it will not — be *administered* by its present incumbents. With my regards to Mrs. S., I am, dear sir,

Truly yours,
DAVID DAGGETT.

The war did not wholly break off communication with men of science whom he had known in Great Britain, as is shown by the following letter : —

FROM DR. JOHN MURRAY.

EDINBURGH, *February* 5, 1813.

. . . . . In a letter which I had very lately from Mr. Griscom of New York, he mentioned to me that you are not a convert to Davy's opinion on the oxy-muriatic and muriatic acids. It does not gain ground, I think, here ; indeed, I have scarcely heard of any chemist of eminence having decidedly embraced it. In one of the latest volumes of the " Annales de Chemie " there are two excellent papers in opposition to it, one by Berzelius, and another a report by Berthollet and Vauquelin. If you have seen the late volumes of Nicholson, you will have observed that the controversy in which I have been engaged on this subject rests much on the experiment of obtaining water by heat from the salt formed by the combination of muriatic and ammoniacal gases. Sir Humphrey visited Edinburgh a few months ago, and at that time performed the experiment with Dr. Hope, and a very inconsiderable quantity of water was obtained. The experiment, however, was conducted in a manner very liable to fallacy. I have repeated it within these few days with Dr. Hope, in a less exceptionable manner, and a larger quantity of water was obtained. None ought to appear, according to Sir Humphrey's opinion. . . . .

CHAPTER XII.

In following up, as far as possible, the annals of our
scientific labors, we now come to the birth of the " American
Journal of Science and Arts." In the preface to the fiftieth
volume of that work, being the index volume of the entire
series to that time, — 1846, — there is a full history of the
rise and progress of the Journal. It is not my design to
recapitulate it on this occasion, except so far as to mark its
origin at this era. Dr. Archibald Bruce of New York, had,
in 1810, instituted an American journal of mineralogy ; it
was ably conducted, and was most favorably received ; but
it lingered with long intervals between its four numbers,
and stopped with one volume of two hundred and seventy
pages. The declining health of Dr. Bruce, ending in apoplexy, rendered any. prospect of the continuance of his
Journal hopeless. His own life hung in doubt, and was actually ended the 22d February, 1818, in the forty-first year of
his age. Anticipating the death of Dr. Bruce, and it being
certain that his Journal could never be revived by him,
Colonel George Gibbs, in an. accidental meeting on board
the steamer Fulton on Long Island Sound, in 1817, urged
upon me the duty of instituting a new Journal of Science ;

that we might not only secure the advantages already gained, but make advances of still more importance. After much consideration and mature advice, I reluctantly consented to make the attempt. It was not done, however, without showing due deference to Dr. Bruce. It was in the autumn of 1817 that I called upon him at his house and asked his opinion, which was given at once in favor of the effort, and moreover in approbation of the plan, which included the entire circle of the physical sciences and their applications. The first number appeared in July 1818, and the Journal, under many discouragements and through some perils, has survived until this time, February 3, 1859, having already had a life of forty and a half years; and the labors of its editors and contributors are recorded in the seventy-sixth volume.

The Journal was often obliged to maintain a dubious struggle for existence; but, when it was most endangered, the friends of Mr. Silliman and the friends of science rallied to its support. This was particularly the case when a discreditable effort was made by an individual to destroy it and to supplant it by a rival publication. Mr. George Griswold, and other liberal-minded gentlemen of New York, came forward at that time with their generous patronage. A few years after the Journal was started, it was recommended to the public by Mr. Edward Everett in an article in the "North American Review," (for July, 1821,) of which he was then the editor. He speaks of it as "a work which does honor to American science," and as "a vehicle of imparting to the world the scientific speculations and discoveries of our countrymen, which is held in honorable esteem by the philosophers of Europe." This last remark truly describes a most important service rendered to science by the Journal. As editor, Mr. Silliman became the recipient of communications without number from every part of the country. Not only such as made science a profession sent him their papers, but unlearned pioneers in the East and the West would give him information of curious objects that fell under their notice in exploring the country. By gathering together so many scattered rays of light, the Journal aided not only in'the diffusion, but also in the advancement, of the sciences. Another result was the intercourse into which Mr. Silliman was brought with scientific men abroad. Their discoveries were also announced to the American public in the Journal, and their articles not unfrequently found a place on its pages. His reputation in Europe was without doubt the effect, for the most part, of his editorial labors.

The following paragraphs record bereavements that deeply affected him, — the death of his mother and of his eldest son : —

Sickness and Death of my Mother, Æ. 83. — Until the spring of 1814 she had enjoyed very good health, when she was prostrated at Wallingford, at the age of seventy-eight, by an attack of pneumonia, and she never recovered her former vigor. She was thrice a widow, and the time when she was at liberty she divided among her children. I brought her from Norfield, the residence of her son, the Rev. John Noyes, in June 1818. She passed a few days in my house, and I then conducted her to Wallingford, which was her favorite home. She was feeble, and continued to decline until July 2d, when she passed gently out of life, — eighty-two years old in the preceding May. I had not received information of the impending event. A letter sent by a private hand was not seasonably delivered. I was therefore deprived of the satisfaction of watching her last hours. On the 4th of July we went, Mrs. Silliman and all my children, in a family carriage to attend the funeral. The Rev. Matthew Noyes conducted the religious services with solemnity; and we remained over the night. My little Trumbull, who was with us, was very ill, and it was the first of those premonitory attacks which ended his mortal life. My brother, Gold Selleck Silliman, did not arrive until after the funeral. Thus was ended an excellent Christian life, and we felt that our mother had been spared to us to a good old age, and was summoned home when she was mature for heaven. She cherished a cheerful confidence in her Saviour, and looked at death without dismay. She told me after her recovery from the attack of pneumonia, that she had no fear of death, and was ready and willing to go at any time. She opened her trunk and showed me her shroud, and all the dress for the grave which she kept by her, that whenever she might be summoned, her death might make little trouble in preparation. She was a heroic woman, and encountered with firmness the trials and terrors of the American Revolution, in which my father was largely concerned. She did not lose her self-control, when three months before my birth the house was assailed by an armed banditti at the midnight hour, the windows demolished, and my father and elder half-brother were torn away from her, and my father detained for a year at Flatbush, Long Island, as a prisoner of war. Blessed Mother! In her widowhood, after my father's death in 1790, she struggled on in embarrassed circumstances, and gave my brother and myself a public education, forming our minds at home to purity and piety. Whatever I have of good in me, I owe, under God, mainly to her, and I look with mingled reverence and delight at her lovely picture, which smiles upon me still.

Her death was soon followed by that of his son, whom he tended, during a lingering illness, with affectionate care.

This lovely and promising child gave us only delight, until occasional ill turns of fever and cough, in the autumn of 1818, began to excite alarm. All his unfavorable symptoms were aggravated in the winter, and my own solicitude and watchfulness at night, after busy and laborious days at College, were increased by the sufferings of his mother with acute rheumatism. His nights were much broken by his cough and fever, but his spirits were cheered by the hymns which I often sung to him during the watches of the night. Spring brought some recreation to the dear child by riding; but it was only too obvious that his progress was downward toward an early grave.

The little sufferer was removed by his father to Hartford, in the hope that good would result from the journey and the change of place.

I remained in Hartford with my precious little patient as long as there appeared the slightest prospect of alleviation. At last, with a bed in the coach as before, we proceeded slowly homeward, and one week of respite was afforded us before death came to his relief. We had a few short rides, and I had arranged a swing for his amusement; but all in vain. The evening before his death, his little brother, Benjamin, came into the room, and, although Trumbull was panting with cough and fever, on seeing his little friend waddling into the room, he smiled, and uttered his favorite expression: "O funny little Bunny!" On Sabbath morning, June 27, I was alone with him when he gently expired, and he put up his cold lips to kiss me a few minutes before he ceased breathing. His mother was brought down in a double chair, and looked upon his cold remains, still beautiful in death, as he lay in his coffin; and she could only follow with her tearful eyes the funeral procession as it moved from the house. We were sorely bereaved; but we submitted without repining, feeling that

He who had given us this child of hope and promise had a right to take him again ; and we blessed His holy name. This bereavement took fast hold on me. The shaft of death, which never before had been discharged in this house, was levelled against my oldest son, a child of the most attractive traits, lovely and beautiful, serious, considerate, and affectionate, but with a slight air of pensiveness, which added to the interest of his character, although a child not yet five years old when he died. We believed that he was accepted by the Saviour, to whom he had been offered in baptism and commended in prayer.

The death of this child inflicted a wound which was never fully healed. All the toys which he had used were carefully garnered up by his sorrowing father, who never ceased to recollect, with tenderness of feeling, the loss which he had sustained.

What with the labors, the watching, and anxiety of the preceding year, followed by this affliction, my spirits drooped and my health began to be affected, when a source of alleviation was opened by my ever kind and considerate brother-in-law, Mr. Daniel Wadsworth, and it was the more seasonable, as death had more recently smitten another lamb in our flock.*

Neither Mr. Wadsworth or myself had ever visited Canada, and we resolved on this journey as a tour of refreshment and observation, without any motives of business. As it is my habit, when circumstances are favorable, to preserve written notices of my journeys, I began to do it in this instance with the design of inserting in the " Journal of Science " any notices that might appear worthy of it ; but the interesting objects and scenes and historical associations were so numerous that my MS. became a small

---

* This was an infant which was born a week before the death of Trumbull. — F.

volume, which appeared in two editions, in 1820 and 1824, entitled, "A Short Tour between Hartford and Quebec in the Autumn of 1819," with pictorial illustrations by Mr. Daniel Wadsworth. To this volume of 443 pages 12mo., I refer for the details of the journey.

. . . .

My little book met with favor. It became a *vade mecum* for travellers to Canada, and might readily have passed to a third edition, had I moved in the matter. . . . . . It was agreeable to me also to find that the book met a very favorable reception in Canada. I received from officers of the British army on service in that country, as well as from persons in civil life, a decided expression of approval. These communications were made to me both by letter and in personal interviews. To this day this unpretending volume is sought for by tourists going to Canada; and repeated applications have been made to me by strangers for the loan of the book, as it was not to be found on sale.

Purchase of the Cabinet of Colonel Gibbs. — In May, 1825, I received a letter from Colonel Gibbs, in which he informed me that he intended to sell his cabinet, but that he now offered to Yale College the right of preëmption. The price named was twenty thousand dollars, with a reasonable allowance of time to make the payments. We were startled, indeed, by his letter, and taken by surprise, although we had no right, as regards the liberal proprietor, to entertain any other sentiments than those of grateful acknowledgment for the long - continued loan of such a treasure. The cabinet had rested with us from thirteen to fifteen years. From it the owner had derived no pecuniary advantage whatever; but he enjoyed the richer satisfaction of doing good to many hundreds of young people, of diffusing useful knowledge through the country, and elevating the reputation and dignity of science. I have already mentioned that he had, at his own expense, and without our knowledge, kept the cabinet insured. It is true that he derived from his liberality a rich reward of honor and esteem by the common verdict of his country, an honor more permanent than that of sanguinary success in war; for, while military heroes enjoyed only a transient fame, the name of Gibbs is enrolled for posthumous fame as long as science shall be cultivated and honored.

On myself as the head of the department rested of course the duty of making the first movement. I had able counsellors; President Day, the Hon. James Hillhouse, our Treasurer, and my brother Professors, were unanimous in the feeling that the Gibbs Cabinet, so long our pride and ornament, must not be removed from Yale College.

The Corporation was called together by the President. The meeting took place at Hartford on the 24th day of May; the Governor, the Lieutenant-Governor, and six members of the Senate of the State, who are *ex-officio* members of the Corporation, being already there in attendance on the Legislature then in session. The clerical members were summoned to meet them, and the subject was at once proposed for their consideration. They also were unanimous in the sentiment, that the Gibbs Cabinet must be retained, and they approved of the measures already adopted in New Haven. The treasury of the College could not afford to make the purchase, and our only resource appeared to be to call again,— as had always been done for the endowment of the College, — upon the loyalty of our *alumni* and the liberality of the friends of science and of the College, — a resource which had never failed-in previous exigencies. (See the appendix to Baldwin's " History of Yale College," for a list of contributors on many occasions.)

Agreeably to the intimation already stated, the Corporation passed votes, in form, approving of our efforts to save the Cabinet, and gave us authority to invite subscriptions and contributions.

The first effort appears to have been made in New Haven.

As a preliminary to a public meeting, a hand-bill was prepared, in which the case was concisely but clearly and forcibly stated, with an invitation to the citizens to attend a public meeting at a time and place named, to hear a discussion of the merits of the case. The hand-bill was extensively distributed in the town, and the meeting, which soon followed, was well attended, and was warmly addressed, not only by gentlemen of the College, but by some of our prominent citizens. Among them was the Rev. Dr. Croswell, Rector of Trinity Church. Although not an *alumnus*, nor sympathizing in the religious organization of the College, he addressed the assembly with powerful arguments, which were, perhaps, rendered more effective by touching a string of policy, and no one knew better than he how to do it. He gave an intimation that if New Haven did not come forward and secure the Gibbs Cabinet, Hartford might secure it, as the people of Hartford were always prompt and liberal in cases where their local interests were concerned, and they too had a college.

The public meeting in New Haven was immediately followed by personal applications to the citizens. The permanent officers of the College subscribed first, and then dividing the town into districts, each solicitor called upon individuals and asked for their donations. This canvass was laborious, and such duties are always irksome; but when the object is a public one, and not personal, we do not feel that we are chargeable with selfishness,—which is a great relief. President Day zealously led in the canvass, and all the gentlemen put forth such efforts as were convenient to them. It is obvious, however, that no one could be expected to labor so much as the head of the department. I was indeed most ably and zealously assisted by Prof. Chauncey A. Goodrich, who was always zealous and efficient in every good cause in which he engaged. He worked with all his might, and he had uncommon tact in approaching people; he could put on the pressure both upon the right man and in the right place, and was not only successful with the willing, but with the unwilling.

When Mr. Edward Everett came to New Haven to deliver his discourse upon Washington, he related in a short speech to the college students, an anecdote connected with the purchase of the Gibbs Cabinet. Understanding that this collection was offered for sale, Mr. Everett had suggested to several friends of Harvard that it might be secured for that institution. " But," said Mr. Everett, " they hung fire; and after the bargain was concluded by Mr. Silliman, I observed to him that I hoped the affair would give a useful lesson to our people against delay in such matters. ' You are welcome,' said Mr. Silliman with a smile, to any *moral* benefit to be derived from the matter; *we*, meanwhile, will get what good we can from the Cabinet."

Other additions were made from time to time to this noble collection, one of the most important of which was the cabinet of Baron Lederer, Austrian Consul-General in the United States, which was purchased by subscription in 1843. From his scientific correspondents Mr. Silliman obtained valuable specimens, and several of these friends, together with their contributions, are noticed in the " Reminiscences," in connection with the history of the cabinet.

A Collection was purchased from Robert Bakewell, London. — I became acquainted early with the system of geology by this gentleman. By profession a mineral surveyor, he was, of course, a practical geologist, and being a man of strong mind, sound judgment, and moral courage, he pursued an independent course, without being committed to existing theories. In commencing my geological lectures, I used the sketch of the Wernerian system, which was annexed as an appendix to Brochant's "Mineralogy," and from this I derived important aid; but I found it difficult to make out all the Wernerian distinctions, and to identify the rocks which they were intended to illustrate. I was, therefore, greatly relieved by Mr. Bakewell's straightforward, common-sense method, which tore away and threw aside useless subtleties and refinements, and took strong hold of the great framework of the subject. I therefore decided to adopt Mr. Bakewell's work as a text-book, and wrote to the author, requesting that any additions or corrections might be forwarded to me. Eventually I published three editions with copious notes and additions, and the work was generally adopted in this country. My first edition was from Mr. Bakewell's third. ·

We became, of course, correspondents, and his letters were always interesting and instructive, and sometimes brilliant with original thoughts. Wishing to see the original types representing Mr. Bakewell's ideas, I obtained from him a small collection of rocks and minerals which came out, numbered in reference to a detailed catalogue which accompanied them. In earlier years I became acquainted, at Edinburgh, as I have already stated, with the geological ideas that prevailed in Scotland, and was familiar with their representative types. Now I had before me the palpable thoughts (so far as stones could represent them) of an eminent English geologist, and I had the satisfaction of finding that I had before not erred in any important fact or opinion.

Mr. Bakewell appeared much gratified that his work had been made so extensively known in this country. In the preface to a new edition, following my first, he quotes from me the remark that I had adopted his book as being one that "my pupils would be willing to read and able to understand," and he justly regarded this as a high recommendation. Such was his feeling of personal and scientific independence that he held himself aloof from the aristocracy of science, and he even declined the proffered honor of membership in the Royal Society, after he had, almost alone, vindicated his claims to rank among the most eminent geologists of the day. His travels among the Alps added to his reputation, — ("Travels in the Tarentaise and Grecian and Pennine Alps, and in Switzerland and Auvergne, in the years 1820, 1821, and 1822, by R. Bakewell Esq.") Dr. Mantell was his warm and constant friend.

I received a French collection from Mr. Alexander Brongniart of Paris. The specimens related chiefly to the tertiary and chalk formations of the basin of Paris, and the collection included also miscellaneous specimens from many other places. Mr. Brongniart forwarded to me his work on the mineral and paleontological history and structure of the basin of Paris. At a later period I received also from him the revised and improved edition of his work, — a great work indeed. He sent to me also a suite of specimens illustrating the materials and the manufacture of porcelain, especially as it is carried on at the Royal Manufactory of Sèvres, six miles, or two leagues, from Paris, of which Mr. Brongniart was superintendent. This collection I left in the laboratory of Yale College, with the catalogue and description of the process in the handwriting of Mr. Brongniart. His letters to me were highly instructive and very friendly. He corresponded with me also on the subject of a collection which he was forming to illustrate the art of pottery in all ages and countries. It was in my power to aid his design in a small degree, by specimens of aboriginal pottery of the American Indians, and by the products of our advancing arts in common ware and in porcelain, — the porcelain especially of Philadelphia, which compared very well with that of Sèvres. We were at Sèvres early in April 1851, and saw this extensive collection in the ceramic art, and surveyed with admiration the splendid productions of the manufactory.

William Maclure: His Contributions. — This gentleman, born in Scotland in 1763, resided some years in London as a member of a mercantile firm, and early became opulent. He retired from business about 1798–9. He visited the United States in 1782, at the age of nineteen, and again in 1796. In 1803 he appeared in London along with two colleagues, as a commissioner of claims upon the French government for spoliations on American commerce. During some years following he visited most of the countries of Europe and collected specimens in geology and other branches of natural history, which he sent to the United States, his adopted home. He then came to America and commenced the exploration of its geology, and the result was published in 1809 in the Transactions of the Philosophical Society of Philadelphia. In 1817, eight years after, he published a revised edition of his memoir, enlarged and made more perfect, and it appeared also in a small separate volume, with maps. His observations were extended through nearly all the States, from Canada to the Mexican Gulf, and from Maine to the Mississippi, — also including the West Indies. In order to obtain correct sections of the Alleghanies, he crossed that chain of mountains fifty times, back and forward. During all his journeys he collected geological specimens which, from time to time, he boxed and forwarded to Philadelphia, or other places of deposit. He came to New Haven in the autumn of 1808, and I passed several days with him in exploring our geology. He had then come from Maine, and had become acquainted with Professor Parker Cleaveland, whom he greatly admired. He travelled in a private carriage with a servant, and a

pair of horses which, as they transported loads of stone
from place to place, were lean and dull. Mr. Maclure was
at that time in his meridian. Being a teetotaller, drinking
nothing but water and requiring only a moderate quantity
of the most common articles of food, his health was perfect,
and his frame robust and vigorous, as his temperance was
associated with much travelling and with mountain excursions on foot; his countenance had a ruddy glow, and his
manners were in a high degree winning and attractive. His
language was pure and elevated, and his mind being imbued with the love of science, he was successful in exciting
similar aspirations in other, and especially in younger, minds.
In 1817, he was elected President of the Philadelphia
Academy of Natural Sciences, and he was annually reëlected
until his death. . . . . . At the meeting of the Geological
Society, November 17, 1828, Mr. Maclure appeared
decidedly marked by age and infirmity. The brilliant man
whom I first saw twenty years before, had now hoary locks;
he stooped as he walked, and an ulcer on his leg made him
lame. His friend, Dr. Thomas Cooper, was with him, and
these two celebrated men did me the honor to attend one
of my lectures in the chemical course, and to call at my
house. The principal topic was the moral relations of
science and the expositions it gives of the mind and
thoughts of the Creator, as they are recorded in his works.
Other topics might have been more agreeable to these
gentlemen. Dr. Cooper was well known as a sturdy sceptic
in religion, and Mr. Maclure's plans of education did not
include the Bible. Still all his efforts, continued through
forty years with an immense expenditure of money and an
unselfish devotion of time and effort without any personal
advantage, bore every mark of benevolence and good-will,
not only to his adopted country, but to mankind. Mr.
Maclure was a punctual correspondent. For about twenty
years, we exchanged letters, rarely, I believe, omitting a
year. His brother, who was his executor, kindly returned

to me many of my letters, but, I should think, not all. There are about twenty-five, five or six of which passed to him in Spain through Paris; the remainder are directed to the city of Mexico; they run from 1821 to 1838, — from my forty-second to my fifty-eighth year, — the meridian and best part of my life. They are, of course, occupied with the busy avocations of that active period of my labors, in which I might have truly said, " Omnia plena laboris." My letters were also responsive to those of my correspondent on the great subjects which occupied his mind, — the education of the young, the diffusion of useful knowledge, and the elevation of the masses from ignorance, degradation, poverty, and vice. His views were noble ; his fellow-creatures were his family, and to carry out his large plans his ample means were munificently bestowed. His own personal wants were few and simple, and a very small part of his revenue sufficed to supply them. Although some of his views were vision-ary, they were benevolent, and he was one of the benefac-tors of his race.

As the companion of Mr. Maclure in his last visit to New Haven, Dr. Cooper is entitled to be mentioned on this occasion, as well as on account of some friendly epistolary relations, for a time, subsisting between us. Dr. Cooper came out from England, I believe, with Dr. Priestley, or soon after, in 1794, during the exciting periods of the French Revolution. Dr. Cooper resided with Dr. Priestley at or near Northumberland on the Susquehannah River, and was familiar with his scientific pursuits ; and being him-self a man of science, he occasionally wrote to me, and always exhibited a vigorous and discriminating mind. I had never seen him before his visit to New Haven with Mr. Maclure in November 1828. On that occasion his man-ners were mild and conciliating, and his appearance was patriarchal and venerable, very different from what I had imagined it to be. Ten years after, 1839, my third edition of Bakewell's Geology appeared. In an appendix I had endeavored to reconcile the Mosaic history with geology, but this gave great offence to Dr. Cooper, who in a letter to me protested against my views, both scientific and moral, and he even wrote a considerable book, principally in opposition to me indeed, but still more to vituperate Moses or the author of the Pentateuch, whoever he might be. In the last letter which I received from him he reviled the Scriptures, especially of the Old Testament, pronouncing them in all respects an unsupported and, in some respects, a most detestable book. To this letter I made no reply, feeling that it was such a violation of gentlemanly courtesy when writing to one whose sentiments he knew to be so opposite to his own, that I thought it better to drop the correspondence, and I never heard from him again. While presiding over the College at Columbia, S. C., he made no secret of his infidelity, and the community in South Carolina was divided into supporters and opponents of Dr. Cooper, until he was constrained to resign. One of his college faculty, Professor Gibbs, informed me that as he — Professor Gibbs — was passing the college grounds on Sabbath morning on his way to church, he met Dr. Cooper going to work in his laboratory, who said to him, — " Come along with me and learn something that is true and worth knowing." When Dr. Cooper resigned his place, some of the first gentlemen — General Hayne, General Hamilton, and, I believe, Mr. Calhoun — of South Carolina, consulted me to know whether I would accept the Presidency of the College. If I had felt no other reason for declining, I should have been very reluctant to sow in a field which had been so ill prepared to receive good seed. I was unwilling, moreover, to become a member of a community where slavery was established. The only reason, however, which I assigned for declining the overture was, that I feared I should not be able to give them satisfaction. I would not forget the friendly maxim — " Nil de mortuis nisi bonum." Dr. Cooper was, I have understood, much esteemed by those

who knew him intimately, and it affords a pleasing indication of his domestic character that he lived in great harmony with an excellent wife. If I am not misinformed,
the ballad "John Anderson my jo John" would have
described them well. In religion and politics he was pugnacious and sometimes bitter. He was considered as the
leader of the disunion party in South Carolina, and to him
was first attributed the sentiment, uttered at a convivial
meeting, that it was "high time to calculate the value of
the Union."

Among the early patrons of the "Journal of
Science," was Mr. Calhoun, whose feeling with reference to Yale College at that time is expressed in
a note to Mr. Silliman.

FROM HON. JOHN C. CALHOUN.

WAR DEPARTMENT, March 26, 1818.

DEAR SIR, — I have received the Prospectus which you
transmitted to me, and I hope most sincerely that you may
meet with ample encouragement.

The utility of such a work, particularly in this country,
must be apparent, and our number, wealth, and intellectual
improvement have now attained that point at which there
ought to be sufficient patronage.

You do me justice in supposing that I still retain an
affection for the institution with which you are connected.
I have every reason to feel the strongest gratitude to Yale
College, and shall always rejoice in her prosperity.

I remain, with esteem,

Yours, &c.,

J. C. CALHOUN.

The principal difficulty in sustaining the Journal
is indicated in the following note from Dr. Hare.

The Essays on Musical Temperament to which he refers were written by Professor A. M. Fisher. Mr. Silliman succeeded in sustaining the enterprise without suffering the Journal to become a merely popular magazine.

FROM DR. ROBERT HARE.

July 28, 1819.

. . . . . I AM grieved to hear the pecuniary result of your publication is so unfavorable. In our city the interest in favor of our own journals is very strong. I have already hinted this to you as operating against the giving of communications abroad, and of course it will operate against subscriptions. There are few in our country who take interest in the profounder branches of knowledge. I doubt if there be a dozen men on the Continent who would peruse some of the essays on musical temperament in your Journal. I was told in New York that many said they could not understand my memoir, who considered their standing such as to feel as if this were an imputation against me rather than themselves. I could not write it for those who are so ignorant, without making it too prolix and commonplace for adepts. There is our difficulty, — we cannot write anything for the scientific few which will be agreeable to the ignorant many. . . . . . .

Among the letters of condolence which he received on the occasion of the death of his son, was one from Mrs. Humphreys, the widow of Colonel Humphreys.

FROM MRS. HUMPHREYS.

BOSTON, *October* 6, 1819.

. . . . . I CONDOLE with you most truly and sincerely on the loss of your darling child. The all-consoling reflection, that you describe with so much feeling, is so just and so true, that it cannot fail to heal the sorrow of every Christian who has faith in the words of our Saviour. I cannot here forbear to mention to you the customs of my native land — Portugal, — in regard to the death of little children under seven years old. If you ask a mother how many children she has, it is usual that she should answer: " I have *two* with me, and *three* in *Heaven*." Or, if she has lost them all, she will say, without hesitation: " I have *so many* in Heaven." The funerals of little children in that country are accompanied by every emblem of joy instead of sorrow; the coffin, or rather cradle, is of pink and silver; roses and myrtles and jasmine are thrown upon the corpse, which is only covered with a transparent silver gauze. A band of fine music accompanies it. After the funeral, all the friends and acquaintance return to the house to congratulate the mother (who is smiling through her tears) on having an angel in heaven and another advocate in her favor. Such are the singular customs in Lisbon.

I pray you to make my best regards to Mrs. Silliman, and believe me to be,

Yours with esteem and friendship,
A. F. HUMPHREYS.

A portion of the journey to Canada is briefly described in the following letter: —

TO PROFESSOR J. L. KINGSLEY.

QUEBEC, *October* 8, 1819.

MY DEAR SIR, — In compliance with your request and with my own promise, I now write you from the capital of the Canadas. Our journey has been thus far prosperous. We left Hartford in the equinoctial gale, September 22, Wednesday; on Friday reached Albany; dined and spent most of a day with Judge Kent, in whose fine library of between two and three thousand volumes *you* would *revel:*

they are choice books, and have cost him $10,000. I was more than ever delighted with the Judge. We were also at the Patroon's, — probably the most like an ancient baronial establishment of anything in America: it is a princely place. At Troy we saw the new and almost ludicrous horse-boat, which two horses, without ever moving a step from the places they stand in, and to which indeed they are harnessed, propel the boat merely by moving their legs, and thus causing a circular flat platform on which they stand to revolve. I will explain it fully when I see you. We lodged at Stillwater, in the house in which General Frazer died, in which Lady Harriet Ackland and the Baroness Reidesel met with those interesting but tragical adventures, which we read together, you may remember. I visited the battle-grounds in company with an old man (a Lebanon man, too), who was a guide to our armies in all the fighting. Mr. Wadsworth stopped that night at Sandy Hill, and I proceeded to Lake George. I will say nothing about this wonderful scene and its interesting forts and battle-grounds till we meet. I rejoined Mr. W. at Fort Anne, half way between the Hudson and Lake Champlain; and, in our ride to Whitehall, we found frequent occasions to wonder at seeing a fine canal to connect the waters of the Hudson and of Lake Champlain, running along almost side by side with, and frequently within a stone's throw of, a still finer natural canal, a wood-creek, which empties at precisely the same spot with the canal. From Whitehall we proceeded down the lake, in the only remaining steamboat; the horse and carriage were taken on board and left at Burlington (Vt.), to await our return from Canada, when we proposed to cross the mountains to Hanover, and so home down the river. At Plattsburgh we saw the scene of Macdonough's victory, as we had seen the trophies of it — the flotilla — laid up at Whitehall; we found out Lyman Foot, who is very happy, and in high repute in the army, at which I was not a little gratified, regarding him as almost my child. We entered St. John's River — the river Sorel — just nine days from our leaving Hartford, and passed by the magnificent stone castle on Rouse's Point, at the foot of Lake Champlain, the guns of which were intended to prevent any more Commodore Downeses from ever escaping from Canada into the Lake; hundreds of thousands of dollars have been expended on it, and it is now ascertained that the forty-fifth degree of latitude falls about one half a mile south of it, so that this work now falls to our friends, the British, who will thus affectionately prevent any armament proceeding by water to St. Johns. At the Isle au Noix, ten miles down the Sorel, we passed a strong British fort, a frigate on the stocks, &c., &c. Everything looked foreign and formidable.

We lodged at St. Johns, and a week ago to-day arrived at Montreal, where we stayed between three and four days. It is a fine, foreign town, much underrated by our countrymen, and the city and environs make together a grand prospect. Two days ago we arrived here, and shall stay several days longer, determined to see everything in and out of town. We are highly gratified with our tour, and everything in Canada is beyond our expectations. The fortifications here, and the natural situation of the town, are so commanding, that it seems as if it could never be taken. We have got acquainted with a noble-hearted fellow, a captain of grenadiers, in the garrison. He was with Sir John Moore at Corunna, and with Wellington in the Peninsula, and has taken us into the Citadel on Cape Diamond, — a favor very rarely granted to anybody. But I must have done. I will, however, tell you a great deal when we meet.

The " Tour in Canada " was the subject of an interesting communication

FROM CHANCELLOR KENT.

ALBANY, *October* 14, 1820.

DEAR SIR, — Your obliging letter of the 9th instant has been received, accompanied with your " Tour to Quebec," and I return my sincere thanks for this mark of your kindness, and for the great pleasure which the perusal of your book has given me. I have read it very attentively, and beg leave to bear my humble testimony to the justness and beauty of its descriptions and the accuracy of its historical illustrations. It has, also, that moral charm and those graces of composition which are diffused over all the productions of your pen. There is not a page too much on geological observations, and no more than what was due to your character and required from your station.

I have not been to the northward this summer as you have been informed, but I have *frequently* visited the grounds over which you passed between the matchless valley of Lebanon and Montreal. The first time I visited the shore of Lake Champlain was twenty-five years ago with Mrs. K., and I shall never forget the emotions excited when we landed for the first time near sunset at *Ticonderoga,* and hastily ascended to the top of its mouldering walls (then a solitary and awful ruin) and caught within the sweep of the eye the majestic scenery around the place, and the distant lofty summits of the Green Mountains. I visited at that time old *Fort St. Frederick* at *Crown Point,* built by the French in 1731, and the near and large fort on higher ground, built by Lord Amherst in 1759.´ There was not then a human habitation on that peninsula. We returned through Lake George in a small sail-boat, and lodged at a dismal old house which had been a military barrack on the shore below fort George. It was all woods where the beautiful village of Caldwell now stands, and we ran over the ruins of Fort William Henry, then most fearfully interesting from historical recollections, for it appeared not to have been disturbed by the hand of man since 1757. I think you must admit Mrs. K. and I had considerable en-terprise, considering the great inconvenience of travelling at that day in what was then a new and wild country. I had learned in early youth from my father and from Carver's "Travels" (for he was present) the tragical story of the Massacre of the garrison, and I trod the ground with highly excited feelings. You have given a very interesting account of that enchanting spot *Monte Video*, and the pencil of Mr. W—— has contributed exceedingly to illustrate and adorn your work. If I ever go to Hartford I think I shall solicit the honor of his company on a visit to his seat, which does infinite credit to his munificence and taste.

All the leisure I have had this season was occupied in a short visit to Governor Jay, who lives at Bedford, about ten miles west of Ridgefield, in Connecticut. I went through Dutchess County and the mountains in Putnam County, and discharged a debt of respect, reverence, and gratitude, which I owed to that venerable man. Mrs. K., as usual, accompanied me, and we stayed a night with him. He is now seventy-four years old, and is feeble but cheerful, and his mind appears to have retained all its acuteness and vigor. He has a grand farm of six hundred acres, and everything about him was plain, convenient, and substantial, and bore the same stamp of solidity and simplicity which has always characterized the owner. He received us with most engaging kindness, and conversed freely on the passing events of the times, and dwelt on the Revolution, in which he bore such a distinguished part. He spoke highly of Dr. Dwight's volumes on theology, and regretted he had not known more of him in his lifetime. He is very religious and performed family worship in the Episcopal form with tender and impressive devotion. He appeared to be a perfect model of a Christian sage, and I am not aware that we have a more finished character in the country. From his house we returned through Danbury, where I lived from 1773 to 1777, and then visited South-east Town, in Putnam County, where my father once re-sided. I went to the house, and to *the very room* where I was born, where I saw my blessed mother die, fifty years ago next December. I never viewed any scene with deeper interest or more affecting recollections. Everything looked decayed and melancholy, and the features of nature seemed to have dwindled since the eye of youthful exaggeration was withdrawn. I was astonished to find how much the enchantment of youth had disappeared, and how much forty years had disrobed the spot of the brightness and charms with which it once contributed to transport me. But, my dear sir, excuse my.wandering pen. I set out to thank you for your friendship and goodness, and to assure you of the interest I take in whatever concerns your wel-fare and your character. I am, with the highest esteem and regard,

Yours, &c.,

Prof. Silliman.   James Kent.

The letter of invitation to the Presidency of South Carolina College, with Professor Silliman's reply, is presented below.

FROM HON. ROBERT Y. HAYNE.

Charleston, *January* 19, 1835.

Dear Sir, — You have probably seen that the trustees of the South Carolina College have made a radical reform in that institution, the president and all the old professors (except one, Mr. Nott) having gone out with a view to give place to others to be chosen.   Three only have as yet been elected professors : Dew, of William and Mary, to the pro-fessorship of History and Political Economy ; Professor Davis, of West Point, to the professorship of Mathematics, and Mr. Cogswell, formerly of Northampton, to the profes-sorship of Languages ; the presidency with the professorships of Moral Philosophy and Chemistry, still remaining vacant. We are very anxious to fill these with men of high character and commanding talents. To accomplish this, a committee has been appointed by the trustees, consisting of Governor McDuffie, General Hamilton, and myself, to make inquiries and find out suitable persons for these stations. The president will not be chosen till the annual meeting in November next; the professors, if we can find proper men, may be elected in June next, to enter upon the duties of their respective offices in October. Now it has occurred to me that as the presidency of the South Carolina College is in many respects the most desirable literary office in the Union, it might suit your views to accept it, and believing that there is no man better qualified for the station, none who would be more acceptable not only to the trustees but to the people at large, I take the liberty of submitting the question to your consideration. The salary is $3000 per annum, with a good house; the tenure during good behavior. The salary is certain, being paid out of the public treasury. The number of students it is not expected will exceed one hundred for several years to come, and probably never extend beyond one hundred and fifty. There is an annual vacation from June to October, which includes the whole season in which autumnal fevers *occasionally* (though rarely) prevail in Columbia, which, as you are aware, is a fine flourishing town, the seat of government, and possessing a polished society by whom the faculty of the College are greatly cherished. The president might choose his department, and chemistry could be assigned to you. I am persuaded that there is no station in the Union in which you could acquire more honor or be more successfully employed. Under the new arrangement, I think there will be no serious difficulty in enforcing discipline. With these brief suggestions, I submit to your consideration whether you cannot allow us to look to you to fill the vacancy. I am, of course, not authorized to act for the Board, but I have the sanction of Governor McDuffie and General Hamilton for saying, that we should not only support you ourselves, but we have no doubt that, should you consent, the trustees would elect you without hesitation. I write this confidentially, because it may happen that you would not desire (even should you be willing to be a candidate for the office) that it should be publicly known, with reference to your present situation.   I shall be much gratified to hear from you on this subject, and also to have the names of suitable persons suggested for the other vacant offices in the College.   I am, very respectfully,

Your obedient servant,

PROFESSOR SILLIMAN.   ,   ROBERT Y. HAYNE.

TO HON. ROBERT Y. HAYNE.

YALE COLLEGE, February 2, 1835.

DEAR SIR, — I have taken a few days to consider the very important subject which you have done me the honor to lay before me, and trust I have not transgressed the limits of propriety in consulting a very small number of trustworthy friends immediately around me.   While I feel much gratified by the favorable opinion which you and the eminent gentlemen, your associates in this affair, are so kind as to entertain of me, it is but candid to say that I cannot discover good ground of confidence in myself, that I should be able to answer the reasonable expectations of your community.   Having from a very early period corresponded with several gentlemen in the faculty of your University, and with others interested in promoting its welfare, it will give me pleasure still to exert myself for that object.   I will therefore keep in mind the vacant offices, and should the names of any persons qualified to fill them occur to me, I will, with your permission, communicate them to you.   I remain, most respectfully, your

Very obedient servant,

HON. ROBT. Y. HAYNE.   B. SILLIMAN.

CHAPTER XIII.

IN 1806 I made the first arrangement for regular aid in the manual service of my departments. Before I went to England, I depended on accidental assistance, by hiring one and another to do the work. But in the autumn of 1806, being at Wallingford, Mrs. Noyes recommended to me a lad of about twelve years of age, by name, Foot, who soon after came to me at the College, and a sleeping-room was prepared for him in the attic of the Lyceum, in which building was my own chamber. He did the work of the laboratory as far as he was able. During the autumnal, winter, and spring seasons, after my return from England, in June 1806, I had my breakfast and evening tea in my chamber, — until October 1809, when I had a better home,

—and this lad arranged everything satisfactorily for my comfort, while his own food was taken in the college hall. In the summer I boarded at Mr. Twining's, in the town. Foot grew in usefulness, as in stature and intelligence; he was studious and exemplary, and became a useful assistant in all my departments, but particularly in chemistry. He remained with me nine years, studied medicine and surgery, received a diploma from our medical institution, and after a short term of service in rural practice, he became surgeon in the army by the recommendation of the Professors addressed to Mr. Calhoun, then Secretary of War. Three of us, — Mr. Day, Mr. Kingsley, and myself, — in addition to President Dwight, had been instructors of Mr. Calhoun in Yale College, and he paid more attention to our recommendation than to that of our demagogues, who presented their own favorites. Dr. Foot reared an interesting family, from whom he was separated by active service in the war with the Seminoles in Florida, and in the Black Hawk war in the region of the northern Mississippi. When more than fifty years of age, he was ordered to join the army in the Mexican war, but his constitution, already impaired by severe service in savage warfare, yielded to the deleterious effects of the climate, and he died of dysentery at Port La Vacca, in Texas. From the situation of a poor boy, of unfortunate parentage, he rose by his merit to the rank of second surgeon, in point of age, in the American army. President Dwight and the Professors gave him their friendly influence, and the medical professors gave him the fees of their respective courses, in consideration of his merits and of his inability to purchase their tickets.

After the resignation of Dr. Foot in 1815, and until 1821, I had no regular trained assistant. The labor of the laboratory was performed by hired men, who lived in my family, serving there in all necessary domestic duties, including the garden and the barn, and at the College, as there was occasion. It may be well supposed that such

persons would not be very adroit adepts in scientific employments. A few of them, however, having acquired some
degree of skill, became very useful assistants, but others
were clumsy, heavy-handed men, and the glass vessels suffered not a little in their hands. During this period, and
at subsequent times also, I was aided by private pupils who
worked in the laboratory for the sake of obtaining a knowledge of practical chemistry. Among the most distinguished
of these were Prof. Denison Olmsted, Prof. George T.
Bowen, and Prof. Edward Hitchcock, — giving them the
titles which they afterwards bore. Prof. Olmsted had been
appointed to the chair of chemistry in the College of
Chapel Hill, North Carolina ; and with a view to render
himself more fit for the duties of the office, he passed a
year with me at the expense of his College, and became
familiar with chemical manipulations and with the various
duties of all my departments. When departing in the autumn of 1818, from New Haven, for his destination in
North Carolina, Mr. Olmsted feelingly expressed to me his
sense of the advantages which he had enjoyed in the course
of preparatory labor and instruction through which he had
passed, without which he said that he should not have dared
to enter upon the duties of his station. In that station,
during the seven or eight years of his professorship at
Chapel Hill, he bestowed important advantage on the College there, and acquired deserved honor for himself. In
addition to his duties of instruction and the necessary labor
of preparing his experiments, he explored extensively and
successfully the geology of North Carolina, whose territory
is rich in valuable minerals, and in facts illustrative of
geological theory, which were presented by him to the
public in a small but valuable volume, — an interesting
early record of American Geology. He deposited, also,
duplicate specimens in Yale College Cabinet. From my
successive classes, and especially from my private pupils, I
withheld no important fact with which my experience had

made me acquainted, and I, in turn, invited a frank communication of their knowledge and of their objections to my views. With Horace I often said to them, " Si quid novisti rectius istis, candidus imperti ; si non, his utere mecum." I had some way of succeeding in every department, but I was always happy to hear from them of a better way. From Chapel Hill, Professor Olmsted returned to Yale College in 1825, as Professor of Mathematics and Natural Philosophy, in place of Rev. Professor Matthew Rice Dutton, deceased.

Mr. George T. Bowen, of Providence, R. I., when a member of the Junior and Senior classes, in 1821–22, made application to me for admission to the laboratory, as a private pupil and assistant in the preparation of the experiments. As such an engagement might interfere with his duties as an undergraduate and a member of one of the College classes, I declined receiving him, unless he could obtain special leave from the President. So earnest was the young man in his application, that the indulgence was granted upon the express condition that he should perform all his college duties with fidelity. Under these conditions he came to the laboratory ; and he proved himself a zealous, industrious, ingenious, and efficient pupil and assistant during the two years when he was with me. He performed several analyses, which are recorded in the fifth and eighth volumes of the "American Journal of Science," and in the fifth volume he recorded the magnetic effects produced by the calorimotor of Dr. Hare. . . . . . After leaving New Haven, Mr. Bowen passed some time with Dr. Hare, in Philadelphia, both for the advantage of his instruction and from social considerations, as Mrs. Hare, who was a lady from Providence, was also his relative. He went also through a regular course of medical instruction in the University of Pennsylvania. From Philadelphia Mr. Bowen passed to Nashville, Tenn., as Professor of Chemistry in the University of Tennessee, where, under President

Lindsley, he was associated with the eminent Dr. Troost. We had occasion to lament that only a brief course of duty was allotted to him. He died of consumption, in 1828, having a decided Christian hope. From his death-bed he sent me an aerolite that had fallen in Tennessee, at the same time that he sent me an affectionate farewell.

More than forty years ago —I believe in the year 1817— I received a box of minerals from a person, then unknown to me, who signed his name Edward Hitchcock, teacher of the Academy of Deerfield, Mass. He stated that he had collected these minerals from the rocks and mountains in the vicinity; and as he stated, moreover, that they were unknown to him, he desired me to name them and return them to him with the labels. I promptly complied with the request, and as the accompanying letter of Mr. Hitchcock was written with modest good sense, and indicated a love of knowledge, I invited him to send to me another box, and I promised him to return it with the information he desired. It came, and was attended to accordingly. The minerals were chiefly of the zeolite family, — chabasie, analcime, mezotype, and agatized quartz, &c., being the usual companions of trap-rocks, such as are numerous in that region. I then invited Mr. Hitchcock to visit me in New Haven. The invitation was accepted, and for a series of years he was often here, and attended all the courses of lectures with more or less of regularity. He discovered an amiable character and an ardent mind animated by the love of knowledge, and he engaged with great industry in the study of chemistry, mineralogy, and geology. The "Journal of Science and Arts" was instituted the next year, 1818, and Mr. Hitchcock appeared in the first volume. His communications have been numerous and important. I have found between fifty and sixty titles of his papers in the tables of contents and in the index; not a few of them are elaborate, and indicate much care and skill.

His starting-point was with us, and we may regard him as a pupil of our scientific departments.

I cannot take time to follow him in his career as a minister of the gospel at Conway, in his office as Professor of chemistry, geology, &c., in Amherst College, as President afterwards, for several years, of the same institution, and as Professor again, after his voluntary resignation of the presidency.

It was rare that I was without private pupils, but of some the term was too short or the result too unimportant to merit a mention, unless very transiently, on this occasion.

Rev. Sereno E. Dwight was with me when a youth, and worked with his characteristic zeal. Prof. Chester Dewey and Prof. Robert Hare both operated with me at different times in making potassium, and Dr. Hare in later periods in galvanism. Prof. Amos Eaton passed a winter here in preparation to become a lecturer, and he became a distinguished teacher. With the same view came Prof. William C. Fowler, although he did not follow the profession; and the same was true of Rev. Gamaliel Olds, a gentleman whose mind was more bent on metaphysics than physics. Prof. Avery, afterwards of Hamilton College, was much engaged as a student of chemistry, and so was Dr. and Prof. Edward Leffingwell, who was, moreover, a very useful assistant, although he could not distinguish colors. Prof. Vigus, of Alabama, observed and recorded everything, and carried his knowledge into the Southern academies. Prof. Ormond Beattie was an earnest student. Others resorted to the laboratory as amateurs, — as Mr. Dill, of Indiana. Mr. George Spalding and Mr. John W. Parker studied and practised to become chemical manufacturers. There were doubtless others whose names do not occur to me, and which could be rallied from my old note-books,—for it was very seldom that the laboratory was without extra students or observers of the operations. Many times I have said to those who as novices have offered to aid me, that they might come and see what we were doing, and I should much prefer that they should do nothing ; for then they would not hinder me and my trained assistants, nor derange or break the apparatus.

Again being at Wallingford, the same good lady, Mrs. Noyes, wife of the Rev. James Noyes, on being informed that an assistant was needed in my department in Yale College, recommended a young gentleman of Wallingford, Mr. Sherlock J. Andrews, a son of an eminent physician of that place, and a recent graduate of Union College, Schenectady. Mr. Andrews readily accepted the offer, and came with me to New Haven, to be ready to commence the business of the term. A pleasant chamber was assigned to him in the North College, opposite to President Day. The choice of Mr. Andrews was a happy one. He was a young man of a vigorous, active mind, and energetic and quick in his decisions and movements ; of a warm heart, and a genial temper and temperament ; of the best moral and social habits ; a quick and skilful penman, an agreeable inmate of my family, in which we made him quite at home ; and in short, we found that we had acquired an interesting and valuable friend, as well as a good professional assistant. It is true he had, when he came, no experience in practical chemistry. He had everything to learn, but he learned rapidly, because he had zeal, industry, talent, and love of knowledge, and before the end of the first term he had proved that we had made a happy choice.

Mr. Silliman interrupts his account of the services rendered by Mr. Andrews, for the purpose of describing his exertions at this time for the restoration of his health, which had become seriously impaired. The death of his son, Trumbull, and also of an infant daughter, in 1819, has already been mentioned.

Within three years, two other infant children were taken from him by death. " Anxiety, watching, and sorrow" had worn upon his health, and in the autumn of 1822 repeated attacks of vertigo warned him of the necessity of seeking some relief. He first undertook a journey to West Point, having been appointed an official visitor to the military school. He was on his way back when he received the appalling intelligence of the death of his friend and youthful colleague, one of the most brilliant young men whom the country has produced,—Alexander Metcalf Fisher.

We passed a night at Kingston, and at Poughkeepsie the morning papers shocked us with the news of the wreck of the *Albion* — a New York packet-ship — in a tempest on the rock-bound coast of Old Kinsale in Ireland, with the loss of all her cabin passengers, except one, and among the lost was our Professor Fisher of Yale College, who was on his way to Europe for improvement. More than forty passengers were drowned, besides numbers of the people of the ship ; and her commander, Captain Williams, was among them. Her spars and topsails being blown away, she could not be kept off from the shore.

Mr. Fisher perished at the age of twenty-six, and his attainments and merits placed him among the very first young men in the land. My companions being devout men, we all kneeled in our chamber in an act of devotion. Resigned indeed we were, but deeply afflicted by this most unexpected event. The disaster might probably have been averted had the ship tacked and stood out to sea until the southeast gale abated. In April 1805, the *Ontario*, in which I was a passenger for Liverpool, was caught in a southeast gale in the same part of the channel, and she tacked in time to escape being driven upon those terrible cliffs of Kinsale. In my last trip to Liverpool, in March 1851, we steamed with a smooth sea so near these cliffs that they were very distinctly visible within two miles, and our captain pointed out the very place where the *Albion* perished, and with her, poor Fisher and his companions.

Having returned home, Mr. Silliman, soon made a second journey with Mr. Wadsworth, southward as far as Philadelphia, and back as far northward as the Catskill Mountains.

— We remained two days in New York, stopping at the City Hotel, where the house was not quiet until past midnight, and the city, with milkmen, sweeps, and moving carriages, was astir again between three and four o'clock, A. M. Of course, there was little time for repose, and I felt little spirit for the interviews of the day. My good Quaker friend, John Griscom, a brother chemist and lecturer, dined with me quietly at the hotel, and his mild and soothing manners and modest good sense formed a pleasant relief from a rather stormy interview with an English travelling geologist, whose arrogant assumption of superiority over American geologists provoked me to a rather sharp rejoinder and reproof, and somewhat agitated my nerves which were prone, in my enfeebled state of health, to vibrate painfully, when roughly touched. This gentleman, however, profited by my rebuke, for he became very much my friend, visited me at New Haven and communicated several valuable papers to the " American Journal of Science." His name was John Finch ; he remained several years in this country, returned to England, and is, I believe, deceased.

Mr. Silliman reverts to Mr. Andrews, and to the valuable aid derived from him.

We acquired the habit, on my part, of dictating, and on

his, of writing, from the living voice. We improved daily in this exercise, until it became familiar and easy. Often when my debility induced me to recline on the sofa, Mr. Andrews wrote for me by the hour, and sometimes for whole days, for it cost me no inconvenient effort to dictate, although I had little ability to write. I began usually by stating the subject; then I gave him the first sentence, or a member of it, if it was long. It being written down, my assistant then repeated the last word of the sentence or clause and another sentence or member was then added, and so on until the subject was finished. Last of all, the writing was read aloud for corrections. I learned these habits from President Dwight, who from the weakness of his eyes, was compelled to dictate most of his writings. Even his great theological work was put on paper by the hand of an amanuensis, generally a regular paid assistant, — but sometimes his friends wrote for him. I wrote after his dictation, his very interesting and instructive sermon, on the close of the century and the commencement of a new century, January 1, 1801, — not January 1, 1800, as many strangely imagined, as if ninety-nine years were a century.

Finding his health not established by these repeated journeys, he with his wife and Mr. and Mrs. Wadsworth spent some time at Ballston and Saratoga.

Among our guests at Ballston were Hon. Martin Van Buren; Mr. Short, formerly of Paris; George Harrison of Philadelphia, and his beautiful wife; the rich bachelor, Mr. Pollock of North Carolina; Harrison Gray Otis and family from Boston; John Dickinson and lady from Troy; Mr. and Mrs. Williams from Mississippi; Rev. Sereno E. Dwight, and many more persons of the higher aristocracy, as well as those of less pretension. Had I not enjoyed the company of my good wife I should, however, have suffered from *ennui*, for we had few sources of entertainment. Our walks were limited as the ground was not very eligible, but I enjoyed riding on horseback through the pine woods, in company with a lady friend, Miss Davenport, now and for many years the wife of Rev. Dr. Skinner of New York, — Mrs. Silliman not preferring that kind of exercise. We had more time than spirits for reading in our chamber; the evenings were generally passed in the parlor, where we were entertained by a band of musicians, who also summoned us to dinner with the Marseilles Hymn, or God save the Queen, or Hail Columbia.

In 1797, soon after leaving College, owing to a wound in my foot from an axe, I was in danger of lockjaw, and a nervous debility followed after the immediate danger was removed. This induced me to pass a month at Ballston Springs. My companions were Mr. John Winn, and the Hon. John Elliott, both from Sunbury, Liberty County, Georgia. We performed the journey on horseback, and of course rode daily at Ballston when the weather was favorable. There was but one hotel, that of Aldrich, and in the street in front of the house the sparkling fountain of chalybeate water, brisk with carbonic acid gas, rose as if joyous, from the earth ; and the area was enclosed within an iron railing. We of course visited Saratoga, which has now become a large and celebrated town, owing to the excellence of its waters. Reverting to 1797, the period of my early visit, it is interesting to mention the condition of Saratoga at that time. We, the little party before named, Mr. Elliott, Mr. Winn and myself, mounted our horses one day and rode seven or eight miles through the pine forest, with its delightful fragrance, and arrived at the place where they said that there were some mineral springs. There was not even a village, but only two or three log-houses standing among the pine-trees. The people were civil, and provided hay for our horses, and for ourselves bacon and eggs. They then piloted us into a morass where nature was unsubdued, and, stepping cautiously from bog to bog, we soon arrived at a spring which they called the Congress Spring, and we drank the water which tasted as it does now. . . . . . . Twenty-six years had passed and what a change ! A beautiful city had arisen where there were only a morass and a pine barren. Beautiful lawns adorned with statuary now meet the eyes, and the fashionable world, in the summer months, throng this favorite resort.

Once more, in May 1824, with his usual companion in journeying, Mr. Wadsworth, he left home and travelled southward as far as Washington.

We were just in time to see both Houses of Congress in session. We dined with Mr. J. C. Calhoun, a distinguished graduate of Yale College, who was the Secretary of War, and who received us with great cordiality. He explained to us his plans for internal improvement, which were extensive and detailed, and included not only a ship-canal between Lakes Superior and Huron, by the Sault St. Mary, but even a cut across the neck of Cape Cod, thus uniting Buzzard's Bay with Massachusetts, or Cape Cod Bay, and saving a dangerous navigation around the Cape. But all this was changed when sectional jealousies arose, and the high-minded, honorable patriot became the antagonist of internal improvement, and was narrowed down to a South Carolina politician. President Monroe was then at the head of the Government. He had been kind to me in 1805, when he was our minister in London, and I called upon him there in company with the late Professor Peck of Harvard. I paid my respects again to him when he visited New Haven on his Eastern tour in 1816, and was promptly recognized. We now called upon him in the official palace, and were received with that mild benignity which corresponded with his amiable character. As we then thought of travelling into Virginia, his native State, he, unsolicited, offered us letters to his friends. Although not a splendid man, he was a wise and good President. Twenty-five years have passed since this visit at Washington, and I will copy from a letter which I wrote at the time, the impression which I then received. " The magnificence of the exterior of the public buildings quite equalled my expectations, and the city itself is more considerable and more respectable in its appearance than some people will allow. As I sit writing in my chamber, the grand Potomac winds and stretches far away, and reminds me of the St. Lawrence at Montreal and Quebec. Arlington House, the seat of George Washington Parke Custis, Esq., grandson of Mrs. Washington, makes an imposing appearance on a high hill upon the opposite side of the river. The carriage is at the door to take us to the Capitol, — for nobody walks here, in this rudimentary city, where, as our Senator Tracy used to say, ' it is three miles to anything.'" In many visits to Washington in later years, I have seen it gradually filling up, until it is no longer a skeleton city, and now numbers 50,000 people. We visited Arlington then (1824), and I was there again in 1852, after the lapse of twenty-eight years, and found everything very much improved. The hospitable proprietor made this brief visit very pleasant. Mrs. Custis was living, and the house was rich in relics of Washington: his plate in many forms; his portrait at the period of Braddock's campaign, dressed in the full and flowing costume of that day ; — and, in the visit of 1824, Mrs. Custis showed me the bed on which General Washington died, and offered it in hospitality for my repose, — if repose would indeed come when memory recalled the death-scene.   Mrs. Custis gave me a terra cotta medallion of Dr. Franklin, which used to hang in General Washington's study or office at Mount Vernon ; and Mrs. Custis sent to Mrs. Trumbull a saucer of the Presidential period at Philadelphia, from a set made for Mrs. Washington in China. A napkin also was sent, belonging to the camp furniture of the military marquee. This grand tent was expanded in full in the garret at Arlington ; it was in perfect preservation, fit for field-service again ; and it was no small satisfaction to me to stand beneath its ample folds, associated as they had been with so many stirring events, and anxious as well as joyous musings. Those who rendered Arlington so attractive are there no longer. Mr. Custis died October 10, 1857, some years after he had returned from a journey to Boston, when I received a call from him at my house, where he passed an hour. His age, when he died, was seventy-seven. Mrs. Custis died before him. . . . . . At dinner, at Gadsby's, I found myself next to General Bernard, the distinguished engineer of Napoleon I. He exhibited the suavity of his country ; and, as he was about to visit the West as an engineer of our government, I, by a passing remark, invited him to speak of our great system of Western waters,— our Mediterranean - like lakes, and our rivers great and full ; and I ventured to add that the regions of the West were admirably adapted to a system of internal navigation.

These journeys were doubtless salutary ; but the principal cause of his renewed vigor was a change of diet, of the nature and effect of which he gives the following description : —

When my health began to fail in 1821 and 1822, I was under the common delusion that debility and functional derangement must be overcome by a moderate use of stimulants. I had used the oxide of bismuth as an anti-dyspeptic remedy, but with no serious benefit. The muscular system was enfeebled along with the digestive, the nervous power was thrown out of healthy action, an indescribable discomfort deprived me in a great degree of physical enjoyment, and the mind became unequal to much intellect-

ual effort.   My spirits, were however, cheerful ; and even
when I was unable to sustain a conversation with a calling
stranger, I still believed that I should recover, for my
physicians, after careful examination, could find no proof
of any organic disease, but only of functional derangement.
I yielded for a time to the popular belief that good wine
and cordials were the lever which would raise my depressed power ; but the relief was only temporary: a flash
of nervous excitement produced an illusive appearance of
increased vigor with which the mind sympathized ; the
transient brightness was soon clouded again, and no permanent benefit followed ; but often disturbed slumbers,
with nocturnal spasms and undefined terrors in dreams,
proved that all was wrong.   No medical man informed me
that I was pursuing a wrong course ; but the same wise
and good friend, to whom I have been already so much indebted, Mr. Daniel Wadsworth, convinced me, after much
effort, that my best chance for recovery was to abandon all
stimulants and adopt a very simple diet, and in such quantities, however moderate, as the stomach might be able to
digest and assimilate.   I took my resolution in 1823, in the
lowest depression of health.   I abandoned wine and every
other stimulant, including, for the time, even coffee and tea.
Tobacco had always been my abhorrence ; and opium, except medically, when wounded, I had never used.   With
constant exercise abroad, I adopted a diet of boiled rice,
bread and milk, — the milk usually boiled and diluted
with water, — plain animal muscle in small quantity,
varied by fowl and fish, avoiding rich gravies and pastry,
and occasionally using soups and various farinaceous preparations.   I persevered a year in this strict regimen, and
after a few weeks my unpleasant symptoms abated, my
strength gradually increased, and health, imperceptibly in
its daily progress, but manifest in its results, stole upon
me unawares.   While this course of regimen was in progress, I met at Mr. Wadsworth's the late Mr. William Wat-

son, who, as an invalid, had pursued a similar course, and, although consumptive, had recovered comfortable health. He gave me,— then beginning to recover strength — the fullest assurance that, as I had no organic disease, I should fully recover, provided I persevered ; and that in his opinion I should by-and-by be able to ride all night in the stage, and to perform all the labors to which I had been accustomed in former years. I was then at the meridian of life, in my forty-fourth year ; and in the almost thirty-six years that have elapsed since, I have resumed no stimulus which I then abandoned, except tea, and very rarely coffee. Tea is a cordial to me ; " it cheers but not inebriates." Tea and water are my only constant drinks ; milk I drink occasionally. I have not the smallest desire for wine of any kind, nor spirit, nor cider, nor beer ; cold water is far more grateful than any of the drinks which I have named ever were. I never used them more than moderately, as they were formerly used in the most sober families. If any person thinks that wine and brandy are useful to him, he cannot, at this day, have any assurance that they are not manufactured from whiskey, with many additions, and some of them noxious. Very little port wine has seen Portugal, or madeira wine Madeira, or champagne wine France ; and if we would have pure wines, and avoid imposition, they must be manufactured at home from grapes or other fruits ; and sugar and age are all that are needed to make them very good.

I cannot dismiss this topic without adding that Mr. Watson's predictions have been fulfilled. Some of my most arduous labors have been performed since my recovery. I have not only been able, as Mr. Watson predicted, to travel all night in the stage, but to travel extensively both at home and abroad ; to lecture to popular audiences in many towns and cities, — some of them far away ; to write and publish books ; to ascend the White Mountains of New Hampshire in 1837 ; to explore copper mines in the Blue Ridge of Virginia in 1856; twice to traverse the Atlantic and portions of the Mediterranean; and to ascend Mount Bolca, near Verona, Mount Vesuvius, and Mount Etna, at seventy-two years of age, in 1851. I record these facts, not with any feeling of vanity or pride, but with deep gratitude to God; and I am influenced more than all by the wish to warn my children, and my children's children, to obey God's physical as well as moral laws, and so remember, if they would enjoy health and long life, that they must not waste their physical powers upon extraneous indulgences, but must be satisfied with nutritious food, water, or watery fluids and milk for drink, regular and sufficient sleep, and a due regulation of all propensities, physical, moral, and intellectual. With a good conscience and a faithful discharge of duty, which will naturally result from the course which I have sketched, they will pass on agreeably and usefully through life, and may expect, under the influence of religious principles and the hopes which they inspire, to meet death without dismay.

Resignation of Mr. Andrews. — I have kept Mr. Andrews in view so long, because his services were of the utmost importance to me during three to four years of feeble or fluctuating health, — from 1821 to 1824. During this anxious crisis, he sustained and served me with much ability, and with the zeal of an affectionate son. Without such aid I could hardly have retained my place in the College. He remained with me until my health was restored; and he has been ever since held by me and my family in grateful remembrance. His chosen profession was the law, in the study of which he had been more or less engaged during his residence with me. In 1825 he resigned his place as assistant in my department, and, soon after, he established himself in Cleveland, Ohio, in his profession, having married Miss Ursula Allen, daughter of the late Hon. John Allen of Litchfield, an eminent lawyer, and a member of Congress from Connecticut, — an estimable lady, still surviving, with a happy family of four daughters and a son. Mr. Andrews has taken a high stand in his profession, both at the bar and as a judge. He served in one Congress; but, not being pleased with life in Washington and with life in Congress, he returned to his profession in Cleveland. He is a learned and eloquent advocate, a man of great integrity and purity of character, ardent and earnest in support of a good cause, and not disposed to engage in one that is bad. His high position and success in life have gratified me very much, as I cherish towards him a paternal regard. The children of Mr. Andrews are among our cherished and personal friends.

Benjamin Douglass Silliman was the successor of S. J. Andrews. Mr. Silliman was graduated in Yale College in 1824. As the designated successor of Mr. Andrews, he was more or less associated with him in the laboratory in the last year of his College life, in order to become gradually initiated into the duties of the department. He also aided Mr. Andrews in writing for me by dictation, or by copying; and these gentlemen being persons of genial temper and temperament, and congenial withal, they brightened the laboratory by their wit and good humor. Mr. Silliman, being the oldest son of my brother, Gold S. Silliman, I may be presumed to have been partial to him; but I would not, on that account, fail to do him justice, although he will, in this narrative, fill a much smaller space than that allotted to Mr. Andrews. This is not merely because he remained with me only one year, — for that brief period was sufficient to develop the interesting and valuable traits of his character, — but to delineate him as he was, it would be necessary very nearly to repeat the account of Mr. Andrews, for *mutato nomine de illo, historia non fabula narratur.* He was equally kind, equally de-

voted, and equally quick and skilful with his pen, — quick
also in apprehension, and judicious and prompt in execution. The affairs of his father and family, and his own
interests, took him from me within one year after Mr.
Andrews left me; but I have long had the pleasure of
seeing him in the first rank at the New York Bar, and
beloved and admired for his winning manners, his talents,
and generous and noble social qualities. . . . . . Mr.
Silliman has, very wisely, avoided being drawn into the
turbulent maelstrom of politics, from which very few escape unharmed. He has pursued quietly his professional
course, with the exception of being once a member of
the Legislature at Albany; and, like his early friend,
Mr. Andrews, avoiding political life, he has acquired both
honor and emolument in his professional course. He
very reluctantly yielded, a few years since, to the urgent
solicitations of his fellow-citizens in the district in which
he resided, to be nominated for an election to Congress,
and I took occasion to congratulate him upon his defeat,
as, had he succeeded, it would have been a serious injury to his professional business; for in Congress it is
rare that any one saves much money, or gains in reputation.

Dr. Burr Noyes was also of my family, his father being
my eldest half brother. He was of the same graduating
class with Mr. B. D. Silliman, and had been engaged in the
study of medicine, at or near his native home, Norfield and
Saugatuck in Fairfield County. He was intelligent, faithful, and studious; and as chemistry had a favorable bearing
on his professional studies, I offered him the place of assistant, when Mr. Silliman resigned. He retained it only
long enough to make me regret losing him so soon. He
passed but one winter with me, and he would have become
a still more useful assistant, had his experience been equal
to his fidelity. In the spring of 1826, after the chemical
lectures were ended, he received temporary overtures for

settlement as a physician at Chester, a parish of Saybrook in Connecticut. I could not refuse to release him, especially as the happiness of another was deeply involved in his success. He so early proved himself an able practitioner that he did not long delay to introduce a lovely partner into his house, but death removed her within a few weeks,— a very noble woman, who left him broken-hearted. A sudden hemorrhage from his lungs, induced by the attempt to hold in a hard-mouthed, running horse, ended in a rapid consumption, and he was laid in an early grave. He died July 2, 1830.

Charles Upham Shepard. — This gentleman had been for a year residing in New Haven as a student of natural science. He had brought with him a reputation for the love of science, especially of mineralogy and chemistry, and he had given lectures to some of the schools in Boston. His manners were amiable and gentlemanly, and his moral character pure. He was not an alumnus of Yale College, but of Amherst. Dr. Noyes had been acquainted with him, and as he mentioned Mr. Shepard's name as a successor to himself, I offered him the place and it was accepted. Mr. Shepard was already a proficient in mineralogy, and his services were at this time particularly acceptable in that department, as I was now to resume the lectures in the Cabinet, which had been suspended or imperfectly given of late. He was also, to a considerable extent, acquainted with geology, and was advancing in both of these departments. He had formed habits of travelling to observe localities of minerals, fossils, &c., and his views were directed to science as the business of life.

Mr. Shepard retained the office until 1831, — five years ; he discharged the duties of his station with zeal, fidelity, and ability. His taste was eminently scientific ; he loved science for its own sake, and found his happiness in its pursuits ; of course, his society was congenial and we proceeded in our mutual duties with entire harmony. His manners were habitually polite and respectful, and his temper so amiable, that during our whole intercourse there was never a moment of irritation, still less of alienation.

Professor Oliver Payson Hubbard was an alumnus of Yale College, of the Class of 1828. He came from Hamilton College at Clinton, N. Y.; and although he joined the Junior Class in Yale, not having the advantage of the instruction of the previous years in that institution, he took a high rank among his classmates, and was greatly respected for his intelligence, his virtues, and attainments. He had the warm recommendation of Professor Olmsted, and was agreeably remembered by me as an attentive hearer of the lectures, and as indicating by his inquiries both intelligence, curiosity, and habits of observation.

Mr. Hubbard remained with me five years, and his services were very important. His intelligence and gentlemanly bearing made him very acceptable to the strangers who very often called upon us. He was also highly acceptable to the students, whom he treated with affability and kindness. His punctuality, his exactness in affairs, and perfect integrity, made him entirely reliable, while his knowledge of science in all the branches that belonged to the department qualified him to render efficient assistance.

Professor Silliman proceeds to speak in warm terms of the eminent ability manifested by Mr. Dana, who succeeded to the post vacated by Mr. Hubbard. " Mr. Dana's works," he remarks, " are of the highest authority, and place him among the first scientific men of the age." He also dwells with tender feeling upon the long - continued assistance rendered him by his son, Mr. Benjamin Silliman, Jr., and his earnest and successful devotion to scientific pursuits. Honorable mention is made of his last regular assistant, Mr. Mason C. Weld, one of the present editors of " The American Agriculturist." Among the gentlemen who were more or less associated with him as occasional assistants are Mr. William Blake, Prof. T. Sterry Hunt, Prof. Charles H. Porter, Prof. John P. Norton, Prof. George J. Brush, and Prof. William H. Brewer, names since distinguished in the annals of American science.

In 1830, Professor Silliman published, in two volumes, his " Elements of Chemistry." This extended work was mainly written in a little room connected with his laboratory, to which he retired after taking his tea, laboring at his task sometimes until near midnight. He says of the work : —

In the preface to the first volume, I find the following statement of my embarrassments. " If it does not excuse, it may account for, some inadvertencies, when it is known that an arduous and responsible work was written and printed under the unremitting pressure of absorbing and often conflicting duties. Life is flying fast away, while in the hope of discharging more perfectly our duties to our fellow-men, we wait in vain for continued seasons of leisure and repose, in which we may refresh and brighten our faculties and perfect our knowledge. But after we are once engaged in the full career of duty, such seasons never come. Our powers and our time are placed in incessant requisition, there is no discharge in our warfare, and we must fight our battles, not in the circumstances and position we would have chosen, but in those that are forced upon us by imperious necessity." . . . . . Its reception by candid men was quite favorable. I received many expressions of approbation ; and teachers of chemistry regarded it as a magazine of valuable facts, disposed in an orderly and practicable way, so that they could avail themselves of its affluence in materials. The work also contains exact and ample directions for the successful performance of experiments, especially of those which are attended with difficulty or danger. I had been a zealous and active experimenter, and rarely met with a failure. I recorded in my work the results of twenty-five years of experience, and my contributions to practical chemistry were regarded as generous and valuable. I had the satisfaction to find that processes, which I had regarded as my own, were, in various instances, similar to, or identical with, those which Professor Faraday had published in his very valuable work on chemical manipulations, which I had not then seen.

Considering the size of the work it went off with reasonable rapidity, and could I have found time to revise and cast it anew with corrections and improvements, and with more condensation, its vitality might have been continued.

If I had found such a work as I had myself written, I should never have undertaken a duty which proved to be extremely laborious, and with the result of which I was dissatisfied, because I had overshot my mark, and therefore, as a manual for those who attended on my lectures, I could not but regard it as a failure. In a more elevated view it was no failure. It was a very valuable work for professors and teachers in colleges who, I have been assured, held it in high estimation. Everything considered, however, I was not well satisfied, and I have never ceased to regret that I committed myself, as I did, by commencing the publication while I was lecturing, and with the vain hope that I could write and print even a brief work so rapidly that I could keep pace with my own doings in the lecture-room.

With the foregoing chapter may be connected some letters of a miscellaneous character, a portion of which relate to the topics of the preceding narrative.

The first of them have a melancholy interest, as emanating from Professor A. M. Fisher, just prior to his departure on board the ill-fated *Albion*.

FROM PROFESSOR A. M. FISHER.

WALL-STREET HOUSE, *March* 28, 1822.

MY DEAR SIR, — I have just time to inform you, before the departure of the boat, that I have concluded to take my passage in the *Albion*, which starts for Liverpool on Monday next, at ten A. M. I previously went, in company with Mr. Doolittle, on board of two Danish vessels bound to Havre; but have concluded not to take passage in either of them, for three very good reasons: 1st. They will neither of them sail under two or three weeks. 2d. They have very wretched accommodations. 3d. They positively refuse taking any passengers. The *Albion* has most excellent accommodations. I have arranged everything to my satisfaction with the captain, and have my passage (all liquors included except wines) for thirty guineas. It is now probable that I shall make the former half of my residence abroad in England, and the latter in France. . . . . .

FROM PROFESSOR A. M. FISHER.

NEW YORK, *March* 31, 1822.

MY DEAR SIR, — I have just received your bulky packet of letters, and need not tell you under what obligations I feel to you for furnishing so many more than I had any claim on you for, or than I anticipated. The few words of advice at the close of your letter are very comprehensive, and I shall endeavor to profit by them. I have picked up a very considerable number of letters, which will be valuable to me, during my short stay here, and that with very little solicitation. Mr. Griscom, alone, besides a great deal of useful information, will furnish me with eight or ten. Dr. Mitchell is now very busy with his medical examination, but promises to send out a number of letters after me for the Continent. I have seen a good deal of the Doctor, and am not sorry that I took your advice in regard to making myself acquainted with him. I trust that I shall hear from some of you every few weeks, and that you will not wait till you hear from me before you begin to write. . . . . . I feel ashamed of sending you two such scrawls as this and my last; but I have not been able to arrange matters so but that it has been absolutely necessary to dispatch a half dozen letters since ten o'clock this evening; and I shall be called up to-morrow at five. With the sincerest wishes for the restoration of your health, and the welfare of your family during my absence, I remain,

Dear sir,

Yours with high esteem and respect,

A. M. FISHER.

FROM PROFESSOR A. M. FISHER.

NEW YORK, April 1, 1822.

MY DEAR SIR, — Since I despatched the letter for you by the steamboat, it has occurred to me that perhaps Dr. Morse would be willing to make me the bearer of a line to Mr. Wilberforce. . . . . . . *Steamboat Nautilus*, half-past ten. —We are now going down the harbor to the *Albion ;* fair weather, and a west wind which promises to take us out of sight of land before night. I will thank you to inform Mr. Twining, as I have no time to write him again, that Mr. Catlin will write him and inform him what is the current value of five-franc pieces; and to get word to Mr. Orr, of Hartford, if you can do it without any trouble, of the receipt of his last communication. This is my last communication to my friends in New Haven. So I bid you and them an affectionate adieu.

A. M. F.

This proved, in truth, the " *last* communication " of its gifted author to his New Haven friends.

FROM MRS. L. H. SIGOURNEY.

HARTFORD, *November* 26, 1822.

. . . . . MY principal object in writing at the present time is to request your acceptance of the volume that accompanies this letter. You may possibly recollect that it was on the eve of publication just before my marriage, — and was delayed in conformity to the wishes of my husband. Since that period, he has been anxious that I should devote my intervals of leisure to its improvement, and after it had received considerable additions, became desirous that it should appear. I am conscious that it retains many defects, and think it will not prove a popular work, since the modern taste seems drawn more powerfully to productions where the entertainments of fiction predominate. My principal anxiety respecting it, is to remain concealed, and to gain something from its sale for the religious charities to which it is devoted. The secret of its publication and authorship are only known in this place to my dear Mr. and Mrs. Wadsworth, beyond whom I hope it will not go. I am happy to be permitted to give you and Mrs. Silliman and your mother this mark of my confidence; and with sincere wishes that the Almighty will send the richest of His blessings upon your heads, both in this life and the next, remain,

Yours, with

Esteem and affection,

L. H. SIGOURNEY.

A frequent correspondent of Mr. Silliman, was his brother-in-law, Mr. Wadsworth, who expressed himself with force and decision on whatever subject he wrote. The letter below discovers a strong impression that a new style of preaching was coming into vogue, though Dr. Beecher would hardly have accepted this representation of his views.

FROM MR. WADSWORTH.

HARTFORD, *February* 14, 1825.

. . . . THE influence which has so long prevailed at New Haven on religious subjects, has extended to Hartford. Mr. Maffit seems to have been the original cause. Mr. Beecher has been here nearly a fortnight, and preaches almost every night to the most crowded audiences in one or the other of our meeting-houses. I have never heard him but once *before*, but now five times. He is certainly a most uncommon man in his way. But I have not been so much surprised at his power of stating in a clear manner, without being tedious, his own views on religious subjects, as at his *entirely* giving up, or *sweeping away*, in as unqualified a manner as its greatest opposers could wish, the doctrine of election. He placed it exactly in the light that you and I have always viewed it. He also expressed his horror at the idea that Christ died only for the elect ; and declared that it was blasphemy to suppose that God had called upon us all to be saved (which he did) at the same time that he had made it impossible for a certain number to accept salvation, which he had offered to *all*, — and they could be *all* saved if they would. On these two points, he was so entirely the reverse of what I had always supposed him, and so explicit, that I take it for granted he has, like many other men, grown *older*, and consequently found out that there are some parts of the administration of the Almighty with which he is not as well acquainted as he *would have been* had his infallibility been as certain as he once believed it. Whether he may not at some other time absolutely contradict the whole of this, I do not know. But he *said* he made no metaphysical distinctions between *will* and *can*,

&c., &c., — and he seemed not to leave himself one knot-hole to creep out at on another occasion. He might as well have knocked down some of the ministers near him (as far as civility went) as to contradict them so to their teeth about what they had so labored to establish.

To a request to contribute to the purchase of the Cabinet, a cordial response was received

FROM HON. J. C. CALHOUN.

August 14, 1825.

MY DEAR SIR, — You do not mistake my feelings in supposing that I take deep interest in the prosperity of Yale College. Besides the feelings with which I regard it as one of her sons, (I trust not less strong than they ought to be,) I consider it one of the lights of the nation, which under Providence, has mainly contributed to guide this people in the path of political, moral, and religious duties. I regret that my contribution must fall so much short of my inclination. I had the misfortune last year to lose by fire my cotton crop and gin-house, which for the present has greatly limited my means. You will place me among the subscribers, and affix one hundred dollars to my name, which will be paid by the time mentioned in the printed address. Should there be any difficulty in making out the necessary sum to buy the collection, and thereby a greater effort become necessary on the part of the friends of Yale, I trust that you will not be backward in informing me, as I would, in that event, very cheerfully increase my contribution. My best respects to Mr. Day and Mr. Kingsley.

With sincere regard,

I am, &c., &c.,

J. C. CALHOUN.

B. SILLIMAN, Esq.

FROM MR.º JARED SPARKS.

BOSTON, *July* 26, 1826.

DEAR SIR, — I fear I can suggest few hints that will be of service to you on the subject you mention. My experience in the business of periodicals, it is true, has been considerable, but you know experience is not always the handmaid of wisdom or profit. In regard to the "North American Review," nothing has been done from the beginning but to let it take care of itself. For the first four or five years, it languished, and its friends aimed at little more than to keep its head above water, and to prevent the living principle from becoming quite extinct. Since that time it has been more successful, and still continues to receive an increased, substantial support of the public. From the nature of this work, it must of course be adapted to a greater number of readers, in this country particularly, than are strictly scientific; yet it cannot be doubted that there are scientific readers enough among us to afford a most liberal patronage to such a work as the "American Journal." The character of this latter is strictly national, and it is the only vehicle of communication in which an inquirer may be sure to find what is most interesting in the wide range of topics, which its design embraces. It has become, in short, not more identified with the science than the literature of the country. In regard to the means of promoting the circulation, I would remark, in the first place, that I am convinced any attempt at a forced subscription by sending out runners to importune people, for this or any other work, will result in more harm than good. There is no difficulty in procuring any number of names in this way, but every name increases the expenses. The greater part will fall off at the end of one year, and many of the remainder will never pay anything. This system has been the ruin of many of our periodicals, and came near destroying the "Edinburgh" and "Quarterly" when first set up in this country.

There are two general classes of people who ought to take the " American Journal of Science," first, — those who are particularly interested in its subjects ; and secondly, gentlemen not particularly devoted to any branch of study, but who seek for valuable and popular works to supply their libraries. In addition to these, every public library in the country should take a copy. A reasonable patronage from these sources would give the " Journal " a wide circulation, and afford it ample support, such as would remunerate the editors, publisher, and writers. In my mind, there is but one mode of effecting this with any tolerable chance of success, and that is for you to send out a circular, directed to certain individuals by name, stating the present condition of the " Journal," the importance it has acquired at home and abroad, the influence it is calculated to exercise on the progress of physical science in the country, by bringing together the acquisitions of men of talents, learning, and ardor ; also, the slender patronage it receives in proportion to the expense and labor of the work ; and such other things as may occur to you. Let this circular be sent only to such persons as you have good reason to suppose will feel an interest in the subject, such as contributors to the work, physicians of eminence, men of skill and practice in the mechanical arts, and professors of the sciences in the colleges. Nor should this be done through the publisher, but as coming directly from you, and with your own name, accompanied with such suggestions and arguments as you think will have weight. Let every one be solicited to procure names within the circle of his acquaintance, and let him be urged to this by motives of patriotism, a love of science, and the desire of encouraging research and the diffusion of important knowledge by affording suitable rewards. Whether such a plan would be successful I know not, but I should think it worthy of a trial, and in every way consistent with the character and dignity of your work. Meantime, the publisher must be spurred up to do his part.

Among those whose appreciation of his labors was grateful to Mr. Silliman, there were none whose praise was more valued than that of the author of the two letters which follow.

FROM HON. JOSIAH QUINCY (SENIOR.)

CAMBRIDGE, *November* 1, 1829.

DEAR SIR, — I had the pleasure some months since of receiving a small volume, containing the outline of your geological lectures, rendered doubly valuable from their being transmitted to me by the author. For next in degree to the satisfaction of being *laudatus a laudato viro,* is that of being remembered by him. I ought immediately to have acknowledged my sense of your kindness. I have, however, never thought it a compliment, and scarcely justice to an author, to return thanks for a work which one has not yet read. It happened in this case, that your volume came to hand while my mind was wholly occupied in preparing for the duties of a new official relation, unexpectedly devolved upon me ; and being myself, in this respect, in a sort of " transition state," by every rule of " chemical affinity," and " post-diluvial action," I thought it my duty to admit nothing into the sphere of operation, whether it were of " aggregation or crystallization," which might disturb the desired result. So I fairly laid your work upon the shelf, until " the activity " of the then " existing chemical agents " had ceased, and the " crust " of things here being duly " arranged," and my " transition " state passed, I should have leisure to attend to matters — speaking with reference to my own then existing necessities — of a " secondary formation."

That period having recently arrived, I have read your work, and permit me to add, with unqualified pleasure. Indeed, the interest was so great and intense, that it absolutely excluded every other thought. I did not lay it down until I had given it a complete perusal. The truth is, it is a work of that general and comprehensive kind, I apprehend, extremely wanted on the subject concerning which it treats; and it is admirably qualified to excite and direct the attention to its object. Be assured, sir, I take great delight in observing the regular and rapid extension of your fame and usefulness, and particularly am I happy to find that the public have given you so substantial and encouraging evidence of their sense of your merits by the recent enlarged subscription to your "Journal of Science." Wishing you every success,

I am, very respectfully,
Your obedient servant,
JOSIAH QUINCY.

BENJAMIN SILLIMAN, LL. D.

FROM HON. JOSIAH QUINCY (SENIOR.)

CAMBRIDGE, March 10, 1831.

DEAR SIR, — I have received your kind favor of the 18th ult., and your excellent work on chemistry of which your letter was a precursor. It will not be, I assure you, among "*the mutes*" of my library. Its station is at present on my parlor-table, where it is seen, examined, and approved by the many intelligent men, who are my occasional or weekly visitants. When it takes its station in my library, it will be often resorted to for reference or comparison, and with the more interest from the deep personal respect I entertain for its profound and laborious author. From the cursory survey I have yet been alone able to give it, I cannot question that the effort has been successful to the extent of your hopes, and that it will be a most useful text-book, subserving powerfully the cause of instruction in the branch to which it relates.

Present me respectfully to President Day and the learned gentlemen in your vicinity to whom you may know I am not unknown. It gives me great pleasure to find that Dr. Webster is reaping late in life the harvest, at least of ap-

probation if not of reward, for which he has been so faith-•
fully laboring.. His dictionary has certainly great merit.
In my own library it stands by the side of half a dozen
others. It never fails to be by me first consulted, and
almost ever with success.· In a manner, it has in point of
fact superseded the use of all others. Again repeating my
thanks for your polite attention,

I am, very respectfully,
Your obedient servant,
JOSIAH QUINCY.

BENJAMIN SILLIMAN, Esq.

"Professor Silliman had met Lafayette during the
progress of the latter through this country, and afterwards received from him several tokens of remembrance.

FROM LAFAYETTE.

PARIS, February 21, 1827.

MY DEAR SIR, — I am requested by Mr. Juillet, who has
been attached to the foreign department, to give him some
letters of introduction to the United States, where he is
making a literary tour, with a view, I suppose, to publish
his observations. The learned traveller cannot but find
everywhere grounds for admiration, but nowhere more
than in his acquaintance with the city of New Haven and
with Doctor Silliman. Happy I am, my dear sir, in this
opportunity, to be affectionately remembered to my friends,
and to tell you once more that I am, with all my heart,

Your grateful friend,
LAFAYETTE.

FROM LAFAYETTE.

PARIS, July 30, 1828.

MY DEAR SIR, — I am happy in every opportunity to
remember myself to you and to our friends at New Haven;
this instance is peculiarly gratifying. General Verveer, a

·very distinguished gentleman, lately the Dutch Minister at the Congress of Panama, now returning to that part of the country, did me the honor of a visit with his amiable daughter. I also called upon them, and both acquaintances left me the regret of their sudden departure, as they are to sail by the next packet. I found Miss Ververer a most agreeable young lady, and what won my heart, a most decided Connecticut patriot, as she has been educated in New Haven, and is returning to your so justly beloved city. I would feel a great pleasure to think I may somewhat contribute to the welcome to which her accomplishments and American feelings justly entitle her, and I thought the object would be in some measure attained by giving her the pleasant charge of a letter to you. My dear sir, remember me affectionately to your family and friends, and accept the affection and regards of

Your most sincere friend,

LAFAYETTE.

Professor Silliman, although opposed to the last war with Great Britain, which he deemed to be unnecessary, felt a warm interest in the achievements of our navy in that contest. The following letter is from the commander of the *Constitution*, and relates to the action which resulted in the capture of the British ship *Guerriere*.

FROM COMMODORE ISAAC HULL.

NAVY YARD, CHARLESTOWN,
October 29, 1821.

DEAR SIR, — I some days since had the pleasure to receive your letter of the 15th instant, but my time has been so constantly taken up on duty since, that I could not give you the information you asked for ; nor can I now, in writing, in a way that you would be likely to understand it. I have therefore endeavored to show you the manner

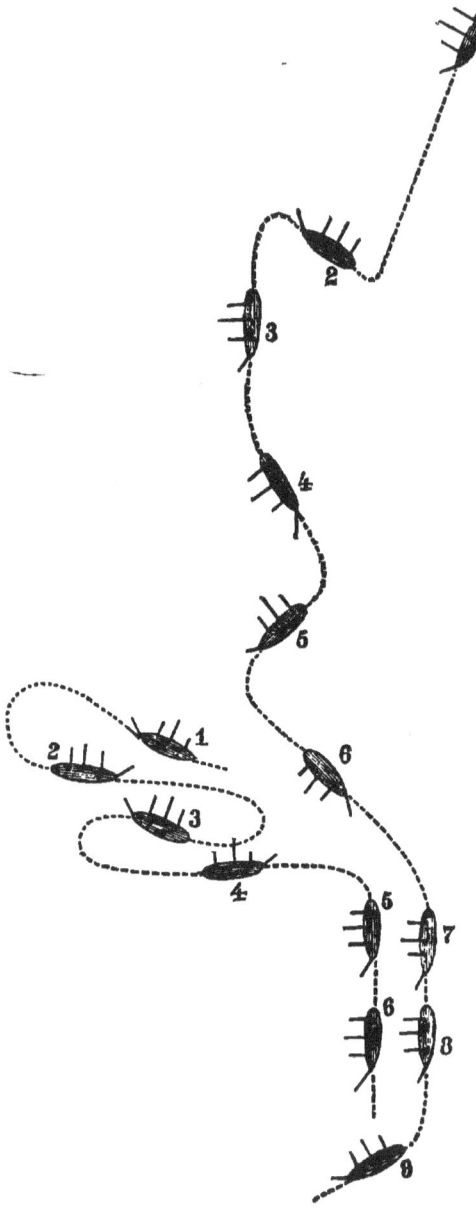

Fig. 1. The Constitution, running before the wind with all sail set, sees the Guerriere on a wind under her topsails, standing to the southward and westward.

Fig. 2. Constitution hauls to; shortens sail, and prepares for action.

Fig. 3. Constitution begins to bear down upon the Guerriere, who is laying with her main topsail aback, and occasionally wearing, as in the diagram. Guerriere commences firing on the Constitution at fig. 12, being about two miles' distant.

Figs. 4, 5, 6. Constitution still pressing down upon the Guerriere and receiving her fire as she wears.

Fig. 7. Constitution alongside the Guerriere. First opens her fire and shoots away her mizzen mast.

Fig. 8. Constitution still alongside the Guerriere, and to windward—*close fighting.*

Fig. 9. Constitution is endeavoring to lay her aboard, on the larboard-bow, shoots ahead and crosses her bows ; immediately after, her fore and main masts fall by the board.

Fig. 10. The Guerriere, under double reefs standing on a wind to the southward and westward.

Fig. 11. Commences firing on the Constitution, then wears and lays with her main topsail aback.

Fig. 12. Fires, and again wears (as short round as possible.)

Fig. 13. Bears up before the wind, to make a running fight.

Fig. 14. Alongside the Constitution. Loses her mizzen-mast.

Fig. 15. Constitution attempts to lay her aboard on the larboard bow, but shoots ahead and crosses her bows ; immediately after her main and fore masts fall.

in which the *Constitution* approached the *Guerriere* whilst in chase, by giving you the track of each of the ships, by which you will see that during the action they were before the wind. Of course no advantage was lost by me in having taken the larboard side instead of the starboard, for, as the wind was directly aft, one was as much the weather-side as the other.

I am proud that my friends are pleased to consider that I possessed humanity on that occasion ; but I should regret that they should for a moment suppose that any advantage that might have offered would have been overlooked by me, as, by doing so, the honor of the nation and my own reputation would have been put at hazard.

For fear that you may not understand the manner in which the ships approached each other, by the tracks accompanying this letter, I have requested my friend Captain Macdonough to call and see you on the subject, and explain any part that you may have doubt about.

I do not wish any remarks I have made published, but leave you to make such corrections as to you may appear proper, after being assured that no advantage on my part was given to the enemy. With very great respect and sincere regard,

I am, Sir,
Your friend and obt. servant,
ISAAC HULL.

BENJ. SILLIMAN, Esq.,
 New Haven.

Interesting political observations are found in the subjoined letter

FROM JUDGE DESAUSSURE.

COLUMBIA, S. C., *November* 1, 1830.

. . . . . I HOPE your fine Institution is in the most prosperous state. The cause of literature is a common cause ; and we must rely upon education as the foundation for the permanency of our Republic and its liberal institutions. God grant that we may have the wisdom to preserve them! There is great and almost universal discontent in this State at the imposition of enormous duties for protection, greatly beyond the actual wants of the government for legitimate purposes, — such as the payment of the debt, the civil list, the army, navy, and other indispensable objects. It is believed that a tariff for protection is against the spirit of the Constitution, and that it is oppressive, unequal, and unjust. It is therefore very generally odious, and is weakening the, attachment of the South to the Union, though the value of that is felt and appreciated, — for you may be assured that all charges of a desire to separate from the Union are fables of a distempered imagination. It may ultimately come to that, because our people would prefer even that deplorable measure to having a government of unlimited powers. At present we are divided into nearly equal parts, — not at all as to the evil, but as to the remedy, and to the degree of forbearance. If the tariff of protection and vast expenditures for internal improvements become the settled policy of the government, beyond all hope of redress, the separation of the Union will inevitably follow; which I pray God I may not live to see. . . . . .

Among the persons who had the misfortune to fall under College discipline, but who did not lose their respect and affection for Professor Silliman, was the distinguished novelist, Mr. Cooper. In a long letter, of which a part is here given, he adds to political speculations on the state of Europe some recollec-' tions of Yale.

FROM MR. J. FENIMORE COOPER.

PARIS, *June* 10, 1831.

. . . . . Now France is guilty of the extreme folly of attempting to imitate a system which is just found out to be intolerable to those who have some relief for its abuses. France has no countries subsidiary to her prosperity, and the sentiment of the nation is opposed to aristocracy, and yet such is the secret object of her present rulers. They do not see that England has got on in spite of her aristocracy, and not by its means, and that when the true agents of her wealth and power are beginning to fail her, that she cannot bear the inflictions of that aristocracy, and is about to get rid of it, too, along with other evils. But there is something so seductive in the social distinctions and the real superiority of the English gentlemen over their neighbors, that it proves too powerful for their patriotism. It is fashionable to say that France is not good enough for free institutions. Surely this involves a fallacy. Free institutions mean the responsibility of the rulers to the ruled; and the worse the former are, the greater is the need of this responsibility. We trust the word of an honorable man; we look for bond and mortgage from a knave. If men were virtuous, government would be unnecessary. A strong police can exist in a republic; the strongest and best in Europe is in Switzerland, — and that is all which is required to suppress ordinary vice; and, as to public corruption, surely the more responsibility the better.

Again, there is no better training for public virtues than publicity and freedom. You will ask me what I expect from all this. It is my opinion things cannot stand as they are. The press is virtually free in France, and five years have made a great change in its tone. The government has been guilty of the weakness of offering a premium to all the revolutionists in Europe to overturn them, since without France no other country can get on. I have little respect for the king, though I think he is rather a weak than a bad man. It is impossible to foretell what course events will take in this inflammable nation, but the movement cannot be stopped. There will be more or less freedom all over Europe fifty years hence, or even sooner. Public opinion has already secured it in most countries, despotic or not in name, and public opinion will exact pledges for its continuance. At present all the efforts of France are turned towards peace. If this were done with a good motive, it would be respectable, though it were weak. But the motive is a narrow selfishness. The powers that be know that a war, in the present state of Europe, would inevitably throw the people uppermost; and this is a result they are determined to avoid at any hazard. They wish to be nobles, and in that vulgar reason you have what just now forms the whole spring of English and French policy — self, self, self.

I am sorry I can tell you nothing of the person you name. I never saw him but on that occasion, and I think I was told that he was a clerk in the office of the " Revue Encyclopédique." It is nothing unusual for men of very indifferent pretensions in Europe to make a figure in America. Still, if he has imparted anything as from himself, you will naturally estimate him by what he has done, rather than by what he is. The journal to which he was then attached is of no great reputation itself, nor do I know that there is a single French literary journal of any reputation. Europe rates our men very differently from what they are rated at home, and we rate theirs in the same way. If we understood each other's terms better, we should not make so many blunders. When I first reached Europe, I was all wonder at the ignorance of this part of the world concerning ourselves, and now that I have leisure to look about me, I am all wonder at the ignorance of America concerning Europe. I see by the returns that your little city grows. I could wish you to mention me to Mr. Day and Mr. Kingsley; I dare say I should say Dr. Kingsley, but of this I am in the dark. I remember the latter with affection. He did his duty, and more than his duty by me; and could I have been reclaimed to study by kindness, he would have done it. My misfortune was extreme youth. I was not sixteen when you expelled me. I had been early and highly educated for a boy, — so much so as to be far beyond most of my classmates in Latin; and this enabled me to play — a boy of thirteen! — all the first year. I dare say Mr. Kingsley never suspected me of knowing too much, but there can be no great danger now in telling him the truth. So well was I grounded in the Latin that I scarce ever looked at my Horace or Tully until I was in his fearful presence; and if he recollects, although he had a trick of trotting me about the pages in order to get me mired, he may remember that I generally came off pretty well. There is one of my college adventures which tickles me, even to this day. I never studied but one regular lesson in Homer. The poor bell, or a cold, or some letter had to answer for all the others. Well, when the class reviewed, I clapped another fifty or sixty lines to the old lesson, and went to recitation. The fact was notorious, — so notorious that the division used to laugh when I was called up for a Homeric excuse. Examination came at length, and Mr. Stuart, between whom and myself I cannot say there were any very strong sympathies, was examining. I had calculated my distance, and by aid of the Latin translation, which I read as easily as English, I was endeavoring to find out what Homer meant in a certain paragraph that I anticipated would fall to my lot. I remember that I sweated. The examiner was not disposed to give me the benefit of my recent application, but skipped me over the whole book. I found the new place amid a general titter, and lo! it was in the very heart of my two lessons. As we sailors say, there was plenty of sea-room, and I had half a mind to ask the examiner to take his pick. As it was, I got through admirably, and I believe greatly to the astonishment of the examiner; and I know it was highly to the amusement of my own tutor, whose laughing eyes seemed to say, "This is what my boys can do without study." If I ever write my Memoir, the college part of it will not be the least amusing. On one occasion, a tutor of the name of Fowler was scraped in the hall.

Now I was charged with being one of his assailants, *by himself*, and was arraigned before you all in conclave. You presided, and appealed to my honor to know whether I scraped or not. I told you the truth that I did not, for I disliked the manner of assailing a man *en masse*. You believed me, for we understood each other, and I was dismissed without even a reproof. You told me you believed me, and I was not a boy to deceive any one who had that sort of confidence in me. This little court made a pleasant impression on me which I remember to this day. I hope to return next summer, and certainly I shall come and take a-look at old Yale. You cannot claim me in public, for the reason that Dr. Busby wore his hat before King Charles; but I hope you will not turn your backs on me in private. I can sit in the gallery at least. Is Mr. Twining living? I could wish to be recalled to the memory of both him and his wife. I trust I have not wearied you with my gossip. If I can be of any use to you at Paris, where I shall pass most of the present year, I beg you to command me.

With great respect and regard,

I remain, dear sir,

Yours faithfully,

J. FENIMORE COOPER.

DR. SILLIMAN, Yale College.

In looking over your letter I see I ought to have explained to you that no moment has Paris been in serious danger of disturbance, except at that when the Ministers were acquitted. Lafayette then saved the king, and the next week he was turned out of his office. He can dethrone Louis Philippe even now, when he shall please, but he acts on principle. The other affairs were mere riots of no great moment, though they looked ominous on paper. You are quite wrong in thinking France in danger of despotism. Bonaparte himself could not now enslave this nation, — rely on it. The new generation is too enlightened, and has too much the habit of liberty for that.

CHAPTER XIV.

His Lectures outside of College. — Course of Geology in Hartford (1834). —
Lectures in Lowell: Daniel Webster and Jeremiah Smith. — Course on
Geology in Boston (1835). — Hospitable Treatment in Boston. — Party at
Dr. Warren's. — Governor Winthrop. — Party at Mr. Nathan Appleton's.
— Judge Davis. — Dinner at General William Sullivan's.— Judge Story.
— Dr. Gannett. — Interview with Mr. Abbott Lawrence. — Lectures in
Salem: Mr. S. C. Phillips: Dr. Prince: Mr. Silsbee: Judge White.

THIS chapter marks a new epoch in Mr. Silliman's
life. Hitherto his lectures had been addressed to
students within the walls of College. He was now
to step forth upon a broader arena, and to become
the teacher of the people.* Popular lectures were
then comparatively a novel thing. Perhaps he, more
than any other person, was instrumental in bringing
this mode of instruction into vogue in the country.
He had some rare qualifications to act in this capacity. He had been for many years an assiduous
student of the branches which he taught, and was
fully possessed of their principles and facts. He
knew how to produce brilliant effects by experiments,
which he so prepared that they almost never failed.
As a public speaker, he was dignified, animated, and
fluent. At the same time his engaging manners in
private conciliated the favor of all classes, and espe-

* He had, however, previously (in 1831–32 and 1832–33) given courses
of lectures on chemistry and geology to the mechanics of New Haven, in
the Franklin Institute, an establishment which, under his encouragement,
was founded and supported by a liberal-minded man, himself a mechanic,
James Brewster, Esq.

cially attracted to his lectures the refined and cultivated. The numerous courses which he gave in all parts
of the land were almost uniformly successful. He
kindled wherever he went a lively interest in the
study of physical science. And he was everywhere
the object of warm personal esteem and admiration.
Especially was this true in Boston. In that city his
lectures were thronged by audiences of the highest
respectability. Marks of personal regard in the form
of hospitality and social attention were showered
upon him. The six courses of lectures which he delivered in as many years in Boston formed, in his own
view, the brightest period in the history of his scientific labors. We quote from the " Reminiscences."

After April 1, 1834, a new era opened upon me. Public courses of lectures by me were called for in many
places, most of them out of Connecticut, and this call continued actively for twenty-three years, — from 1834 to
1857,—nor is it quite ended yet, at the close of twenty-five
years. Those lectures were given while I was between
fifty-five and eighty years of age. . . . . . . I was called
out in the maturity of my powers, experience, and reputation ; and while I enjoy the satisfactory assurance that I
have popularized science, these efforts brought important
assistance to my family at a period when my children were
requiring aid in their settlement in life. I conceive that
in no period of my life have my efforts been more useful,
both to my country and my family ; and' as regards professional labors, there is no part of my career which I
reflect upon with more satisfaction.

The Course of geology in Hartford, in April and May,
1834, was the first that I delivered out of New Haven.
The overture came through the kind attention of Alfred
Smith and Daniel Wadsworth, Esqrs. Their letter, dated

April 9, 1834, enclosed an official communication signed by Daniel Wadsworth, (private citizen,) Thomas S. Williams, (member of Congress and Judge,) Thomas Day, (Judge,) Joel Hawes, (minister of the First Church.) The following passages are extracted : " After the interesting lecture on geology, which you so kindly gave at Hartford last winter, January 10, 1834, a lively interest was felt to hear a full course from you on the same subject." " Our object in writing is to express the pleasure which we should receive from hearing a course of lectures on geology, and to ask whether you will be able and willing to attend here for that purpose." There was enclosed a subscription of two hundred dollars, with an assurance that it would in all probability be largely increased. The actual result was three hundred and fifty dollars.

This course was attended by from three to four hundred persons from among the most intelligent and estimable people of the place. The lecture-room of the Centre Church, — that of Rev. Dr. Hawes, — was conceded to me without charge, and I of course had a welcome home at Mr. Daniel Wadsworth's. I had a considerable collection of drawings, and had selected numerous specimens of minerals and fossils to illustrate my subject; they were stored in a room in the wing of Mr. Wadsworth's house, and every morning before breakfast, I devoted an hour in the lecture-room to meet those persons who wished to see the specimens more fully, and to hear additional explanations of them. The number of individuals who attended this second meeting was not indeed large, but they were attentive and interested. The number of lectures in a week was two and three, and the audience manifested decided satisfaction, while by this first experience out of New Haven, I was encouraged to listen to the next overture. I received a warm vote of thanks from the gentlemen who invited me to Hartford.

In the autumn of the same year, he accepted an invitation to give a course of lectures in Lowell. Among his auditors at one of these lectures was Daniel Webster.

I ought not to omit that the Hon. Daniel Webster, then in the very height of his power and fame, attended one of my lectures on geology. The subject was diluvial action and the deluge. As he lodged at our hotel I had an interview with him after the lecture. He entered into the subject with zeal, and discoursed upon it with energy and eloquence, showing that his great mind had not overlooked this subject; and many years afterwards our conversation was renewed.

The Hon. Jeremiah Smith, colleague with the Hon. Daniel Webster and Jeremiah Mason, in the famous cause of Dartmouth College and the State of New Hampshire, came to Lowell and delivered a lecture on the moral principles and character of Washington. It was a beautiful production, and to a gentleman who asked my opinion of it, I replied that it went right to my heart. Mr. Smith has much vivacity, and when my remark was reported to him, he replied that it could not go to a better place. It was one of those gay sallies which such men make without inquiring into their truth.

Boston Course on Geology, March and April, 1835. — So long ago as when the Hon. Josiah Quincy was President of the Boston Atheneum, I received, through him, an invitation from the trustees of that institution to deliver in their hall, for the public, a course of lectures on any subject which I might choose. The proposition interested me deeply as an unexpected honor. Being much inclined to accept it, I consulted my colleagues, and they unanimously encouraged me to make the attempt. My course of instruction in Yale College at that time filled the entire season of public lectures in the cities, and I was therefore constrained to decline.

Several years elapsed before the subject of lectures in Boston was again presented to me, but from a different source. Mr. William J. Loring, a lawyer in Boston, addressed me on behalf of a Boston society for the promotion of knowledge, desiring me to give a course of lectures in their city. I accepted the invitation, thinking that it presented a fair opportunity of introduction to the Athens of New England; I demanded nothing more than an honorable endorsement from the Society. Waiving all pecuniary stipulations, I agreed to take my chance, and to depend solely upon my own efforts for a favorable verdict and a competent remuneration.

He gives an account of his stay in Boston on this occasion, partly availing himself of brief memoranda written at the time. A portion of this account is presented below : —

Monday, March 2, (1835). — Dined with Mr. Edmund Dwight and friends, and the next day with Mr. William Lawrence, — a beautiful entertainment, and great hospitality. The morning of March 3d was passed with Robert* in the Temple in arranging the specimens into groups, and in preparing for the first lecture.

As I had never before appeared publicly in Boston as a lecturer, I thought it both fair towards my audience, and prudent as regards myself, to afford the citizens an opportunity to hear me before any of them should have been committed. After consultation with some friends, I decided upon a lecture which I believed would be interesting, as I felt assured it would be novel. As it was to be gratuitous, it would also be an indication, by the attendance, whether any interest was felt in the stranger now come among them. I gave the lecture at the instance of the Natural History

* Robert Park, his faithful colored servant. — F.

Society, and was introduced to the audience by Mr. William J. Loring, the gentleman through whom I had received the invitation to Boston. I dined once at Mr. Loring's, who had a lovely wife, — a Thorndike. He died the next year. A brother survives him, an eminent lawyer, with whom I also dined. . . . . . I entered the lecture-hall through a private door leading from my study. A large and brilliant audience was before me, — much larger than any one that I had ever addressed. I was awed but not abashed, and I entered upon the duty with good courage and entire self-possession. The room was more than full, — alleys and all, — the people filled the stairs, and were clustered around the door in crowds. My friend, Dr. Woodbridge Strong, told me that those who went away because they could not gain admittance, were more than the actual audience. They were differently estimated, by different persons, from 1000 to 1400; perhaps 1200 might have been nearer to the truth. Such an audience of intelligent and attentive persons was sufficiently encouraging. The subject of the lecture was Meteors. I spoke seventy minutes, — giving first an introductory view of luminous meteors, including lightning and shooting stars, — this being merely introductory to the meteoric fire-balls. Then followed a historical sketch of the arrival in our atmosphere of fire-balls, throwing down stones and iron, preceded and accompanied by violent explosions and cannon-like reports. The Weston Meteor of December 1807, was fully described, and a summary of the facts was given from my own investigations at the places and among the people where the event occurred. Specimens of the meteorites were then exhibited; their external characters and mechanical and chemical compositions, were explained. Theoretical views were then presented.

At the conclusion of the lecture, Mr. William J. Loring endorsed me, as being invited by the Society for Promoting Useful Knowledge, and he announced the ensuing course of geology; the first lecture in that course to be given on the next evening, March 4. The lecture on the meteors, having been designed merely to make myself known in Boston as a lecturer, was not properly a part of the intended course. It answered the object I had in view. The course of geology that followed, was my first great success, both as regards reputation and remuneration. The courses in Hartford and Lowell had gained for me a high reputation as a lecturer, and a moderate remuneration in money,— say $500 for both, and with the addition of the Lowell gift, about $600.

March 4, Wednesday. — After the evening lecture I went with the Rev. Dr. Channing to Rev. Mr. Parkman's,— both some years since deceased ; Mr. Parkman by a mysterious suicide, — to meet a literary and social club of sixty years' standing, — a very agreeable interview.

March 5. — In the morning I was almost entirely at home; received many calls; gave Robert liberty to go and amuse himself; wrote to B. S., Jr. Dined with Mr. Thomas Lamb (he and his lady and family are warm and constant friends to this day, — 1859). At Mr. Lamb's, met the Rev. Mr. Gannett, — a small and agreeable family circle. P. M. —Wrote to my English friend, Mr. Mantell, to Mr. Lyell, and others, to go by Mr. Henry Barnard. Did not go out in the evening.

March 6, Friday. — Ascertained at Mr. Wm. D. Ticknor's the state of payments for the lectures, — very satisfactory. Went to my private room in the Temple ; wrote to Robert Bakewell and O. Rich, London, by Mr. Barnard, and to Agassiz, Neufchatel ; to Mrs. S., at home. Made gases with Robert for the afternoon lecture. Dined at home ; was at the Temple in the afternoon. Received a very warm call and reiterated welcome in my Temple study, from Mr. John Parker and son, persons of high consideration here. Mr. Parker, the father, said that no stranger in such a character had ever had such a reception in Boston.

At Dr. Bigelow's in the evening, — a *soirée*. Present: President Quincy, President Kirkland, Alexander Everett, and many other eminent men, thirty to forty in number. All stood in two rooms; a table of refreshments was spread in one of them; came home at ten P. M. Met Dr. Wainwright, who says that the impression concerning the lectures is favorable.

March 7. — Called on Willard the painter, who wished to paint my portrait, and I am to sit for him on Monday, March 9th. At home, looking over my notes. Called at W. D. Ticknor's about the tickets; on Dr. Bowditch for missing volumes of the Academy, — very kindly welcomed; invited to tea. Dined at home.

"The first week of my very important and interesting probation in Boston is now closed, and very happily. · We have been signally prospered in everything. Nothing has failed, either in the lecture-room or in the city. The interest excited and the numbers in attendance are far beyond my expectation. I suppose that in both the courses there are twelve hundred persons. Surely goodness and mercy have followed me hitherto, and I will humbly and audibly acknowledge them in my chamber, and privately in my thoughts in the house of the Lord."

March 8th, Sabbath. — A storm of snow and rain; and a cold I had taken kept me at home in the morning. Read Dick's "Philosophy of Religion." P. M., attended in the Stone Chapel, — it was the King's Chapel before the Revolution; sermon by Mr. Greenwood, Unitarian, on the Temptation of our Saviour. After coffee at Dr. Wainwright's, went with him to the Boylston Hall to hear the Oratorio of the Handel and Haydn Society.

March 9th, Monday. — I sat one hour for Willard the artist, and wrote business letters. I dined with Dr. Jackson in his family, one son and four daughters, and two gentlemen friends. The sitting was rendered agreeable by rational and animated conversation. Tea at Mr. Edmund

Dwight's in the family, and at Professor Ticknor's. Showed the meteoric stones, and stated the case of the "American Journal." Professor Ticknor says, that I speak loud enough, but drop my voice near the end of a sentence and some words are lost. I attended a great Government party at Lieut.-Governor Armstrong's, — hundreds of gentlemen without one lady. At nine o'clock, I retired to read and write at home. Governor Armstrong, formerly a bookseller, is a man of noble person and mien, and courteous manners. I am well, and all goes well — charmingly indeed, — cordiality and interest and numbers far beyond my expectations. Robert * is well and does exceedingly well; he is much admired in his station, and is regarded by the audience as a sub-professor! . . . . .

March 11th, Wednesday Evening. — Room very full, seats all filled. I should think there were from eight hundred to nine hundred people, — the day-course notwithstanding. Great interest was manifested by the most profound attention, and I am assured that there was great satisfaction. In a letter of March 13, 1835, to Mrs. Silliman, I say: "Many people have been denied evening tickets, the seats being entirely occupied; and we are not willing to admit a crowd to annoy each other in the alleys and spaces. In consequence the day-course grows, but I cannot tell to what extent." "In addition to the remittance of $1022.50, already made to you, there is enough more paid in to make $2000; the expenses will be, all told, about $500, and $1500 will remain as my reward. Besides the money, my success here is really a triumph. The audience is not surpassed in numbers and intelligence by the assemblies at the Royal Institution in London. The interest is already intense, and the moral influence is said to be of the happiest kind. Clergymen, both Unitarian and Orthodox, thank me warmly for the manner in which they say that delicate points are treated. They tell me that the success of the lectures is

* His colored servant. — F.

without a precedent, even in the case of Dr. Spurzheim, as to the numbers attending and the interest excited." . . . .

March 12, *Thursday Evening.* — I did not think that I spoke as well as on the preceding evening; and have noted in my observations on this lecture that it is very important to be cool and deliberate. I had supposed that the subjects of this lecture might be rather dry, but I was assured that the audience manifested great interest and great satisfaction, while they gave profound attention and behaved with perfect decorum. The room was entirely filled, and all the seats occupied by apparently eight hundred or nine hundred persons. A few stood, and many were excluded at the door for want of room.

Day Lectures. — *Friday and Saturday.* — The two preceding lectures were repeated on the afternoons of Friday the 13th, and Saturday the 14th, to audiences from four hundred to five hundred persons. I began to feel and act naturally, and thought that I improved in speaking, and it became more easy. The audience on Saturday afternoon was larger than ever before, — nearly or quite five hundred. The audience was very attentive, and appeared to be deeply interested. In my notes I remark : " Everything goes well ; it must be my endeavor to sustain the interest, and this will be done by effectual preparation ; but my time (the people are so cordial and kind) is much cut up by calls and engagements, — sometimes fifty or sixty cards on the frame of the mirror, all reminding me of attentions to be returned. . . . . .

March 13. — After tea at home, went to Mrs. Lamb's party ; and then to Dr. Warren's *soirée* at 8½ o'clock, — a large number of gentlemen without ladies. Dr. Warren's is a splendid house. He showed us the Psalm-Book that was in the pocket of his uncle, General Joseph Warren, when he was slain at Bunker's Hill, June 17, 1775. It was taken out of his pocket by an English soldier, who carried it to England, where it was purchased by an English clergyman,

Dr. Wilton, who gave it to Dr. Gordon, the English historian of the Revolution, and he, I believe, sent it out to the family. It was of the Geneva edition of 1500 and some years, — a very small volume, and in very good order, containing the Psalms of David. . . . .

Saturday, March 14. — I called on the venerable Governor Winthrop. Arranged for the afternoon lecture at the Temple, and dined at home. Then to Dr. Bowditch to tea. We sat down at table in Connecticut style, — a rational and profitable evening ; a charming family, and Dr. Bowditch a delightful man. The translator and annotator of the "Mechanique Celeste" is at his fireside a bright and cheerful man, with buoyant spirits and the kindest manners. . . . .

March 15, *Sabbath.* — At Dr. Lothrop's — formerly Dr. Buckminster's and Dr. Kirkland's — church. In the morning, sermon on Hope, — a discourse very well written and well spoken. Dr. Lothrop ranks as a Unitarian ; — is much esteemed. Mr. Abbott Lawrence attends here. Afternoon at Dr. Wainwright's church, — Episcopal. A very good sermon. Evening, — tea at Mr. William Lawrence's ; supper at Professor Ticknor's. . . . . . .

March 16, *Monday.* — Forenoon at the Temple. Packing things that have been exhibited and are not wanted here again. Arranging for the next lecture. Calls from Hon. Edward Everett and Warren Dutton, Esq. and Hon. Samuel Hubbard, — the two latter distinguished sons of Yale ; Mr. Everett, the pride of Harvard. Dinner at three, at Mr. Charles G. Loring's, — eminent at the bar. Mrs. Loring was Miss Brace of Litchfield, Connecticut. . . . . .

March 16, 17, *Monday and Tuesday.* — At Mr. Loring's table met General William Sullivan, — a handsome man, of fine presence, of very polished manners, and very entertaining. He is the author of the "Familiar Letters" describing the manners of the Court of General Washington, and of the American gentry of that day. I remember him at a ΦBK anniversary dinner at Cambridge, when he gave, as a volunteer toast: "Woman, man's social and intellectual companion." The sentiment did him honor, and was received with enthusiasm. At the dinner at Mr. Loring's, he remarked that the men of the American Revolution have been overrated. I suppose he thought as to talent, and that veneration for the cause gave them in the minds of the people an exalted rank. General Sullivan, sipping with moderation his glass of wine, said he did not know what wine was good for, except to set "a fellow's tongue a-running," — meaning that it was a promoter of sociability. Many years after, being at the public dinner in Cambridge given in honor of the inauguration of President Everett, water and lemonade were served without wine, and I did not perceive any want of wit and vivacity, comparing the occasion with similar ones at Cambridge when wine was freely used. . . . . .

March 17. — From the pressure of the subjects, I became a little hurried towards the close of the lecture. The presence of a great audience, too, and the heat of the room, contributed to a degree of discomfort, and near the close of the evening a lady fainted quite away, which created a little confusion; but the interest excited appeared to be intense ; and as this was only the fourth geological lecture, I hoped that with God's blessing it would be sustained and increased to the end. . . . . .

Thursday. — I dined with Mr. Peter C. Brooks, father-in-law of Mr. Edward Everett. At his table I met Mr. Edward Everett, Warren Dutton, Esq., Mr. Isaac P. Davis, who said that in 1817 I had shown him civilities at New Haven, — forgotten by me; but I did not tell him so. Also Rev. Dr. Wainwright and Rev. Mr. Frothingham. I retired in season to prepare for the lecture. A violent snow-storm in the morning, but rain and melting before noon. The walking at evening being still wet, the audience was not quite so full as the evening before; but the seats were all occupied, and everything went well. . . . . .

After lecture, I attended a splendid party at Mr. Nathan Appleton's. The drawing-rooms were magnificent, with princely furniture and appendages. The Scotch lady, Mrs. Inglis, with her daughter, was there. One of the daughters was taken sick at the Tontine in New Haven, and we, being informed of it by Dr. Lieber, bestowed some attention upon them, for which they were very grateful.* They conduct a female academy in Boston.

March 20, *Friday.* — Made many calls in the morning, arranged for the next lecture at the Temple, and dined at home. At three quarters after six o'clock P. M., I went with Mr. Josiah Quincy, Jr., and a gentleman of the name of Loring, to Cambridge, in a close carriage. The meeting at President Quincy's was that of a regular Friday Evening Club, instituted during the last year. Most of the College gentlemen were present, and many others. I was treated with great kindness and attention. Mrs. and Miss Quincy appeared before the meeting was over, and I had a brief but pleasant interview with them. We returned to Boston in the same carriage that brought us over. President Quincy and lady hold Oliver Wolcott, Esq., of Connecticut, in high admiration. They knew him when in the Government of the United States at Philadelphia. Mr. Josiah Quincy, Jr., kindly took me to Cambridge, and attended me in the same way back to Boston. . . . . .

March 22. — In the evening I had not indeed quite recovered my full physical energy, but I believe that my audience gained by it, for I was more calm and deliberate in my manner; and this lecture, chiefly on the early organic remains, appeared to me to excite more attention than any preceding one. I took tea at Judge Davis's. At his family table (I believe a sister presides, as he is a widower) everything was rational and agreeable. He is a very estimable and respectable man, cordial in a high degree, and full of the love of science and of good learning.

* One of these ladies married Don Calderon de La Barca. — F.

His manners are gentle, modest, and winning. Among
many good friends in Boston, I have not one more devoted
than Judge Davis. He holds, by Washington's appointment, the high office of District Judge of the United
States for Boston and the District of Massachusetts.

March 22. — Colonel Pickman of Salem, Speaker of the
present House of Representatives, fell dead this morning
in an apoplectic fit. His residence was under our roof, in
another tenement in the same block of buildings. " In
the midst of life we are in death ; " let us be always ready,
and then we need not fear the summons. While I remain
in this world, may God grant me both the ability and the
disposition to do good, and perfect willingness to go whenever, and in whatever manner, He may call me ! May God
bless my dearest wife and my lovely and beloved children,
and their children also ! May we be all saved by the
great and glorious redemption, by a second creation unto
righteousness ! In the afternoon I attended the church
of the Rev. Mr. Winslow, where I heard an excellent sermon by a young man, a stranger. The evening was stormy,
and I remained at home.

Dinner at General William Sullivan's. — When General
Sullivan led me up to introduce me to his wife, he said : " I
present you to the best woman in the world," and I sportively admitted her claim, making only a single reservation.
In this delightful family I met several eminent men, —
Judge Story, Rev. Dr. Wainwright, Mr. George B. Emer-
son, Professor Ticknor, Rev. Mr. Greenwood, Mr. Dexter,
and Professor Farrar.

Judge Story having extraordinary colloquial powers,
great resources for conversation, and a most agreeable
voice and manner, with a noble person and fine presence,
had been regarded as the monarch of table-talk. To-day
he seemed conscious that he might be regarded as too engrossing, and when he advanced to pay his respects to

Mrs. Sullivan, he said: "Now, madam, I am not going to talk to-day." He took a seat, and kept his promise for a few minutes, when the gushing torrent broke forth, and flowed almost without cessation, very pleasing and instructive. There was, however, an interval, which Mr. —— made use of to introduce an anecdote. He was, as he said, one evening in company with Professor Parr at Oxford, when the conversation grew more and more interesting, and they passed the night in high converse on exalted classical themes; "but," added Mr. ——, addressing Judge Story, "it was a dialogue, Judge, and not a monologue." The Judge felt the application, and bowed with a smile. I had been before somewhat acquainted with this eminent man, having met him more than once in the New Haven steamers, passing along upon his judicial journeys. In the letter to Mrs. Silliman, which I quoted above, I find the following remarks:— "Everything goes on most agreeably in the lectures; everything is said and done that can gratify and encourage me; and I believe I have completely won the confidence and gained the favor of my audience: there is the most breathless attention at all the lectures." "All this, however, although it cheers, gratifies, and encourages me, so far from producing an emotion of vanity, serves only to increase my sense of responsibility to my generous audience and to Yale College, that I may not fail to sustain its elevated character." Again: "I wish I could tell you all that passes here; if it were in my power, I would record every dinner and every party, and all that is said and done; but, as this is impossible, you will be satisfied with selections. I must decline going to great evening *routes*, where I must stand for hours; dinners fatigue me much less. I can sit and enjoy conversation without indulging in wine and luxuries. I am habitually very careful that my health may not be deranged and the activity of my mind impaired." Referring to personal religion in the children, it is written in the same letter: "I hope our dear boy will put himself in the way of the good influence which F—— writes me is hopefully abroad in the College, and I wish that the dear little girls may feel it too."

March 24.—Dinner at Dr. Shattuck's ; met a very agreeable party of gentlemen; among them were Rev. Dr. Charles Lowell, Mr. Bowditch, Jr., Rev. Mr. Adams, Dr. Charles T. Jackson, and Mr. Washington Allston, the distinguished artist in painting. I saw Mr. Allston in New Haven many years ago, then a bright young man with black hair, now an old man with snowy locks. Dr. Lowell, a moderate Unitarian, almost Orthodox, remarked to me that theology was not always Christianity. Dr. Shattuck said there were some ideas so established that we could not go behind them to examine their origin,—*e. g.*, a man's paternity.

March 26. — Dined at Governor Winthrop's, a noble and perfect gentleman of the old school, — his person grand, being large and handsome, and his locks white, — manners dignified, but courteous and encouraging to strangers. Guests: Edward Everett, Jared Sparks, Alden Bradford, Judge James Savage, Mr. Williams from Northampton, Judge Davis, Rev. Dr. Harris, and two sons of Governor Winthrop. Thus this noble house is continued from the pilgrim ancestors down to our time. Dinner and entertainment excellent. I, rather early, retired with French leave, and, as I afterwards thought, too abruptly, as I sat on the Governor's right hand. I went home to rest, and to prepare for the lecture of the evening, which went off very well. After lecture, although fatigued, I was prevailed upon, contrary to my resolution, to attend a large and brilliant party at Mr. Abbott Lawrence's. Mrs. Lawrence kindly provided me a seat, and insisted that I should occupy it. I made some efforts for the "American Journal of Science," and wrote a circular which was approved by Dr. Ticknor and other judicious friends.

March 29, *Sabbath.* — In the morning I went with Mrs.

John Tappan to the church of Mr. Adams, — in the afternoon to Dr. Channing's, but did not hear him. In the evening, I heard his colleague, the Rev. Dr. Gannett, at the Temple, where he gave an excellent Sabbath-school address; the subject was the Temptation of Christ. His thoughts were excellent, his manner fervent, and his style eloquent. He reminded me of his venerable grandfather, Rev. Dr. Stiles, President of Yale College. They say that he is one of the most engaged and warm of the Unitarian clergy; and if I may judge from this instance, he approaches very near to orthodoxy, nor could I discover anything in his very interesting discourse to which any reasonable Christian could object.

Monday, March 30. — Good news from home: seriousness prevails in College, and, I thank God, my dear boy is a subject of it, and many more with him. May God carry it through the Institution! Letters from Mrs. Silliman and Professors Goodrich and Kingsley.

The arrangements for the lecture of this evening occupied a very snowy day and evening; but this did not hinder ladies from coming to the lecture in the usual numbers. I took tea at Mr. Louis Dwight's, the celebrated inspector of prison discipline. I declined attending the lawyers' club at Mr. Mason's. Invitations are numerous. I have just written six notes of acceptance or refusal. . . . . .

April 1st, Wednesday. — In the morning with Willard the artist. As far as I can judge, he is succeeding well with the second picture, which is spirited; the first was too mild, even tame. After arranging the preparations for the evening lecture, I went with Robert in a gig to Cambridge, — the weather being very fine, — and made calls on Dr. Palfrey, Dr. Beck, Dr. Webster, President Quincy, and George Gibbs, returning to town in time to call on Rev. Dr. Channing, and on Gen. William Sullivan, — he not at home, — but with Dr. Channing and ·lady I had a very pleasant interview. I have already mentioned that I had, in 1807 and 1808, a very agreeable acquaintance with Mrs. Channing in her native city of Newport, when she was Miss Ruth Gibbs. I dined at Judge Prescott's, the distinguished son of a distinguished man, the Revolutionary Col. Prescott, of Bunker-Hill memory. Mr. Loammi Baldwin, the celebrated engineer, was of the party; also Dr. Bigelow, late Rumford Professor of the Useful Arts at Cambridge; Mr. Isaac P. Davis, always joyous and cordial; Judge James Savage, the genealogist; the Rev. Dr. Kirkland, always sparkling; Rev. Mr. Young, Unitarian; and Mr. Codman and others. We had a very agreeable time, and I retired early to review my lecture for the evening, when there was a very full house. Although I spoke eighty minutes, the audience was exceedingly attentive, and appeared deeply interested in the history of the saurian and iguanodon age. I spoke to-night more satisfactorily to myself than at any other time since I have been in Boston. I was cool, self-possessed, deliberate, and I believe easy and natural. This manner I must endeavor to retain and improve. The partiality and special kindness with which I am treated gives me confidence, and places me at ease.

April 2. — I dined with a small and agreeable party at Mr. Dunn's, a merchant living in Mount Vernon Street. Mr. Dunn has taken so much interest in the " Journal of Science " as to purchase an entire set. At Mr. Dunn's I was introduced to Rufus Choate, Esq., a young advocate then beginning to figure at the Boston Bar, and giving more than indications that he would reach the eminence which he afterwards attained. On this occasion he was very silent and reserved, while the keen glance of his brilliant and piercing black eye seemed to scan me as I yielded to the efforts of the company to draw me out upon professional subjects, which in mixed society I aim to avoid. That chilling impression remained until an accidental interview at the Court Room in Boston, where I came as a witness in a case managed by Mr. Choate. He then cheered me by the warming influence of his manners, so cordial, courteous, and winning, that I could hardly believe him to be the same gentleman whom I had met twenty years before. The evening lecture was very fully attended. The weather was very warm, but people go an hour beforehand in order to secure good seats, and appear very attentive during lectures of seventy-five and eighty minutes. Not to lose time while they are waiting, individuals often bring their work, — knitting, sewing, reading, and proof-reading, not to mention newspapers. After lecture I went for a little while to a party at Mr. Cary's, and was to have gone to Mr. Abbott Lawrence's, but I was too much fatigued. Good letters came this evening from my dear wife, from Prof. Olmsted, and other friends. The interest in the course appears unabated and indeed increasing, and on all sides they assure me that I am doing a great deal of good. I bless God for all the mercies that have attended me in this anxious undertaking. Everything has gone delightfully, and the pecuniary result is very important to the interests of my family.

Friday, April 3. — At Mr. Amos Lawrence's, by appointment, I met Rev. Mr. Taylor, the noble and warm-hearted chaplain of the seamen. He, with much interest, is an attendant upon the course; wished to hear me on the relation of Geology to the Mosaic History. The family and a circle of friends gathered around, eager listeners to the statement of his difficulties by Mr. Taylor, and to my efforts to remove them, in which I was generally successful; and when we were through, the honest and honorable man and fearless minister caught my hand, and said warmly, "My dear friend, I am satisfied, — may you live a thousand years."

Saturday, April 4. — At half-past six I went to Mr. Abbott Lawrence's in Somerset Street, to family tea, — myself the only guest. All the Lawrences were my friends, and Mr. and Mrs. Abbott Lawrence had shown a particular

interest in my labors. On the present occasion Mr. Lawrence brought on a free, frank, and confidential conversation respecting the lectures. With warmth, he said that
no man before me had ever drawn together in Boston such
audiences, both for numbers and character ; and that he
had heard animated expressions of delight and of surprise
at the wonderful developments of geology, quite novel in
Boston. He added, " You must come again next winter,
and give us a course of chemistry." I replied that there
would be difficulties.

These difficulties Mr. Lawrence labored to remove, and strenuously urged Mr. Silliman to return
to Boston.

April 10. — I took tea at Mr. Dutton's, who expressed
great satisfaction in the lectures. He was a college contemporary, and always a friend. My last call was at Professor
Ticknor's. I have already mentioned that at the concluding lecture I discussed the question of time, and the coin-
cidence of the Mosaic History, and I concluded with a
moral and religious application to the young men. There
was a crowded audience who showed the most fixed attention and, I thought, satisfaction, — but I may have erred.
Dr. Channing heard the same subject, — Geology and the
Scriptures, — discussed in the day-course ; but as he can-
didly told me, he was not well satisfied ; he did not explain
in what particulars, but he added, — " We do not trouble
ourselves much about the Old Testament." I presume he
may have referred to its relation to questions of science,
for example, Astronomy, between which and the literal
reading there is an entire disagreement.

April 10. — I had received many manifestations of 'approbation of my labors during the whole progress of the
course, which had occupied six weeks. The narrative
which I have given proves, also, that proffers of hospitality

were more numerous than I could comfortably accept. I concluded the courses, therefore, with a mind not elated and vain, but soberly satisfied with what I had faithfully and laboriously done for the people, and with what they had done for me. But there was a concluding act which touched my feelings, and the effect of which remains to this day. When I had made my bow, and the crowded audience were beginning slowly to retire, a committee of ladies, five or six in number, came upon the stage, and their leader requested me to linger a moment. She then expressed for herself and her companions, their satisfaction and grateful estimation of my efforts for their instruction and entertainment, and on behalf of the ladies who had attended the course, they earnestly requested that I would return the next season and give them a course of chemistry. I thanked them, of course, and engaged to take their request into respectful consideration, but did not allude to the overture of Mr. Lawrence. One of the ladies, the leader, a matron, gave me a little book on Christian Union, on a blank leaf of which was inscribed by her, — " I thank my God upon every remembrance of you." . . . . .

Saturday, April 11. — At six o'clock A. M., in company with my faithful Robert, I left Boston for Providence. As objections might be made to the admission of a colored man into the passenger cars of the first class, and being unwilling to disturb the feelings of one who had served me so well, and contributed materially to my success, I went with him into one of the unoccupied cars of the second class. I was the more willing to do this, as my mind having been for many weeks under great tension and excitement, repose and quiet were very grateful to me, and I gladly avoided the necessity of conversing with strangers or of reviving the accidental acquaintances which I had formed. ·I had just concluded successfully an arduous and responsible enterprise. I had been permitted to sustain the honor of my College, and to justify the favorable opinion of my sponsors. Everything had been entirely prosperous; nothing of all my undertakings had failed, and I was not without a pensive religious impression, deeply seated in my mind, that goodness and mercy had followed me all the time, and in our solitary car, it was pleasant to me to indulge in silent gratitude.

In May 1835, he was called to deliver a course of geology in Salem. Here he was received with the same cordial hospitality. The next passage relates to the introductory lecture.

Rev. Mr. Williams, Professor Park,. of Amherst, Rev. Mr. Worcester, and Ex-Senator Phillips, walked with me to Crombie-Street Church, which was almost full when we arrived, and soon was crowded. Mr. Phillips, in a very handsome manner, introduced me to the audience, and I addressed them during one and a half hours. I was assured on all hands that the lecture gave great satisfaction, and such was the appearance of the audience. After the lecture, ladies came up to the table to see the meteoric stones and meteoric iron. The evening was warm, and the effort of speaking so long to a crowded audience, was somewhat fatiguing. . . . . . Theodore D. Prince, at seventy-four years of age, was still performing his duties as a Unitarian clergyman, and had been established there between forty and fifty years. He said to us that when, after his probationary preaching was finished, and the question was raised in the meeting of the society, whether, in New England phrase, they should give a call, that is, invite him to become their minister, — at this moment a venerable man rose in his place and said, " That he had but one objection to the young gentleman ; his health was so delicate that they would probably be called to bury him within the first year." " But," said Dr. Prince, " I have lived to bury every individual of the assembly that voted on that occasion." Dr.

Prince was a venerable man ; he had a commanding person, and dressed in the costume of the gentlemen of the old school, — with small clothes and stockings, and a white wig. He made us at home among his instruments and in his extensive library, so closely arranged in his apartments that we walked among the books through narrow alleys. Dr. Prince was distinguished by an extensive knowledge of natural philosophy, and by great skill in the construction and use of philosophical instruments. He manifested much pleasure in showing us experiments with his fine instruments. As a compliment to myself as a geologist, I suppose, he showed us a mimic volcano, — an artificial Vesuvius, in fiery eruption, — in a darkened room ; an exhibition resembling that of Dr. Bourg's cork models, which I witnessed in London. . . . . . Hon. Mr. Silsbee and Hon. Leverett Saltonstall, both eminent in Congress, were among those whom we knew in Salem. Mr. Senator Silsbee, being intimately acquainted with maritime affairs, was always Chairman of the Navy Board, and rendered important service in that arduous and responsible station. We experienced much kindness from the Silsbee families ; and Miss Silsbee — now Mrs. President Sparks — was one of the most intelligent and interesting of my female auditors. Hon. Leverett Saltonstall was absent at Washington, as a member of the House of Representatives, until near the end of our course, but he returned in season to enable us to form his acquaintance ; and in 1839, he visited New Haven with his two daughters, when we had the pleasure to show them particular civilities, and to conduct them to the old Saltonstall House, by the lake of the same name, once the residence of Governor Saltonstall, a distinguished member of their family. . . . . . Among the eminent men in Salem who honored us by their kindness and friendship, no one is entitled to stand before Judge White, — a person of distinguished literary attainments, a finished scholar, with a beautiful refinement of thought and style, simplicity and purity of language united with force, in manners a refined gentleman, with a modest gentleness, creating assurance and ease in the stranger, and inviting confidence in one whom you would fain make your friend. He has a large and select library, chiefly literary, for although he appreciates science, his taste has not led him so much in that direction as into the fields of literature. He did me the honor to attend my course of lectures, and after they were finished, he in conversation reminded me of an opinion which I had early and strongly expressed in the lecture-room, namely, that after astronomy there was no branch of natural science which possessed such grandeur as geology, and none which was sustained by so many and such interesting facts. He was so candid as to add: "I could not at the time admit the correctness of your opinion, but now that I have heard the entire course, I am ready to say that you have sustained your statement, and as I judge I should give the case in your favor." I am happy to say (November 28, 1859,) that this venerable gentleman, some years over fourscore, is still living in the full possession of his powers, intellectual and moral.

We returned to New Haven in the last week of May. All our geological establishment was transported back to Yale College, and was ready for use there in the regular academic course. I had little respite from my foreign labors, when I opened the College course of geology in the first week in June. Much enthusiasm existed respecting geology, and there was a great pressure from without to attend on the lectures. Ladies attended in crowds, and the students were induced from politeness to relinquish their seats, greatly to their inconvenience. I was, therefore, induced by request to give a distinct course of geology to an audience of about seventy persons of both sexes. I gave this second course parallel with the College course,—allowing one hour between the lectures to afford time for rearrangement of specimens, &c., and for a little rest. It was, however, a fatiguing service. Both lectures were in the forenoon, and after the second lecture I often found an hour's repose at home quite necessary.

The extra course given to ladies and strangers was satisfactory, and was continued several years, but I did not attempt again to lecture twice in the same morning, but took a different hour, or gave the extra course after the July examination.

After a few years, however, I relinquished the extra course and transferred it to my son, who gave it for several years more, on his own account.

CHAPTER XV.

Lectures in Nantucket. — Intercourse with John Quincy Adams. — Arduous Labors. — Chemical Course in Boston (1836). — Dr. Channing. — Miss Martineau. — His Success in Boston. — His Investigation of the Culture and Manufacture of Sugar. — Interviews with General Jackson and Mr. McLean. — Visit to the Gold Mines of Virginia. — Slavery.

. The favorable impression resulting from the four public courses of geology, which I had given during the last year (1834), three of them in Massachusetts, in and near Boston, was extended to Nantucket. Mr. James M. Bunker, a graduate of Yale College in the class of 1832, and his brother, on behalf of the citizens, made overtures to me for a course of lectures in their maritime city, and the correspondence resulted in an engagement.

In this course, as previously at Salem, he was assisted by his son, Mr. Benjamin Silliman, Jr.

In a letter to Mrs. Silliman of September 8, are the following remarks : — " I have lectured one hour and a half, and have not felt the worse for it. Our son is a great comfort and an important aid to me ; he has had no recreation except one excursion with his gun, in company with an older friend. We have both been so completely occupied that we have had no time for study. Our chemical experiments have given us much employment, and all of them, especially those with the calorimotor and compound blowpipe, have been very successful. The people are astonished to see intense ignition coming out of cold fluids, and the rocks themselves melting under a stream of burning gases. Such experiments demonstrate to the observers that the mighty power of heat is inherent in the earth as well as in the sun.   There is, as far as we can learn, universal satisfaction with the lectures, and great surprise is expressed at seeing experiments — even the most difficult — always successful.   I have now no doubt of the entire success of the course, life and power being continued.   We are both well, and have become accustomed to bad water."   The following is an extract from a letter to Mrs. Silliman, dated September 18, 1835 : "I must not postpone a reply to your letter until next week, as there is much work on hand for another lecture this evening.   In addition to a great and increasing audience from the town, we had last evening at the lecture, the Hon. John Quincy Adams and son, the last a son-in-law of Hon. Peter C. Brooks ; Isaac P. Davis, Esq., who does a great part of the honors of Boston ; and Mr. Paine, the astronomer.   These gentlemen are on a visit of curiosity and observation to this Island, which I believe most of them have never visited before."   " Postscript, Saturday, A. M., September 19, 1835.   The four lectures of the week are safely through.   The great folks having passed the day at Siasconsit, nine miles from town, on the other side of the island, returned in season for the lecture, — the second which they have attended.   President Adams sat on the platform near me, and was very attentive ; but how much interested, I do not know.   For a week past we have had daily invitations to tea, to dinner, to rides, &c. We find the society very friendly and agreeable, and the people universally kind.   A very high degree of interest is manifested in the course, and they are feeling my pulse for a course of chemistry another year.   Everything here promises to wind up with great and mutual satisfaction." Again : " The great folks are here in the Hotel with us, and are very agreeable.   Mr. Adams especially is very patient of inquiries, and quite ready to impart information." I had seen him on several occasions before, and was first introduced to him by the Hon. Rufus King, in his office, in January 1804, in New York, when I was preparing to visit Europe. Mr. Brooks I had seen in New Haven, with Mr. Everett, when he came on as our orator. Mr. Paine I had long known. Mr. Isaac P. Davis was an old and warm-hearted friend, with a great disposition and equal power to be useful to me. The interlude of the visit of these gentlemen was therefore very agreeable, and broke up a little the monotony of my life in Nantucket.

The Nantucket gentlemen being desirous to honor these eminent visitors arranged a walk about the town and its environs, for Saturday morning, September 19. A companion was assigned to each for the proposed walk, and I had the honor to walk with Mr. Adams. The lions were few in a town so much better acquainted with whales, and our excursions therefore, did not lead us far, and were limited by the hour of the departure of the boat.

A principal object in our excursion was a garden and grapery belonging to a Mr. Mitchell. I was more interested in my distinguished companion than in the horticulture, and I took the liberty to make some inquiries respecting his early life, particularly at what age he began his career. He replied, that he was fifteen years old when he acted as private secretary to his father, then Minister at the Hague. The reason why he was employed at so early an age was that he both wrote and spoke the French language fluently, and therefore could be very useful to his father. At that time very few persons in our country were acquainted with the French language. This was his beginning; and he had been, more or less through his whole life, occupied with public affairs. I had seen Mr. Adams at Washington in his office when he was Secretary of State, during the Monroe administration, and again in his chair as a member of the House of Representatives, and again at the table of the

Hon. R. S. Baldwin, in New Haven, at which the gentlemen of the College were invited to meet him. It was a few
years before the death of Colonel Trumbull, November 22,
1843, who then resided in my family; and I invited Mr.
Adams to ride home with me and call on his old friend,
the venerable Artist. To this he readily assented, and he
passed about two hours with us in very cheerful and animated conversation. He sat at the tea-table with us, — Colonel
Trumbull, Mrs. Silliman, myself, and, I believe, several
of our children. I had never seen him before so easy and
communicative. There was nothing of the stateliness of
the public man, but perfect affability and a mellow renewal,
with Colonel Trumbull, of the scenes of earlier years in
Europe. He declined to eat or drink, saying that this was
his habit when about to speak in public, as he was engaged
to pronounce a lecture that evening before our citizens.
We sat long at the table, and I took the liberty to remark
to him that I honored him much, as the fearless advocate
of freedom in the right of petition which he had fully vindicated; and no other man could have done it against the
powerful assaults of the united South. He had stood firm
like a rock in the sea, over which the billows broke and
moved it not. I thought he was not displeased with my
frankness. This led to conversation regarding his Presidential career, when he said without reserve that the presidency
of the second term, which he was by precedent entitled to
expect, was lost to him by the strenuous, bitter, and persevering opposition of John C. Calhoun, who of course carried
the entire South with him, and such others as he could
influence. His own eye was doubtless fixed upon the
Presidency. There was still an hour or two before the
time for the lecture, and as Mr. Adams expressed a wish
to call on the family of Vice-President Gerry, I drove with
him to their house, then, I believe, as now, in Temple Street,
and the call appeared highly gratifying to Mrs. Gerry and
her estimable daughters. I believe I left Mr. Adams at the

Tontine Hotel for a little quiet before lecture. His appearance before the audience was very impressive. Although, I believe, then in his seventy-third year, his appearance was almost youthful. He wore a blue coat with yellow buttons : he had a slight tint of red upon his cheeks, and as he kindled with his subject, he forgot his years, rose on his feet with energetic and graceful action, and spoke eloquently and beautifully upon the progress of human society from barbarism to Christian civilization. He spoke emphatically of what woman had gained by passing from the condition of a mere chattel, liable to be bought and sold, to the condition of the rational and cherished companion of man, and the wise guardian and instructor of his children.

There was little time for repose after our return from Nantucket, September 28, 1835. The past year had been one of incessant labor. In addition to all the College courses, which were given in ·full, I had given four extra popular courses of geology with full illustrations, both pictorial and chemical, in Lowell, Boston, Salem, and Nantucket. Now, with scarcely a breathing-spell, we returned to the chemical course in Yale College, occupying the months of October, November, and December, and a few days in January. This course is always arduous, and examinations were held weekly with both the Senior class of the College, and the Medical class. Still, there was to be no rest. I was called to New York in the January vacation, 1836, the College recess of two weeks, to give a brief course of geology. . . . . . The lectures were generally two hours long, or nearly so, and the last exceeded two hours, so great was the pressure of the subject; but no restlessness was manifested. At the concluding lecture there were, as was supposed, thirteen hundred people. I might fairly infer the approbation of the public from the increasing numbers, and from the zeal and enthusiasm which they manifested.

I refer back for a notice of an important overture made to me in Boston, by Mr. Abbott Lawrence, regarding a proposed chemical course to be given in Boston by me in the spring of 1836. Not many weeks after my return home from the geological course of 1835, I received, in affirmance of the proposition of Mr. Lawrence, a written overture inviting me to return in the ensuing season, and then to deliver a course of· lectures on chemistry. The communication was signed by fifty of the principal citizens of Boston, among whom were President Quincy, Dr. Nathaniel Bowditch, Hon. Judge Davis, all the Lawrence brothers, Col. Thomas H. Perkins, W. W. Stone, &c. The invitation was full and cordial in its terms, and placed me in a proper position.

Mr. Silliman made an auspicious beginning ·of his second course in Boston.

I wrote to Mrs. Silliman (March 9) : " You will to-morrow morning receive mine of yesterday, informing you of the splendid success of the course. Hitherto the higher-priced ticket has sold more rapidly than that of last year, of a lower price, and the receipts up to last evening were $1000 more than the entire receipts of last year. I have just now received a call from the Rev. Dr. Channing, who said he was very glad to see me again in Boston. I am to go to his house this evening with Mr. Hubbard to meet Miss Martineau. There is also a visit to be made at Prof. Andrews's. Great admiration is expressed at the experimenting on Monday evening; they remark to me : ' We were delighted to see how everything went just like clock-work, — no confusion, no hurry, and everything beautifully successful.' A few words regarding Miss Martineau. Knowing that she was deaf, I asked Dr. Channing how loud I must speak. He replied, ' Speak in your usual voice; only speak slowly, and articulate distinctly.' I was no sooner seated by her on the sofa, than she handed me her ear-trumpet, which I held, and she placed the other end of the flexible tube in her own ear. But there was little occasion to prompt her. She was very communicative, and discoursed freely about this country, — not always in laudatory terms, — and I thought her to be bold and opinionated, but very intelligent and extremely fluent."

Last year a repeated course in the day was found to be very useful, and in the present course, also, it was early resolved upon, after due consultation. In a letter to Mrs. Silliman, dated March 8th, the day after my first lecture, is the following passage: "Our battle is won; the course opened charmingly last evening, with an attendance of at least a thousand persons. We were obliged to refuse selling any more evening tickets, and we now turn over all applicants to the day-course, — to begin on Wednesday, March 9, at four o'clock, P. M. Our new galvanic instrument, an immense deflagrator, was put into operation yesterday, and its performance was splendid, far beyond anything I ever saw, or anything known here."

On Monday night, after my successful opening lecture, I was too much excited, and too agreeably, to permit me to sleep much. My mind had been overwrought, and in the morning I indulged in the relaxation of writing letters. In the journal I remark: "Invitations to dinner are coming in, but I decline them all, on the score of my urgent engagements. I intend to reserve the day for our experimental labors, and for some little relaxation in excursions, and in seeing interesting things." We finished the preparations for the first day's lecture by eleven o'clock, A. M., which enabled me to come home and rest, so as to be prepared for my duty. . . . . .

. . . . . In a letter to Mrs. Silliman, dated March 17, after all the three lectures had been given and repeated, I find the following passage. In reference to the severe labor of the double course it is said: "I assure you that I am in perfect health, and am quite equal to all my labors, although I think I never encountered so severe a trial; but a liberal flow of money, — always acceptable when honestly earned, — and the delight expressed on all hands at the style of successful experimenting and the course of statement and reasoning, gives me full assurance that I am now as firmly established here chemically, as I was last year geologically."

" In the fifth lecture, I made a very liberal use of potassium and sodium, which are not only splendid subjects of experiment but are highly illustrative of chemical principles. Everything went beautifully. After the sixth lecture, at a large party at Deacon Walley's, great satisfaction was expressed to me regarding the lectures. The Mayor, Mr. Armstrong, said that he thought the subject very interesting and instructive, and was pleased that a moral and religious aspect was given to the science ; and similar views were expressed by others. I communicated to-day, at the lecture, the discovery that cast-steel of the first quality is formed directly from the ore, and that malleable iron is manufactured from cast-iron without melting it again ; specimens furnished to me by the manufacturers were also exhibited, and I was assured that the subject excited great interest, and gave much satisfaction. My mind is working like a steam-engine in perpetual motion, but the night succeeding the last lecture gave me refreshing sleep, and I awoke the next morning in remarkable strength."

I make some remarks upon the important crisis which brought me before the public as a popular lecturer. I was called out, as I have said, in the maturity of my powers, experience, and reputation, at fifty-five or fifty-six years of age ; and the results of the years 1834–35–36, in Hartford, Lowell, Salem, Nantucket, and Boston, were of the greatest importance to me and my family. The two Boston courses were peculiarly important, and I have, therefore, given a particular account of them. I have given also, without reserve, the impressions which they produced upon the audience and the public. The entire success by which they were attended I can truly say never produced in my mind any feelings of vanity and self-exaltation. I was too sensible of the responsibility of my position, and of the difficulty of presenting those great subjects clearly and attractively to such large and intelligent audiences, — too sensible of this to permit any other feeling than that of the most earnest sincerity, attended by the most strenuous efforts to perform my duty well. I was also most ably assisted; and never, in the two seasons, and in the forty-nine or fifty lectures which I delivered in the two double courses, was there any failure in an experiment or in an illustration.

I had, moreover, the happiness to obtain the good-will of the people of Boston. The Orthodox and Unitarian influence was united in my favor. I had many warm friends among both classes, and was equally cherished by both. The moral and religious bearing of the lectures was decided in illustration of the wisdom, power, and benevolence manifested equally in the mechanical and chemical constitution of our world. These deductions of natural theology were out of the bounds of politics, and were equally acceptable to the wise and good of all religious denominations. The language of the press was entirely friendly, and even laudatory; nor have I ever seen or heard of an unfriendly paragraph. I was deeply gratified and deeply grateful to God, and to a community which had thus generously adopted me, and entertain no doubt that the successful issue of these Boston courses produced the still more important engagement which four years later brought me back to the metropolis of New England, the account of which I hope to give in due time. It was, indeed, a bright era in my life, a brilliant and remunerative success which diffused the benefits of science, honored the Creator, cheered

my excellent wife, and drew in its train beneficial consequences which are felt to this day.

In February, 1836, Mr. Silliman received an invitation from many of the leading citizens of New
York, to give a geological course in that city. This
he complied with, and the lectures were given in the
ensuing April and May. Of this course he says: —

The course was quite successful, both as to the number
of hearers and the interest excited. Among the audience
were many of the first people of the city; there were many
ladies, and, I suppose, a solid mass of intelligence from the
middle classes of society. The excitement was almost as
great as in Boston.

Mr. Silliman introduces here some account of
other labors which were partly contemporaneous
with the delivery of his public courses of lectures,
but which extend back, also, to an earlier date. He
first notices a visit of exploration, made in 1830, to
the valley of Wyoming, and to its coal formations
in the State of Pennsylvania.

Of the labor of the investigation, in a letter to Mrs. Silliman of May 25, 1830, it is remarked: — "We have finished
the investigation. We have examined, I suppose, one hundred mines and localities of coal extending through forty
miles in length, and as we have explored both sides of the
valley with many crossings and doublings back and forward, we have investigated one hundred and twenty to one
hundred and thirty miles of mountains, forests, swamps, and
excavations. We have travelled occasionally in wagons,
principally on horseback, but much of our movements have
been on foot, especially in regions incessible to wheels or
horses. I have never in my life gone through a week of

such arduous exertion, not even in the mountains and mines of Derbyshire, in the centre of England, nor in those of Cornwall, at the Land's End in the same country. If I was able to perform those early labors at the age of twenty-six, I have not shrunk from similar efforts at the double age of fifty-one, and I have not succumbed under them, although I have, from exposure, become as brown as a Cherokee. My report was finished between ten and eleven o'clock last night, when I read it aloud to the gentlemen assembled at the hotel to hear it, and it appeared to give good satisfaction." It was, after my return, printed, and I presented two hundred copies to the people of the valley.

In 1832–3, by the appointment of the General Government, he engaged in a scientific examination of the subject of the culture and manufacture of sugar. It was a part of the aid which he rendered in the development of the physical resources of the country. The "Reminiscences" contain an account of this investigation.

A resolution of the House of Representatives of the United States was passed, January 25, 1830, requiring the Secretary of the Treasury "to cause to be prepared a well-digested manual, containing the best practical information concerning the culture of the sugar-cane, and the fabrication and refinement of sugar, including the most modern improvements." Being at Angelica, N. Y., on a visit to my daughter, Maria T. Church and family, in September 1832, I received from home a letter from the Hon. Louis McLean, Secretary of the Treasury, dated August 31, 1832, in which he desired me to take charge of the proposed investigation. I replied that, as it was impossible to visit all parts of the United States, where sugar was grown or refined, I would undertake the proposed duty, provided

I might depute competent persons to the remote parts of the field, while I would myself examine the central portions. In a letter of October 19, the Secretary assented to my proposal. To Professor O. P. Hubbard, I committed the Eastern States, especially Boston ; to Mr. Charles U. Shepard, the Southern States, particularly Louisiana and Georgia. In the course of the ensuing winter, we resorted to our respective fields of labor. The gentlemen associated with me in the enterprise were active and zealous in their efforts, and they received kind and generous aid on the part of the proprietors and manufacturers in the several places which they visited. I also experienced similar treatment in Baltimore, Philadelphia, and New York ; and in the last-named city, I was aided by my brother, Gold Selleck Silliman. I omit the details of our investigation, as the results were embodied in a report to the Hon. Louis McLean, Secretary of the Treasury, in which we blended and assimilated our information into a harmonious whole.

I finished the report at Washington, May 27, 1833, and communicated it to the Secretary on the following day, May 28. It was approved by him, and was printed in a pamphlet of 121 pages, with all necessary wood-cuts and copperplate engravings. After reading my introductory letter addressed to himself, the Secretary said that he reposed entire confidence in me, and should at once accept my report. He then directed Mr. Dickens, the Secretary of the Senate, to pass the document through the forms of office — half a dozen offices in number — which occupied three hours ; but it was all accomplished before dinner, and to my entire satisfaction. My intercourse with Mr. McLean, who was an honorable and very intelligent man, was entirely agreeable. He introduced me to President Jackson, who received me with the courtesy and dignity for which he was distinguished. He did not appear to have been informed of the duty in which I had been engaged, and when it was mentioned to him by the Secretary, he said he was glad I had undertaken it. My charge of $1200 for the investigation, was readily allowed by the Secretary, and the necessary papers, as already stated, were furnished me for passing through the different offices of the Treasury. The expenses of my coadjutors were also paid, I do not remember whether on this or on a subsequent occasion. Altogether, I presume the investigation cost the government $2000. I never heard that the government took any action upon the report, nor do I know what was thought of it by any one at Washington, except the Secretary. However this may have been, I had some evidence that the report was favorably appreciated by those interested in the subject, because I was very often called upon to furnish copies of it. I was liberally supplied from the Washington government press with, I believe, one hundred copies, and only one is left, the others having been given away, and even that is, at this late day, occasionally borrowed. . . . . . I have already mentioned that Mr. McLean introduced me to the President. In a letter to Mrs. Silliman, dated Washington, May 27, 1833, I find the following more particular notice : — " At the palace I met not only the President, but Mr. Edward Livingston and General Cass, Secretaries of departments. The President received me with great kindness, and much as I have heard of his dignified and courteous manners, I was more agreeably impressed than I expected to be. He is not only a dignified but a winning gentleman of the old school of manners, which brought up to my mind your father, the late Governor Trumbull. He informed me that he was soon to visit the Eastern States, and should stop in New Haven. I tendered him the civility of showing him the Colleges, which he said he should be very happy to see. He said he should leave Washington in a week or more, and that he wished to pass quietly along." General Jackson was strongly marked by time, but there appeared to be no abatement of physical or mental vigor. A Connecticut man whom I had long known — Commodore Hull — kindly found me out, and was earnest that I should remain through the next day to dine with Mr. Vaughan, the British Minister, as it would be the King's birthday; and he would hardly let me off from a strawberry party of Mrs. Hull's, on Wednesday evening.

In August, 1836, at the request of proprietors in New York, Mr. Silliman, in company with his son and Mr. Eli Whitney, made a professional tour among the gold mines of Virginia. Extracts from his narrative of this visit follow.

The morning of August 27th found us at the landing-place in Virginia, and a train of stage-coaches was in attendance to convey the passengers of the steamer on their way. Heavy rains had made the road muddy and deep, and we consumed two or three hours in going ten miles to Fredericksburg. In that city there resided a highly respectable Scotch merchant, James Vass, whose sons having been placed under my care in Yale College, an extended correspondence had been maintained between us for several years. I had not informed him of my intended visit to Virginia; but, one of his sons having met us at Washington, and having returned home by an earlier boat, had informed his father, who was already at the station waiting the arrival of the stages. They had hardly come to a stand, when I observed a gentleman stranger passing rapidly from carriage to carriage, apparently looking for some one. I had never seen him before; but, as he approached our carriage, I heard him inquiring for me, and, as he came up, I responded, when he announced Mr. Vass. Of course he gave me a cordial greeting, and at once invited me to his house, when the following dialogue ensued: — "I thank you, sir; but as I visit Virginia on a professional visit among the gold mines, I may be very irregular in my movements, and ought not to tax your hospitality." "No matter for that," was the reply; "go and come as you please, making my house your head-quarters." "But, sir, I may be a month in this region." "So much the better," was the answer. "Nor is that all. I have two young friends with me, — my own son and an only son of a friend, — a widowed mother, — and I cannot part from them." "So much the better," was the generous reply; "you will be more than welcome at my house, and my wife and children will be most happy to entertain you with Virginian hospitality during your sojourn." As there was neither time nor occasion for more debate, I therefore accepted the hospitable offer of my friend Mr. Vass, and we received a cordial welcome from his good lady and their household, and our home was now established in their house. Never was a home made more comfortable and agreeable to those who came as strangers, but were now adopted as friends.

In our travels, and in the prosecution of our researches among the mines, we had of course met with slaves everywhere, and in general they were, as far as we observed, treated kindly.

Slaves were employed about the mines, and the strong arms of athletic black men were employed to crush the quartz for us in heavy iron mortars, preparatory to the washing for gold; they also broke the quartz from the veins; and we had always as many of these men at command as we desired for the accomplishment of our labors. As we were quietly reading in our apartment at a tavern, on the Sabbath, the landlord entered, with an apology for the intrusion, and, opening a glass case in the corner of the room, took down a large riding coach-whip, which we supposed was wanted for some excursion. Within a few minutes, however, we heard through our open windows the sharp reverberations of the lash rapidly repeated, and accompanied by loud cries of distress. We found, by the voluntary reports of the servants, that the sufferer was a negro man whom we had seen about the barn where our horses were stabled. His offence was being seen near the jail, where two negroes were imprisoned for an assault on their master. It did not appear that he held any communication with them, and it would appear very improbable that he should attempt it in broad daylight, and in full view of all passers-by. Slavery, begun in wrong, is sustained by a cruel despotism.

CHAPTER XVI.

Double Course of Chemistry in New York (1838). — Accident. — The Lowell Lectures: Plan of the Several Courses. — First Course (1840).— His Introduction to the Audience by Mr. Everett. — Popularity of the Lectures. — Dinner at Mr. Tuckerman's. — Mr. John Lowell. — Mr. Jeremiah Mason. — Courtesies Received. — Second Course in Boston (1841). — Interest Manifested in the Lectures. — Presides over the Geological Society in Philadelphia. — Third Course in Boston (1842). — Dr. Walker's Lecture. — His Opening Lecture. — Social Civilities. — Fourth Course in Boston (1843). — His Concluding Reflections. — Correspondence with Professor Kingsley, Chancellor Kent, &c.

RESUMING the narrative of his efforts as a popular lecturer, Mr. Silliman makes mention of the double course on chemistry, which he delivered in January, 1838, in Clinton Hall, in the City of New York. He had given, a year before, a brief course on geology, by invitation of the Lyceum of Natural History. During the former course, — of which he preserved no detailed memoranda, although it was fully successful, — an accident befell him, which gave room for the exertion of remarkable self-control.

Although there was no failure of an experiment, I met with an injury, which, however, I was able to conceal from the audience and from my assistants. I was exhibiting the elements of water, and the generating of heat by the combustion of oxygen and hydrogen gases, in the compound blow-pipe of Dr. Hare. A suspended gasometer was used for each of the gases, and weights were placed upon each of them to create a pressure for the expulsion of the gases, — the rate of efflux being regulated by stop-cocks. The platform on which I stood with the apparatus was of limited dimensions ; and, while passing by the gasometers, I hit a six-pound iron weight which lay on the top of one of the gasometers, when it fell from the height of four to four and a half feet upon my right foot, the great toe of which received a severe blow, causing me to draw a long breath ; and, before I could recover my natural breathing, I became satisfied that I should not faint, although the pain was intense. The sensation of the foot was as if standing in a fluid, which, in this case, was blood, as appeared on drawing off my boot at the hotel, — the stocking being soaked with blood. The nail of the large toe was torn up at the root, and merely hung like a loose shingle on a roof. I went on half an hour or more, and finished the lecture. Blood continued to issue from the wound during ten days,— the bloody dressings being removed every morning ; and bleeding kept the inflammation down. The nail grew out again very slowly. At the end of eight months it had not entirely covered the original surface. In my childhood I had split this toe with an axe, and the nail grew out after that accident, carrying the mark of the axe along with it. This marking was still preserved in the recent restoration, but the parts of the nail were not united, or only at the root, and grew out separately, but side by side, and are not perfectly united now (1861), twenty-two years after the injury.—In connection with the subject in hand, I exhibited the formation of water from its two elements, — oxygen and hydrogen, — and adverted to its three physical conditions of vapor, fluid, or water and ice. In speaking of the permanence of ice in very cold climates, I quoted *memoriter* Cowper's graphic description of the palace constructed of ice, in 1740 or 1745, on the river Neva, near St. Petersburg, to celebrate the marriage of Prince Galitzin.

> " Silently as a dream the fabric rose;
> No sound of hammer or of saw was there;
> But, ice on ice, the well-adjusted parts
> Were soon conjoined, nor other cement asked
> Than water, interfused, to make them one." — &c.

My brother, from Brooklyn, was present, and hearing in the morning that I had received an injury during the lec-·ture, said to his family that it could not be so, as he heard me lecture to the end, and that it was concluded by poetry. The injury made me lame, but no lecture was omitted. I finished the courses both of the evening and the day, and there was no occasion to mention the occurrence to the audience.

Mr. Silliman was called upon to open the Lowell Institute, which had been established by the munificence of a citizen of Boston, as a means of public instruction. For four successive years he had the pleasure of presenting the truths of science to large and approving audiences. These courses of lectures he regarded as the crowning success of his professional life. In all of them he had the assistance of his son. Mr. Silliman had been consulted by Mr. John A. Lowell, the trustee of the Lowell fund, as to the best mode of organizing the Institution.

In consequence of previous correspondence, Mr. Lowell came in the month of June, 1838, to my house ; an interview took place in the library, and we occupied the greater part of the forenoon in presenting views of what such an institution ought to be, and in suggestions as to the lectures. From the experience of thirty years in the departments of science which had been committed to my care, I was able to give Mr. Lowell exact information as to the necessary apparatus, materials, and illustrations, with estimates of the probable expense, or approximations to it. As I supposed it probable that an overture for my services would be made, I was desirous to impress upon the mind of Mr. Lowell that to give effect to lectures and demonstrations in science a liberal expenditure would be required.

The invitation followed, and a plan was adopted for the lectures which were to be given.

Mr. Lowell at first suggested an arrangement for three years, but yielded to my view that the work would be more thoroughly done upon a basis of four years ; the first year, or rather the first winter, to be for geology, and chemistry to be given in the three succeeding seasons ; the non-metallic ponderables for the second year ; the metals for the third ; the dynamics of chemistry, namely, the powers that effect the changes of matter, for the fourth.

In due time Mr. Silliman presented himself in Boston to fulfil his engagement.

By the request of Mr. Lowell, the trustee of the Institute, His Excellency Governor Edward Everett pronounced an historical eulogy upon the Founder of the Institute, — Mr. John Lowell. On December 31st, 1839, this address was delivered in the Odeon, as an introduction to the lectures, and it was repeated in the Marlborough Chapel on the evening of January 2. On the latter occasion, I was present with my son, and we listened with great satisfaction to this beautiful eulogy, which has been published in the collection of " Orations and Speeches on Various Occasions, by Edward Everett," Vol. II. p. 379 (Edition of 1856). Mr. Everett remarked that, with the exception of the bequest of the late Mr. Stephen Girard of Philadelphia, the sum appropriated by Mr. Lowell was the largest ever given by any private individual in this country, and he was not aware that there is in Europe anything of this description on so large a scale. His will was written before he left this country, and was finished on the ruins of Thebes, and a codicil added at the Arabic village of Luxor, the whole of which is situated on the remains of an ancient palace. In this codicil he gives his kinsman, Mr. John A. Lowell, detailed directions for the administration of his trust.

Governor Everett announced to the audience the name of the individual who would have the honor of opening the Institution, by giving the first course of lectures. He remarked thus : — " The first course of lectures is now about to commence on the subject of Geology, to be delivered by a gentleman — Professor Silliman of Yale College — whose reputation is too well established in this department of science, both in Europe and America, and is too well known to the citizens of Boston to need an attestation on my part. It would be arrogant in me to speak farther of his qualifications as a lecturer on this foundation. The great crowd assembled this evening, consisting as it does of a moiety only of those who have received tickets of admission to the course, sufficiently evinces the desire which is felt by the citizens of Boston, again to enjoy the advantages of his instruction, while it affords a new proof, if further proof were wanting, that our liberal founder did not mistake the disposition of the community to avail themselves of the benefit of an institution of this character." — (p. 383.) The Orator added : — " The few sentences, penned with a tired hand by our fellow-citizen on the top of a palace of the Pharaohs, will do more for human improvement than, for aught that appears, was done by all of that gloomy dynasty that ever reigned." . . . . . . I thought it was proper, in opening the course, to acknowledge, in guarded language, Governor Everett's generous announcement of myself; and I therefore pronounced the following exordium : —

" *Ladies and Gentlemen*, — By invitation of the trustee and director of the Lowell Institute, I have the honor to stand before you this evening, charged with the fulfilment of an important duty. We have all listened with delighted attention to the history of the origin of this Institution, and to the biographical sketch of its noble founder. The simple narrative of the facts was clothed with a deep and touching pathos, and the distinguished orator imparted to them an intellectual and moral beauty, alike honorable to the dead and useful to the living. His generous confidence, bestowed on me in advance, while it enhances to an almost painful degree my sense of obligation, created by my present position, at the same time checks the expression of those more than reciprocal sentiments which glow in my mind. His pure and elevated fame office cannot enhance nor retirement eclipse.*

" In commencing our appropriate duties in this place, and in opening the course of instruction to be given in this Institution, we are happy to recognize in the views of its lamented founder a moral purpose, elevated far above merely physical or even intellectual advantages. While aiming to secure these highly important results, his mind was devoutly directed to his Maker. The investigation and exhibition of physical laws, while they are to be applied, by his direction, to the illustration of the attributes of the infinite God, are to be summoned also to prove the harmony of his revealed word with the visible creation, and of both with his holy character. With such a design, worthy of the noble and virtuous mind of Mr. Lowell, — a design cherished from youth to middle life, from his quiet walks in this city through all the vicissitudes of his eventful travels, renewed in sickness and sustained in death, — may we not hope that the blessing of God will descend upon this Institution, and that those to whom its important trusts are committed may be guided by wisdom from above in the fulfilment of their high and responsible functions. With feelings then in perfect harmony with the testamentary injunctions of our founder we turn to our more immediate duties." . . . . . .

---

* A single vote, in a then recent election, had superseded Governor Everett, and made Mr. Morton his successor.

Although geology had been, five years before, discussed by me successfully in the presence of a Boston audience, the present occasion presented some advantages. The subject had been more thoroughly studied by me, and I was still an anxious and faithful student, having with me a collection of the best books on the subject. The liberal views of the trustee, Mr. Lowell, had enabled me to obtain many new and excellent illustrations, so that the lecture-room could be beautifully decorated, and the lectures made both intelligible and attractive, by drawings, diagrams, and pictures, which through the eye informed the mind and sustained the positions that were to be assumed. . . . . . I have already copied the exordium of the introductory lecture of the course. I now approached this public duty with intense anxiety, and the more so as my voice was not perfectly clear. I spoke, however, in the first lecture apparently with good effect during an hour and a half. Owing to my hoarseness, I was not perfectly heard by every one, and I ran into my old fault of being too rapid; but still I was assured that the lecture was successful.

The second lecture (Saturday, January 4) gave me confidence. My voice served me well; I was deliberate and animated, and was heard in every part of the house. From the aspect of a very large and attentive audience I felt assured — as I was informed was the fact — that the lecture gave great satisfaction. I spoke two hours on the foundation-rocks of the globe, allowing an interval of five minutes at the end of an hour. It gave the audience a brief season for conversation, for changing position, and for retiring, should they wish so to do; but I believe few or none of them withdrew. I wrote home, January 10: "My second lecture was warmly commended. Mrs. John A. Lowell, wife of the trustee, said to my son, at the end of the two hours, that she should be willing to sit two hours more. The elder Mr. John Lowell, father of the trustee, heard the lecture, and is very warm and cordial. He is a very eminent man.

The battle is now won, but I shall have an anxious and laborious task through the entire course." On the next Sabbath, with our excellent friends, the Rev. G. W. Blagden and lady, we attended worship in the Old South, of which he is pastor; we listened to an interesting New Year's sermon, and participated in the solemnity of the sacrament, which was administered after the morning service.

The following passages having respect to his stay in Boston on this occasion, and partly drawn from notes made at the time, are extracted from the " Reminiscences " : —

Mr. Webster, having recently returned from a visit to England, was invited by the Whig members of the legislature to speak in the State House, on Monday evening, January 7. He was introduced with much ceremony, and addressed by Mr. King, chairman of the senate. His address on the national currency and the reigning policy was very powerful. He had returned from his travels in fine health. His manner was exceedingly energetic and impressive, with much action, great deliberation, good pauses, and perfect self-possession. He was highly excited, and it was considered as one of his happiest efforts. I had seen him in private, and had only once before * heard him in public. His manner now exceeded my expectations. I went with others, after he had finished, to congratulate him on his happy return, and we were courteously received.

Friday, January 10. — Except calls at Mr. Bancroft's and Mr. Lamb's in the morning, I was engrossed by my studies with reference to the great subjects of the evening lecture. The tertiary contains amazing revelations, and the Mosaic deluge, with all the phenomena of floods and moving waters, powerfully arrests the attention of all listeners. The audience was all that the house could contain:

* At the laying of the foundation of the Bunker Hill Monument, June 17, 1825.

the alleys were full, and the third gallery as well as the second was occupied. I had, in two preceding lectures, given a recess of five minutes at the end of the first hour, and I now informed the audience that, as my subjects were very extensive, and would take me into the second hour, I should, as a regular thing give them that relief of five minutes, and to this notice they gave a warm response. This suspension was doubtless felt to be a relief to them, and it was most acceptable to myself. I then retired at once into a private room near at hand, threw myself upon the sofa, closed my eyes, and neither spoke nor was spoken to, until the five minutes were past; in the mean time the excited respiration and pulsation subsided to their natural condition, and a glass of water enabled me to return quite fresh to the audience, and to resume the speaking with renewed energy. The impression of the lecture appeared to be strong and vivid. I concluded that I had won the audience, and that with great exertions I might hope to go through successfully.

I record again that the assistance of my son was invaluable to me in these labors, and a great consolation by his amiable conduct and filial devotion. In our apartment we daily commended ourselves and our friends to the Giver of all good, and invoked a blessing upon our public efforts.

Thursday.— Dinner at Mr. Edward Tuckerman's, Beacon Street. A very delightful occasion in a refined and polished family; conversation of a high moral tone. Among the guests were the Rev. Dr. Stone, of St. Paul's Church, and Prof. Greenleaf, of the Cambridge Law School. Geology was introduced, but not by me, as I never obtrude professional subjects upon mixed circles, or upon any uninitiated individuals. Dr. Stone has no difficulties as between geology and the Scriptures, and we agreed entirely in our views. The other gentlemen and Dr. Stone will accept a copy of my printed remarks on this subject. . . . . .

January 17th, Friday. — The interest appears to increase. Some people come at six o'clock, at the opening of the door, and therefore remain three hours; and curious individuals remain half an hour longer after the lecture to examine the specimens, which are explained by my son and Dr. Wyman, as I always retire at once to my room.   After half an hour's rest, I resume my reading for an hour or two. My voice served me well at the last lecture.   I have already mentioned my deep sense of responsibility in introducing to the public a splendid institution.   It is the greatest honor I ever received, to be selected for such a service, when there are so many able men of their own here and in this vicinity.   I am therefore very anxious to discharge my duty with decided ability, that the institution may not fail in my hands; and I need not say that a failure would be most unhappy, and to me calamitous.

January 19, Sabbath. — In the morning, at the Marlboro' Chapel to hear President Mahan preach on perfectionism.   In the afternoon, with Mr. and Mrs. Lamb, we attended their place of worship, — Dr. Channing's and Mr. Gannett's.   The latter gentleman's subject was, "A double-minded man is unstable in all his ways."   He urged fervently the duty of immediate repentance, and exposed very forcibly the sin and misery of being half in earnest. These ministers are fervent and devout men; in doctrine they are Unitarian, in spirit, Christian. . . . . .

January 31. — In a morning which was bright after the rain, Mr. John Lowell, father of Mr. John A. Lowell, the trustee, called in his carriage, and took us both to his country-seat in Roxbury, where he kindly entertained us for more than an hour, by explaining to us in his beautiful green-house some of the more rare plants, among which were the *Pandanus* or screw pine, the Auracaria pine, the *Dracena* or dragon-plant, many palms, the *Ficus elastica* or elastic gum-plant, some of the *Orchidiæ*, and many more. Most of these, in relation to their fossil analogues, possessed for me a high degree of interest.

My first knowledge of this eminent man was at the mineral springs at Ballston, in 1796, when he appeared with an equipage and servants; and although a young man, he arrested the attention of all by his high conversational powers. I met him next in London, in 1805, where he displayed the same superiority, only intensified; next in Boston, at the table of his brother, Francis Cabot Lowell. During my present engagement, we passed an evening at his house in Boston, when he told me that he had read every article of the "American Journal of Science," including the mathematical papers, which I considered as a strong mark of his approbation. He had been recently in Cuba, for his health, and there he learned that the Caribs prefer to inter their dead on the sea-shore, next to the tidal wave, and he thought that practice might account for the famous fossil skeleton of Guadaloupe, which has figured so much in geology. I thought the suggestion valuable. It is supposed that the Charibs thought that their friends might pass by water to another world. Mr. Lowell met in Cuba a distinguished English botanist who had visited the island on purpose to see tropical plants in their native climates, but was deterred from exploring rural scenes from fear of yellow fever.

Saturday, February 1. — In the morning a walk to Mr. Alger's foundry, where we saw the boring of large cannon for the United States. We then rode to Cambridge in a close-covered sleigh, as it snowed rapidly. Made calls at President Quincy's, Prof. Lovering's, Mr. Sparks's, Mr. King's, Mr. Worcester's, &c. Mr. Worcester occupied the Dr. Craige house, which was General Washington's headquarters in 1775 and 1776. Tea at Mr. Jeremiah Mason's, sitting around the table with his lovely family,—Mrs. Mason and daughters, with the noble head, a magnificent man, both physically and mentally, and, withal, most kind and gentle in manners and disposition; his conversation enlightened and instructive.

Sabbath, February 2. — Morning at the Old South, and partook of the sacrament. In the afternoon at the Brattle-Street Church, — preacher, Mr. Frothingham. The regular incumbent is Rev. Dr. Lothrop, a moderate Unitarian, and an excellent man. Mr. Abbott Lawrence and family attend here. Mr. Lawrence said to me that he could not go along with Dr. Channing.

February 4. — A very agreeable dinner-party at Mr. William Lawrence's. Among the guests were Lieutenant-Governor Hull and Dr. Charles T. Jackson. We inspected, on our return, Wightman's chemical apparatus, which he is constructing for our next course, and found satisfactory progress and skilful construction. There were five invitations for the evening, of which we accepted three and declined two. We called at Mr. Winslow's, then at Mr. Edward Tuckerman's, and finished at Mr. Armstrong's, where there was an elegant party assembled in superb rooms. Having been much fatigued during the day, I found it inconvenient to remain standing during so many hours as the party might last. But the retreat which I had contemplated was prevented by an unexpected honor. Mr. Armstrong committed his lady to my care to lead the company to the supper-table, and to do its honors, at least as an auxiliary. Of course I braced myself up to the requirements of the occasion, and literally stood it out. I was at home by eleven o'clock, and found time and strength for reading Darwin's delightful work on the " Natural History and Geology of South America." Darwin was the naturalist of the exploring expedition of the British ships *Adventure* and *Beagle*, between 1826–1836; making a voyage around the world. The reading of this work has been a recreation at night, after the labors of the day and evening.

After the lapse of a year, Mr. Silliman was again in Boston, to commence the first of his three courses on Chemistry.

February 19. — The course of lectures on Natural Religion, in the Odeon, by the Rev. Dr. Walker of Harvard College, on the Lowell foundation, was to be finished the evening of our arrival, and we availed ourselves of the opportunity to hear that eminent man. His lecture was able, instructive, and interesting, and his manner was dignified and impressive. One year and one week had elapsed since I finished the course of geology in the Odeon ; and, as we entered this evening by the private door facing the audience, there was a quiet movement of welcome, which showed that we were not forgotten. It was significant, although not boisterous, and was returned by me with a bow of acknowledgment. Rev. Dr. Walker did not partake of any narrow feelings towards me.; but, on the contrary, when I afterwards saw him at Cambridge, he expressed much satisfaction that I was a fellow-laborer with him in the Lowell Institute.

February 22, *Monday.* — This being the day for the beginning of the course, I passed the time in revising, correcting, and reading my introductory. It was written with great care, and contained a comprehensive generalization of all science, with a portraiture of physical science in all its departments, divided and mapped out, so as to show the distinctive features and boundaries and connections of each, coming down finally to the one science — chemistry — which was to engage our immediate attention. This lecture was read, quite audibly, I believe, to an audience estimated to amount to fifteen hundred persons or more. They were very attentive, and perfectly quiet during the hour and a quarter which the discourse occupied. I was glad to have got well through this lecture, — the only one in the course which I expected to read, — which I very much dislike to do, as in reading my manner is artificial, and lacks the genial tone and expression which an earnest speaker, full of his subject, and looking his audience in the face, naturally assumes. I had, however, no reason to be dissatisfied with this first effort of the course. . . . . .

March 8. — My health is good, and my voice clear, so that I fill the house without difficulty; my son is very efficient; and at both lectures the theatre is quite full. Good news from home; and the best news is, that my two younger daughters, H—— and J——, have become deeply interested in religion, and I wrote to them to bid them God-speed on their way to the celestial city.

Sabbath, March 14. — Yesterday I received from them a very gratifying answer, in entire sympathy with my parental counsels; and their response shows that their young minds —their ages are seventeen and fourteen—have already taken the right direction in deciding to embrace the offered Salvation. I was so happy as to receive similar intelligence respecting my only son, Benjamin, when I was engaged in my first course of lectures in Boston, in March, 1835; and now, in the same city, during a similar engagement, I am again favored in the same way. I have been permitted here to unfold to an excited and interested community some views of the secrets of God's material world, as displayed in its structure and constitution; and thus, I trust, I have been enabled to contribute not only to the mental illumination of the people, but to the increase of their reverence for God. But I am much more favored in hearing, on this beloved spot, that my two younger children are determined to walk in the truth, so that thus all my dear family are hopefully enrolled in the Book of Life. Not unto us, O God! but unto Thy great and holy Name be all the honor and glory!

Immediately after his return home, at the completion of this course, he went on an important scientific errand to Philadelphia.

It would appear strange, even to myself, that, after so

long an absence, I should pass only one day at home before leaving it again; but the reason was one that I could
not resist: it was an official call to Philadelphia. As the
object was geological, it falls in naturally after a course of
professional duty in Boston.

In the spring of 1840, a meeting was held in Philadelphia of those gentlemen who had been professionally engaged in geological surveys under public authority. This
meeting was preliminary to the formation of an association
of geologists for the purpose of promoting the progress of
the science and its applications in this country. A constitution was formed, and officers appointed, preparatory to
the first meeting during the present week. They saw fit
to name me as the first President; and this was the call
that took me to Philadelphia at this time. I proceeded,
on the 5th of April, to that city, arriving with my friend
Mr. Wm. C. Redfield at midnight. We found a shelter at
the Washington Hotel, and in the morning I resorted to my
old home at Mr. Charles Chauncey's, where, as usual, I was
affectionately received. On the morning of the 6th of
April, I found my way to the hall of the Academy of the
Natural Sciences, and took my place as presiding officer.

The week was most busily employed in geological meetings. Many gentlemen were present from different States,
and many interesting discussions took place, which were
ably sustained.

The society formed in Philadelphia, was after a
time succeeded by the "American Association of
Geologists and Naturalists," and later by the "American Association for the Advancement of Science."
It was the starting-point of those annual meetings
of scientific men, which continued, with happy results, until the civil war broke out, in 1861.

In the middle of February, 1842, Mr. Silliman

opened the third of his courses before the Lowell Institute.

Dr. Walker's lecture, as happened on our arrival last year, was to be delivered on the ensuing evening; and as we found our friend, the Rev. George Jones, a fellow-lodger with us in our hotel, we took him along with us to hear the lecture — which was excellent, and delivered with dignity and force — on the question, "Whether man can live and improve without religious education?" The house was entirely full, stage and all, and a breathless silence prevailed. We were received into the box of Mr. John A. Lowell, our patron, with warm greetings from him and his family; also, from President Quincy, who advanced promptly to meet us with his usual cordiality and kind inquiries. To Mr. Lowell, I remarked: "I am very glad, sir, to see that the Institute does not fall off." "Oh no," said he, "the interest keeps up, and there have been as many applicants for your lectures as last year, which you will remember was about ten thousand, and each ticket drawn is entitled to two or three seats."

I was told that on the day of applying for tickets, Federal Street, leading to the Odeon, was entirely filled for a long distance with a dense mass of people, waiting for hours for a chance, and content to advance slowly as the front melted away. The tickets at once commanded two or three or more dollars, and they are often drawn by servants and others for the purpose of selling again for money.

February 21. — On entering the hall I was saluted by, I think, the largest audience which I have at any time seen there. Every nook and corner was filled, and all the galleries, even the uppermost, and all the alleys.

I gave a concise notice of the course last year, and introduced this course with an exordium which I thought was intelligible and apposite, and, what was still better, it was brief. I gave a classification of the metals, and enumerated their leading properties, — the chemical first, and the physical last. This gave me an opportunity to close the lecture with those fine mechanical experiments, which are at the same time beautiful and instructive. I allude to the evolution of heat by percussion of metals. The experiments were performed on lead and copper; they were entirely successful, and appeared to give satisfaction to the audience. Although I was diffident as to the success of this lecture, I spoke deliberately, and, I believe, clearly.

February 22. — I had two full audiences, exceedingly attentive, and the repeated lecture went off very well. I am told, indeed, that the audience are much interested in the organic chemistry; and I am now persuaded that what I feared might be dull, will make only a pleasant transition to the splendors of heat and light, of electricity and galvanism, whose history will be given near the conclusion of the course.

The fourth year of the Lowell lectures brought a repetition of the social attentions with which Mr. Silliman had been honored in Boston, and witnessed no diminution of the popular interest in his instructions.

February 27, *Monday.* — Tea at Mr. R. H. Dana's, Sen. Met there Mr. R. H. D., Jr. (author of "Two Years before the Mast") and lady, and passed an hour and a half most agreeably, — Professor Brown, of Dartmouth, being in the circle.

February 28, *Tuesday.* — Evening at Mr. Andrews', Mount Vernon Street, with a large circle. A Mr. Ford and his wife, professional mesmerizers, exhibited for the entertainment of the company. She was said to be magnetized by her husband, and in the early part of the evening made, as was reported, some successful hits, but after we came in she was not fortunate in every instance, although she brought out some things very well. But the phrenological exhibition was ridiculous, and it appeared to me mere acting.

Tuesday, A. M., *February* 28. — On board the *Emma Isidora,* a small ship bound for Smyrna; and were present at the parting scene with Mr. D. B. Stoddard, late Tutor in Yale College. We saw the Rev. Mr. Perkins and lady, now returning with the worthy bishop, Mar Yohannan, and with them several young missionaries. A solemn religious service was performed, a large crowd of people being assembled in and around the ship. The scene was touching, and the impression solemn and happy. . . . . .

Saturday Morning, March 26. — Another week of labors and cares is finished, and our public exertions have been crowned with entire success. Civilities and various engagements have multiplied upon us, until all our fragments of time are taken from us. A cluster of social interviews, especially in the evening, almost used us up, and it was a real relief to sit at Mr. Mason's table, with him and his most agreeable family; and we had quiet interviews at Mr. Pliny Cutler's, and a delightful family sitting at Mr. R. H. Dana's, Jr., with themselves alone, in their quiet, elegant parlor. . . . . .

Last evening we finished our labors in the Lowell Institute, with entire success in the whole series of four years (besides the two years before the Lowell courses began). God be praised! There has been no failure of health, or of punctuality, or of any experiment, during the popular course of geology, 1835, and of chemistry in 1836, and of the Lowell courses, — six years in all. The last lecture on galvanism gave great delight to both audiences. I have been very ably assisted by my affectionate son, and by our devoted artist, Mr. Wightman.

The following paragraph is from the "Boston Transcript" of March 30, 1843: —

"Professor Silliman, whom all the Bostonians love as a Christian, and honor as a man of science, concluded his series of valuable and instructive lectures to one of his audiences, and will complete this evening, before another audience, his engagements in the Lowell Institute, which, as is well known, have been continued for four years, and have diffused among our people much useful knowledge, exciting, as we do not doubt, many a dormant intellect, and compelling the awakened mind to renewed activity and investigation. Admiring as we do the perfection of science exhibited continually by the lecturer in all that he has undertaken to explain, we have yet a higher love and reverence for that beautiful exhibition of divine truth to which Mr. Silliman constantly alludes, as seen in the wonderful works which he has successfully presented as designed by the Almighty power, and made known to man by human intelligence. This is the source of our respect for this accomplished Professor, in comparison with which our admiration for his scientific attainments sinks into insignificance. In the conclusion of last evening's lecture, Mr. Silliman paid a just encomium to the progress of art and science in Boston, and ended with a heartfelt tribute to the city itself and its excellent citizens. 'This noble city,' he said, 'for which his prayer was, that peace might be within her walls, and prosperity within her palaces.'"

He thus finishes the record of his work in Boston: —

In concluding my labors in Boston during *the six anxious years*,— the most arduous scientific engagements of my life, — I did not indulge, and have never felt any sentiment of pride or vanity. Deeply impressed with my responsibility for the honor of Yale College, and with still higher moral obligations, and being ably assisted by my excellent son and a devoted artist,* I labored earnestly to fulfil every

* Mr. Wightman, philosophical instrument-maker in Boston.

duty. By God's blessing, to whom be all the honor, our efforts were crowned with glorious success, and I was satisfied.

The following are letters interchanged between him and Professor Kingsley, in the period covered by the preceding chapter. The first gives an account of the ceremonies at the commemoration of the first settlement of New Haven.

FROM PROFESSOR KINGSLEY.

NEW HAVEN, *May* 2, 1838.

. . . . . . THE anniversary of the 25th of April is past, and you will readily believe me when I say that I feel relieved from a heavy burden. You have seen, from the newspapers, the printed accounts which contain the chief particulars, but with some circumstantial errors. I advised Benjamin * to send you the " Palladium " and " Register " of this town, as well as the " Herald." You will see from the statements in all these that the affair has upon the whole gone off very well, and without the intervention of any disturbing political or sectarian feeling. The exercises in George Street were very impressive. Mr. Hotchkiss, as you know, has a stentorian voice, and the thousands on the fences, houses, and trees, as well as in the streets, must have heard him with perfect distinctness. The tunes from Sternhold and Hopkins, selected by Mr. Bacon, were sung with great effect. The house was crowded to overflowing ; and I was at first doubtful whether I should be able to make myself heard by so great a multitude. By the time, however, I had uttered a few sentences, I was satisfied that there was no cause of fear on this account. This new conviction gave me of course confidence and strength ; and I spoke about an hour and a half, without much difficulty.

* Mr. Silliman, Jr. — F.

When I found my voice failing, I called to my aid Mr
Goodrich, who had read over, the evening before, a part of
the manuscript, so as to be ready for such an emergency.
My friends have expressed quite as much satisfaction in
the performance, as I could wish; and more than, in my
own conviction, the piece will give when read apart from
the excitement of the occasion. In reply to some of your
questions, I am able to state, that the ode first sung in the
house was written by young Mr. Bacon, who graduated last
Commencement; the hymn at the conclusion was written
by Rev. Mr. Bacon, who selected likewise the words of the
Anthem, which were set to music by Mr. Fitch.

Mr. Croswell was invited to read the Scriptures, but for
some reason declined; and this service was performed by
Mr. Bennett. You must excuse my saying so much of
what relates more or less directly to myself. I know the
interest you took in this anniversary; and have supposed
that these details would not be unacceptable. The historical discourse is about going to press.

FROM PROFESSOR KINGSLEY.

NEW HAVEN, March 24, 1841.

DEAR SIR, — Your letter of Monday was quite refreshing. Not that I have felt any apprehensions about the success of your lectures, especially after your former experience
in Boston; yet it is gratifying to have it under your own
hand, that you have reason to believe that "Mr. Lowell
and the public are satisfied." The attentions you have received must have made your time pass more pleasantly,
and perhaps may be considered as evidence not only of
personal regard, but of kind feeling, or at least of the
absence of all unkind feelings, towards our College. I am
sure that there is here no hostility to Cambridge; indeed,
I have always considered the prosperity of that institution
as highly favorable to the prosperity of ours. I have obtained a copy of Mr. Quincy's history, and of course do not

wish you to purchase one for me, as I told you I possibly
might.   On reading the work more attentively, my first
impressions are confirmed.   Not that I suppose that it
contains any designed misrepresentation, but for some reason or other, there are in it demonstrable errors in point
of fact, particularly as respects Yale College ; and I think
likewise that there are in the book very manifest errors in
point of opinion.   The latter, of course, it would be more
difficult to prove to the satisfaction of the public; yet even
here I should not despair of some success.   The work as
a literary performance has certainly great merit; and the
body of the information in it is without doubt correctly
given.   Whether I shall make any remarks on this work
publicly, is still uncertain.   If I should determine on it,
I shall find it necessary, perhaps, to visit Boston to consult a few books, which I cannot procure here ; or I have
thought of trying to borrow several volumes through my
friend Mr. Worcester. . . . . College is very quiet.
There are some things in the present religious movements
which I can hardly approve of; but I hope for the best.
One evidence of the "genuineness of the work," is, that our
Faculty meetings pass off with little or no business. . . . . .
I have received from Dr. Beck a copy of the pamphlet on
the proposed changes in the studies at Cambridge.   This
is a much more *radical* proceeding than I anticipated.   I
am a little curious to see the operation of the new system.
I am not bigoted in my attachment to old plans of study ;
nor am I disposed to be caught with every novelty.   Let
them at Cambridge try experiments, and we will try to
profit by them.   They are better able to experiment than
we are. . . . . .

TO PROFESSOR KINGSLEY.

BOSTON, *March* 22, 1841.

. . . . . . WE have received many kind attentions, and they have been much increased by Susan's * residence with us, which has brought in *a great wave* of ladies, — some of the most noble and famed being on the top of the billow. The Quincy family have been particularly attentive and kind ; nearly every member of the family has called, — the President very early. . . . . . I suppose Mrs. S. told you that Mr. Q. presented two copies of his history, — one for our library, and another to myself, — with a friendly letter. Probably Mrs. S. read to you his rejoinder to my thanks for his civility. . . . . . Dr. Walker is a very interesting man. I have made no allusion to your criticisms on the history, except in conversation with Mr. Jeremiah Mason, who did not appear to be aware of the facts, and I much doubt whether there is any purpose to do injustice. Mr. Q. is a very ardent man. Mr. Gannett is laboring very hard to illustrate his views of the doctrines of grace. I heard him last evening for two hours and twenty minutes on Regeneration. He was very able and impressive and eloquent, and said many excellent things. I cannot pretend to enter on his peculiarities. I can tell you something about them when we meet. One thing, however, I will add. His allusions to the views of the Orthodox were candid and decorous, and such as become a Christian gentleman. His house is every Sunday evening crowded to the utmost, aisles and all, to hear these lectures. From what I hear of the religious influence in College, I trust you have had quiet times, and will have. May God prosper every genuine religious influence upon the hearts of those young men, so interesting to their friends and their country.

* Mrs. Silliman, Jr. — F.

TO PROFESSOR KINGSLEY.

BOSTON, *March* 20, 1842.

. . . . . I HAVE been particularly gratified to learn from Mr. Larned, that you had a *half hour* Faculty meeting, and that everything is quiet at College : I trust it will continue so, as examination is impending. Mrs. Silliman, I suppose, informed you that President Quincy was almost the first gentleman to salute me, and with much cordiality of courtesy, on the stage, at the conclusion of Dr. Walker's lecture, the evening of our arrival. He called at our lodgings the next day, and left his card, as we were not in. Yesterday week I dined at his son's, Mr. Josiah Quincy, with a considerable party of the *aristoi* and the *plousioi*, where he and the President were very polite, and yesterday we made our calls in Cambridge, — at Dr. Beck's ; at the new library, and on Dr. Harris, the Librarian ; and last, at the President's. There was no abatement of kindness on the part of the family, — and ladies are more sensitive, and not always as well disciplined in suppressing riled feelings as men. I have not heard a word from any Unitarian or college man or college friend, which would enable me to infer that they had or had not read certain criticisms.* . . . . Dr. Taylor regretted that the articles had not been struck off separately for extensive distribution, and we concluded that the author ought to pursue his investigations, and publish a complete history of Yale College, to which these criticisms and all others that are, or may be, digested may be appended. I hope you will not neglect this subject, for there neither is, nor ever will be, any one who can do the work well but yourself. . . . . .

While Professor Silliman was gaining his great success in Boston, he had the satisfaction of know-

---

* Professor Kingsley's articles on President Quincy's *History of Harvard College.* — F.

ing that his labors were appreciated in foreign countries.

Too long have I neglected to express my obligations for
the letters with which you were pleased to honor me when
about to embark for England, and my regret that I saw so
little, while there, of your excellent friends, Dr. Daubeny
and Professor Buckland. I enjoyed, however, repeated
interviews with both, and had the happiness to hear from
them sentiments of the highest respect and regard for yourself. From both I was requested to bear to you the assur-
ances of their warm esteem and friendship. Dr. Buckland
I first met at the British Association, in Glasgow, when at
a public dinner in the theatre, to about one thousand
gentlemen, I was favored with an opportunity of publicly
expressing my admiration of your character, and my regret that you were not present to represent, better than
any other American could do, the cause of science in
our country. And you may be assured, that among the
purest pleasures experienced by me while abroad, was
that arising from the applause which your name excited
throughout that great and learned assembly. Dr. Daubeny
kindly invited me to Oxford, but it was not in my power to
visit that place. I subsequently dined with Dr. Buckland,
Lord Northampton, the sculptor Chantrey, Professor Whe-
well, and other gentlemen of science, at the Geological
Club, and attended the meeting of the Society in the evening. I cannot but hope, my dear sir, that having by arduous efforts in the cause of science and humanity, won so
bright a fame in Europe, as well as America, you will yet
revisit England to renew your personal intercourse with
those who love and admire you there, thus receiving and
imparting happiness, which you never fail to do in every
intelligent and refined society.

In 1842, Professor Silliman gave the Address to the Alumni of Yale College, the reception of a copy of which was thus acknowledged in a letter

FROM CHANCELLOR KENT.

NEW YORK, *October* 30, 1842.

My DEAR SIR, — I thank you for your address before the Alumni of Yale College. Though I heard it delivered, I have read it with renewed, and indeed increased, interest. I delight in the visions of ancient reminiscences, and, when I was at New Haven I saw, with a pang, the desolate ground where the President's old house stood.

Your pamphlet affords me an apology for writing to you, for you must know that I was deeply attracted by your earliest publication, and the charm of your style, taste, ability, learning, and moral character, has been ever since growing with my years and strengthening with my judgment. You are aware, I presume, that I take your " Journal of Science," and have it *ab initio.* The address in the October number before the geologists at Boston, interested me exceedingly, and I have much to regret that I am so ignorant of the sciences, except, perhaps, that I may be permitted to claim some skill in the *science of law.* Of the physical sciences, I am much attracted and delighted by astronomy and geology. I ran over lately, by way of a refresher, Mrs. Somerville's delightful sketch of the " Connection of the Physical Sciences," and some of the earliest of the English Quarterlies first drew my attention to the sublime science of geology. I spent an evening with a party in this city, where Mr. and Mrs. Lyell were present. I had not much conversation with him, for everybody was about him, and I was occupied very much with the attractive conversation of his wife. He told me he was the author of one of the early reviews on the geology of Central France. I own, and have read and studied, his two volumes on the " Elements," and his four volumes on the " Principles of Geology," and

yet I feel humble at the reflection how little I know of the
sciences in which you are so great a master. But you must
pardon my intrusion. I ventured lately, for the first time
in my life, to address an English judge, and I stated in a
letter to *Lord Denman*, (Lord Chief Justice of the King's
Bench,) that "though I had never the honor of a personal acquaintance with any judicial character in England, yet, that my familiarity with the English law, and
with the decisions of the English courts for the last half
century, made me feel as if I was in some degree addressing a companion." He replied more liberally, and said,—
" He adopted the expression, and desired to add to it " (in
its application to me) " a Guide and a Friend." Now, after
that, I need not be afraid of addressing you as familiarly
as I do. I have long since made up my mind that the
discoveries in geology are not unfavorable to the Christian
faith in the Bible. The argument is conclusive, that the
Holy Scriptures were intended for man as a moral and ac-
countable being, and not to teach him physical philosophy.
The boundless antiquity of the elements of geology, and
the recent creation of man, are indisputable facts. No fossil evidences of the existence of man, prior to the Mosaic
date, are to be found, and that fact discloses awful and sublime results, and shows that man might have been created
perfect in his mind and body, by extraordinary and omnipo-
tent agency, as told in Genesis. The fact gives vast energy
to the doctrine of the immaterial soul and immortal destiny
of man, as disclosed in the Scriptures.

Wishing you every success and every happiness, I am,
with my best respects to Mrs. Silliman,

Your obedient servant,

PROFESSOR SILLIMAN.　　　　　　　　　JAMES KENT.

English travellers, not unfrequently, brought to him
letters of introduction. His kindness and hospitality
never failed to leave upon them agreeable impressions.

FROM CAPTAIN BASIL HALL.

EDINBURGH, *February* 22, 1837.

. . . . . IT affords me much pleasure to have an opportunity of sending you Mrs. Hall's compliments and my own, and of assuring you that we remember, and ever shall remember, your very kind attentions to us, and those of Mrs. Silliman and your two daughters. Our little girl, also, to whom you were so kind, though she has forgotten all about her transatlantic travels, is kept in the full knowledge of the hospitality with which she, as well as her papa and mamma, were received in America. We have been great wanderers since we had the pleasure of seeing you; but we always look back to America with the warmest feelings of gratitude, not merely to those friends to whom we were personally known, but to the country generally, and if I had not become old and stiff and lazy, I might venture again across the Atlantic; for I should suppose, from all I hear, that in the few years which have elapsed since I visited the United States, the circumstances have changed so as to make it a different country. I wish you joy, with all my heart, of your railway sort of speed, and hope that your happiness and success, in all respects, may keep pace with your speed in national progress.

Ever, very dear sir,

Most sincerely yours,

BASIL HALL.

www.ingramcontent.com/pod-product-compliance
Lightning Source LLC
Chambersburg PA
CBHW021336110726
47900CB00005B/1497